Laila
Hietamies

RED MOON OVER WHITE SEA

NOVEL

Translated by Börje Vähämäki

ASPASIA BOOKS
Beaverton, Ontario, Canada

Red Moon over White Sea

Published in 2000 by

Aspasia Books
R.R. 1
Beaverton, ON
L0K 1A0 Canada
www.aspasiabooks.com

Translated from the Finnish *Vienan punainen kuu*
First published in Finnish 1992 by Otava Publishing Co. Ltd
First published in Canada 2000

Cover design by Martin Best based on original
oil painting by Canadian artist, Helen Lucas ©

ISBN 0-9685881-4-X

Canadian Cataloguing in Publication Data

Laila Hietamies, 1938-
Red moon over white sea

Translation of: Vienan punainen kuu
ISBN 0-9685881-4-X

1. Finns--Russia (Federation)--Karelia--History--20th century--Fiction. 2.
Karelia (Russia)--History--Fiction.
I. Vähämäki K. Börje II. Title.

PH355.H46V5313 2000 894'.54133 C00-900857-8

Between two ice blue seas
A land lies dormant,
Whose landscape to this day
On maps is vaguely drawn.
It is the land of Viena Karelia.
Endless its forests,
Huge its hills,
Enchanting its rivers.

ILMARI KIANTO

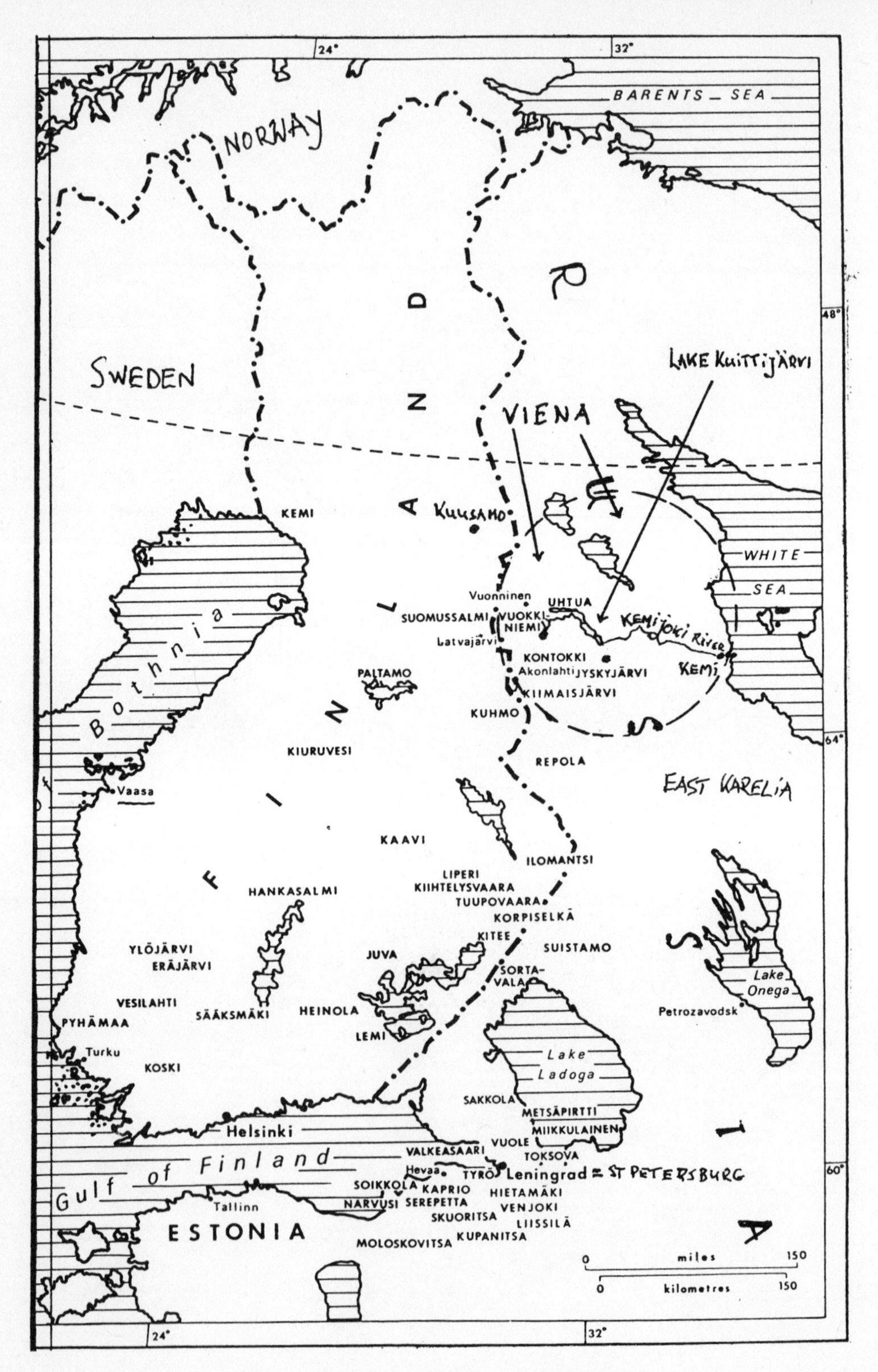

Map of Viena, Finland, and Western Russia

PART ONE

Childhood

IN MEMORY OF OUR PARENTS

Kreeta Rauvala

AND

Axel Wilhelm Solander

ARVO - BERTHA - ROBERT

WINCHENDON, MASS.

The snow had been whirling about all day and was still falling when the first loads arrived. It was only a week since the ice on Lake Kuittijärvi had become strong enough for sleighs to ride on. Only the rapids murmured softly from behind Small Bird Grove; the winters in Viena never got cold enough for the rapids to freeze into a ghostly castle.

In the afternoon light some twenty horses and horsemen approached along the ice with cargo. The farm people stood on the Uhtua side of the point looking at their arrival.

Katri and Teppana were out emptying the nets. They skied toward the shore with their knapsacks on their backs.

"We got some white fish," said Katri, jumping off her skis in front of the sauna. She turned to look at Aniviisu, who was wearing a black coat and a scarf wrapped around her head several times.

Before Aniviisu had a chance to answer, Nasti, who was looking out over the ice, began to speak in an excited voice.

"*Hospody*," she said pulling her scarf tighter. "They're coming here."

Teppana frowned as he turned to look in the direction his wife pointed.

"From Uhtua … What are they coming here for!"

They stood there silent, all four of them, looking at the approaching sleighs. Soon they could discern three men sitting in the lead sleigh. The first horse came straight to the shore by the sauna and stopped right next to them. The others remained a little ways behind. A man dressed in a homespun winter coat, wearing a huge fur hat and leather boots with high shafts, clambered up from the sleigh.

"Huovinen is my name," the man said through lips stiff from the cold. "This is Huotari Point, right?"

Nobody answered at first. Aniviisu's face crumpled up, she looked anxiously at her aunt Katri. Aunt should have answered by now …

"That's right… This is Huotari Point," Katri said with a clear, ringing voice. "Why do you want to know?"

The man – who called himself Huovinen – pushed his fur hat back with his thumb.

"There is a house going up on the point. These men are from Archangel, construction workers. Just so you know."

For a moment no one said a word, then Teppana almost jumped forward into Huovinen's face.

"A house, you say! But there already is a house here. And the girl – the one over there – she owns both the point and the house."

Huovinen reached inside his coat and pulled out a piece of paper. He gave it to Teppana.

"Read this.'

Teppana didn't know how to read, and so Katri took the paper and read it. Then she gave the paper back to Huovinen and turned to look at Aniviisu.

"There is indeed going to be a house built here, and the one who is having it built … is your *buobo*, your grandfather."

The house reached its roofing stage before Christmas. Such an enormous house had never been seen in Uhtua before – probably not in the entire Viena Karelia. Men came and went with their horses, the sleighs laden with giant logs from Kemi in Viena. People were saying that a ship had brought building materials and supplies from Archangel while the sea was still open and that a large warehouse had been rented for that purpose in Kemi.

"There are water tanks, windows and furniture, and lots of other stuff …" Huovinen explained.

The Huotari Point people were silent – out of sheer shock. And so a house was erected at the tip of the long and wide Huotari Point. There was no stopping it. Not even by Katri, who, despite several attempts, had not managed to get a hold of the girl's grandfather's address in Canada.

One evening a letter arrived. It was delivered by someone from Likopää village in Uhtua. The letter read:

To my grandson – whose name I don't know – in Uhtua, Viena Karelia.

Toronto, Ontario, Canada
7th September 1909

Dear grandson,

As far as I know you are now going on ten. Consequently I assume you can read. I got word of your parents' drowning last spring, and it saddens me. I am now your only surviving relative.

I will come to Finland from Canada by ship. The ship is expected to arrive in Finland's capital in late summer, and before that the building materials and furniture for a new house. It will be built on the shore of Kuittijärvi on the point. I do not intend to live in the old house, and you'd better get used to the idea that you too will live in the new house. We will meet in the year to come, because I intend to settle and live in Uhtua.

Written by your grandfather
Ilja Huotari

"Good God ..." Katri stood with the letter in her hand in the sacred icon corner and bowed deep. "Grandson, she whispers quietly.

A terrified expression had crept onto Aniviisu's face.

"Katri! I am a girl – a girl!

Katri took her into her arms.

"A girl, of course …"

Aniviisu pressed her head into the folds of Katri's white apron, and with her hand Katri stroked the child's hair, her silken, curly hair.

"Don't cry, Aniviisu," she said comfortingly. "Surely the man can't be evil …"

"Will you leave me then, when he arrives?" Aniviisu asked sobbing.

Katri pressed the girl closer to her.

"I will never leave you. I promised your mother once that I would look after you, if anything were to happen … And I always keep my promises."

The moon was blood-red and surrounded by an enormously large halo, which colored the entire vault of heaven and flared so mysteriously that people were afraid to look at it. Aniviisu glanced quickly at the sky as she pulled her felt boots on after the day's lessons and sped with her sled down to the shore.

The old house – that's what she and Katri had started to call their home – stood, gray and lonely, on a small hill at the edge of the forest. It was almost buried in snow, which reached up to the windows, covering the thick logs. In Aniviisu's mind it was a wonderful home – it had a large living room, an alcove and enough outbuildings. It also had a covered farm path, along which one could get to the cowshed, and so the animals were safe and close to the people. Of course, the house was of Russian style and more modest than the large Finnish style houses in Likopää, but it was still a home – a safe place for a small orphan child.

The distance from the old house to the shore was about 150 feet.

The slope of the hill was steep and the sled Teppana had built gathered good speed. The snow whirled around Aniviisu and the sled rushed far onto the ice-covered lake – far, far. When the sled finally came to a stop, Aniviisu found herself looking straight at the new house. It rose on the tip of the point, gloomy and large – so huge it covered from view the grove behind it as well as the expanse which opened on the other side of the point. It had windows on two levels, and on the very top they had started to build some strange contraption, a tower of some sort. She could see men and horses near the building. The men were shouting to each other, carrying boards and other building materials; someone laughed loudly.

Quietly, furtively Aniviisu kicked her sled to the tip of the point, into the shelter of a big spruce. She stood there looking angrily at the house. It loomed in the dusk of the evening like some wooden mountain, and the blood-red moon shone through its empty windows.

Aniviisu sat on her sled deep in thought. She appeared exceptionally mature for a little ten-year-old girl. She had always liked being by herself and had become even more contemplative after her parents drowned in the raging rapids of Kemijoki River. That had happened the summer before. She skated past this thought now – she had learned to put aside sad thoughts. Then Katri had come from Finland to look after her – and Katri didn't go away, but stayed to be her teacher, since she was trained as a teacher. In Katri's opinion the girl had had such rough experiences that she should not exhaust herself further with lengthy travel to school. It was more than seven miles from Huotari Point to Uhtua. Aniviisu had been making her trips to school on skis in the winter or with Teppana and his horse; in the spring and the fall she had gone to school by boat.

After the accident Aniviisu's life returned only gradually to normal, but now this new house was being built. The girl looked at the bustle of the construction site in a state of powerless indignation. Almost every day more materials had arrived from Kemi in Viena. The lathered horses had pulled the fully loaded sleighs on the trip, which took almost all day. Dozens of loads had arrived across the open lake that spread like a desert of snow. Logs and timbers were brought in by the hundreds, round ones, square ones, and planed ones.

Where do all those trees come from, Katri had wondered standing by the window watching the loads come in.

Nasti, Teppana's old crone, had shrugged her shoulders. And Nasti wasn't really a crone, but in Uhtua women were customarily called crone. Nasti Miikkula daughter Jyrkinen had been given to Teppana for wife and she was thereafter known as a 'crone' despite being only ten years Katri's senior.

"Teppana was saying the timber comes from Archangel," Nasti offered.

"Good grief – all the way from Archangel ... although I have heard it said that they have big sawmills over there."

"He's got to be a rich man today, that Ilja Huotari, I can't think of any other explanation!" Nasti said. "God knows - those timbers may be coming straight from Canada for all I know."

"Haven't seen those kinds of timbers around here before," Teppana marveled aloud from the living room bench. He scratched the top of his head and lifted one leg across the other. "They have indeed been brought from Canada to the Archangel sawmill, that's what Huovinen said ... He said the house will be built partly of hardwood, wood that has not been seen in Viena before."

"*Hospody*," Nasti sighed in wonder. "Real hardwood trees, are they?"

Aniviisu was mulling all of this over in her mind while she sat on her sled. She stared at the unfinished house with her head tilted to one side. The empty window holes gaped at her like the devil's eyes. In every respect the house was like some hunchbacked beast, at dusk lying in ambush waiting for its prey. In Aniviisu's mind the monster home became one with her *buobo*, the unknown man, whose letter had been on its way for several months. Now it was already April and with a horror-struck heart Aniviisu awaited summer, when the ship her grandfather had talked about was due at port of Helsinki.

What kind of a man was her *buobo*? He had never been interested in his family in Uhtua. How cold-hearted he must be! Teppana had told her that some thirty years ago her *buobo* had gone abroad and forgotten Uhtua altogether. In any event, not a word was heard from him.

Suddenly Aniviisu heard steps from behind her and turned around abruptly.

Here you are Aniviisu ... said Teppana and turned her sled around. "You must be cold. You shouldn't sit motionless on the sled in this icy wind. I'll take you home now."

As Teppana set the sled in motion with a push, some workers came out of the house and began to harness the horse that was standing by the hitching post.

"They are leaving for Uhtua to spend the Sunday," Teppana grunted. "But come Monday morning, they'll be here before six o'clock."

The wind swirled the fine snow on the ice and lifted it up in the air in the shape of a statue. A dog barked somewhere at the tip of the point. Aniviisu looked behind her. The big house defied the wind and the cold; it rose almost up to the level of the treetops, although it was still empty and open.

The foreman Huovinen took to the ice in the first sleigh. The remaining eight sleighs followed suit. The lead horse stopped next to Teppana and Aniviisu.

"On Monday the windows will be coming," said Huovinen amidst his furs and pelts. "Would it be possible to store them in the farmyard of your house until it's time to install them in the new house? We'll bring the necessary tarpaulins. And there'll be other things as well ..."

Teppana's face was stiff from the icy wind, and his voice cracked as he attempted to speak.

"What other things?" he roared.

"Paints ..."

Teppana said nothing. With one angry gesture he again pushed the sled in motion and began to kick it toward the shore.

"I don't understand your hostility," Huovinen shouted after them. "It's your house and you're gonna move in there! No use fretting about it to me, I'm just a hired hand!"

Teppana did not stop until he reached the shore, where Aniviisu stood up, looking behind her. The horses rode side by side on the ice and became smaller and smaller until they turned around the point toward Uhtua and disappeared altogether.

Teppana looked at the girl awkwardly. The death of the child's parents still pained him. He wanted to help, but didn't know how. He just felt that something was irrevocably broken.

"That they had to go and drown themselves," he mumbled to himself not realizing it sounded like an accusation to the child's ears.

"That's what I think too," said Aniviisu mournfully and jumped off the sled. "I wish they were alive."

Teppana didn't notice anything, but Aniviisu herself certainly did: small, clear tears welled up in her eyes, fell onto her cheeks and froze there instantly. The wind was unspeakably biting.

The Huotaris had lived in their house for centuries. They had originally come to Uhtua from southern Finland, it was said. They still had relatives on the Finnish side of the border, and even in Canada, where some Huotaris had gone among the very first emigrants. It was in their footsteps that Ilja Huotari had traveled in search of his fortune.

Ordinarily people emigrate in the hope of making a better living, but the Huotaris had always enjoyed a reputation of being wealthy – in fact, so wealthy no one in Uhtua knew the full extent of their might. The Huotari household and the lives of its people had always been shrouded in secrecy. They isolated themselves too, only the hired folk and head hired man Teppana and his crone, Nasti, had occasionally gone to the Ryhjä church, but they had never told anyone anything about the Huotari farm. And after the last master of the farm, Moissei, had drowned in the rapids with his Finnish wife, Helena, the sister of the deceased farmwife arrived from Suomussalmi to care for the orphaned girl. The woman's name was Katri Jääskeläinen, teacher by profession. She took the child out of school and began to teach her at home. To the Uhtuans she seemed haughty. Katri herself thought it wise, since after the accident Aniviisu certainly was not up to being picked on and teased by the other kids, that is how shaken she was.

The large old Huotari house was of Russian style, which was not in harmony with the Finnish roots of its inhabitants, regardless of the fact that their religious tradition was Eastern Orthodox. The farm also had lots of land, at least a six-mile stretch along the shore of Middle-Kuittijärvi Lake. When one goes west from Likopää village in Uhtua, the shore line almost immediately becomes winding and those winding shores belong to the Huotaris. The nearest neighbor was about a mile from Uhtua, a jolly and ruddy woman named Outi, who lived there with her old and sickly father. Once, Moissei had courted Outi, who now was in her thirties.

Huotari's old house had a large living room that was entered through a vestibule. Across from the vestibule was an alcove for guests, and outbuildings. There was also a farmyard, which one crossed to get to the cowshed. Steep stairs led to the upper level of the cowshed.

When Katri arrived the previous summer to care for Aniviisu, the dark and smoky living room had annoyed her at first. It was natural for her to start sleeping in the warm and clean alcove with the girl. The furnishings and the linens in the guest room reminded Katri of the kind of life she was used to at home in Suomussalmi.

All things considered, seen from the lake side Huotari was a beautiful house with its blackened logs and chimney. It was surrounded by ancient spruces that hid it almost entirely from view. The long and wide point grew mainly birches. The windows faced toward the wide expanse of Lake Kuittijärvi. Adjacent to the rear of the house lay crown land upon which stood a primeval forest, which seemed to extend indefinitely.

On the shore of the point stood a gray log sauna – the new house had risen some hundred feet away. Now in the winter the sauna looked lonely and bare, but in the summer red flowers grew on its moss-covered roof.

If you walked a few hundred yards from the old house you arrived at Small Bird Grove, which had a lovely pond in the middle. Some distance away was a meandering river, which over a stretch of three miles turned into thunderous rapids. Then the river flowed into the wilderness and was joined by two other rivers. Aniviisu used to visit the pond even in the winter. She was a brave girl. She wasn't afraid of wolves or bears, though they were known to dwell in these forests. The rapids attracted her both in summer and in winter – they were as if enchanted, as they roared free or flowed as a rippling little brook among the ice.

As Teppana and Aniviisu entered the yard with the sled, Nasti was standing on the path with a water pail in her hand.

"Go get water," she told Teppana, giving him the pail.

Whether autumn or winter, or the worst kind of cold weather, Aniviisu had never seen Nasti with her coat on. She always threw a large gray wool shawl over her shoulders, and dressed in that she was warm enough to ski to the Uhtua church. Otherwise Nasti dressed like most Uhtuan women: a red *kosto* or skirt, that reached down to the ankles, a white shirt decorated with embroidery, and a *sorokka* or married woman's headdress. It was years since Teppana had bought the large gray shawl for his young wife from an East Karelian peddler. Nasti was so fond of her wrap that it became her favorite piece of clothing. She also had a black scarf, with which she sometimes covered her headdress tying it under her chin – during her trip to church or at home when fetching water.

Obediently Teppana took the pail and went to the shore, where a hole had been cut in the ice. Nasti turned to Aniviisu.

"Come on in, Katri is preparing to go to the sauna," she said. "Nasti's own little orphan girl ... soon we'll wash your hair."

They hurried through the yard to the house.

"That man told Teppana they are going to bring stuff to the farmyard for storing," Aniviisu said as she crossed the threshold.

"Stuff?"

"Window panes and paints ..."

"*Hospody* ... Where will we fit them! Who knows, they may reach all the way to the living room ... What a cross we have been given to bear, with this house-building and all!"

"Yes, a cross indeed," Aniviisu said precociously and looked toward the icon corner as if pleading for help.

Katri stood by the door smiling.

"The sauna is ready," she said.

Katri was over thirty years of age, a pretty and educated woman. She had big dark eyes and long blond hair that she always kept twisted into a bun at the nape of her neck. She was a neat and organized person, very energetic and active, though she was sometimes overcome by a strange sorrow, and would sink into her own thoughts, which she would not share with anyone.

After the accident the previous spring, Nasti and Teppana had sent word immediately to Katri that the child had been orphaned. She had come at once; she was herself widowed, having lost her husband a couple of years earlier. She understood the child's anguish and sorrow. She had been a teacher in Suomussalmi, but left the job when she realized what her niece's situation was. Teppana had fetched her things as soon as the lake was free of ice. Katri had been in Uhtua ever since, but now, having read Ilja Huotari's letter, she had a premonition she would be returning to Suomussalmi or Sortavala in the fall ...

The letter from Canada gave rise to all kinds of questions on Huotari Point. Katri knew that when Ilja Huotari went abroad as a young man some thirty years ago he had left the farm to his younger brother, Ohvo, and a girl in Uhtua pregnant. Moissei was born a few months after Ilja's departure. The Huotari firstborn was reported to have gone to sea ... And now a letter from Canada! What had happened in the thirty years in between ... Katri smiled at the thought. At least he must have come into money; no pauper would have a house built like the one that was now going up on the point. Had Ilja Huotari out there in the world ever given any thought to the home he had left behind? Had he thought of the people who had stayed behind ... of Moarie, who gave birth to his child?

After the child was born, Ohvo had taken the girl in, married her and accepted the child as his own. The child was a boy and was given the name Moissei. When the boy was fifteen years old, his stepfather drowned on a fishing trip, and five months later Moarie succumbed to childbirth fever along with her baby. Moissei was left alone to run the Huotari farm, which had only some old woman as a servant.

Young Moissei, however, was not made of candle wax. He attacked the farm work with youthful enthusiasm. A kind farmer guided the boy in cultivating the land, raising cattle, and fishing. Around the same time, Nasti and Teppana Jyrkinen, just married, appeared in the area, and at the young master's request they moved to the farm – and stayed on. And so Huotari farm did not, as many had expected, go under after all. In a few years the farm was stable enough to allow Moissei to go one summer with a farmer friend of his on a peddling tour. When he returned in the fall, he brought with him the slender and blonde Helena, Katri's younger sister from Suomussalmi. Nobody had heard anything from Ilja Huotari over the years. No one even knew whether he was alive any more, because his parents too had died before the boy reached fifteen.

"It is a curse," Moissei had told Teppana and Nasti. "Helena and I will also die for sure before the girl is fifteen …"

They died when the girl was ten. And Nasti would stand for hours in the *opreza*, the sacred icon corner, cross her eyes and pray that the curse would be lifted …

Once a letter had arrived from Finland's capital with questions about the people at Huotari – who they were and what ages they were. That was ten years ago. Helena had been about to give birth to Aniviisu, and Moissei had marked down on the questionnaire that a child would soon be born. It must have been Ilja Huotari who was behind the questionnaire, and he must have imagined the child was a boy.

Moissei had never had respect for his real father, rather, he had hated and despised him. The father was not interested in them, not in Uhtua, not the Viena Karelians, nothing. And when the man did not have the guts to write and ask for information, he asked the Canadian Embassy to do it. That is how they had figured out that Ilja Huotari must have gone to Canada …

Katri sat in the alcove by a small table, which was lit by a candle, writing a letter to her friends in Sortavala. She put down her pen when Aniviisu entered. Usually children would rush in with a rumble, that is at least what her pupils in Suomussalmi used to do, but this girl slipped inside quietly as a mouse and slipped through the low door secretly, with a frown on her little round face. Without a word she went to stand next to Katri, pressed against her side and looked at her with a searching look. Katri was almost always thrown off balance when the girl looked at her; she had never seen such deep blue eyes on anyone else, ever.

"So … you've been outside? I am writing a letter to Sortavala. If everything works out right, we will move there next fall. You will go to the girls' school and I'll start teaching at the teacher's seminary." Katri looked at the girl with a smile. "Then you'll have to start using your given name, the name you got at baptism. How on earth did you as a little girl manage to twist Anna Liisa into Aniviisu?

The girl laughed. "Did Mother never tell you? It was just very easy to twist the name …" Then the girl became serious. "But what will this Ilja Huotari say if we leave for Sortavala?"

"… This Ilja Huotari is your grandfather. You'll have to learn to call him *buobo*!

Katri grabbed the girl by the arms.

"Anna Liisa Huotari – student at the girls' school! Doesn't that sound grand?"

The girl nodded, but then, a little worried, she said: "Anja will be going to Sortavala, too, won't she?"

If she is conscientious in her schoolwork," Katri said. "And why wouldn't she, since her schoolmistress mother teaches her?"

Aniviisu thought to herself for a moment.

"Listen, Katri, they are bringing stuff to the farmyard, window glass and paints …"

"Did Huovinen say that?"

"Yes" – and Teppana only grunted and Nasti carped that they'll dirty the farmyard altogether if they store that kind of material. "I'm scared."

"Why are you scared?"

"Yesterday I went to Vaahtovuori rapids and the Water Spirit was sleeping. She's frozen because she has no blood in her veins, only water. But as soon as the veins melt, the spirit wakes up … although she does hear what happens around her even when she's sleeping. And when she wakes up she'll be mad, because there isn't a water spirit who can stand the sound of an axe. And she could hear the sounds of axes from the construction site quite clearly.

"What will happen then?" Katri asked.

"Terrible things…If the owner of the axe goes to the rapids he might fall in the gorge, and the Water Spirit will not rescue him because someone who has felled a tree has hurt the Tree Spirit."

"So one is not allowed to fell trees?"

"No," Aniviisu said ardently. "Except for old ones, those which have died standing and have rotted. Healthy big trees you are not allowed to fell. They have lived for centuries and then people would just cut off their life in a few minutes."

"That is true of course, you are quite right," Katri said quietly.

She was not always able to make the girl distinguish between what was imagined and what was real. Lately the girl had been engaged in her imaginary world more deeply than before. It sometimes frightened Katri a little.

"Put your sauna robe on, let's go to the sauna, Nasti is waiting outside," said Katri in order to expel the Water Spirit from the child's thoughts. But the girl still had things on her mind:

"When the new house is finished, we have to fetch a bucket of water from Vaahtovuori rapids, walk around the house and throw water at every corner with a whisk … If we don't do that, a fire could burn down the house, and then all the trees on the point would die. The Water Spirit would never forgive us if we didn't do that. And I'm not moving into a house that has not been blessed. Although I'm not moving in there anyway.'

"So the blessing is important then?" Katri said, helping Aniviisu take off her shirt."

"It's important, that's what Mother would say, too."

Katri watched with a smile as Aniviisu threw on a linen robe, which drooped on the floor, and slipped her feet into felt slippers.

"Now you are just like a little gnome."

"Let me undo your bun," said the girl, "you have such beautiful hair."

The fresh air rushed against them as they stepped into the yard. The little knoll was steep enough for Nasti to take the water sled, seat Aniviisu in Katri's lap and then step onto the runners herself. The sled glided smoothly down the knoll to the shore and stopped right in front of the sauna.

The shore already showed signs of spring. The snowdrifts gave off a strong fragrance, somewhere in the dusk a bird chirped, and the wind in the forest rustled mysteriously. A severe wind had swept across the ice all day and whirled up the snow. Now the moon had risen behind Lake Kuittijärvi; it was blood-red and made the whole lake glow red.

"In the old days, people used to say that a moon like that means war," Nasti said.

The red glow of the southern sky frightened them. Even Nasti could not recall having ever seen a moon of such strong color. They stood unmoving at the corner of the sauna looking at the sky. The snowy expanse that opened before them seemed to continue indefinitely. From the corner of the sauna, they had earlier been able to see across the narrow point to the other side, but now the new house blocked the view. It stood tall and empty-eyed.

It filled them with dread to look at it.

"Now, into the sauna, otherwise we'll be frozen stiff," Katri said.

Katri motioned for the girl and Nasti to go in. The raw wind raging across the lake had penetrated to their very bones while they stood there. The sauna, however, welcomed them with a wonderfully warming heat as they opened the door. Katri helped Aniviisu take off her dress and got undressed herself while Nasti used a scrap of board to lift the glowing rocks into the water tub. The rocks had accumulated heat for hours on the hearth and now they warmed up the water in the wooden tub also.

Aniviisu climbed up to the highest bench in the sauna with Katri right behind her. Nasti lifted the water basin. No one spoke, no one had anything to say at this time. The steam hissed up to the ceiling and began to spread throughout the sauna making the women gasp.

After the first steam had settled, Aniviisu began to look at Katri and Nasti, who sat on the bench opposite her. They were already chatting quietly; one doesn't raise one's voice in the sauna. The Sauna Spirit doesn't like it. As the women talked away they forgot about Aniviisu whom they considered to be just a child. The girl was, however, already a young woman, even though she looked like a child. No one knew her thoughts or her knowledge about life. Katri would have been surprised at what matters her protégé pondered quietly in her mind or what she talked about with her friend Anja. Anja was one year older than Aniviisu and lived in Uhtua, where her mother Darja Mihailovna Remisova worked as a teacher. They had moved to Uhtua from St Petersburg, and it was rumored that there was something very strange about both the mother and the daughter … Aniviisu had heard Nasti tell Teppana even before Katri arrived, that they should not let Aniviisu keep company with Anja, because her mother was a socialist. Aniviisu did not know what that meant but Nasti had been quite serious.

Aniviisu had always enjoyed being with Anja. They had sat together on the shore of the pond in Small Bird Grove, pondered about life and talked about things. There was something in the life of human beings that frightened and fascinated at the same time. Birth and death. Next to those two, everything else lost its meaning. To be born naked and bloody and to end up in the dirt of the earth naked again. However much one had gathered during one's life, however fine the clothing one had worn, what remained was the same nakedness one was born with.

Anja liked to discuss death, but Aniviisu would always lead her thoughts elsewhere. Aniviisu sometimes felt as if Anja were ten years older than she, as if Anja had been born an old person.

"Surely not!" Nasti said to Katri in a voice loud enough to snap Aniviisu out of her thoughts. "And why would they build a new one, this sauna is old and good – and what excellent sauna steam!" And where would one wash the laundry if they took away the dock?"

Aniviisu looked at Nasti. She looked somehow shrivelled on the sauna bench without her red shirt and her headdress. Her breasts were drooping and the thin stomach was concave; her hair reached down her back like the thin tail of a mouse. There was a strange discrepancy between her dried-out body and her round, cheerful face. Nasti had no children of her own, and therefore she loved Aniviisu as her own.

Katri was quite the opposite of Nasti. Katri was in Aniviisu's mind even more beautiful than her mother had been. Her breasts were large and soft, the skin shimmering white; her hips were round and curved and the stomach small and flat. Aniviisu thought Katri was at her most beautiful in the sauna, in its warmth and soft light.

"How old is this Ilja Huotari?" Katri asked Nasti as she threw more water on the rocks. "I wonder if he is over sixty."

Ilja was nineteen when he left and Moissei was born a few months later.

"Moissei would have been thirty this year, Katri said. Ilja is then just about fifty … And already a grandfather, a young man," Katri smiled. "Too bad, he has such a bad reputation. Did Moissei look like him?"

"I don't remember what Ilja Huotari looked like," said Nasti. "Kind of big and dark his whole being. So was his mother, too, they say, a tall and handsome woman. And mean; she didn't like Uhtuans near her, being from Finland herself. Isolated herself like everyone else before in this house …"

"I wonder why he went off to sea," Katri thought aloud.

"Who knows," Nasti snorted, "a restless blood. Now that he has seen the world, he suddenly remembers that he owns some land around here. I wonder if he is even rich, who knows, he might have the house built on credit, imagining that this land plot will eke out a living for him … Comes here from the big wide world to this little hole of a village to criticize and mock people. Who knows, he might get rid of me and Teppana first thing, tell us we're no longer needed. Maybe he brings a wife along, what's going to become of us then …"

"A devil, that's what he is," Aniviisu said vehemently, provoked by Nasti's musings.

"All right," said Katri quickly. "Come on down, I'll wash your back …"

Teppana always cut a hole in the ice next to the dock, where they could fetch water for the sauna. All the tubs were filled with Lake Kuittijärvi's clear water. Katri washed Aniviisu's hair, then she rinsed her own blond and thick hair several times. The wash ritual took a long time, but soon even Nasti's mouse tails were washed and a contented smile appeared on her good-humored face. The women kept talking as they added some more steam:

"Remember I said so, he's got a wife," said Nasti. "Maybe even a foreigner – how could a man be without a wife! But not a word about that in the letter. And so ignorant about things in his home region that he thinks the girl a boy. What kind of a person is he anyway?"

"This will lead to my departure," Katri sighed. "Luckily I have managed to get a teacher's position in Sortavala. And I'll take the girl with me, nothing can stop me from doing that, I promised Helena …"

The women could not see Aniviisu's face in the dim light of the sauna. They did not notice how tears had begun to roll down the girl's cheeks. The involuntary swell of tears annoyed Aniviisu: they welled up instantly when she felt lonely or feared abandonment. Now it was Katri's words that made her cry. Deep inside she felt that something frightful was about to happen. Oh, how she hated her *buobo*, whom she had never seen, that "big and dark one," as Nasti called him. She hated that unfeeling man who suddenly chose to remember that he had a home somewhere in Uhtua in Viena. A man who just announced his arrival without any consideration for messing up their lives altogether. How she hated, hated, hated! And she was frightened, for after all, she was only a child.

The previous spring, when her mother and father had died, Aniviisu wandered the forests alone. Anja had tried to join her a few times, but since she was unable to comfort her in any way it had felt forced to be together, and eventually Aniviisu told her she'd rather be alone. And Anja had understood. One day while walking on her own, Aniviisu had met a boy. It happened at the time of the marsh marigold, when the last patches of snow had melted dissolving into tiny rivulets. She had walked from her yard to the pond in Small Bird Grove, where the liverworts were about to bloom. She sat in her favorite spot, on the trunk of a fallen tree near the Vaahtovuori rapids, whose murmur she never tired of listening to. She was so dreadfully sad that she felt her heart in a tight squeeze. Never could she have imagined that grief could hurt so badly … She had sometimes thought that sorrow existed only in your mind, but now she knew it was a pain felt by the whole body.

In school in Uhtua the spring report cards had been handed out but she did not go to get hers. She did not attend school after the accident. Every day she escaped into her loneliness, as she had done now in the middle of the funeral. She could no longer stay in the house crowded with strangers. She was suddenly roused from her reverie when she saw someone move in the forest. Had they sent someone to look for her?

A boy emerged from the birch grove carrying some kind of a small case. First, when he saw Aniviisu he stopped, then he walked toward her. The boy was tall, a lot taller than Aniviisu. He was wearing knee pants and a striped jacket, his stockings reached up under the pants and his shoes were black.

Aniviisu began to feel embarrassed that she was staring at his clothes. It was just that they were so different from what any of the Uhtua boys would wear. Then she looked at the boy's face. It was thin but beautiful in its own way. The brown hair had been allowed to grow long. It became curly at the ends and flopped over his eyes, when he moved his head.

The boy stopped and looked curiously at Aniviisu. She was wearing a red skirt and a white blouse, but her hair was not tied with the ornate headband that was typical of young women in Uhtua. It was allowed to flow freely. The boy thought the girl was exceptionally pretty with her dark blue eyes and blond curls – a dreamlike vision suddenly appearing before him in the middle of the wilderness.

"Who are you? What are you doing here in the middle of this gloomy forest?"

Aniviisu stared at the boy in surprise, then she began to look around her.

"The forest isn't gloomy, I am …"

"Why then are you so gloomy?"

"My mother and father were buried today."

The boy lowered the case to the ground and sat down next to Aniviisu on the tree trunk.

"My name is Aniviisu Huotari. My home is near here."

"I've never heard such a crazy name," the boy said.

Aniviisu laughed. “I came up with it myself when I was little – my real name is Anna Liisa,” she explained shyly.

“It’s of little consequence what a person’s name is, but it’s of great significance that your parents have died,” the boy said. “Both, your mother and your father … that is sad.”

The boy bent down and took his case from the ground. When he opened the cover it revealed a violin whose surface reflected the sun-light. The boy lifted the instrument gently as if afraid to disturb it. He caressed the top of it, touched the strings and lifted it under his chin.

He took the bow into his other hand. Then he began to play the saddest of melodies. Aniviisu had seen pictures of a violin but never heard what it sounded like. She looked at the boy spellbound. Never could she have imagined that an object made of wood could make sounds like that; the violin sang a lament, weeping quietly, but its song was also comforting, soothing, calming … Aniviisu almost stopped breathing, as the tune dissolved high into the still bare crown of the trees around them.

They were quiet for a long while and looked at each other. Then the boy put the violin back into its case and lifted it into his lap.

“My name is Kaarlo, Kaarlo Meinander. My aunt lives in Likopää in Uhtua, in the large house with the blue window frames.”

“I know it,” Aniviisu said. “Then your aunt’s name is Elma. She is from Finland. When Mother was alive we sometimes visited her …”

“My father is an ethnologist,” the boy said. “We live in Sortavala, but Father spends half the year in Helsinki. He studies this area, Viena Karelia. We come here at the beginning of summer after school is out and then move to Terijoki for the rest of the summer.”

“What’s there to study about Viena Karelia,” Aniviisu said, almost to herself.

The boy smiled a little puzzled, he had never come to think of things like that.

“I am fifteen,” he continued the conversation. “I go to Sortavala high school, although Father thinks I should go to school in Helsinki.” The boy reflected a moment and then he said:

“My mother is dead, too.

Aniviisu had to lean forward to hear, the boy said it so quietly.

"You play so beautifully," she said. The boy laughed, not at all amused or haughtily, but warmly.

"I've played since I was a little boy. It is my whole life. I'm going to become a violinist."

The boy stood up. He gave Aniviisu a long look.

"Come here to the same place tomorrow, we'll talk."

Then the boy walked away in the direction of the clearing. Before he disappeared among the trees, he lifted his hand and waved.

Aniviisu remained seated on the tree trunk gazing after the boy. When the forest had concealed the wanderer, she was not sure whether he had been real or imagined.

"Aniviisu, now get washed!"

Katri's voice woke Aniviisu up. She was sitting in the sauna. On the lower bench. She glanced at the women as if afraid that they might have seen her thoughts. Then she began to wash herself.

They ate dinner late that evening, after Teppana had returned from the sauna. Teppana was the only man in the household; he went fishing every day, hauled timber from the woods with his horse, did bush-work, and split firewood in the yard. He worked from early in the morning till late at night. In addition he tended the cattle, milked the cows, and gave them food and drink. Generally in the Uhtua area women took care of the animals, but Teppana would not allow it. He saw how much work Nasti had taking care of the house; that is why they had a clear division of tasks. Nasti did the housework: the baking, cooking, laundry, and ironing. In her spare time she wove rugs and cloth, and worked her spinning wheel in the darkness of the room, humming her own songs.

Usually Katri taught Aniviisu at the living room table beneath the window. Nasti often interrupted her chores to listen to the teachings, and that way she learned new things about the world. She had got along well with Katri. Katri had not started to tell them what to do when she came into the household, but concentrated on raising Aniviisu, letting Teppana and his Nasti take care of the farm. Somehow they had even become friends. And now, after the letter from Ilja Huotari they had pulled together so well that there was no doubt about it.

Katri had brought a slate and pieces of chalk from Suomussalmi for Aniviisu. The girl did not have to be told to do her homework, she had a bottomless desire thirst for knowledge. Katri had hardly answered her questions when she would ask a new one. In the evenings, Aniviisu read the *Tales of a Field Surgeon*. Katri had brought both her volumes to ease the girl's sorrow. And the novel by Topelius had opened a world to the girl into which she delved with heart and soul.

"Listen!" She said sitting by the window after the sauna. "Listen to this poem! The twelve-year-old Princess Ulrika Eleonora always walked the king's pet dog Pomppe on a rose-colored ribbon leash. When the dog died, the following poem was composed for his grave:

Pomppe, the King's own dog,
Slept in the sovereign's bed.
Then he died tired and old
By the master's feet, it's said.
Many a pretty maiden would surely
like Pomppe have liked to live high,
And many a hero had often desired
like the blessed dog to be allowed to die.

All three of them listened to the girl's rippling laugh. When she laughed her face lit up, her eyes shone with joy as they had done before her mother and father died, and her speech bubbled.

"... and during the ballet one would occasionally see the widowed queen inquiring with furtive glances whether her beauty and charm had not finally made an impression on the heart of stone of the seventeen-year-old! But the day will come when a beautiful princess will enchant Your Majesty and the Swedish Empire will have herself a queen."

When Aniviisu stopped Teppana whispered,

"Read more, girl, read on!"

In the furthest corner of the living room was an icon of the Mother of God from the convent of Konevitsa. All lessons began in front of it, and were also finished in front of it. Around the icon, Nasti had hung a white cloth, which was embroidered at both ends with red thread. In front of the icon was a tall kneeler for praying and on top of it an old copper cross and a book of prayers. They kissed the crucifix both coming and going and always at night, before bed.

Aniviisu knew that Katri wanted to bring her up exactly as her mother would have done. But however dear Katri had become to Aniviisu, she could never replace her mother and father, those two people, so faithful to each other, who perished deep in the lap of the rapids. Aniviisu felt like crying each time she thought of her parents, who had been found between two large rocks – as if embracing each other, someone had said. Every time the image appeared before Aniviisu's eyes, she shuddered and had to get up and move about, and make herself busy. That way she could make her painful thoughts fade away.

"They are talking about our loads in Uhtua," said Teppana, lighting his after-sauna pipe. "Huovinen told the people at his lodgings that all the material had been brought by ship to Archangel already last summer. And then from there to here … That is some trip for the material! Katri, you who understand things better, is it far from Canada to here, I wonder?"

Katri let out a cheerful laugh.

"One can't even contemplate that long a trip! But I've been thinking about this – did he already send the material from Canada before he heard about the accident? Did he intend to come here to Uhtua anyway? That's what I think. How else is it possible that the material began to arrive in Archangel around the time the accident happened …"

Was there word sent to Canada about Moissei's death?"

Teppana and Nasti looked at each other.

"That Sortavala lawyer …" Teppana said. "He said he had sent word to some embassy. There was no address for Ilja Huotari."

"But he must be rich," said Nasti while carrying the food from the stove to the table. "That's what people are saying in Uhtua ... They feel sorry for us, because everybody knows that the rich are also mean."

Katri decided it best not to correct Nasti. She turned toward the icon corner and asked for a blessing for the food. They ate in silence as was their custom. However, Aniviisu's mind was bubbling with ideas and she almost forgot to eat. After Katri brought her back to reality, the meal was finished peacefully.

"Soon the snowdrifts will all be melted," Teppana said sitting down on the living room bench after the meal. "What did the letter say again – he will arrive at the end of the summer."

Nasti clapped her hands. "*Hospody* – May the Mother of God help us!"

Aniviisu ran through the living room to the alcove. The adults did not notice her fear.

That night the bulk of the snow came down off the roof. First they could hear a distant roar as if a giant bird had clapped its wings together. Then they heard thumps as if someone had slid on the roof. The snow kept sliding for a long while – soft thumps, the gliding of large blocks of snow. In the dark, the noise sounded frightening, as if a horde of ghosts were moving about.

Aniviisu was awake. She awoke with a start and in a state of terror, but calmed down as Katri whispered that it was only the snow making noise. She put her hands under her head, closed her eyes and tried to fall asleep again by thinking of the events of the previous spring.

The boy had come to the clearing the following evening and they had walked to the pond together. They had sat down on a rock, and Kaarlo had taken off his shoes and socks.

"The water is still cold," Aniviisu cautioned. "You'll catch pneumonia, if you get chilled."

Then Kaarlo laughed: "You speak as if you were older than you are."

"I'm ten.

"One wouldn't think so … next summer you'll be eleven and I'll be sixteen," he said putting his shoes back on. "There's a five-year difference between us. Where do you go to school?"

"In Uhtua …" Aniviisu muttered, "but I haven't been in school at all in May, not since it happened … Katri, Mother's sister has come from Suomussalmi to stay with us, and I am supposed to study with her."

"You should come to the Girls' School in Sortavala," Kaarlo said. "It's a good school; it has girls from all over Karelia. From there you could then go on to the teachers' seminary – you will become a teacher, I can see that."

Aniviisu looked searchingly at the boy's mischievous, smiling face.

"How can you see that?"

"It's in the eyes … You have what it takes. You're interested in the world and in people – just like me. I want to go abroad one day to study violin. I do have a good violin teacher in Sortavala, but I might find one even better abroad …"

Aniviisu was surprised at the fact that the boy spoke to her like an equal, as if she were a friend. She had had so few friends, only Anja and one other girl from Uhtua, but never a boy …

Now, lying in the dark surrounded by mysterious noises, she remembered everything they had spoken about. For two weeks they had met every single day. Aniviisu's grief had not yet let up at all, but she was able to talk about it with Kaarlo, even to say the word "mother" without bursting into tears. The days just flew by too fast, the time to say goodbye came before they knew it.

"Goodbye, Aniviisu," Kaarlo said, using her name for the first time. "We'll meet again next spring as soon as school is out."

Before he left, he played the same sad yet comforting tune he had played when they had first met. Then the boy disappeared into the forest, and once again Aniviisu pondered what was real, and what was not.

The snow that had fallen during the night reached up to the windows; only very small patches still lingered on the roof, and they, too, began quickly to melt as the sun climbed higher. In the afternoon, the first drops of water fell from the eaves. The people out in the yard noticed this, lifted their faces toward the sun and sniffed the air. Spring was in the air! You could see it everywhere, even if the joyfully dripping drops still formed into icicles at night.

Aniviisu was standing on the steps of the house when two laden sleighs stopped in the yard. Huovinen sat in one of the sleighs. He asked Aniviisu to go and fetch an adult.

"What's it about?" Aniviisu asked. She didn't feel like telling him that Katri was out lifting nets with Teppana and that Nasti was doing laundry on the shore by the sauna.

Huovinen looked at Aniviisu with displeasure.

"Adults!" he barked. "Can't you hear me!"

"There are no adults at home," Aniviisu answered without yielding to Huovinen's glance. "And what's more, this is *my* house! You can take your paints and your window panes to the shed on the left, it's empty."

Huovinen glanced at the girl again with a trace of an amused smile. Then he ordered the men to carry in the material. Aniviisu stood on the steps looking as determined as she could, with a scarf over her shoulders and with reddened cheeks.

Huovinen urged the men on, looking every once in a while at Aniviisu. The man was clearly irritated that the girl appeared to supervise the men's work.

"So, you're the owner of the house," Huovinen said as he finally stopped in front of the girl. "It's your house, is it?"

"Yes, mine," Aniviisu said.

"I say, the girl has a temper," Huovinen muttered groping for his pipe in his pocket. "Standing there, clad in scant clothing, watching over things, you could be frozen solid."

The man tapped his empty pipe and left, the others followed, laughing.

Now Aniviisu herself realized how cold she was, but she waited until the men had left with their sleighs; only then did she go inside –

and straight to the recently heated hearth. Her thoughts were confused, she hated and loathed everything to do with the new house.

She sat down at her desk and stared out the window. There was snow everywhere, the tree branches were bending under the weight of the snow. As Aniviisu was sitting there deep in thought a large spruce was suddenly freed of its burden: there came a great swoosh and the girl was startled; the dark branches sprang upward as if born again.

The Girls' School in Sortavala … Aniviisu drifted back into her thoughts. That could now become reality. Katri would get an apartment in Sortavala and they would live together – far away from the dark figure of Ilja Huotari.

Once again Aniviisu was drawn back to the present when she heard clattering at the front door. She thought it was Nasti, but instead a happily smiling girl slipped into the room.

Aniviisu sprang to her feet and flung her arms around the visitor.

"Anja!"

Anja was the only daughter of schoolteacher Darja Mihailovna Remisova, who was the teacher in the Uhtua primary school. She had arrived a few years ago from St Petersburg and immediately aroused conflicting emotions among the Karelians. The language of instruction in the school was Russian, but Darja Mihailovna spoke fluent Finnish, which was rare for Russians. It was also rumored that she held socialist views; someone who had visited her tiny house in Lamminpää village was said to have seen issues of Russia's Social Democratic Party's magazine, *The Spark*. Darja Mihailovna was considered a strange and a dangerous woman, and many would have gladly taken their children from her care, particularly as she was said to be speaking disrespectfully even of the Czar. There were, however, only a couple of schools in Uhtua. And since most of what Darja Mihailovna spoke about seemed like incomprehensible rubbish to the children's parents, they settled for avoiding this peculiar woman, some casting sullen glances at her, others feeling downright afraid.

The teacher herself did not care about people's attitudes. She treated everyone equally brusquely. She knew she was hated and feared, but she also knew she did her job properly. She taught the children to read and write. And so she twisted her hair even more tightly into a bun and kept an ever more undecipherable expression on her reticent face. Only the piercing gaze of her dark eyes revealed the fury that raged inside her. In her black jacket she would ski in the winter from Lamminpää to the Ryhjä school, and in the summer she would walk the same distance with brisk, purposeful strides. And Anja was always with her but no one had ever heard the mother speak a single word to her daughter; they journeyed in silence. In school Anja was shunned because of her mother and she had no friends other than Anna Liisa Huotari.

"Did you come all the way fom Uhtua?" Aniviisu asked her friend.

"Yes, I did, since I haven't seen you for a long time," Anja said, taking off her jacket. "You seem to be doing fine."

Aniviisu nodded quietly. The memory of her parents' drowning was no longer constantly on her mind, although it still hurt. Then she looked at Anja smiling; it made her feel good that Anja had come. At the same time Aniviisu was a little concerned about her friend. The black dress Anja had on did not seem to suit a young girl like her, and there was something else shabby and worn about Anja's appearance.

"I kept pestering Mother to let me come and see you," explained Anja. "Then when she had to visit the Paakkinen school near Pistojärvi, and had borrowed a horse for the trip, I got to go along … Mother will come and pick me up tomorrow. Is it all right if I stay overnight?

"Of course it is!" Anviisu laughed. "We can both fit in my bed."

Anja was silent for a while and looked a little secretive, then she said:

"I've been accepted by the Girls' School in Sortavala! Mother first thought she would send me to St Petersburg, but when her sister Natalia took a job as a nurse in Sortavala, she wrote to Mother that I should take the entrance test. Well – Mother organized the examination and the test, and here we are!"

Aniviisu laughed. "I have not been accepted yet, but Katri will organize the same tests for me."

"You'll do fine, I'm sure!"

The girls were quiet a while, then Anja said: "That new house sure is huge! When is the man coming?"

"The man…" Aniviisu thought. It felt strange to hear Anja speak of Ilja Huotari the same way she did.

"In the letter we got, it said the ship would be coming to Finland's capital in late summer … You know what, I hate that man already! Oh, I hope I can go to Sortavala and be in the same class with you, that would help. I wouldn't have to live here under Ilja Huotari's watchful eyes."

"Aren't you going to move into the new house?" Anja asked surprised.

"No!" Aniviisu shook her head vehemently. "Never! Come – let's go out, I'll show it to you. We can take the sled down to the tip of the point and then you can see the monster with your own eyes."

Anja put on her worn-out overcoat. Aniviisu thought it was Anja's mother's old coat. Aniviisu's sensitive nose had always detected the smell of the Remisova cottage, which told of poverty and want. During her first year at school Anja had been sick a lot, and then it became known that Darja Mihailovna couldn't afford decent food for her child. Now they had a cow, and Anja's cheeks had become considerably rounder, having had milk to drink and butter on her bread.

They slid down to the sauna shore. Anja sat on the sled and Aniviisu kicked. The sled glided smoothly on the ice towards Huotari Point, and Aniviisu steered it to the very tip of the point. The new building basked in the brilliant sunshine. A tower had just been completed on the roof, and Anja looked at it wide-eyed.

"What's that?" she asked Aniviisu.

"The house has two ordinary stories and then stairs to the tower," Aniviisu explained as she had heard Katri say. "It's probably the man's secret room … Huovinen had said a water tank would be brought in there somewhere and that when you turn some kind of faucet, water comes through a pipe."

"He must have lied," Anja said. "Water must be carried in from the lake or the well. Everyone knows that."

Aniviisu shook her head.

"This house is not like any other – you should have seen what large windows they brought from Archangel."

At the top of the tower two men were working. They were putting shingles on the roof. Anja thought they must be able to see all the way to Likopää from that high up.

"Why don't you call him *buobo*?" she said suddenly looking at Aniviisu. "Why do you always call him "that man" or Ilja Huotari?"

"If he had wanted to be a *buobo* to me, he would have written ten years ago. He hasn't shown any interest in anything around here. If it hadn't been for Nasti and Teppana, who knows, I might have ended up in the poorhouse. They were the ones to let Katri know that a little orphan girl was living here."

Anja understood Aniviisu's sorrow; her own father was also dead, although she had been four when he died. She sighed to herself and thought of St Petersburg, where they had lived at the time. She could not understand why her mother had insisted on coming here to this village in the wilderness and refused even to visit St Petersburg. She knew the reason: her mother hated czarist Russia and hoped for revolution. The Czar's power was, however, so firm that nothing could bring him down. In his day, Grandfather Remisov had belonged to a group that had attempted to assassinate the previous Czar – and with what result: Grandfather had been convicted and executed. That was something Darja Mihailovna could never forget or forgive. Over the years, she had managed to pass on her own hatred to her daughter. Even now Anja found herself thinking that Ilja Huotari was an evil person – a house of that size would be able to house ten families, yet Huotari had it built only for himself.

"What kind of a person is he?" she wondered aloud. "He probably doesn't care about the poor at all! Comes here playing the bigwig, sticking out his stomach covered with wolf's fur and orders you to live with him and, as his first command, tells you not to keep company with me."

"Where did you get ideas like that?" Aniviisu asked perplexed.

"There you see!" Anja said. "You are already defending him."

"I'm not defending anybody," Aniviisu said angrily. "How would we know if he's rich or poor."

"Would a poor man build something like that?"

"He might have done it on credit!"

"In that case he is crazy!"

With that they ended their squabble. Aniviisu asked Anja to sit on the sled and began to kick it along the ice toward the sauna shore. Anja cast a glance at the house they left behind, which after all fascinated her.

Katri was glad to see Anja and Aniviisu sitting together absorbed in the *Tales of a Field Surgeon*. Aniviisu was always so much alone, and it was plain to see that Anja's visit had cheered her up. Katri's feelings toward Anja were mixed. The girl had adopted her mother's ideas, which in Katri's opinion were quite strange. She had herself always felt a slight suspicion towards anything to do with Russia or Russians. After her husband's death, she had become even more suspicious. Anja was, however, dear to Aniviisu, and that's why Katri's eyes shone with affection as she watched the girls, who were no longer children, but not yet women either, rather something in between.

"It's really good, Anja, that you were accepted by the Sortavala school," Katri said. "Did you specifically want to go there?"

"Aunt Natalia has recently moved there and Mother thought I could live with her.

"Yes, of course," Katri said. "Aniviisu will live with me the same way. Well, then you'll get to see each other every day."

Katri looked at Aniviisu affectionately, but when she glanced at Anja she had a strange premonition. She did not know what caused it. Could it be the girl's shabbiness, her mother's small dark eyes, the self-assertive tilt of her head, the fact that she was constantly on her guard? Katri could not help but feel a tinge of aversion toward her, however hard she tried to fight it. She forced her mind to think; she had to let go of her petty criticisms; she had to take joy in the fact that someone brought a smile to Aniviisu's face.

That night no one slept in the Huotari house. The northerly wind swept across the open sea, brushing the remaining snow toward shore. It howled and whined in the corners.

The following day in the afternoon, teacher Darja Mihailovna rode her borrowed horse to the sauna shore, tied the horse to the dock post and walked with brisk steps up the slope to the old house. She had on the same black coat as always, and her hair was covered with a black scarf. She knocked on the door and without waiting for an answer pushed the door open. The people were having a meal. Without a word, Darja Mihailovna unbuttoned her coat, took it off, put it on the bench by the door, took off her scarf, arranged her hair quickly and took one step forward.

"Good day to you all," she said with a clear, resounding voice.

"Good day to you, Darja Mihailovna, come on in," Katri said in a friendly voice. 'Please join us at the table, though we're having only fish and potatoes ..."

"A person needs nothing more than that to eat," replied Darja Mihailovna and looked at her daughter. "How have the girls enjoyed being together?"

"They had a good time, said Katri. Nasti and Teppana did not dare open their mouths; that's how harsh and unfriendly Darja Mihailovna's tone of voice was.

Nasti did, however, fetch a plate and utensils, and made room at the table.

"There you are," she said, motioning with her hand.

"It is not proper for poor people to refuse food," said Darja Mihailovna, which caused Anja to blush. "I have been inspecting the old Paakkinen school; they say the children have been sickly all winter. I discovered the reason: the place is too drafty, the stoves aren't hot enough, and the children are shivering with cold and keep getting fevers. The young male teacher is quite helpless ... Perhaps some help would be available from this house?

Teppana coughed hard, staring at the table. Darja Mihailovna gave him a disapproving glance.

"The school's stove should be repaired," the teacher said. "But who can you talk to about it, when there are no men in the village, everyone out peddling on the Finnish side of the border ... Could you make a trip there?

"I guess I could go there ..."

Nothing else was said. Darja Mihailovna only sized Teppana up with her eyes, but then concentrated on eating.

Anja cast a glance at Aniviisu, but the girls didn't speak, and it would not have been appropriate. When the meal was finished, Darja Mihailovna offered a curt thank you and went to get her coat.

"I heard that Aniviisu, too, wants to go to Sortavala, she said having got her coat on and while tying her scarf.

"Yes, she does," Katri responded. "I have a teacher's position at the Sortavala teacher's seminary, and Aniviisu can live with me."

Darja Mihailovna nodded with her face expressionless. She did not like this woman who had come to Huotari, taken the girl out of school and begun to tutor her herself for the girls' school. Did the woman even have the proper training? However, she didn't want to start asking about that. She waited, fully dressed, until Anja was ready for the journey. Then she nodded, thanked them for the food, and walked out with the girl in tow.

Aniviisu ran out to the front yard after Anja and asked her to visit soon again. Anja waved eagerly, but Anja's mother did not invite Aniviisu to their home.

The mail moved slowly between Viena Karelia and Sortavala, but the news finally arrived that Aniviisu had been accepted and could attend the Girls' School in Sortavala in the fall. She was allowed to skip fifth grade and was placed in the sixth grade. Because she lived so far from Sortavala, the entrance test was taken under teacher Katri Jääskeläinen's supervision. Aniviisu had no problems; she labored for a day with the test that arrived in the mail. She solved both the algebra problems and the geography questions. Katri had even taught her Swedish and when a sample of that was also attached to the answers, it was no wonder Aniviisu was accepted to the Girls' School.

Otherwise the days passed, morning till night, doing everyday chores. The construction site was bustling with activity. The new house got fireplaces and brick chimneys, light interior walls were erected, and a great many bundles of insulation were carried up to the attic, where a large water tank was indeed installed.

That went beyond Teppana's comprehension. One day after he had chatted with Huovinen by the sauna corner, he ran in, threw his mittens and his work clothes into the basket in the vestibule, and rushed into the living room quite agitated:

"A water tank! Up in the attic – you understand? And pumps in the living room!"

"The living room ...," Katri gave a short laugh. "There probably won't be a living room similar to this one here!"

"In the attic, the attic!"

"The attic?" Nasti lamented. "The water is coming from the attic, you say?"

Aniviisu found Nasti's horrified expression amusing. She felt a strange thrill deep inside when people spoke of the water tank and other contraptions in the new house. She did not yet like the house, not at all, but she realized it represented something new, something that had never existed in Uhtua before. It represented a completely new era.

"The house will be finished before June," Teppana said almost with a sigh.

"And what then is to become of the Sortavala school?" Nasti asked. "What will Ilja Huotari say to that?"

Katri raised her head from her knitting.

"I tell you, I'll take Aniviisu to Sortavala without Ilja Huotari's permission if need be. He has never shown an interest in the girl and he'd better not fancy he'll be giving orders about anything. I have a teacher's position and an apartment ... If Ilja Huotari wants to deny his granddaughter the opportunity to study, he will soon find out whom he is dealing with.

Nasti and Teppana became quiet when Katri spoke, sometimes her strong determination scared them.

May, June, July Aniviisu counted in her mind. "The ship will presumably arrive in Finland's capital in late summer..." What did that mean? July or August? The further spring advanced, the more frightened she became.

How wonderful it was to run around in light shoes in the grove and look at the Vaahtovuori ridge! How exhilarating to see the rays of the sun glittering and sparkling between the spruce tops, and then suddenly to hear the roar of the rapids. The closer Aniviisu came to the rapids, the quieter the forest grew, until the deafening roar of the rapids was the only sound you could hear. At last she stood by the edge of the rapids.

She had to take a deep breath when she saw the foaming arc of water that gushed over two giant rocks down into the cascade. It was a familiar view for her from many springs before, yet it never ceased to fascinate her.

Now the atmosphere had an added attraction, for she had promised to meet Kaarlo here.

When Aniviisu turned around she thought she saw a human shape further away between the trees. Kaarlo! She felt her heart throb, but when she took an impatient step closer, she noticed it was not Kaarlo ... It was some older man – leaning against a tree, unmoving. He was about sixty feet away. The man was clearly on his guard ... he had on a dark jacket, and was smoking a cigaret.

Aniviisu instinctively felt she was in danger. She turned quickly and started walking away. The man followed her. When Aniviisu walked faster, the man also picked up his pace. By a large boulder next to the road to the village the man caught up with her.

"Stop! I have something to tell you."

Aniviisu's heart jumped into her mouth. The man's voice was raw and unfriendly. Aniviisu looked around in panic; she'd have to run across the road over there and dash into the grove and she would be almost home ... Then the man reached out his hand and pulled the girl close. Aniviisu tried to struggle free, but his grip was like a vise.

He used only one arm, the other one hung limp. He pressed his face almost into the girl's face. Aniviisu was terrified.

"You are from the Huotari house? Answer me!"

Aniviisu managed to nod her head.

"Did your aunt from Suomussalmi come here?"

"Yes ..."

"Did she move here for good?"

The man's grip tightened and Aniviisu yelped.

"No, only for a while ..."

At that moment, Huovinen's horse appeared around the bend in the road. The man did not release his grip in time, and Huovinen realized something odd was going on.

"Stop it, man!" he yelled jumping off the wagon. "What kind of a bloody good-for-nothing are you! Going around scaring children in the woods ..."

The stranger let go of Aniviisu and ran into the woods.

His heavy steps disappeared into the thick spruce grove. Huovinen stared after the man with his fists clenched, and then turned to Aniviisu who stood there her face white as a sheet, lips blue, and trembling as if in a fever.

"What did he say?"

"He asked about Katri… my aunt."

"Why don't you come with me, I'll take you home. You don't need to be afraid any more, I'll find him and I'll squeeze the truth out of him, find out what this is all about ..."

Huovinen accompanied Aniviisu through the little grove to the yard of the old house.

"Now, you go in and tell your aunt every word the man said."

After Huovinen had left, Aniviisu remained standing on the steps. For the first time in her life, fear of evil had entered her world. It affected her deeply and she was still shaken. Suddenly she realized the world was not the kind of place she had thought it to be. All people were not good – that man in the forest was truly evil.

Aniviisu sat down on the steps trying the get her thoughts to calm down. But the feeling of horror that had flooded her when the man grabbed her arm kept returning again and again. She sat there shivering, and that is how Katri found her.

"Good grief, what has happened, you poor child?"

In May of that same year people in Uhtua were talking about Halley's Comet. The newspaper *Echo* from Oulu, which Katri read regularly, told about people who warned that the comet was a sign that the end of the world was near. The comet had not come near the earth for two thousand years, but now it would crash into it. Finally, on May the eleventh, the comet passed by the Earth at a safe distance, and the end of the world did not come after all.

Unlike Nasti, Katri did not fear Halley's Comet, but the Czar's manifesto, on the other hand, gave her a great shock. Czar Nicholas II had issued a manifesto designed to bring Finland under the jurisdiction of Russian law. The darkness that now hung over Finland – which had been able to live quite independently after the national general strike – was to her comparable to the threat of the end of the world.

"And the human spirit is again in new shackles ...," Katri had sighed one night while sitting in the dark living room with Aniviisu.

"Is that from some poem?"

"Yes, it's from Kaarlo Kramsu's poem "The New Era".

Aniviisu did not ask anything more, but to herself she was thinking how sad a person must be who even in the new era sees only the bad things returning in a new form. Was the world really like that? She did not want to believe it.

At the time of the general strike there had been huge riots, tens of thousands of workers had marched on the streets and the events were brought to a tragic culmination on the day that since then had been called Bloody Sunday. On that day, the army had started shooting at the demonstrators and hundreds had been killed. Even the rural areas experienced unrest because the abolition of serfdom had not eliminated poverty and inequality; the peasants had rebelled and many manors had been burned down. Even in Uhtua strange men had been seen roaming about after the general strike. They tried to hold meetings in different villages, and they tried to turn people against the Czar. Uhtuans did attend the meetings, but the strangers' speeches were so lofty that no one really understood them. And also, they disapproved of the fact that the strangers spoke disrespectfully of the Czar.

One evening Darja Mihailovna had called such a meeting. A moon-faced socialist with a pointed beard had arrived from St Petersburg to give a speech. He had shouted in a loud voice and banged his fist in his hand for added effect. When he got all worked up about how the church, and even God, were oppressors of the poor, some of the men took it upon themselves to calm him down. But the visitor only brusquely told them that they did not understand their own best interest but let themselves be treated any which way. When the man from St Petersburg had finished, Darja Mihailovna had taken the floor and spoken at least as doggedly and vehemently.

"Uhtuans!" She had shouted. "Is the Czar helping you? Are the Finns helping you? Who hates you more than the Germans! Join the common front to defend Viena. The Socialist revolutionaries support you and will help against oppressors who come from all directions! You are waiting in vain for the Czar to show you humanity. All power to the people!"

People did not quite know what to think. Someone had wanted to ask the St Petersburg man some questions, but he had disappeared as inconspicuously as he had arrived.

The following Sunday, Nasti and Teppana had returned from church all agitated.

"People at church were saying that the Russians have started to send people to Siberia. That half a million people have been sent there already."

Alarmed Nasti had asked Katri if it was possible that Viena could be emptied based on an order from the Czar ...

"He probably wouldn't dare touch Viena ..."

Some time passed, but a quiet horror remained in the hearts of the Viena people. After the general strike, The Viena Karelia League had been established in Uhtua. The village meeting had demanded that the Russian Duma grant democracy and constitutional status for Karelia. The request had not been granted, the Czarist government had not agreed to deal with the problems of the Karelians, nor with their wishes. The inhabitants of Viena felt great uncertainty about their future because they felt they were alone in some sense between Finland and Russia. Both the Finns and the Russians tried to convert them, and they both promised them freedom.

When Aniviisu told Katri about the man she had encountered in the forest, Katri's face suddenly turned white and she went into the alcove, almost running. Nasti looked at Aniviisu, and the girl went in after her aunt. Katri was standing by the window gripping hard the back of the chair. Her face had a strangely agitated look as if she had wanted to scream out loud.

"Aniviisu, come in," she said turning toward the door. "Tell me what the man was like."

Aniviisu pondered. What did he look like ... evil ...

"Tall ... he was pretty tall. Dark hair ... And – yes, one of his arms was somehow peculiar!"

Katri nodded gravely.

"He's paralyzed. That's right – it was him ... Aniviisu, sit down on the chair, I'll tell you about him. I know that man, he was an agent for the revolutionaries, and he tries to get people to believe in doctrines that may lead to great destruction. Don't ever tell that man anything should he ever come back."

Aniviisu listened wide-eyed with fear in her eyes.

"Why did he ask for you?" she asked almost with a whisper.

"He was involved in the death of my husband – but you are too young to hear about that. I will tell you in good time."

Aniviisu looked at Katri's serious and pale face. Katri, too, was afraid; Aniviisu felt it instinctively. She did not dare think what the strange man had done to Katri's husband. Something bad, no doubt.

"Do I dare walk in the forest again. The boy said we were to meet by the rapids as soon as school was out."

"Yes – I can even accompany you. It's so much more fun to walk together. Now go and take off your coat and give Nasti a hand. We'll still have time to study later."

After Aniviisu left, Katri sat on the bench deep in thought. She knew that the changes that had occurred in Russia after the general strike had given the Viena people new hope of independence. The people were fed up with the fact that teachers and priests were almost exclusively Russian. Neither the children nor the churchgoers understood half of what they were being told.

And the more the people shunned the priests and the teachers, the more sullen and less friendly their behavior became. The Russian authorities were a breed apart, and were hated by everyone. Under the seemingly calm surface there was a constant surge of emotions, and the Karelian people were just waiting for the moment when they could be freed from their oppressors. Their reactions were monitored both by henchmen of the secret police and the agents of the revolutionaries alike.

The appearance of the new house had changed as the materials had been gradually transported to the construction site. The house now had glass panes covering the window openings, the tower had developed into a little room on top, the window frames had been decorated and the enormous water tank had been heaved up to the attic. They were now cleaning up around the building, which was not easy since the snow had melted and turned the entire area into a soggy, muddy field.

One evening Teppana came into the living room looking mysterious. He watched the others with a sly look on his face, speaking about this and that until finally he could no longer hold back the news that Huovinen had invited him to look at the new house – inside and all.

Nasti had to sit down.

"So, tell us, tell us ... What was it like?"

Teppana began at a leisurely pace:

“Two stories, upstairs and downstairs. In addition, a staircase to the tower.”

“Start with the downstairs,” Katri requested.

“Well, when you go inside under the big overhang, first there is the vestibule. From there you enter a huge room, which has such a row of pillars that you get dizzy. Hallway is what Huovinen called it’.

“The front hall, yes…” Katri said, urging him to go on.

“On the right is a room where they are supposed to eat. That, too, was big, they could fit an army for meals in there. And the windows behind it belong to the cooking room.”

“Kitchen, that’s what that room is called,” Katri knew to tell them.

“On the left is an even bigger room than that hallway and those pillars are in front of it … And the water tank is in the attic and the water is pumped directly from the lake.’

Nasti squeezed her hands and said blessings; Aniviisu listened with her eyes squinting, but tried to look disinterested.

“What about the upstairs?” Nasti egged him on. ‘Did you go upstairs?”

Teppana dug out his pipe with deliberate slowness.

“Yeah, I did – a wide staircase led upstairs from the hallway, and there were at least five, six bedrooms … It had an indoor box to pee in, no need to visit the outhouse; you only need to sit on a wooden chair and go. That, too, is rinsed with water, that’s what Huovinen said.”

“Hospody!’ Again Nasti said blessings. “You don’t need to go outside! You can let go there! Oh my goodness, they must have pulled your leg!”

“Such things do exist,” Katri hurried to defend Teppana. ‘You can also heat the water and it runs in pipes inside the house. There is a lot in this world that we have not seen. But how does it look otherwise – does it have floors and doors?”

"It has floors and it has doors," Teppana said. "The floors reek badly, but the surface is so hard and shiny that you can see your reflection in it ..."

That was something for the women to digest. Katri was dying to see the house on the inside, and she tried to think of some excuse to make her wish come true. What if she were to tell Huovinen straight out that she wanted to see everything that had been finished during the last few months.

"They said the furniture will be brought in in two weeks' time," Teppana continued.

"The furniture?" Katri wondered; she had not seen any furniture.

"It, too, has been brought here from the warehouse in Viena Kemi," Teppana said. "Everything has been taken to Uhtua during the winter, they will now be shipped here by boat. And they say he has so many books that there is a separate room only for them."

"A room only for books!" Nasti again wagged her tongue.

Books ... Aniviisu looked out the window and a strange yearning began to stir in her mind. Books ... the man had books. But were they in the Finnish language, what if they are in a foreign language, one she didn't understand. Yet her *buobo* was, of course, from Viena, I wonder if he even knows the language of Canada ... And who knows, he might not even let anyone near his books. If he does not let me go to Sortavala, then all my dreams of books will end as well.

Books ... Katri pondered. Enough books to require a library. I wonder if they are in English or Finnish? If there are so many that they need a room of their own, then there really have to be a lot – and such quantities of Finnish language literature would probably not be available in Canada. The majority of the books must be in English ... That's good, Katri thought. If I get to live here this summer taking care of Aniviisu, then I will surely dare ask to borrow a few books; and I have done some studying on my own after the teachers' seminary and above all when Juhani was still alive. Juhani spoke English quite well, in addition to Swedish ...

They talked about the new house and its wonders all evening. When they went to bed it was the last day of May. Finland's Parliament had requested that the Czar continue to honor Finland's constitution. There was no reply yet to the request, but when they woke up on the morning of June 1, great things were about to happen out in the world, things that would have an impact even on their lives.

It was already summer in Finland, but Viena was still experiencing late spring. The snow was gone, the newly emerged ground was glistening, and the waves were billowing on Lake Kuittijärvi. The previous week's rain had warmed the ground enough that the leaves of the birches were budding, the cowslips and the wood anemones were blooming. The leaves of the midsummer roses' were large and green. One day Teppana saw the first swallows. One of them had flown very low and suddenly a rain shower had arrived. The sun was quickly covered as dark clouds gathered above Lake Kuittijärvi, and then large rain drops began to pelt the sauna roof and the sand on the shore. Teppana had watched the swallow, which hid under the eaves of the sauna looking at the rain. When the shower had passed and the clouds moved on toward the north, another swallow swooped in from the direction of Uhtua to join the first one. Teppana recounted this with a smile.

"I guess they became a couple then ..."

The next morning a strange fog rolled in; it blanketed the surface of Lake Kuittijärvi like a mysteriously creeping wall. Everybody could follow the advance of the fog with their own eyes and when it reached the shore it spread at the roof level and spread to the pond, to the river, and to the rapids. The fog was thick and mobile; Teppana could not recall ever having seen one like it, but that, too, was part of spring in Viena. The rains continued with brief showers and afterward the shore of the entire Lake Kuittijärvi region gave off a wonderful fragrance of cool soil.

One day Huovinen brought word from Uhtua that the man who had been sneaking about in the woods was a revolutionary, an agent from St Petersburg. He had been arrested and sent to St Petersburg. Now once again Aniviisu was free to walk alone in the forest.

Around the same time, Katri had received a newspaper from Oulu with a news item that gave them things to ponder:

> The Russian Duma approves a proposal to extend its national legislative authority over Finland. Russia's hold on Finland tightens. This proposal is a further step on the way to annexation of Finland to the Czar's empire. According to the new law, all issues that do not explicitly concern only matters internal to Finland are to be dealt with in accordance with the empire's general legislation, i.e., by Russian legislative branches, thus by-passing the Finnish Parliament altogether. The Parliament is left with only an advisory role.

"What is to become of Finland now?" Katri spoke aloud. "What will happen to Viena Karelia?"

That very question was on the minds of all thinking individuals in Viena and in the Finnish border region. The news aroused bitterness and defiance; it was clear to each and every one that new forms of oppression had been instituted. But they had also awakened a new yearning for independence.

Aniviisu walked briskly in the forest. She was wearing soft brown shoes with laces tied around her ankle. She had put on a red skirt, and over her everyday white blouse she had wrapped a red-striped shawl – it kept her warm in the shade of the forest, it held off the mosquitoes, and the spruce needles did not penetrate it as she walked in the dense spruce grove.

Nasti had been nagging Aniviisu for quite a while now to wear the *otsipaikka*, the headdress for young women. Aniviisu paid no heed, and let her hair flow freely; she abhorred anything that would tie her down by rules and regulations.

Her spirit was free and light as she walked in the forest that abounded with the smells and sounds of early summer. The brooks rippled and the birds chirped looking for nest-building materials. The sun shone warmly drying up the mosses after the long, wet spring.

The roar of the rapids became louder, and Aniviisu increased her pace unconsciously. When she came to the pond, she stopped abruptly: Kaarlo was sitting on the tree trunk with his back toward her. At that moment the boy turned, having heard Aniviisu's footsteps.

"You came," he said with a smile which brightened his face.

Aniviisu blushed.

"It's summer now," she said, sitting down on the tree trunk next to the boy. "You are now sixteen and I am eleven, just like you said last summer. How was your winter?"

"Rather dull, to tell you the truth – work and studying."

Aniviisu looked around searchingly and then she asked: "Where is your violin?"

"It is being repaired – Father will bring it to Uhtua next week."

After a short while they were talking away without inhibitions, just as if there had not been any winter in between. Kaarlo said he was now going to stay in Uhtua all summer.

"Oh, would you like to come over to our house?" Aniviisu suddenly suggested. "Katri is home, she is my aunt. Nasti and Teppana are off to Uhtua by boat."

Kaarlo was immediately ready to go. They walked side by side through the grove until they came to the old road. From there they could see both houses. Kaarlo stopped as if frozen.

"What's that?" He said, pointing at the new house.

Aniviisu turned up her nose.

"My *buobo,* Ilja Huotari, is arriving from Canada at the end of the summer. He had that monster built on our point. Suddenly last fall logs and other materials began to arrive … The inside has now been finished, and they say the furniture is coming next week. There are about twenty men working there."

They walked along the old road to the west side of the point and stopped to look at the house from the rear. Then they took the flat-bottomed rowboat and began to row and circle the tip of the point. Kaarlo couldn't take his eyes off the house. From inside they could hear hammering and men's voices. Somewhere behind the house a horse neighed. When they reached the tip, they saw six boats pulled up on the shore and a barge at anchor a hundred and fifty feet out from the tip of the point.

"That must be the furniture," Aniviisu said bewildered. "It must have arrived late last night – the lake view was blocked by the foliage of birches."

Kaarlo rowed silently, still looking at the house.

"What an odd tower!" he said finally. "I have never seen a house like that."

They soon arrived at the sauna shore, and Kaarlo pulled the rowboat onto the sand. The sauna roof was covered again with green moss, and a bench was placed beside the sauna.

"You must be pretty happy to live in a place with such charm, Kaarlo said.

Aniviisu stopped and looked at the boy with surprise. Happy – she whose mother and father had died and who now, with a cold heart, awaited a strange man she was supposed to call *buobo*? What did he mean ... She was not happy, she was full of fears, she was afraid of almost everything. She glanced at him from the corner of her eye – she realized he was not from around here; people here were not in the habit of talking about happiness.

Katri was shaking rugs when the youngsters walked into the yard.

"Katri, this is the boy I met last summer by the pond. His name is Kaarlo."

Katri offered her hand with a smile.

"Hello, Kaarlo. You are from Uhtua, are you?"

"From Sortavala..." The boy said, offering his hand, and bowing.

"All the way from Sortavala..."

"My name is Kaarlo Meinander. I attend the high school there."

"Meinander? Is your father Henrik Meinander, the ethnologist?"

"Yes, he is," the boy said astonished.

Katri gave a cheerful laugh.

"Well, isn't that a coincidence. When will you see him next?"

"Today, I guess."

"Tell your father that Katri Jääskeläinen is here on Huotari Point."

"I will, of course."

The boy was embarrassed. Katri looked at him as the youngsters sat on the steps. His father's son, not the slightest doubt; the same refined features, shy pleasant demeanor, remarkably sensitive hands, and dreamy eyes. Too bad Aniviisu had not happened to mention his name before. Or maybe she had mentioned it – Katri had to admit she had thought the violin-playing boy a figment of the girl's imagination.

"We are planning to come to Sortavala next fall, Aniviisu and I," said Katri. "Aniviisu has been accepted by the Girls' School in Sortavala.

"Didn't I tell you," Kaarlo chuckled, "they have the best school there."

They talked away all afternoon, and Katri took a real liking to the boy, who, despite his poet-like appearance, seemed very sensible. She found herself wishing he would visit the Huotari Point often, so that Aniviisu would not have to be alone. It would be good for the girl to spend time with people other than Anja ...

Late in the afternoon Kaarlo returned to Uhtua. Aniviisu took the boat and rowed him far in the direction of Likopää. Halfway they met Nasti and Teppana's boat; Nasti's mouth gaped as Aniviisu just waved her hand and rowed past with a laugh.

On the Huotari Point side of the Uhtua embankment, Kaarlo got out of the boat saying next time he would come with his aunt Elma's boat.

"Are you coming tomorrow?"

Aniviisu's voice sounded very thin and she did not dare look at him.

"Yes, I'll come tomorrow."

As Aniviisu rowed back home she steered the boat close to the dock where their neighbor, Outi, was sitting dangling her legs in the water.

"Aniviisu, come here and talk to me!" Outi shouted. Aniviisu steered the boat to the side of the dock. Outi had only a white slip on. Aniviisu thought that if she were to swing like that on the dock, Nasti would come and pull her away by the hair. But Outi did not care what people thought, she just laughed away and wiggled her toes splashing the water.

"When is he coming, your *buobo*?"

"Nobody knows," Aniviisu said. "In the summer, I guess."

"Is he a handsome man?"

"I don't know."

"At least he's rich," Outi said with a laugh. "The house, I'm told, is the biggest and grandest in Uhtua. I can hardly wait ... What does he look like?"

"Nobody seems to remember."

Outi pursed her lips disgruntled.

"You are reticent today, aren't you. Well – go away, row home, now off with you ..."

Outi was always very impatient, she got excited in a second, but lost her enthusiasm just as quickly. She never talked at length with anyone, but was off somewhere else – like now. When she did not get any information from Aniviisu, she got tired and impatient, got up from the dock and started walking slowly to her house. Aniviisu rowed ahead, and soon she could see the brown walls of the new house.

In the evening, Katri asked Aniviisu to go for a walk. In a short while they came to the road behind the old house, and as if inadvertently ended up in the yard of the new house. Huovinen and two other men stood by the gable having a smoke. Huovinen noticed the women first.

"Hello there!" he exclaimed. "How about a little tour of the house?"

"It was easier than I thought," Katri whispered to Aniviisu. "Let's pretend it was his idea."

Slowly they turned and walked up to the men. Huovinen looked at Katri with the curiosity of a ladies' man. So there are blond beauties living here in the Viena wilderness...

"You were saying?" Katri said looking inquiringly at Huovinen.

"Madam isn't from around here, I take it ..."

"No – I'm from the Finnish side, from Suomussalmi. I am this girl's aunt."

A smile spread across Huovinen's face.

"Oh yes, the house owner ... Would you esteemed ladies be interested in seeing what the house looks like on the inside? Everything is about finished."

Katri pretended to give it some thought, then she agreed.

Huovinen went in first, the women followed. Aniviisu had resisted Katri's suggestion at first, but now Huovinen's phrase "esteemed ladies" flattered her. It included her as well.

Close up the house was stunningly huge. On top of the main entrance was a large terrace, and the door was made of some dark unknown wood. The door handle was of shiny metal. They stepped into the entrance hall, which had a small room on each side. Aniviisu stared wide-eyed at the room on the left. There it was, the box Teppana had talked about, and it was really indoors. There was a hole in the seat of the chair, and from above hung a string with a porcelain weight at the end.

"It's a water closet," Katri said hurrying on, driven by her curiosity.

Next they entered the large hallway – and stopped to look around, holding their breath. In the middle of the hallway a wide staircase rose to the second floor. The hall was lined with white pillars, four on each side and between them they could see a large room on either side.

"On the right is the dining room, which seats twelve people at once."

In the corner of the dining room was a fireplace, and an entrance to the kitchen. Katri had read about American-style kitchens, but had never seen one. The kitchen had a counter on each side. The stove was ridiculously big, and on the back wall was the door to the maid's room and the pantry. Katri walked around the kitchen, touched the shining counter tops; there was enough room to cook for ten people or more every day ... They returned to the hallway and entered the room on the left, which Huovinen called the parlor. It, too, had a fireplace and the windows overlooked Lake Kuittijärvi. From the parlor, they went to the rear of the house, which had three additional rooms. The walls of the library were lined with tall shelves and between the two windows was a mirror, almost from floor to ceiling.

Aniviisu was wary of looking in the mirror, neither did she dare look at Katri, who was strangely quiet as they walked towards the staircase.

"Tomorrow we'll start bringing in the furniture," Huovinen said. "They have already been shipped here on the barge."

"So I've noticed," said Katri curtly.

Upstairs were six spacious bedrooms and bathrooms and bathtubs. The entrance to the terrace above the main entrance was from the upper landing.

"The infamous water tank is in the attic," Huovinen said with a smile. "That was a lot of work."

Katri did not answer, she simply had no idea what to say about the water tank. Then she noticed the stairs to the tower. She turned toward them, but Huovinen said sharply, "You are not allowed to go there! The tower is not to be shown to anyone, that is Ilja Huotari's own order."

Katri stopped and turned back. Raising her head a little higher she once again went through all the bedrooms and bathrooms and headed for the steps leading downstairs.

"So – what do you say?" Huovinen asked downstairs. A smug smile played on his lips.

"Will there be an army moving in here?" Katri retorted taking Aniviisu by the hand. "Thank you for showing us around."

Huovinen remained standing in the middle of the hallway, bewildered. He did not understand why the women were so reticent.

When they reached the sauna shore, Katri sat on the bench rubbing her forehead.

"You know, I'm in a total shock," she told Aniviisu. "I never imagined the house to be so enormous … Is the man a megalomaniac – or is he just crazy?"

Aniviisu looked at her aunt thoughtfully.

"Maybe he's not crazy at all – maybe he is serious."

Katri nodded.

"You're right – maybe he is simply so rich that this style of living is normal for him."

"What do you mean?"

"I mean when we wonder about all of this luxury, fourteen rooms and what not, to him it may be quite ordinary. He may well have a similar home in Canada. It is we who are marveling like country bumpkins ..."

"Country bumpkins, that's what we are," Aniviisu said laughing, although she, too, found it incomprehensible that someone would have a home like that.

Katri joined in Aniviisu's laughter, and when Nasti a while later came to the sauna to fetch water, she encountered two exhausted women wiping their eyes.

"Now we've seen it!" Aniviisu announced to the perplexed Nasti.

"It must have been terrible, since you are so drained."

"Nasti – you are such a country bumpkin," Aniviisu said. "A library has to have a gold-framed mirror and the water closet has to be flushed with a porcelain knob."

Before the haying season, Aniviisu and Kaarlo met every day in the same place on the shore of the pond in Small Bird Grove. There were two rocks in a little cove in the pond; Kaarlo used to sit on one of them waiting for Aniviisu to arrive.

Then the haying season started. Kaarlo arrived one morning at the Huotari farm and reported to Katri for work.

"I have some free time now, is it all right if I come?"

"Doesn't Elma have any hay fields?" Katri asked. "Your aunt ..."

"No, she is running a store."

"Well, come on then, my good man, join our team," Katri said cheerfully. "Strong men are always in demand."

It was agreed that Kaarlo would come to Huotari to do haying for the whole week. In the mornings, the youngsters together with Katri and Teppana left to go to the remote meadows, and they returned at night. Aniviisu's cheeks were glowing; it was wonderful for her to see Kaarlo hard at work in the field, stacking hay.

The new house was somehow external to everything, becoming unreal. What went on at the old house had been going on the same way for decades, even for centuries. The work was done, the land cultivated, the cattle tended to. Everything was as natural and uncomplicated as the rising and setting of the sun, as the changing of the seasons.

One sunny afternoon, when they were stacking hay on the stakes on the meadow behind the pond, the talk turned to the new house, for there was no denying that it did arouse curiosity.

"Fourteen rooms!" Katri exclaimed. "I wonder who is moving in besides Ilja Huotari? Maybe he has a large family?"

"He might have gotten married," Nasti said, "and is bringing ten kids."

"Oh, my goodness," said Katri.

Kaarlo leaned on the rake for a while and looked at Aniviisu.

"You'll be moving into the new house then, too."

"Never, never... I'm not going anywhere from my own home!" Aniviisu shouted from the horse cart. As before, Aniviisu drove the horse. By each spot where a hay stake was to be erected, she dropped one stake and a peg to go with it, and the horse lumbered up and down the field.

"That girl does know how to work," Nasti said looking after the moving cart. "One would think that she'd be spoiled, always around adults, but no. I wonder how things would have been if the parents were still alive ..."

"Aniviisu is an intelligent girl," Kaarlo said cautiously, because Aniviisu's outburst had frightened him a little. "It's very good that she's getting away to Sortavala."

"With Katri's help," Nasti said, lifting a big stack of hay in one motion.

The memory of the accident quieted the farm people. For over a year they had tried to get used to the thought that Helena and Moissei were gone. The cheerful, laughing Helena, who always had something positive to say, and the large, dark and awkward Moissei, always reliable. The farm now lived on without them.

Later in the afternoon, the last stakes were finally standing and the last stalks of grass were raked, and so they were ready to go home. Aniviisu drove the horse with Kaarlo; Teppana and the women walked home with the pitchforks and rakes on their shoulders.

At home Aniviisu steered the horse to the back yard, where she brushed, fed, and watered it. Kaarlo stood beside her amazed how skillfully the little girl cared for the large animal.

"Why don't you go swimming before supper," Teppana advised them. "The water is getting pretty warm by now."

The youngsters did not need to be told twice. Aniviisu ran to the sauna and changed into Katri's old bathing suit, which reached down to her knees. Kaarlo swam in his underwear and was already doing the crawl far out when Aniviisu came to the shore. The girl stopped and looked at the dark-haired head bobbing on the open lake. A quiet thrill of happiness stirred in her chest. Kaarlo was a friend ... Besides Anja she now had another friend. But Kaarlo meant something else too, something that confused her. Something that she did not understand.

The summer had arrived so quickly it was nearly impossible to grasp. It felt like only yesterday that the ground had been steaming where the sun was drying the bare spots in the snow – and they had already harvested the hay in the remote meadows! The last couple of days had been so hot that Kaarlo had burned his neck and Aniviisu her cheeks and nose.

In the evening they went again to the pond in the forest. Kaarlo watched silently as Aniviisu spoke to her spirits. The girl greeted invisible goblins sitting on the tree branches, she hugged the large pine tree that seemed to like her touch. She bowed to the rock spirit and the spirit of the rapids, waved her hand to the cloud spirit and to the forest spirit. Aniviisu knew that the others considered the spirits as figments of her imagination, but that didn't bother her – it was enough for her that she knew they were real.

Aniviisu remembered how she had once visited an old woman in Uhtua with her mother. The woman had talked about her spirits as if they were living beings. And Aniviisu's spirits were also living beings, only hidden. She knew the adults did not understand her if she spoke about them. So she kept quiet. To Katri she had occasionally spoken about the spirits and now to Kaarlo – they did not laugh.

They had been together from morning till night for a whole week. After their stint with haying they had still walked to Small Bird Cove, sat by the pond and talked about all kinds of things. And each time Aniviisu had begged:

"Play something, Kaarlo – please play!"

Kaarlo had taken his violin from its case and played. And so he did this evening again. Aniviisu was not familiar with the tunes but they were always beautiful. They mixed joy and sorrow in such a heart-stirring fashion that sweet sadness filled her spirit and sometimes brought tears to her eyes.

Aniviisu looked at the age-old weeping birches whose branches bent down to the water. The surface of the water lily-adorned pond was mirror-smooth, only some insects rippled on it. The sound of the violin made the entire pond seem like a dream that Aniviisu never wanted to end.

But finally Kaarlo stopped playing, and the spell was broken.

"You have tears in your eyes," Kaarlo said and smoothed away a tear from her cheek with his finger.

Aniviisu wiped her eyes and smiled, embarrassed. Kaarlo put the violin back into the case and put it down on the moss. Then he came to sit next to Aniviisu.

"Just cry," he said quietly. "It helps. I know you miss your parents. I still miss my mother …"

Aniviisu lifted the hem of her white slip under her skirt and wiped her eyes with it. Kaarlo looked at her a little shyly. He thought Aniviisu was very attractive with her blond curls and dark-blue eyes. The face was narrow, the nose small, the chin small, the forehead white and pure. The eyes, however, were large, looked frightened – it seemed like they didn't fit in her narrow face. Kaarlo had to remind himself that Aniviisu was only eleven – for the girl age did not seem to have any significance. He felt great affection toward her, he found her feminine and sweet, as if she were his age.

Kaarlo took Aniviisu's hand gently and unselfconsciously in his. Her hand was tiny and rough. Aniviisu lifted her eyes startled, but turned them away instantly. Her shoulders were shaking, and then she burst out weeping. The small gentle gesture released her, and shattered the dam. Kaarlo waited silently until Aniviisu's crying came to an end.

"There," the boy said. "I cry that way, too …"

"You do? Do boys cry too?"

"Yes, they do," Kaarlo said. "People cry when they are unhappy. It doesn't matter if you are a boy or a girl. Crying has strange power, it gives relief and it helps.

Aniviisu was quiet for a moment. Then she looked at him shyly. She let her hand stay in his.

Aniviisu told Kaarlo the story. It took a long time to tell because Aniviisu was honest and left nothing out.

The previous spring around the time the ice began to melt, the floods had been the worst in living memory, and the water level in Lake Kuittijärvi had risen exceptionally high. A little before the final melting of the ice there had been heavy rains, such heavy rains that nothing like it had been seen for decades. The water flooded the fields, the ponds and rivers rose above their banks, and the lake flushed the steps of the sauna.

Snow was still melting in the woods. The marshes were completely covered with water and one had better not walk on them. Teppana had tried on a hunting trip to walk on the causeway, but the planks had started to sink under his feet. He had narrowly escaped by grabbing on to a tree stump and pulling himself to safety.

One weekend in May, when the ice was about to break up, the people at Huotari Point had planned a trip to Kemi in Viena. Moissei had killed a bear in the winter and now he had heard about a tanner in Kemi. They also needed salt and other household goods that were not available in Uhtua.

Helena and Moissei had been to Kemi before by boat. The route was familiar: From Middle Kuittijärvi Lake one sails through the Luusalmi sound to Lower Kuittijärvi Lake and from there via Jyskyjärvi to the Kemi River along which one gets to the city of Kemi, save for a few roaring rapids. The rapids were so bad one had to pull the boat to the shore and carry it past them.

The planned trip became reality. Helena and Moissei had planned to go with their own boat to Jyskyjärvi where they would change boats. They had indeed spent the night in Jyskyjärvi, and then continued their journey to Viena Kemi. It was called a city although Helena had always thought it looked more like a village. There were two-story buildings, that's true, where rich merchants and government officials lived. There was even a large, white Orthodox church. Helena and Moissei had stayed at the inn, the same building that also housed the police station. At night they had walked on the rocky islet by the shore of the White Sea, and watched the ships and barges, which went to the monastery island of Solovetsk. They had made a short boat trip to the big sawmill, where the large ships bound for Kemi unloaded their passengers to await boat transport into town.

Helena and Moissei had been happy, said one Uhtuan merchant, whom they had met while having dinner at the inn.

They had never before been on a trip by themselves. Now they were and behaved like young lovers. As a thin mist had hovered above the White Sea, they had listened to a Russian singer who had come to Kemi to give a concert in the inn's backyard; he had sung melancholy, old songs to lyrics by Lermontov.

Then it was time to return home. They had salt, coffee and fabrics. They had traveled alongside Kemi River on the new road and got a boat as soon as they needed one.

The Kemi River had flooded and the strong current slowed their advance because they were going against it. But they were in no hurry. Every now and then they had rowed ashore and eaten some of the food they had bought in Kemi. Settlements along the river were sparse, only an occasional, wretched little village with a few houses and outbuildings. The trip was not yet arduous, although the long and narrow Usmana rapids could be quite ferocious during the spring floods. The water roared and rumbled with no rock islet in view, and so they bypassed the rapids on foot, respectful and cautious. After this they could again embark on a stretch of water a few miles long. Moissei had been pulling the oars until one o'clock at night. Then they had gone ashore in order to sleep in a small fisherman's hut. When they arrived, a couple from Uhtua they knew were departing for Kemi into the night. They had wished Helena and Moissei good luck on the rest of their journey, which was filled with rapids.

Aniviisu told her parents' story as if she had been there herself. As the girl's voice trembled and weakened, Kaarlo squeezed her hand as if prodding her to continue and finish her story. Kaarlo's heart was moved as he realized how many times Aniviisu must have gone through her parents' last journey in her mind, how bitterly she must have felt it in her imagination. The girl had to let it all out, otherwise it would consume her whole mind. Kaarlo knew that the most difficult part of the story was still ahead.

They both knew how the journey ended, but oh, how Aniviisu had imagined the actual accident …

The water ran into the gorge surprisingly calmly. It didn't splash, but glided as a smooth arch to the spot where the falls began. Then it fell with a rumble down into the riverbed; it did not yet splash, it was still smooth and clear. Only when it came down from high up did it foam and roar. There the water was a tumultuous, roaring whirlpool and was whipped white as snow. Water rushed down the falls incessantly only to be thrown a dozen feet up in the air, and the rapids boiled and splashed. The tiny drops that rose up in the air were blown far and wide by the wind.

The shores of the rapids were luscious and tall. The water had polished the bedrock into a shiny surface. The marsh tea that grew on the shore leaned toward the water, the rocks next to them were green and slippery. Somewhere a solitary birch stood right by the edge of the water.

All around was endless primeval forest, gloomy impenetrable wilderness. Here and there from the hidden depths of the forest a little brook rippled into the river. Somewhere on the shore stood a cross where travelers had attached fluttering prayer ribbons. Perhaps someone had drowned at that spot or perhaps the cross had been erected for the protection of travelers. Here and there, dotting the shoreline, were fishermen's huts, where one could find shelter from rain and cold.

The boat sped along the smooth surface of the water as soon as they were past the turbulence of the rapids. On the return trip from Kemi they had to push against the waves, and the river did not like anyone to rise against the current – it put obstacles in the way of those who tried. Downstream the river aided the traveler; in the surge of the rapids it hastened the boat on, even over rocks.

In one spot the rapids in the Kemi River were different from all others. They lay between Paanajärvi and Jyskyjärvi. They were tall and mean. Masses of water quickly smashed on the talus of sharp rocks, and then changed into gentle waves. But a dark danger lurked under that gentle surface.

At this moment Aniviisu became silent. Kaarlo pressed her little hand once again. He felt as if he were holding a young little bird whose frightened heart was throbbing.

"Was that where they perished?" he asked quietly.

"Yes."

After a short interval, Aniviisu continued.

Helena and Moissei had pulled the boat up on shore and they pulled and carried it past the rapids. A few times they had to stop and rest because the boat was quite heavy to pull.

As they were struggling with the boat, another boat with three men on board on their way to Kemi came downstream from the direction of Jyskyjärvi. They helped Helena and Moissei push their boat back into the water. Then they pulled their own boat up on shore.

To their great horror, the men suddenly saw a powerful whirlpool begin to drag Helena's and Moissei's boat backward toward the rapids. Moissei was rowing, Helena steering. Moissei tugged with all his might, but some unseen force pulled the boat irresistibly toward the rapids. The men on the shore quickly pushed their boat back into the water, but before they could be of any help, the young couple's boat had disappeared out of sight. The men returned to the shore and ran to the lower end of the rapids. They found Helena and Moissei between two large rocks, where they lay as if in embrace, rocked by the waves. The men lifted the drowning victims into their boat and returned to Uhtua.

The rapids had reaped their grim harvest.

When Aniviisu had finished her story, all was quiet. The light filtered through the crowns of the tall trees, danced among the leaves, and made the dark surface of the pond glimmer. Somewhere behind the pond a red fox flashed into view, but it did not catch the attention of either of the two people sitting on the tree trunk. Aniviisu had reached the end of her story with her voice trembling; her last sentence had been only a whisper. But telling the story had eased her anguish, she was no longer weeping.

"Now I know you better," said Kaarlo and pressed the girl's hand.

Some strange link seemed to join them together, a little girl and a young man. In the eyes of adults they were still children, but Kaarlo felt responsible for the girl. And he felt it was predestined that he should walk all the way here from Uhtua last summer and meet Aniviisu in the woods.

"Now I'll play for you," Kaarlo said and took out his violin.

Aniviisu closed her eyes and leaned her head against the trunk of the tree. Kaarlo's soft music turned into images in her mind; with her mind's eye she saw a clear pond where fish were swimming. One of them swam toward the shore and rose to the surface so that ever widening rings were formed. She took water into her palm and let it seep between her fingers. It was so clear, so pure …

The sun hung low in the western sky, when Aniviisu and Kaarlo walked back toward the old house. As they passed by the new house, they saw large packing crates, some of which had been opened. Driven by curiosity they went closer, and Aniviisu peaked into one of the boxes. It was full of books.

"He reads books," Aniviisu said quietly, almost surprised.

She stole a glance around and then she took one book into her hand. "*Laivanrakennuksesta*" ["How to Build Ships"] it said on the cover in plain Finnish. Kaarlo, too, reached for a book.

"The title of this one is *Visiting Immigrants in Canada*."

They put the books back in the box and continued their walk. Having crossed the little knoll, they came to the edge of the forest by the old house. Nasti was just returning from the sauna and greeted them cheerfully. The youngsters followed her to the yard and into the living room to have a cup of the coffee Katri was making. They had just been seated when there was a knock on the door and a dark-haired man stepped in.

"Father," Kaarlo said perplexed, and stood up.

"Good evening … This is the Huotari house, is it not? Some woman on the tip of the next point directed me here …"

"Did she give her name as Outi," Katri asked lightly.

"Yes, she did."

Katri rose to greet the man with an outstretched hand.

"Henrik Meinander, it's been a long time," she said with a smile.

The man smiled too and his dark eyes sparkled.

"I couldn't believe it when Kaarlo told me you were here."

"Come, have a seat," Katri urged him. She introduced Teppana and Nasti to him. An affectionate smile lit Katri's face when she noticed Aniviisu curtsying deep.

Kaarlo's father, Henrik, was an old acquaintance of Katri's from her days in Suomussalmi and Ilomantsi. He had also been an old friend, a schoolmate, of her husband, Juhani. The years had not changed him one iota. The dark-haired, pleasant-looking Henrik Meinander – a sophisticated university man – adjusted quickly and behaved as if he had known them all before. He told them about his trips to Lapland and elsewhere in the far north and spiced his stories with witty comments, which made Nasti laugh out loud.

"Well, isn't that something ..." Even Teppana would mumble to himself now and then.

Katri and Aniviisu accompanied the father and son team by boat to Uhtua. The trip took an hour, perhaps two. There was not a ripple on the water, the boat glided on its mirrored surface. The evening sun gilded the western horizon, and the entire region was wreathed in shades of green. Henrik Meinander did the rowing. Katri sat opposite him and the youngsters sat in the bow. After a short while they passed by the tip of a point with a small run-down house and a gently leaning sauna by the shore.

"I dropped into that house because I wasn't sure where the little road would lead," Henrik said.

"It belongs to Outi," Katri said with a short laugh. "Tell me, what did she say to you ..."

"She asked me to come in and promised to make me some tea."

"I know," said Katri. "A man can't come to Uhtua without Outi getting excited ... Oops – the kids are listening, although I guess it doesn't hurt them."

"Don't even think, Katri, that we are kids any more," Aniviisu said.

Henrik Meinander looked at his son; one really could no longer call him a child, rather a young man ... sitting there next to the girl so full of feeling, he might as well have held her hand. The father reflected on the fact that the boy was showing a new kind of warmth. He had always been a dreamer – yet since childhood he had been quite precocious, just like Katri's niece. The girl was very young, of course, but it is sometimes possible that people find each other at a very early age, Henrik Meinander pondered while he was rowing and looked approvingly at the youngsters in the bow.

Uhtua came into view behind a long peninsula. Further away the cupolas of the church shone faintly. Likopää village was closest to

Huotari, and the first house was a Finnish-style one with blue window frames. Henrik Meinander rowed to the small dock at his sister's house.

The whole shoreline was crowded with boats of many kinds. Nearly all people living on Lake Kuittijärvi earned their living fishing and peddling, and, therefore, it goes without saying that the children were accustomed to being in boats even before they learned to walk. Usually the women did the rowing because the men would go on their peddling journeys to Finland immediately following the summer chores.

Henrik Meinander had rented a small cabin on the shore of the lands that belonged to his sister's house. He and Kaarlo had decided to live there all summer although they had another summer residence in Terijoki.

The youngsters went on a walk down to the shore and Katri and Henrik sat down on the ground under the window of the cabin. The summer night was quiet and clear. The talk turned to Katri's husband's death.

"I never really got to know what happened," Henrik said.

Katri glanced out over the lake. The soft light made the surface of the water glimmer ethereally. It was still hard for her to talk about her husband's death.

"I am certain he was murdered. And the murderers are free, a bunch of socialists. I am afraid one of them has showed up here in Uhtua. Aniviisu saw a man in the woods some time ago. They are saying, though, that he has been captured now and sent to St Petersburg."

Henrik's face had taken on a grave expression. He nodded quietly.

"Juhani was an activist, and that's always dangerous. His dreams were too grand."

"Before he died he went to Germany," Katri said. 'I'm afraid he learned something there that he had to pay for with his life.

There was fear in Katri's voice. Henrik Meinander guessed that she, for her own and the child's safety's sake, wanted to get away from this remote area, and be surrounded by people in Sortavala.

"What if they come face to face with you, how will you cope with seeing your husband's murderers eye to eye?"

Katri lifted her face. Her eyes did not show signs of crying, but a new worry had entered them.

"I wouldn't be able to cope ..." she said quietly. "But they're not interested in me as a person, I was only Juhani's shadow. But both Juhani's friend, Tuomas Carstén – he's a lawyer as I'm sure you recall – and I are absolutely clear on what happened. The murderers just never ended up in court. They know that we know. And the man who scared Aniviisu in the woods is one of them. He came all the way to Uhtua to snoop around."

"How did it all happen?" Henrik asked quietly.

Katri told the story. Exactly as Aniviisu only a few hours earlier had unburdened her heart by telling Kaarlo about her parents' death, so did Katri now relieve the sadness of her soul to her husband's old friend.

Juhani Jääskeläinen had been an officer and an academic. When he met Katri he was over fifty years old. Katri was at the time a young teacher who had just graduated from the Sortavala teachers' seminary. Their marriage was generally considered harmonious and happy. Juhani confided in Katri from the very beginning. Katri knew there were political secrets associated with his officer's career. Katri was under the impression that the secrets were related to the assassination of Bobrikov, Governor General of Finland, although Juhani had not been a known friend of the assassin, Eugen Schaumann.

It was now six years since the assassination – and although the letter Schaumann left behind stated clearly that there had been no conspiracy behind his act, a number of Juhani's friends had visited their house, arriving secretly late at night and leaving only in the early morning hours. In Bobrikov's place Prince Ivan Obolenski was appointed Governor General of Finland, and he continued his cessor's policies. It was an irony of fate, that Juhani was murdered by socialists, opponents of Czarist despotism. Katri was convinced that Juhani had learned sensitive secrets both in St Petersburg and in Germany about Russia's revolutionaries – and these could not trust a Finnish officer ...

Katri was silent for a while. Telling the story took its toll on her, both physically and mentally. It had been two years since Juhani died, but it felt as if it had happened only yesterday.

"You don't need to go on, if it's too hard," Henrik said. Katri shook her head. No, she would now unburden herself of everything. She looked at the Uhtua village scenery that lay before them. About two hundred houses clustered at the very base of the deep bay. Additional houses could be seen on the treeless ridge along the shore. There were also two churches, one old and one new. The storage shed along the shoreline cast a long shadow out over the lake.

"This is a beautiful spot," Katri mumbled to herself. "I have been here only very seldom ... Since last summer only a couple of times."

Henrik nodded silently. He knew Katri was gathering strength to continue her story.

Katri had been a teacher for one school year in Suomussalmi. Juhani had lived in Helsinki, but made the long train journey once a month to be with his wife. They had bought a small cottage near the border, on the shore of a beautiful lake in the woods. There they had lived for two summers the two of them. In the summer of 1908, after the schools had closed their doors, Katri was taken to the Sortavala hospital. She had a miscarriage followed by several complications.

Juhani had accompanied Katri to town, he trusted only one doctor in Sortavala. When he saw that Katri was well on her way to recovery, he traveled to Helsinki, planning to come back to bring his wife to Suomussalmi. Then a letter arrived:

My little girl,

I have now been here in Helsinki three days and met with different people. I am convinced that our great dream will become reality and that this country will be free one day. I know that our activist group stands for the right cause. When we become free from the yoke of the people who try to Russify us, Finland will be on its way to independence! Some problem individuals are still obstructing our efforts; they confronted me yesterday. I will not write about it here, I will tell you later. They are dangerous because they are supported by Russia's socialist revolutionaries. I told them straight that we will not share the same road – we will win, they will have to yield.

My Darling – I am not able to get you from the hospital. Can you go back by train to Suomussalmi alone? I will travel directly to our cottage from here and wait for you there. I'll bring you some really nice gift … You have been so brave, my little darling. Your recovery is now the most important thing in my life.

I miss you my girl! Juhani

Katri had traveled home to Suomussalmi. Juhani was not at the school, but he had passed by and continued to the cottage. On the table at the school were some welcoming gifts from Helsinki: a couple of English language books, a beautiful hat for Katri, a white and blue one with a narrow brim. There was also a piece of paper on the table:

Katri – hire a driver and come to the cottage.
It's important. Juhani.

That same day, Katri had got a driver and had been driven to the cottage. The road was bad and toward the end became so narrow that the horse almost couldn't make it to the yard. However, the driver who had driven them there before knew how to avoid the large potholes in the road. When they finally got through to the yard, the cottage door was wide open and Juhani's clothes strewn all over the floor.

Katri was scared. It was not like Juhani to leave his clothes and belongings in a mess. She had asked the driver to stay and help her look for Juhani. After searching for a good while, they finally found him …

"In the lake, next to the dock," Katri said in a weak voice. "He was lying face down, wearing only his underwear. I fainted … When I came to, I was lying on the grass and the driver was sitting beside me. When he had made sure I was all right, he placed Juhani in a blanket and carried him to the cart. We drove quickly to Suomussalmi and brought Juhani to the sick room. He was dead – he had drowned. It was impossible to comprehend, Juhani was an excellent swimmer. The matter was reported to the police, and it turned out there had been three men besides Juhani at the cottage. Whether they were those that Juhani had written about – Russians … that has never been found out. But one thing is certain: Juhani was murdered."

Henrik was silent, he touched Katri's hand and looked in her eyes.

"The letter had a sentence 'we will win, they will have to yield,' he said. – It may well be a matter of revenge. Does anyone know that you are living here in Uhtua now?"

Katri shrugged her shoulders.

"Anyone can get that information," she said. "And I'm moving to Sortavala this fall."

"That is good," said Henrik. "In the city you'll have friends protecting you, Tuomas Castrén and others. Could Juhani have left some papers – dangerous papers?"

Katri nodded.

"I have sent all of Juhani's papers to Tuomas."

Their conversation was interrupted when Aniviisu and Kaarlo returned. They brought Anja with them and she was carrying a wooden milk bucket.

"Look who's here – Anja," she said and greeted her. "Are you out walking this late at night?"

"No – I have a little boat; I'll row home in that. I brought some milk my mother sent to a neighbor."

Katri turned toward Henrik.

"Henrik, this girl is also coming to Sortavala this fall, she is a classmate of Aniviisu's …"

"Isn't that something!" Henrik Meinander said with a laugh. "Two girls from the heartland of Uhtua – and both of you going to the Girls' School! That is quite exceptional."

The girls smiled shyly, and Katri stroked Aniviisu's hair.

"We should be going, it's almost ten o'clock," she said.

"Can you row all the way to Huotari Point," Henrik asked with concern in his voice.

"Of course," said Aniviisu, and jumped into the boat. "I'll row, I've rowed this route at least a hundred times!"

Katri and Aniviisu's boat glided quietly in the pale night. The air was warm, the surface of the water rippled, the shores were peaceful and silent. When they pulled the boat to shore by the sauna and tied it to a tree trunk, Aniviisu looked at the new house in plain view behind the sauna.

"I'm not moving to that house ever!" she said in a quiet, but fierce voice. "I'm not going anywhere from my own home! No use him writing "you better get used to the idea ..."

Katri didn't know what to say, Aniviisu looked at Katri, her eyes flashing with vexation.

"I will never get used to it, and Mother and Father wouldn't have gotten used to it either!"

June became July and the hay had been gathered. It didn't need drying for a long time; that is how bad the grass was on these meadows.

In the morning it rained. It rained so hard that the window panes appeared to be crying. Melancholy, Aniviisu looked outside. For weeks she had not had time to read the *Tales of a Field Surgeon*, because there had been so much work to do. One evening she had fallen off her chair from sheer exhaustion. Teppana had lifted her in his arms and carried her off to her bed.

"Just wait till the hay is in the barn, then this little hero will read to us again." Now would have been a good time to read, but the rain made her depressed – nothing appealed to her. After mid-day the rain stopped and a rainbow appeared in the sky.

Aniviisu was getting ready to go out when Teppana stormed into the room, almost pushing the girl over.

"Good grief – they're ... coming!" The man stuttered clutching his chest.

The women did not understand. Who was coming?

"Well, the ship, of course!" Teppana almost shrieked. "It's coming from Lower Kuittijärvi Lake, from the direction of Vuokkiniemi! A big ship with its sails open. Come on out!"

The women looked at each other in horror. Aniviisu grabbed on to Katri's skirt.

"No need to be afraid," Katri said. "They are not cannibals."

She threw her sweater over her shoulders, took Aniviisu by the hand, and went outside. Nasti and Teppana dashed after them, and so the four of them ran down the hill to the sauna and stopped on the dock, quite short of breath.

A ship indeed: white with one sail. Rarely had any ship like that been seen in these waters. The bow of the ship pointed straight at their dock. Aniviisu could barely breathe as she peered across the ship's deck. Could you see anyone there? There were people, yes, but one couldn't make out their faces. Then the ship stopped almost completely, and began a slow approach toward the new dock that had been built on the west side of the tip of the point.

They could only see the sails. They couldn't see if anyone got off the ship.

"What are we going to do?" Katri wondered out loud. "We are not going to the dock ... Everybody inside! Quickly!"

They ran hurriedly back to the old house and went to the back yard.

"Teppana, why don't you stay outside," Katri said. "He might just come to ask a question and introduce himself ... And if he doesn't come, you go and visit him in the new house."

Teppana crossed his heart and let out a deep sigh. Nasti too crossed her heart, something that they had to do morning and night. She felt pain in her heart when she thought they might have to leave ... The women all went inside to the icon corner, crossed their eyes in real agony.

"*Hospody, Isus Kristos* ... Have mercy on us!'

They sat down by the window and began to wait for Teppana. Hours went by.

The sun scorched from a cloudless sky. Where did the heavy rain clouds suddenly disappear to?

PART TWO

I – Ilja Huotari

Why did it suddenly feel like thirty years had been wiped away! As the ship glided on Lake Kuittijärvi toward Huotari Point, Ilja Huotari felt a strange pang in his heart. As the ship sailed closer to home, homesickness tore through his chest worse than it had ever done in foreign lands. The feelings had been bottled up during the long years, and as the dam now broke, the yearning squeezed him like a sharp pain.

Seen from the ship, the point had changed. At its tip now stood a house, the very house whose blueprints he had approved. There it was, transferred directly from paper into the perfect spot, exactly where he had decided it should go while he was still in Canada. He had to admit that the house was huge. Two stories and a tower … large windows on all sides. The building was a challenge to its environment. Ilja Huotari knew it would have an impact on the rest of his life by its mere existence. A thin smoke rose toward the clear sky from the chimney. That must mean they were expecting him. Maybe the boy wanted to welcome his *buobo* this way.

Then the sauna caught his eye. It stood at the end of the bay below the old house just like it did thirty years ago. Some people were standing by the corner of the sauna; he tried in vain to make out who they were. Not one of them lifted their hand in greeting, which he thought that was odd. Maybe they were hired hands. That must be it, an eleven-year-old boy couldn't of course care for a farm all on his own. He must have servants helping him.

The ship turned toward the point and began to slow down as it coasted toward the side of the shining new, wide dock. When it finally docked the crew got busy. One jumped on the dock to take the ropes. Another one began to lower the sails. Ilja's wife, Greta, came to stand next to her husband.

"Not too bad," she said in pure Finnish. "Although the architecture is a little rustic."

"I think the house is beautiful," he said without looking at his wife.

The Huotari entourage also included two servants, old Samuel and Mrs. Jenny, who began in her high-pitched voice to direct the porters.

"First the food stuff! Then the rest!"

Ilja could not take his eyes off the point, or the forest behind it, or the far end of the bay where he could see the sauna chimney. He searched for the old house with his gaze until he realized the forest had grown taller in thirty years and now hid the house from view.

The old Ostrobothnian sea dog Samuel sensed his master's emotions. He came slowly to his side and grabbed him by the arm.

"Let's go ashore, the others have gone already. Beautiful point, I must say ..." Then he doddered along carrying a lampshade.

The amount of cargo in the ship's small hold was quite incredible. First, out came some huge trunks and packing boxes, clothes, lamps, pots and containers. Even a large stuffed fish with a long bill was brought out.

"Careful! Careful!" Shouted both Samuel and Mrs. Jenny who were supervising the porters' work.

Next, the women, Greta and Mrs. Jenny, started walking in their high heels toward the house, trying to keep their balance on the narrow path. Huovinen had come to the main entrance to welcome the new owner. When he saw the women looking around the exterior of the building, he quickly apologized for the fact that the landscaping was still unfinished.

"So it seems," Mrs. Jenny said in an icy tone of voice, "but it won't be for long."

Finally, Ilja Huotari arrived and stopped in front of the building to absorb the smell of fresh wood. Then he saw a man, about his own age and somehow familiar-looking, approaching from the forest behind the house. Ilja racked his brain, but could not conjure up a memory of the man. He wore oddly familiar light pants and a linen shirt. His birch bark shoes were tied to the ankles with laces. Didn't they have leather boots yet?

"Do I know you or not?" Ilja asked the man, who, looking timid, remained standing a short distance away.

"We have met, sir – when we were young," Teppana said and stretched out his hand. "I'm Teppana Jyrkinen. I came to Uhtua from Finland around the same time you left for Canada. I have been living in the old house with my wife as the Huotari hired hand".

Teppana felt a little awkward calling Ilja Huotari sir, but he couldn't think of any better term. He was the master of the house.

Ilja greeted him with a stern look. Teppana dared hardly glance at the impenetrable face of the man whom he had all along recognized as Ilja. The man was tall, almost six foot six, but relatively slim. His face was sunburned and his dark eyes were surrounded by a network of wrinkles. He looked handsome in a masculine kind of way, and his posture was quite stately; even the clothes signaled that he belonged to landed gentry.

"Where is the child?" Ilja asked abruptly in a somewhat surly voice.

Teppana squinted his eyes. He motioned with his head.

"Over there ..."

"Could the child come and say hello?"

Teppana shrugged his shoulders. "I guess I can ask."

Ilja looked around and noticed the women by the main entrance.

"Greta, come and say hello," he said turning toward Teppana. "This is my wife."

Never in his life had Teppana held such a soft silky hand. And never had he been that close to an angel – this is how he pictured Huotari's wife in his mind. Some faint and strange fragrance hovered around the woman ... Teppana woke up to reality again and saw the petite and round Mrs. Jenny, who peered at him with suspicion.

"Oh, yes ... I speak Finnish," the wife said in a shrill voice.

Teppana greeted them and bowed. His face was serious as he looked at these people who were entering the new house for the first time. Ilja went first, the others followed. Teppana remained standing alone on the path. Ilja's homecoming did not seem to bring any good feelings.

Ilja Huotari made a house inspection. He started downstairs, walking with his hands behind his back from room to room leaving no detail unscrutinized. The two women also participated in the inspection. When they returned downstairs to the hall, Ilja sat down on a chair. He declared the house to be perfect.

This was akin to absolution for Huovinen. His work was now completed. For three weeks he had slept in the little servant's room behind the kitchen waiting for his boss to arrive. What was left for him now was to gather his clothes, collect his fee, and take the boat to Uhtua where he had another project waiting. Huovinen had to admit that he had been afraid of criticism from Ilja Huotari, for he knew how uncompromising he could be.

"Please follow me upstairs," Huotari said to Huovinen.

They walked up the stairs and went into a bedroom on the left.

"Is there a safe here?"

"Yes."

"Is my wife's bedroom the next one over to this one? What about the child's room?"

"It's across the hall where you wanted it. Although I'm not so sure the skinny little thing will be coming here – seems attached to the old house."

"Is the child skinny?"

"Yes, unfortunately."

"We'll raise the child to be ready for the big wide world."

Huovinen nodded, he was already thinking of his fee. They went over the combination for the safe, then Ilja Huotari paid Huovinen's fee in cash. It was no small sum of money; in fact it was such a large amount, that if a robber knew Huovinen was about to go to Uhtua with that kind of money, he might have had quite some catch.

Huovinen had now finished his work and it was time to leave.

"Good bye," he said shaking Huotari's hand. "And thanks."

"Thank you for your good work. I'll probably come to visit Uhtua as soon as I get settled in."

"Uhtua probably doesn't look like much after Canada," Huovinen said as he walked down the stairs.

"Doesn't matter," Ilja said. "It's Uhtua."

Ilja looked through the window as Huovinen walked down to his boat and started rowing across Lake Kuittijärvi. He stood there somberly thinking about the fact that the boy would soon come.

But the boy didn't come. It took most of the afternoon to unload the ship's cargo and find the right places for the things.

The quiet new house came alive. A while ago a sofa and armchairs upholstered with dark-red plush velvet were brought in. Ilja sat in his spacious parlor and waited. Aided by old Samuel, Mrs. Jenny was hanging heavy dark-green drapes in the parlor. Crystal vases and candlesticks decorated the mirrored tables with gilded frames. A tall palm tree, which to everyone's surprise had survived the long journey, was placed in the corner. The oriental rugs on the hardwood floors were thick and ornate. They also had come from Canada; not a single one had been lost on the trip across the ocean. The room was very similar to the one in his previous home in Toronto. The view from the window, however, was totally different – and so dear to him ... stunningly beautiful, clear lake as far as the eye could see.

On the other side of the point were two small islands, one of which was now under water; the dead trees stood erect, like ghosts. Ilja thought it was a symbolic view – it was trying to tell him something. Now he neither wanted nor had the energy to think serious thoughts. He realized he had always loved Lake Kuittijärvi, its leisurely rolling waves that caressed the shores of Huotari Point. Clear, translucent waters surrounded the point on all sides. He felt a lump in his throat and had to swallow. He had not anticipated becoming overwhelmed by such a swell of emotions. And no one here understood it; there wasn't a single person with whom he could talk about his innermost thoughts and feelings.

"The drapes are hung," old Samuel announced.

"Thank you," Ilja said, awakening from his thoughts. "How do you feel now?"

"Good," the old man said with a grin. "We've come home."

Ilja too smiled. Faithful old Samuel ... Together they had sailed the seas of the world for years. In those days Samuel had been in his prime, but now he had shrunk and was bent over. His hair had thinned, and his blue eyes that once shone in his weather-beaten face now had a watery gaze.

"If the boy comes, would you send him to me," Ilja asked.

"*Aye, aye, sir*!" old Samuel said in English.

But they had to wait for the boy. And Ilja could do nothing but wait, for he did not think it proper for him to rush to the boy, rather the boy should run to his *buobo*.

In the afternoon Mrs. Jenny brought in a tray of food to the parlor and asked the lady of the house to have a little meal. When Greta had eaten, she went back to her room where she was putting away her clothes in the closets. As Mrs. Jenny was taking the tray back to the kitchen, the door to the large entrance hall opened and a blond woman came in with a little girl.

"Good afternoon, do you speak Finnish?" the woman asked.

"Of course," said Mrs. Jenny. "Of course I speak Finnish. What do you want?"

"We would like to meet Ilja Huotari."

"Oh, I see," snorted Mrs Jenny. "That won't be possible right now."

The blond woman raised her head higher.

"I do believe it is possible," Katri said and squeezed Aniviisu's hand hard. "Surely he will want to meet his grandchild."

Mrs. Jenny almost dropped the tray. She stared at Aniviisu unable to believe her eyes.

"A girl ... Good God, it's a girl!"

"Yes, she is," Katri said. "In spite of that, we would like to come and introduce ourselves."

The shocked housekeeper put down the tray on the nearest chair, hurried to the parlor door and knocked.

"There are vistors ..."

"Ask them to come in," they heard someone answer.

Aniviisu looked at Katri with a pleading look, as she walked from the front door to the parlor door; she stayed right beside her aunt. Her face was pale, and she was short of breath. Katri had supervised as the girl got dressed, and so she was very pretty in a red-striped skirt and white blouse with embroidered roses on the front. The girl's hair was combed in braids, which made her face look even smaller than usual.

Katri herself was wearing a summer dress with red flowers and a white lace collar. She realized that she, too, was nervous, which both annoyed and amused her. What kind of human being did they think this Ilja Houtari was?

They stopped on the threshold to the parlor. The furniture in the large room was upholstered with dark-red velvet. The overall effect was so overwhelming and luxurious that they could only gape.

A tall man stood up from the sofa by the window. He took a couple of steps toward the newcomers – and then he froze.

The man's face trembled, but then it became impenetrable, almost frighteningly severe. At that moment, Aniviisu peered out from behind Katri – and looked into a pair of eyes whose expression was stern and fierce. The girl pulled her head back.

"A girl, the child is a girl!"

The man almost groaned the words.

Katri pushed the girl forward.

"Good afternoon," Ilja Huotari. "This is your granddaughter Anna Liisa Huotari."

A hush descended on the room. All three of them just stood looking at each other. After a moment, which felt like an eternity, Ilja Huotari nodded to the women, bidding them to sit. Aniviisu squeezed herself into the same armchair as Katri, despite the fact there was another chair next to it.

Katri was overcome by the desperate sense that everything was going all wrong. She was on her guard, Aniviisu was frightened, and Ilja Huotari's whole being exuded disappointment and anger. The conversation was painfully slow to start; Ilja lit his pipe and began to pace the floor slowly, from the window to the door and back. Then he sat down on the sofa across from Katri and the girl and looked inquiringly at Katri. Katri regained her composure; a moment ago she had felt so completely at a loss, so disappointed at seeing the man's anger, that she had lost her self-possession. She had not anticipated the man would be this cold and rejecting.

Finally Katri regained her speech.

"I'm Katri Jääskeläinen, born in Finland. As you know, the child's parents drowned in the spring of last year. The girl's mother was my sister. When she was orphaned, I came here to look after her. That is, of course, if you are at all interestd in these matters ..."

Ilja's face darkened even more, as he contemplated the woman's words. That is, of course, if you are at all interested in these matters. Did she think he was a monster?

He glared at the woman from under his eyebrows. The woman's voice suggested she tolerated no objections. She appeared as uncompromising in her speech and accusations as he was himself. Ilja thought it was unfair. Did she forget that Moissei was his son! He had received word that he had a son ten years after Moissei was born. What realistic chance would he then have had of doing something for the boy? His brother had already done everything. He had married the abandoned girl and taken the son as his own ... What could he have done? Now Moissei was dead. Drowned, and these people expected him to grieve. How could he grieve the death of someone he had never even met? What were these people expecting of him?

Ilja cast a searching glance at the woman. Civilized woman, beautiful open face, deep soft voice, speaks in a polished fashion, like a teacher. Dressed tastefully – and calculatingly, no doubt. With the eyes of a man of the world and a ladies' man, Ilja Huotari looked at the woman the like of whom he could never have imagined finding here in the remote regions of Viena. He consciously avoided looking at the girl who sat next to the woman, reticent and uncommunicative. Such a skinny little girl ... He could see that the girl was mature for her age, already a young woman and that her eyes had a deep darkness, which suggested determination and intensity – but the one thing that was wrong was thereby everything: his late son's child was a girl!

But that is an inescapable fact, he finally thought. He took his pipe, began to clean it, tapped its bowl on the corner of the table and with a silver-plated small spoon dug out the dottle and put it into the ashtray.

"The girl can move in here right away tomorrow," he said curtly looking at his pipe.

"Never!"

Aniviisu's voice rose to a shriek. It took both Ilja and Katri by surprise.

"I am never moving to this house!" the girl screamed again. "I have my own home!"

Ilja noticed a faint trace of a smile on the woman's face. So, there was a conspiracy ... this had been agreed in advance. The girl refused to move to the new house even though a nice-looking room had been furnished just for her on the second floor. Everything in the room was planned for a boy, that's true, but still ... what ingratitude!

"Ungrateful child!" Ilja Huotari said thunderously.

Katri's eyes flashed. She was just about to get up from her chair, when the door opened and a woman dressed in a light-blue chiffon dress came in. She walked across the floor, small and light as a fairy. Katri didn't realize immediately who the woman was.

"My wife Greta," Ilja said in an indifferent voice.

Greta offered her delicate hand, first to Katri, whom she glanced at with a faint smile on her face, then she glided over to Aniviisu, grabbed her cheeks and pressed her head to her bosom. Aniviisu became so frazzled she did not know what to do; then she wiggled herself loose, red-faced, and leaned closer to Katri.

Greta gave a short laugh, but her voice was unnatural. Katri noticed it immediately. She also noticed Ilja Huotari's weariness. The woman pretended not to notice, but tiptoed to sit beside her husband and began to fidget with the buttons of his jacket.

"Why don't you ... introduce us," the woman said in an artificial little girl's voice. "Introduce us, please."

Ilja's face was like a wooden mask as he began to speak.

"This lady is the sister of my my late son's wife. She has come to take care of this girl, who I mistakenly thought was a boy."

"Oh – that must be a horrible blow for you to find out that your grandchild isn't a boy after all!"

The woman's voice was scornful, but her face was still smiling. Katri thought they probably always spoke like that, pecking at each other.

"As Aniviisu said..."

Greta's hand covered her mouth.

"What a horrible name!"

Annoyed, Katri glanced at the woman, but she, too, was able to keep up her friendly smile.

"Her real name is Anna Liisa. Children often invent names for themselves, adults do it for each other. Anna Liisa gave herself the name Aniviisu."

"Oh, well, that's much better," Greta said. "Anna Liisa is a proper girl's name."

"As Aniviisu was saying," Katri started again, "we have been thinking that she should not move to this house. The child has lived all her life in the house where she was born and it would be difficult for her to move. I ask you, therefore, to consider the matter again. I don't think it's right to force her to move in with strangers."

"Strangers ..." Ilja smiled. "Who is living in the old house?"

"Teppana and Nasti Jyrkinen, the hired help. They served as the hired help already for the girl's parents," Katri explained. "I, of course, will leave in the fall."

"Why did you come here in the first place?"

Ilja Huotari's voice was so impudent and arrogant, that Katri's cheeks reddened.

"I should hardly have to explain even to you, what a shock the death of her mother and father is to a child," she said. "And I do not want to speak about it in front of her. And there is something else I wish to say right now. Aniviisu has been accepted at the Girl's School in Sortavala directly to start in sixth grade, and I'm taking her with me when I leave for Sortavala in the fall."

Katri trembled inside, but she had now said what she had on her mind. Ilja's face had turned ominously dark. The smile had disappeared from his wife's face, which was painted like the face of a doll.

Just as Katri grabbed Aniviisu by the hand, and they turned to leave, the door opened and Mrs. Jenny entered carrying a coffee tray.

"Coffee, coffee is being served."

"Thank you, we don't feel like coffee right now! Good bye!"

Without a word, Ilja sat looking as Katri and Aniviisu walked to the door and disappeared from view.

Ilja and his wife remained sitting in the parlor. Mrs. Jenny took the tray back to the kitchen and stayed there tending to her chores; she disturbed her employers no further. Greta rose from the sofa and began to move about the room fingering the drapes, the tablecloths, the candlesticks. Her behavior was so nervous, that finally Ilja got nervous too.

"Sit down, why on earth are you running around like that."

"Admit it, I am right," said Greta from behind the palm tree. "Confess that you are disappointed with your crazy idea of coming here! What's there to do in a place like this? A house that is finished to the last detail! I put my clothes in the closet, I put my powder box and my hairbrush on the vanity, I take a book and read … I wasn't even allowed to organize the library, that Uhtua man had already arranged it in alphabetical order. I'm sure he would have folded my underwear and put my corset in the dresser drawer, had they been sent in advance."

"Stop it!"

Ilja's posture was menacing, but Greta did not stop. She continued her pacing back and forth, swinging her skirt every now and then, or arranging her short hair – back and forth, back and forth.

"Only Mrs. Jenny is pleased," she said. "She has returned to be near her old home after so many decades. But you are not satisfied and you will never be satisfied. You sit there like some totem pole, tormenting all the rest of us. You torment that girl, too, who you believed to be a boy. I could see how angrily you glared at the girl. The woman you looked at quite differently. There's a woman to your liking, more full-blooded than us Finland-Swedes. She has the body, we have the spirit ..."

"Stop it!"

Ilja saw his wife's derisive and triumphant gaze, and he had to close his eyes. At the same time he closed his ears. That was a skill he had acquired over the years. The scornful, mocking, hurtful words flew all around him, but he deflected them. That's what he had always done. He knew how this game would be played out. They had been here in this new place for six hours and already their never-ending struggle was in full force.

Ilja felt a great void deep within himself. He could tell no one in the whole world his innermost thoughts. But he also knew he would ultimately sort out these matters. He would pay all his debts.

Late that night Aniviisu sat by the window in the pale summer night watching Katri sleep. Katri slept quietly, but Aniviisu knew her aunt's sleep was deep. She pondered for a long time if she would dare ... But she had no choice, she had to dare. Quickly and as quiet as a mouse she put on her skirt and blouse, put on her socks and tied her shoes. Over her shoulders she wrapped a wool sweater. Then she opened the door and slipped into the vestibule. From the shelf in the vestibule she took a wooden bucket. By the living room door she listened; not a sound came from there, not even Teppana's snoring. The whole house was in deep sleep. Aniviisu sneaked out to the back yard and was on her way.

The summer night was light, but totally silent. Even the mosquitoes appeared to be sleeping; their familiar whine was missing in the forest as Aniviisu walked briskly swinging the wooden pail. She went past the pond and found the little path and began to run. Soon she could hear the familiar murmur and in just a few minutes she stood at the foot of the rapids. She leaned forward to scoop water into her pail, filled it up just in case, although that made it heavy to carry. Now she had to walk with caution so the water would not spill, because she didn't have the strength to go to the rapids a second time tonight.

Aniviisu's arms hurt as she walked along the path back to the village road. Now quickly to the new house ...

Fortunately the house did not have a dog that could awaken the inhabitants. Still, Aniviisu was frightened – there was something eerie about the new house. And that is why it had to be blessed in order for it not to catch fire and burn down the entire forest.

Cautiously Aniviisu approached the north end of the house. She stopped at the corner, took water in her palm and threw it at the joint.

"Be you blessed ..."

Then she crept alongside the house to the south side.

"Be you blessed," she whispered again, tossing water.

She had to go past the main entrance very carefully, so that no one would see her. Minding the pail, running as lightly as she could manage to the next corner, she fretted at how far it was. Again, a handful of water and

"Be you blessed ..."

The last stretch along the side of the wall was the most challenging, because under the windows of the parlor she had to walk around piles of building materials covered by a tarp. Aniviisu peered cautiously at the windows to ascertain that Ilja Huotari did not stand looking at the lake at night. She could see no one. Aniviisu went around the woodpiles and arrived at the last corner. She scooped up water with both hands and threw it at the wall.

"Be you blessed!"

This she said out loud – and gave a sigh of relief. Now the house was blessed with water consecrated by the Water Spirit. Now it would never burn down and would not burn the birches, spruces and pine trees around it. It would remain standing there regardless of the kind of people who lived there. Whatever Ilja Huotari was, the house was innocent.

Aniviisu sat down on the steps with her pail. Behind her was the quiet house, everybody was sleeping, not a sound was heard anywhere. She turned to look at the front door and saw to her surprise that it was ajar. Suddenly she had a thought. Carefully she poured the remaining water on the ground and placed the pail beside her on the steps. Then she took off her shoes and socks. Now she had to be daring … Everyone was asleep, and she would be able to move about silently barefoot in the house. Bravely she opened the door just slightly and slipped inside.

She did not remember much at all of the previous day's visit – only the spacious hall, the staircase and the door to the parlor behind the pillars. Now she slipped in quietly through the vestibule to the hall and stopped to look at the gilded candlesticks, the wide stairs and the decorative cast-iron balustrade. She tiptoed up the stairs quietly. She was driven to this nightly adventure by a desire she had not dared breathe a word about to anyone: she wanted to see the room intended for her. And there it was, on the right off the upper hallway, and the door was invitingly open. Aniviisu slipped in and sat down on a chair by the door. She then began to look around.

The room was designed for a boy, no doubt about that. It was sparsely furnished; the furnishings consisted of a narrow bed, a desk of light-colored wood and bookshelves. There was a globe on the table under the window. On the windowsill stood two armies of tin soldiers. Aniviisu got up and moved about carefully in the room. On one side of the room was a door leading to a smaller room intended for clothes. There was also the same kind of water closet as the one off the vestibule downstairs. Aniviisu did not know what to think. On the one hand she was thrilled by the thought that all these fine things would belong to her: a fine room, a clothes closet and even a water closet with a wooden seat, where she could sit and not have to go to the outhouse – that would be wonderful in the freezing cold of winter. Yet it all felt so alien to her ... Aniviisu closed her eyes, held them shut for a while and then opened them wide. She had made her decision. She would never move to this room! Suddenly she began to long for her own clean, cozy alcove, where Katri slept, knowing nothing of her night's adventure.

Quickly Aniviisu tiptoed back to the hallway and hurried to the steps leading downstairs. The people of the house were sleeping, they must have been tired after their journey through Finland, and from the boat trip and all the new experiences.

Outside Aniviisu let out a deep sigh and drew the fresh air into her lungs. Only now did she realize what a crazy thing she had done. What if Ilja Huotari had woken up after all and come to see what caused the rustling in his house. Aniviisu shuddered at the thought. She would surely have died on the spot!

Katri was asleep when Aniviisu crept quietly into the alcove. She undressed quickly, climbed into bed and fell asleep happy that the new house was properly blessed and that no fire would devour her forest and her trees; these meant everything to her.

Ilja Huotari had dinner with his wife. They were separated by an eighteen-foot-long dark-brown mahogany dining table, whose empty chairs on the long sides emphasized the silent, oppressive atmosphere.

Mrs. Jenny served the food. Samuel stood unmoving behind his mistress' chair. Greta had observed this practice at a dinner hosted by the Lieutentant Governor of Ontario, and so it was to be followed here in Viena as well. Ilja could not understand what business Samuel had there, standing next to the wall, but he did not want to meddle in his wife's doings. Samuel himself did not care; he stood there, his weather-beaten face expressionless, his eyes fixed on the ceiling panels, and let the wall support him when his back got tired.

Mrs. Jenny had made veal cutlets. She had already let Teppana know that she had to have blocks of ice and sawdust for maintaining the freshness of important foodstuffs. She was satisfied with the cellar built under the kitchen at the end of the house: all the barrels and all the canned and preserved foods would fit in there.

The couple ate their meal in silence. Greta could see from her husband's expression that he would tolerate no conversation. She guessed that his thoughts were occupied with the girl – the girl's determined refusal to move into the house had been a shock to him. Greta felt pleasurably tantalized by the thought that her husband would be defeated. The blond woman had also been so headstrong that he would come second also to her. Greta looked at her husband from under her half-closed eyelids, taking care not to let her expression reveal her thoughts.

Ilja was concentrating on eating as if nothing was more important in the world.

Greta looked at him spellbound. The fork and the knife moved irritatingly calmly, and the light seemed to mock her as it played on the crystal decanter, which held red wine. He had wine with every meal, red and white.

But he absolutely denied Greta all wine … The man was cruel and heartless; he refused to understand that Greta's whole body craved wine – and not only her body, but her soul as well. But he had compelled her by force to give a promise that the move to Viena meant the beginning of a new, alcohol-free life – Greta was done forever with her wine and brandy drinking. She had no choice but to promise, but now, in the middle of the wilderness, she resented having agreed to something like that. And what was worse, that she had agreed to come here beyond the reach of all civilization … She longed to go back to Toronto, Ontario, and she missed her son, and she decided to observe everything from the sidelines and to await the right moment to return home. She had known all along while they were onboard the ocean liner that she would soon be having fun on the same ship – alone!

Greta sighed silently: one day in Uhtua and it already felt like an eternity.

Ilja's face did not reveal what went on in his mind. He ate peacefully, drank his wine in long drafts. He was dressed in a light summer jacket, and Greta had to admit that the man was handsome and that he had style. She had once fallen for those dark-blue eyes at a pavilion dinner party ... and two months later they were celebrating their wedding. Well, they shared the fact that they each had their roots in Finland. Greta had been beautiful, but poor as a church mouse; she did not even have enough money to pay for her son's schooling. Besides, she had become quite an alcoholic, although she had never admitted it to herself. Ilja had entered her life and proposed marriage. He had paid for her son's tuition in medical school in New York. He also paid Greta's debts, and rescued her from her predicament. Not a drop of brandy, not a drop of wine after they got married five years ago. Except in secret ...

Greta had a few bottles hidden away at the bottom of her clothes trunk. She had to, she could not cope otherwise. Greta again sighed inwardly; she felt bitter. Ilja had used her up. That was evident also from the fact that she had been given a bedroom of her own next to Ilja's. He no longer wanted to share his bed with her! Greta shoved her plate to the side and glanced at Samuel. She felt as if she were in prison. What the hell had got into him that he had come to this godforsaken place! Who could one talk to here – the beasts of the forest?

Greta knew she had to settle for what she had.

She could not afford to offend Ilja. The man had saved her from a fate even more horrible than death. There had been plans in Canada to put her in a mental hospital, because it was rare for a woman to drink as much as she did. Ilja had taken her under his protection, guarded her around the clock at first, so she would not have any alcohol, and had hired Samuel to be her private servant. As if she didn't know he was hired to keep an eye on her, to follow on her heels, and to watch over her activities. And to tell Ilja Huotari his findings.

It all cost a lot of money, but money Greta's husband had. Tired of moving from one place to another Ilja had tried his luck in the gold fields of Yukon and had found a rich gold deposit. He had also managed to invest his money so well that he could live off the returns for the rest of his life. Greta didn't even try to deny that his money interested her. But the man was attractive to her otherwise also – he was a good and passionate lover. That was why Greta felt so hurt when she was banished to a separate bedroom. There wasn't even a door connecting their rooms! Greta also knew that Ilja wanted a child in the beginning, but for some reason no child arrived. Later Ilja had begun to speak about his grandson, and she, too, had been prepared to care for and spoil this grandson. But there was no grandson – only a hotheaded, skinny girl and her haughty aunt. Greta had been as much disappointed as her husband. The move here to Viena Karelia had been a big mistake. It was impossible for her to imagine spending the rest of her life here. Not a chance!

She just had to devise a cunning enough plan because Ilja would certainly not let her go freely. Consequently she would have to flee … But how?

Greta's thoughts were interrupted when Ilja raised his crystal glass to his lips. Greta looked at the sparkling red wine, mesmerized. She was willing to do anything for just one mouthful … It was cruel to be drinking wine in front of her. Oh, how she hated that man!

The meal was over. Ilja got up, nodded to Mrs. Jenny who was standing by the kitchen door, and picked up his pipe and tobacco pouch. Greta also stood up and thanked Mrs. Jenny who began to clear the dishes off the table. Ilja stepped into the great hall, but Greta went into the library. She had to busy herself with something, otherwise she would scream. She started moving books from one place to another, with quick mechanical movements.

"Samuel," said Ilja in the hall. "I'm going for a brief walk. You take care of my wife, her nerves seem to be on edge. She is ominously quiet – have you noticed anything?"

Samuel shook his head.

"I have not found a single bottle …", the old man hesitated, then continued, "Is it wise under the circumstances for you to drink wine with your meals? I saw her hungry look …"

Ilja Huotari sucked on his pipe and blew out smoke.

"She will have to get used to the fact that others can drink, but she can't!"

"All right, I just thought ..."

Ilja glanced after old Samuel as he hobbled up the stairs. He would have liked to let the man retire, but Samuel would not hear of it.

Ilja Huotari came out of the new house and walked to the tip of the point where he remained standing under a large tree. The point was about 150 feet at its widest. Its shores were low and old trees grew right by the water's edge. The long and wide dock was deserted; the men who had been hired from Vuokkiniemi had left the day before with their boat.

In front of Ilja stretched the grand expanse of Lake Kuittijärvi colored by the slowly diminishing light. Ilja watched the play of light for a good while, deep in thought. Then he walked slowly to the far end of the bay to the old sauna and sat down on the bench. The sauna walls emitted a familiar smell of smoke, which appealed to him much more than the smell of newness in the bathroom off his master bedroom. He had missed the smell of the sauna! He had missed the weeping birches that bent their branches almost down to touch the water. He had missed the whispering forest, the quiet lapping of the waves, the rustle from the evening breeze in the treetops. He felt the yearning as a pain in his heart.

It surprised him. He had not felt anything there before. His chest was strong, strong as a bear's. And he knew that the pain came from deep inside, from his soul. It was a pain that arose from the drowning of his own son – the son he had never seen. So this is how it wounded, even though he had decided to forget it, even had forgotten it? Against his will he suddenly became aware of his weakness and loneliness. Everyone here was against him! He could hear in his ears the words of judgment among the Uhtuans:

"There's a man for you, comes back after several decades having been in contact with no one – for the house's sake? Certaunly not for the child's sake..."

"Rumor has it that he is rich. He won't fit in Viena any more!"

"Arrogant, that's what he is – and so is his wife."

Ilja Huotari sighed half aloud. His own thoughts. His own imagination. Generated by his conscience.

The evening breeze was gentle, it caressed Ilja's cheeks. He leaned his back against the sauna wall and inhaled the fragrance of the summer evening. Far out on the lake a woman was in a rowboat, he could see a red headdress and the rhythmic motion of her arms. The image reminded him of his own late mother, who had died when he was fifteen. How often had he waited for his mother on the shore, watching her row across the open lake, which sometimes was calm, reflecting the light, and sometimes she had to row through foam-crested waves. Mother was a strong woman, she did the farm work alone because her husband was working in the bush or secretly peddling in Finland. Mother cared for the animals, tilled the soil, gave birth to four children of which the three girls died before they were a year old. Now they lay forgotten in the old Uhtua cemetery …

Ilja touched a sun-warmed log in the sauna wall. Here they had taken a sauna bath every single Saturday evening. What could the sauna have told him if its blackened logs could only speak …

While he was lost in his thoughts a boat was approaching the dock, and Ilja was abruptly returned to reality. As he turned he saw a woman in the boat, laughing, her whole round face beaming. A bright flowery shawl covered her shoulders, her arms were bare, enticing. Beside her sat a girl, four or five years old.

"I came to look, that's what I did!" The woman said laughing again.

Her voice rang out clearly; it was charming and seductively audacious at the same time.

"There is talk in Uhtua that Ilja Huotari has arrived, and so it seems …You are a handsome sight. I'm Outi, you know my father – the old *buobo*, not far from his grave."

Ilja stared at the woman, speechless. How could anyone speak that way about their old father and the grave, and at the same time make a play with their eyes, which were so full of unconscious sexuality, that even he felt his knees buckling.

The girl sat apathetically beside her mother who now grabbed the oars with her strong arms, and turned the boat around. Then she began to row forward.

"The tip of the next point … you come whenever you like!"

The eyes, which had narrowed to mere slits, laughed at Ilja's bewilderment as the boat glided along the calm water. Ilja stared after the boat. Was this a dream? He caught himself thinking of the white arms and the bubbling laugh. Oh, my God – it was an invitation!

He rose from the bench and looked at the old house standing on top of the little hill. It was even more blackened than before, just like all the houses in Uhtua. He knew he was expected there, he the master. He also knew the people in the house were suspicious of him, perhaps even hostile, and therefore it was with heavy steps that he started walking up the hill.

When he entered the vestibule, he heard a girl's voice.

"Now it has been properly blessed, Katri – blessed! That's why I went out last night."

"Why didn't you wake me up …"

Ilja knocked on the door and stepped in. He stopped on the threshold and held his breath; he could not see the people sitting within. Everything was so familiar – so very familiar! It was as if time had stopped when he left and only started again right now. Had anything changed here? The yard was as before, the cowshed as before, the living room as before …

All the things were in their place, the dishes in the wall cupboard, the large hearth in the corner, next to it the door to the pen. The long table was under the window at the far end, the benches around it, even the water bucket and the wash stand were in the same place where they had been when his mother was alive! He had been dreaming of this wonderful living room for decades …

"There are people here, too," Katri said after a long silence.

Ilja Huotari returned to the present and saw the girl sitting by the window, and the woman next to her. Their blond heads were bent together, the fading light of the dusk playing on their hair. Teppana Jyrkinen sat on the bench, a pipe clenched between his teeth, a woman was busy by the stove. The room was silent, everyone looked at the newcomer.

"Pardon me for intruding like this uninvited," Ilja said and surveyed his surroundings, ill at ease.

The woman by the stove came closer, wiping her hands on her apron. She nodded toward Ilja Huotari and stretched out her hand.

"I am Nasti, Teppana's wife. Please have a seat."

The woman had a round face. She was thin and nondescript. Her forehead was exceptionally high and on her head she sported some ugly head gear, which allowed her ears to stick out. Her voice was, however, feminine, gentle and friendly; she was obviously the one occupant of this house who realized who Ilja Huotari was.

"Thank you," said Ilja and sat down at the end of the bench.

He sat there saying nothing and breathed in the smell of the living room the same way he had inhaled the smell of the sauna a few minutes ago. Then he forced himself to look at the people in the room. The girl and her aunt had adopted a reticent attitude; you could tell from the way they sat. They sat next to each other like allies, without turning their eyes away from him. Ilja could see how they tensed as he began to speak.

"As far as I understand, I am the child's only guardian after her parents' death," he said in a sterner voice than he had intended. He saw the women startle, and that annoyed him even more.

"No need for any judges," he growled irascibly. "A grandfather is a closer relative than an aunt, any fool knows that. I have come here all the way from Canada to care for the girl. She is moving to the new house – to live with me."

The girl grew pale, and Katri pulled her closer than before. Ilja's voice grew sharper.

"What kind of upbringing have you had that you should defy an older person!"

His face had darkened, his appearance signaled clearly that he did not tolerate opposition. The girl stood up and took a cautious step toward her grandfather. She stopped in the middle of the floor and stood with her hands behind her back and her head proudly erect. Ilja observed that the girl was no longer a child, but a young woman, whose slender body held more strength than he had realized.

"I am going to Sortavala Girl's School in the fall!" the girl said. Her voice rang clear, but its tone was defiant. "Katri is coming, too – we already have a place to live. The rest of this summer I will live in this house, because this is my home!"

"Your home is in the new house," Ilja Huotari thundered. "It has a special room for you!"

The girl's dark-blue eyes flashed – she wasn't far from stamping her feet.

"Why do you come here from some place called Canada to order me around! I remember what Father always said. He said he had never had a father of his own. He said his father had never cared for him."

Ilja lost his patience. He jumped up from the bench and shouted, "You ungrateful brat! How dare you speak to me like that!"

The man had raised his hand as if to hit her. Katri hurried to take the girl in her arms. The grandfather and the girl stared at each other with flaming eyes and trembling chins. Then the girl tore herself free and rushed to the door. At the threshold she turned and shouted, "I hate you, I hate you. Why did you have to come here and mess up our lives?"

The door slammed shut. Katri thought first of going after the girl, but then she returned and sat down. Nasti stood by the stove looking quite shocked. Even Teppana's face was creased with concern, and his pipe was no longer in his mouth; he fingered it in his hands.

"If I were you, I would abandon the idea of forcing her to live in the new house," Katri said. She sat on the bench with her hands in her lap and calmly looked at Ilja Huotari. "You should remember that she has lived in this house her entire life. She is a sensitive child, a dreamer. You may not be interested but she walks in the forest and speaks to spirits, which she sees everywhere. Last night she went out alone at night, went to the rapids to fetch water in a pail from her Water Spirit and then went to your house and blessed it by throwing a handful of holy water at each corner. She blessed your house so it wouldn't be destroyed by fire. She cannot stand the idea that the trees would burn down. And then you arrive like a hurricane and want to change this child! Can't you at least understand that she is still grieving her parents, that she is far from settled!"

Ilja's face had turned red.

"How can a girl like her be unsettled, she has the temperament of a bear hunter."

"That's true," Katri said. "I am wondering how come you don't have the good sense to understand how to treat a girl like that. Why don't you let her live the rest of the summer in this familiar place. In September we'll move to Sortavala, and I'll take responsibility for her. She wants to go to school, she is an intelligent and talented girl."

Ilja's jaw was clenched. The woman was right – he came second, regardless of how one looked at the matter. He seized the tea glass Nasti had given him, drank the hot beverage eagerly and quickly, like a shot of whiskey. Then he looked at Katri.

"I can't get anywhere with you," he said with a strained voice. "But you are alienating her from me."

Katri smiled.

"You're not claiming that she's close to you, are you?"

Ilja's head shot up.

"No I'm not."

Again silence settled in the room. It was broken only when Teppana suddenly got up and went into the alcove. When he returned he held a bundle of papers in his hand. He sat down diffidently next to Ilja and gave him the papers.

"I thought … these papers," he said quite embarrassed. "They are all here, the old house papers. We've bought what we've needed, but since we haven't had a master, I've handled all the affairs."

It was Ilja's turn to become embarrassed. The thought had never even crossed his mind that they might suffer from a shortage of money in the old house. He cast a friendly glance at Teppana; since the previous spring, this man had actually cared for the farm without the help of a master.

"I'll take care of the money matters," he said. "What about your own wages? Nobody's paid them, I take it?"

Teppana shook his head.

"Nobody."

Nasti came to sit beside her husband; she arranged her headdress and wiped her eyes with the corner of her apron.

"I would like to ask if we have to leave now that the new house seems to have servants of its own."

"They don't know how to care for the animals," Ilja said surprisingly peaceably. "No reason to do away with the cows. You just continue as before. You keep this old house, live here, take care of the animals, the harvest, and fall plowing. Without the land there isn't much to live on, and I am no good at tilling the soil."

"You mean, sir, that we don't have to move to the new house?" Nasti asked, sounding relieved.

"Why should you move to the new house …"

Katri said nothing, she only listened. She was happy to see Ilja Huotari show compassion for the first time. She looked at him sitting at the end of the bench, his gentleman's clothes and appearance. But there was something else too: an obviously handsome face, big hands, which showed signs of work, the bearing of a man aware of his station. And when he spoke, his voice was sincere, and he spoke the Karelian dialect – living abroad had not made him forget his own language.

Katri did not manage to find anything else redeeming about the man. She did not understand how he could be so shortsighted when it came to Aniviisu, so cold and unyielding. Exploding like that in front of the child and demanding that she suddenly change her whole life ... The man had money ... there was no doubt about that, but was he wise, could he see clearly? Had Ilja Huotari imagined when he left Canada that he would be welcomed with open arms? Katri realized that her mind was poisoned on Aniviisu's behalf.

Ilja's thoughts moved in similar grooves, as he sat on the bench without speaking. He was disquieted by the blond woman sitting by the window, her intelligent eyes, and her peaceful calm. What was a woman like this doing here in Uhtua, far away from all civilization. He had to admit he had imagined that Uhtua had remained the way it was when he left thirty years ago. Of course, change had occurred here as well. But Katri was still a surprise – and the girl. He could not call her Aniviisu, it was just too awful a name. It was high time to return to the girl's real name, Anna Liisa – that he could accept as the proper name of a Finnish girl. Ilja glanced at Katri from the corner of his eye. There she sat, looking calm and determined, ready to fire off her impudent remarks, formulated in proper, literary Finnish … What kind of a she-devil was this woman? Where did she come from?

Ilja hardened his facial expression and turned to Katri.

"May I ask from where you have come to Uhtua?"

Katri thought about it for a moment, then she answered.

"Nasti and Teppana wrote to me immediately after the accident. I had a teaching job in Suomussalmi, but I left it and came here. I stayed all winter because the girl was in a deep shock the whole summer and fall. I took her out of school, which was a good decision, as I was able to prepare her for her entrance exams directly for the sixth grade, skipping fifth grade."

Only now did Ilja realize he would have to decide what he thought of this whole Sortavala trip.

"Well," he said hesitatingly, "of course I have nothing against the girl going to school in Sortavala. I am all in favor of education. I think it is important – especially language skills. The girl should learn English."

Ilja took the papers Teppana gave him.

"Could you come by in the morning before noon. I'll give you some money, I'll pay your wages. And you, madam?" He turned to Katri. "You have cared for the girl for almost a year. I want to compensate you for it."

"Thank you – I am fine," Katri said. "I have some inheritance from my late husband, I didn't come to care for my sister's child for money."

Ilja frowned.

"You want me to be indebted to you?"

"Certainly not," Katri said irately. "I just feel that everything cannot be measured in money ... She was quiet for a while, then she continued, "Do you want me to leave for Sortavala immediately or can I stay here until I travel there with Aniviisu?"

Ilja's face had turned pale.

"You are trying to offend me – and you have succeeded. Who has poisoned all of you against me?"

Katri stood up as did Ilja Huotari.

"The deceased," she said.

It was late at night, but Ilja Huotari was still walking alone on the shore. He looked around the place, circled the point slowly, and arrived at last at the pond where he too had played as a child. He thought about his granddaughter, who according to Katri Jääskeläinen had blessed his house the night before. He didn't know what to think of that. Something in him aroused an enormous curiosity toward this little woman – that is what the girl was deep down, at least she was no ordinary child. Ilja sat down on a rock he remembered sitting on as a child. His eyes caught a piece of paper beside the rock. He dug it out. On the paper was written in a child's handwriting: "The Mainiemi castle" He didn't know what it meant and where such a castle was to be found, but he had a feeling the girl had written it, perhaps from some book she had read.

It was clear that the piece of paper had been dropped inadvertently, it had not been left there on purpose.

Ilja sighed audibly. How to understand women … For example, the three women he had had the pleasure and honor of meeting here. They were all so different: Katri Jääskeläinen, feminine and intelligent; Teppana's Nasti like Martha of the Bible; and then jovial Outi, who had laughed in her boat and whom he could not get out of his mind. "You come when you want …"

It meant come when you feel the need, you'll get relief for your problem … Had he ever needed that kind of help? Greta had never denied him lovemaking, not once, but he did not enjoy it with Greta. How did it feel to make love to a hysterical woman who lay there in her silk fineries surrounded by a cloud of perfume and who clung to him like a vine. No – that did not match his fantasies. He remembered a girl he used to meet here by the pond, a beautiful and soft woman, who opened her arms and took him into her embrace. He still remembered how the difficult choice had driven him crazy; on the one hand he had desired to go to sea, and on the other he had wanted to stay here with that girl. The longing for the sea was stronger than his love for the girl. How many times had he gone to the city of Kemi on the White Sea to look for seamen whose stories he could have listened to from morning till night. He remembered his trip to Archangel, where he had met the captain of a large Ocean liner.

"Come here a month from now and you'll get on the ship!" the captain had told him.

Ilja had not dared tell anyone about his plans, least of all his brother or mother. He had already made up his mind, when one day Moarie, his girl, came to the pond in tears.

"I am going to have a baby!" Moarie had announced. "*Moamo* told me to get married. She said that in our family we don't have children unless we get married."

That same evening Ilja had confided in his brother, Ohvo, and said he was running away to sea. He did not want to tie himself down with Moarie and much less with a child. Ohvo had called him a coward and a wretch, and they had had a fight here on the shore of the pond. Ilja won the fight and the next evening he had left, leaving behind his home and the girl who was expecting his child. He had been irresistibly propelled by the dream of getting out to sea; it had burned in him like a fever.

He remembered that flight very well, every detail and every moment – hurrying in the dusk to the boat at the shore, then across Lake Kuittijärvi, and down the Kemi River past the dangerous rapids toward Viena Kemi. Upon his arrival in Kemi he went from ship to ship begging for work. He was prepared to do whatever it took to get hired. Finally he was lucky; the captain of an English ship took him on to Archangel to wash the ship's deck. He made it to Archangel two days before the ocean ship SS *Emilia* left the port of Archangel, first for Murmansk, and from there to Canada. The ship swept him along and he had been on that voyage until he returned home. The circle was closed.

Ilja's thoughts were interrupted by a bird, which walked on the shore of the pond and looked at him in distress, letting out odd whistling sounds. He rose cautiously from the rock and took a closer look. It was a hazelhen and she was surrounded by a tweeting choir of chicks.

"Excuse me," Ilja Huotari whispered. "I'll leave."

He felt lonely as he started to walk slowly back to the tip of the point. The new house protruded in the silence of the night like an image in a dream. And a dream it was – his dreamhouse, one that he had thought about ever since SS *Emilia* lifted anchor in the port of Archangel. Now the dream had become reality, but he did not feel happy. He felt nothing, only loneliness.

He opened the main door and went in. He climbed the stairs to the second floor and peeked into his wife's room; Greta slept, breathing heavily; she was of course tired from the trip. Ilja pulled the door shut discreetly.

The upper hallway was still full of travel trunks and boxes. Samuel had been emptying them for two days, but all the things had not yet found their rightful place. Poor man ... Samuel had a room downstairs, the room behind the kitchen. Mrs. Jenny slept upstairs in the room next to the one designed for the child. Ilja Huotari had always cared well for his employees. Some ten years ago he had still had a great number of them, but then he had given up on domestic help almost altogether. He wanted to bring only the two faithful old servants with him to Viena.

Ilja got undressed in the small dressing room next to his bathroom. He washed, dried himself and put on his pajamas. He sat down on his bed, but did not yet lie down. He looked around pensively in the bedroom. The mahogany bed had head and foot boards decorated with ornate carvings. Dark-brown velvet drapes were tied with green cords. The large desk stood between the two windows at the gable end, and the chair in front of it was upholstered with buffalo hide. Then his eyes fixed on the wall next to Greta's room with its bookshelves and the books whose gilded spines glowed dimly in the light of the oil lamp. Everything was perfect, nothing material was lacking. That which was missing was not material.

Ilja blew out the lamp and lay down under his soft comforter, but he could not sleep. He lay leaning on high cushions and contemplated his life. He remembered how in his childhood they had gone sleigh riding along the shore to the Uhtua church in winter. He remembered the white snow-covered spruces, the jingle bells, the crackling snow under the runners. He remembered his mother, a proud woman, whose fate it was to die very young. And he remembered his father, the man who had become a distant stranger, who had never taken an interest in the fields that belonged to the Huotari farm. His father's wanderlust had driven him to the road; caring for the farm had remained his mother's responsibility. Ilja also remembered his brother, Ohvo, who had married Moarie to preserve her honor. Had they loved each other? Had Moarie been as passionate in Ohvo's embrace as she had been in his? Ilja suddenly felt a painful emptiness, and he closed his eyes. He had lost Moarie's love, and he had never found new love. He knew nothing about love, did not understand it. He had had many women, but he had always used them to satisfy himself, he had not loved a single one.

Ilja Huotari had achieved everything in his life, but he had not achieved love. Not since he had left Moarie, who had pressed herself against him on the moss, removing her skirt herself. From that embrace Moissei had been born, the son whom he could not think about now. The son who died before his father had a chance to see him.

Ilja opened his eyes again and stared into the darkness. Sometimes he felt as if a curse were hanging over him.

Mrs. Jenny had set the breakfast table in the dining room: coffee, buns, ham, eggs. She ran back and forth with flapping slippers to the kitchen and back, carrying things with a worried expression on her face. She was wearing a light-blue dress covered by a white apron that reached down to the floor. Mrs. Jenny was going on seventy, but was healthy and vigorous.

"You should really have some more, sir, eggs and ham!"

The benevolent expression on Mrs. Jenny's face was amplified by the second chin under the small soft chin, but her voice was sharp and shrill. Now it was also demanding.

"All right, maybe a little," Ilja muttered, and Mrs. Jenny's face melted into a smile. She immediately began to busy herself with another matter.

"Mrs. Greta is not awake yet ... sleeps until midday, sleeps, the poor thing – she's tired! Samuel, the old scoundrel, didn't remember to speak to the man in the old house about the ice, we have to have ice! Well, now the man seems to be coming here!"

Ilja tried to keep his facial expression in check, even though he found the old woman's fussing amusing.

"Ask him to come in. His name is Teppana Jyrkinen. I've asked him to take me to Uhtua – I have to report our arrival to the police and also your arrival."

When Teppana came to the door, Mrs. Jenny pushed a chair to him, rushed a coffee cup into his hand and poured coffee without asking.

"We need ice here," Mrs. Jenny said sternly. "Could you, Teppana Jyrkinen, please ask around in Uhtua to find out if there is any ice to be had for our cellar? We need some now."

"Sure I'll ask," Teppana said blowing on his steaming cup. "For the most immediate need we do have some stored in sawdust. But we'll ask around in Uhtua, that we will."

Teppana slurped his coffee with an expression of great pleasure on his weathered face. He had never had something as delicious as this before. He took a second cup, and a third, but then Mrs. Jenny took the pot away.

Ilja let Teppana take his time drinking his coffee. The blissfully smiling hired man had no idea he was being buttered up for a reason. In the future Mrs. Jenny, with the aid of her coffee pot, would get help with this and that from Teppana.

"Well then, shall we go," Teppana said finally, licking his lips.

Rowing to Uhtua took an hour. Teppana sat in the boat with his back to Ilja Huotari, pulling the oars vigorously with his pipe between his teeth. They did not speak much. Ilja looked at the shoreline, the small coves and bays of Lake Kuittijärvi. Last night's wind had subsided, and the surface of the water was calm; only here and there small eddies were generated by fish. They passed the tip of the point with the gently leaning gray cottage. The sauna looked as if it were sinking into the water.

"Whose house is that one over there?" Ilja asked, although he immediately guessed the answer.

Teppana turned his head a little and smacked his lips with the unlit pipe dangling.

"Well, that's Outi's … You must have met her father some time way back. He conceived this Outi in his old age and is languishing now in the cottage. Outi has a girl of her own, what, maybe four years old … Nothing wrong with Outi," Teppana spoke to the rhythm of the oars, mostly to himself. "A jovial woman she is, but she doesn't have a husband."

"Is the child's father known?" Ilja asked.

"Said to be unknown …"

There was no activity at Outi's place. For a long while Ilja watched the shack, and time after time the image of the woman with laughing eyes, sitting in the boat appeared before him. He tried several times to chase the image away, but it reappeared each time, vivid and irritating.

Finally, the houses of Likopää village in Uhtua came into view. Farther away he could see a white church and behind it another one.

"There are two churches?" Ilja asked, instinctively using the old Karelian term for church. "Before there used to be only one."

"They built a new one," Teppana said. "The old one was dilapidated. This new church is nice and warm even in the winter."

After rowing a little longer they came upon a high bank with a partly submerged dock. Ilja perused the environs in a state of excitement; there were many new houses in Uhtua, both Finnish- and Russian-style structures. They just sat there in a row along the embankment. Teppana's face reflected his annoyance, a small fishing boat blocked their access to the dock. Three men sat in the boat about to go fishing: the lines and the nets were ready for action. Teppana could not understand why the men were blocking their passage. He was just about to ask them about it when he realized the men were staring at a woman who was descending toward the shore.

The woman was barefoot and walked purposefully toward the dock, her head erect. She was handsome and voluptuous, with a spring in her stride. The men in the fishing boat could not take their eyes off her. They were dumbstruck and just stared.

Behind the woman a tiny little girl scampered down the slope. The woman squatted down on a rock off the shore and motioned for the girl to come to her. She took off the girl's dress and threw the screaming child into the water.

She began to show the girl how to swim and managed to calm her down.

Ilja watched this drama with curiosity. The faces of the men in the fishing boat exhibited undisguised desire; the woman aroused in them such shameless lust that it felt like voyeurism just to look at them. All three of the men displayed signs of animals in heat.

"You gave him the brush-off, Outi … we know! Why did you do that?"

The woman laughed, her white teeth flashing. She swayed on the rock holding the child who was splashing about in the water. Her skirt crept upward baring her dazzling white thighs. The men got even more excited.

"He was such a rascal!" Outi laughed. "Not good enough for me! But the other one is a real charmer."

"I know him," one of the men teased her. "The charmer already has a wife. He's a tough Russian peasant, he wants to have them all."

"But he hasn't had me yet!" Outi giggled.

Ilja started to feel hot. He had never met such a child of nature. The woman's breasts almost welled completely out of the neckline of her blouse; they were large and beautifully shaped. The men in the boat were like cats on a hot tin roof. One fumbled for tobacco in his pocket, but he could not take his eyes off the woman, who now flirted deliberately, swayed, wriggled, and swung her hips. Every gesture was intended to inflame the men's desire. She shook her breasts, threw her head back and laughed out loud, as the child splashed water on her.

"*Hospody* …" Teppana blessed himself and tried to steer the boat to the dock.

But the boat did not make it to the dock, for the woman's play had rendered the men in the fishing boat both deaf and blind.

"Say, will you turn me down if I propose to you?" The man sitting farthest back in the boat asked. He scratched his hair, which was thick and reached over his ears. His pockmarked face seemed to be hewn out of wood, the chin robust and the mouth wide.

Only now did Ilja figure out what was going on. He watched as the third and quietest man stood up.

"You've already been fooling around, Outi and Iivana! What do you say – you're just teasing us, you won't put out for anyone but Iivana. For him you put out easily …"

The woman did not take offense – she laughed even harder. Iivana did not get mad either, a pleased and smug smile spread on his rugged face. Ilja could not help but grimace: so she had put out for him … Ilja devoured the woman with his eyes, her wide and sensuous mouth with its flashing white teeth. The white arms were round and delicious, her bottom broad, and her waist slim. Her entire being radiated a lack of restraint, which aroused men. She revealed herself ever more daringly, she let the hem of her skirt slip up high enough for the men to catch a glimpse of her rounded buttocks. The men sighed deeply.

Ilja could not remember ever having witnessed such a display. He found himself wanting it to last as long as possible. Suddenly Iivana, who was sitting at the stern of the fishing boat, could no longer remain calm; he jumped off the boat onto the dock and yanked the woman onto the shore with one hand. Then he slapped her on her buttocks and jumped back into the boat. Even this did not annoy Outi, she just giggled as she watched her child swim. Her eyes narrowed as she gazed at the crew of the boat. It was obvious that she enjoyed the effect her body had on the men. Then the child got out of the water; Outi wrapped a towel around the girl and took her into her arms. She began to climb up the slope, still swaying her behind teasingly. Halfway up the embankment she turned to look back, moistening her lips with the tip of her tongue.

Ilja let out the air from his lungs quietly. The men in the fishing boat also calmed down, as Outi disappeared from sight. They still had to go fishing despite the fact they were all consumed by desire for a woman. Iivana took to the oars and turned the boat toward the open bay. Only then did the men notice Ilja and Teppana. Their laughter and joking around ended abruptly. The men were young and did not remember Ilja Huotari, but they knew Teppana and immediately guessed who the well-dressed man sitting at the prow was. So that's what he looked like, the seafarer who had at last returned to his home region!

Ilja felt the curious glances the men cast from the departing boat.

As they climbed up the slope Teppana explained that Outi was a real hussy, tempting all men with her bottom.

"Who was the man who lifted her off the rock?" Ilja asked.

"The pockmarked one? His name is Iivana, a real beanpole of a man. They say he has killed three bears. He's a fisherman, I believe, at least I can't remember him going on peddling tours."

Ilja nodded in silence. They continued their journey along the Likopää route toward the police prefecture when unexpectedly, Outi hurried toward them. Teppana quickened his pace, but Ilja slowed his almost to a halt. He could not take his eyes off the woman coming toward them. Outi had taken the child somewhere and was walking alone. Her white blouse was brilliantly clean and her wide red skirt reached down to her ankles and swayed around her feet. The neckline in her blouse was generous, revealing her breasts almost down to the nipples. Ilja could not help his uneasy thoughts when the woman stopped in front of him.

"Greetings and good health!" said Outi crossing her arms on top of her breasts.

"And the same to you," replied Ilja as an echo of a long time ago. He was shocked by his own voice; it got stuck somewhere in his throat and came out as a wheeze.

She looked deeply in his eyes.

"We met the other evening at the Huotari shore. What are you doing in Uhtua?"

She was a big woman; her eyes were almost level with Ilja's. Ilja did not know what to say or how to talk. Finally, he managed to clear his throat.

"We have to report to the police chief ..."

"When did you arrive?" The woman asked.

"Two days ago. This is my first visit to Uhtua since I left as a young man."

Outi gave a cheerful laugh, which sounded like a the ringing of a bell. Her laugh was on the one hand annoyingly shrill, on the other it held a promise that made one's stomach tingle. Ilja did not understand why the woman would laugh at such an ordinary matter-of-fact answer. But he could not bring himself to worry about such matters;

the woman had set his blood churning and he was just as weak-willed as the men in the boat had been.

Teppana had continued walking, slowing down just a little. Ilja was still standing on the path in front of the woman looking into her eyes, which were full of promise.

"I was so hoping a real man would show up. But then you came."

"Aren't I a real man?"

"Well, you're a bear! Wouldn't I just love to feel those muscles in your arms!"

"Do you always feel the arms of people you meet?"

"I feel them when I feel like it."

"And you feel like it now?"

- I do, I do … Come over to the cottage some evening, for a sauna … I'll heat it for you. You'll see the smoke pushing through the cracks of the sauna. Go fishing, you'll see our place."

"You don't live alone, you've got a child."

"*Buobo* stays in the house, he hasn't been outside in ages. He looks after the girl when I'm busy. No one will disturb our sauna.

"What if the other bear – Iivana – shows up?"

"He may come today, but I'll give him the brush-off. I'll tell him it's over. I'm the one who decides."

Outi locked eyes with Ilja once more, then she started walking toward the boat cove. Ilja's eyes followed her. He could not believe what he had just seen and heard. Less than ten minutes ago, the woman had flirted outrageously with other men and now she had invited him for a visit to her sauna. And why not, Ilja suddenly decided. He saw in his mind's eye Greta's weary face and her body, which was like the body of someone who was dead; it did not throb, or stir, however hard one tried to bring it back to life. This Uhtua woman, however, was just the right kind for him, an emotionally deficient man.

By now Teppana had slowed down almost to a standstill. He gazed at the two islets in front of Uhtua, which were not visible from Huotari Point.

"Quite some houses around here," said Ilja as he caught up with sour-faced Teppana. "There sure weren't such splendid-looking houses in the old days."

"You mean women, sir... and they are new too, just like the houses, Teppana said, still resentful that Ilja had stopped to talk to a slut like that. – But then your own house is the biggest and most splendid of all."

"Different at least, yes," Ilja agreed.

"They say the Ondrono house is over in Lamminpää north of Uhutjoki River. It's rumored to have seven windows to the west and just as many to the south. It's even painted and has siding."

Ilja Huotari laughed.

"So the number of windows determines the size of a house?"

Teppana did not answer. What was supposed to say to something like that; he knew it just as well himself, having been out in the big world.

They walked on silently, and Ilja admired the settlement on the embankment. Uhtua was indeed romantic and charming. He sometimes had to walk faster, to keep up with Teppana who pushed forward looking morose, even though Ilja wanted to take his time and look around. That house over there he remembered, and that one used to belong to Moarie's uncle … He became a little apprehensive about walking cockily in this neighborhood; what if he were to meet some male relative of Moarie who could accuse him of abandonment. He had not thought of that before. Then he calmed down – who would still be alive? They had forgiven him long ago. He cast a glance at the river. It was the only means of transportation; there were no roads to speak of. During the spring thaw all the villages were completely isolated. That will have to change, Ilja thought. He knew how to do it, he had money.

"There is the police chief's office," Teppana said suddenly and motioned for Ilja to follow him.

The police chief's office was located in a derelict old house near the church and the elementary school. The front door was dangling partly open, a cat was lying next to the steps. They went in. There was no one in the front room. The door to the back room was open. Teppana called out, "Is anyone here?"

He shrugged his shoulders. Then, through the window they saw the policeman coming from the outhouse, buttoning his trousers. The man was small and swarthy, unkempt, even dirty. As he came to the door he nodded his head and, with a reddened face, said in Russian, "Good day."

"Does he speak Finnish?" Ilja asked Teppana in a voice clearly audible to the man.

"I do speak Finnish," the police chief replied. He took a jacket from a chair, put it on and fastened the uppermost button. Now he was once again the Czar's loyal civil servant. He brushed back his few hairs with his fingers, straightened his posture and cast a stern glance at his visitors.

"What is your business?"

Ilja Huotari pulled out a bundle of documents and placed them on the table before the policeman.

"Here are my wife's and my passports, here our servants'."

The policeman looked at Ilja from under his eyebrows, examined the papers, fumbled with them and tried to understand – but didn't.

"Maybe I could translate for you?" Ilja asked courteously.

The man did not answer; he kept spelling out the English-language text of the documents, all flustered. The scrutiny lasted ten minutes. Then the police chief took out a stamp pad from the cabinet, looked for a suitable stamp and stamped each document twice, to be on the safe side.

"You must show these again in the fall," he said, wiping his brow.

Ilja Huotari bowed, collected the papers from the table, and looked into the man's beady eyes.

"You seem to be still lacking roads around here," he said as he took a step toward the door. "Can't you do anything about that?"

The police chief waved his hand.

"There are boats – yes boats."

"Yes, there are boats," Ilja admitted. "I believe they were invented long before the first people came here to Uhtua. But I am surprised there is not a single decent road leading to the east or to the west from the largest town in Viena."

The police chief's face had become even redder than before. He could not stand a creature like that who came here from somewhere else where they didn't even know how to write in a decent language. Surely he must have been thinking of some kind of scheme even now – he better look out. The man nodded coldly and went into the back room.

Ilja and Teppana waited a while, but since he did not return, they assumed the audience was over. Ilja did not, however, leave immediately. He went up to the door, that led into the back room and peeked in.

"If you Russians are interested in negotiating about some kind of roads to Finland, I'll certainly consider financing it."

The police chief lumbered through the door so quickly he nearly bumped into Ilja.

"If there is a road to be built, it'll be to Russia!"

The man put his hands behind his back and rose up on his toes. Ill-tempered, he glared at his visitors.

Ilja and Teppana nodded their goodbyes and left. Outside Ilja let his suppressed anger fly, but Teppana said meekly, "He hasn't bothered us."

Ilja looked sharply at Teppana. So this is how things have contiinued on here? Again the people just resign themselves … Suddenly he felt he had a lot of things to do here in Uhtua.

As they were returning to their boat, they saw a woman and a child coming toward them. The girl looked like Aniviisu, but appeared much older in her black dress. The woman walked with long strides. She was wearing a black skirt, buttoned shoes, and over her shoulders she wore a fringed shawl that hung far down on her back. Her braided hair was pulled into some kind of a bun at the back of her head. The woman's thin face wore a withdrawn, uninviting expression.

"Aniviisu's former teacher," Teppana whispered. "You have to greet her."

Of course he had to, because Darja Mihailovna stopped in front of the men and waited to see Ilja Huotari's reaction. For a moment they stood face to face, then Ilja stretched out his hand.

"How do you do, my name is Ilja Huotari from Huotari Point."

Her facial expression did not change one bit.

"I see, you have arrived."

"So I have."

"Then you will certainly know that your granddaughter dropped out of school a year ago," the woman said. "It is not good for a child, to have some obscure Finnish teacher teaching her."

Ilja frowned.

You are speaking about my granddaughter and her aunt. I would ask you to use a more respectful tone of voice. If the girl gets admitted to the Sortavala Girls' School with the same grades as your daughter, there surely is no difference in the quality of teaching!"

The woman raised her eyes. Ilja had never seen such eyes before. One eye was an indeterminate brown, the other pale blue. There was nothing indeterminate about her gaze: it was full of hatred.

"You speak of respect ..." the woman said as if to herself. A contemptuous smile appeared on her face. "Never mind, you are of no interest to me, but the child is. Even the law says that she should have attended school in Uhtua last fall."

"We have a different law than you," Ilja Huotari said. "In my house we live by the laws I lay down."

He did not wait around to hear Darja Mihailovna's response, but departed for the shore at a furious pace. He could not quite understand why he was so upset – but there was something about the woman that made him lose his temper completely.

Teppana did not keep pace with his master. He stood in front of the woman and the girl, fingering his pipe in silence.

“What a cold man,” Darja Mihailovna said. “That’s the way they are, the rich people, they don’t think that poor folk are even entitled to human dignity. I pity Aniviisu who has to live with someone like that. Now, move on,” she huffed irritably to her daughter who had been standing there all this time with a frightened look on her face.

“You come and see us, Anja,” Teppana said gently and went to join his master.

Ilja was waiting by the dock, as Teppana arrived puffing on his pipe.

“This is what it’s like here in Viena,” Teppana said, loosening the boat’s rope. “The Russians decide about everything.”

The men returned home just after noon. Teppana rowed the boat to the sauna shore. Katri and Aniviisu were rinsing the washing, while Nasti was busy inside the sauna.

Now in the summertime the cows were taken to the back meadows behind Small Bird Grove. A rain shelter had been erected there for the animals and they slept under it. Teppana walked to that wilderness meadow to milk the cows every morning and evening, pushing the wooden milk tubs on a cart he had built himself. At the edge of the meadow he strained the milk and brought it to the yard.

Teppana was in a hurry to get to his chores, but Ilja stayed on the shore near Aniviisu and Katri. They didn’t pay much attention to him.

“I met your teacher in Uhtua,” Ilja said to Aniviisu. “Quite a busybody; she wanted you to go to school.”

Aniviisu’s expression darkened, as she looked defiantly at her *buobo*.

“I am never going to Uhtua to school any more.”

“Well, we know that well enough,” Ilja said. “I, too, told her that.”

Katri laughed.

“She didn’t like that, did she?”

“No, she called you ‘some obscure Finnish teacher.’”

Katri smiled.

"She did, did she? Well, she knows my late husband was an activist. She also knows that I, too, am inclined to oppose the oppressive policies of the Russians. The woman is a socialist. Everyone knows that."

Katri slapped some sheets in a big wooden bucket and wrung the water from them with her strong hands. Ilja stood looking on, until he was brought back to reality by the little girl's stare. What's with me, Ilja pondered in his mind. I am looking at these women as if I had never seen a woman before.

As he began to walk toward the new house, Katri turned to say to Aniviisu, "He is not totally impossible."

Aniviisu did not answer.

During the course of the morning the house was being put in order with vim and vigor. Before long all things were in their right place. The shelves of the pantries were filled with dry food goods, sugar, and flour. After Teppana had hauled a large chunk of ice on his cart to the cellar, even the more delicate foodstuff was safely stored. The clothes and the linens were already in their cupboards and dressers, the books were on the shelves, and the paintings on the walls. Mrs. Jenny cleaned up the verandah in front of the house, and together with Samuel she carried out a table and chairs for afternoon coffee. Mrs. Jenny was a master of adaptation. She was never in a bad mood, but always responded with a smile to her mistress' fretting and fits of ill temper, which invariably were due to her craving for alcohol.

Life had settled into its tracks in Huotari's new house. There was no further talk of Aniviisu moving in with her *buobo*.

Katri and Aniviisu had not paid another visit to the new house, but there were frequent visits from there to the old quarters. Even Mrs. Jenny had given herself an excuse to go there, and it turned out she had grown up in nearby Vuokkiniemi. She sat at the table in the living room sipping coffee from the saucer through a sugar lump, with her eyes closed, just like Nasti. Mrs. Jenny had brought American coffee with her, and with that she had won over Nasti's heart. They had a good time together and Nasti took the opportunity to relate what fates had befallen each farm in the area, the old families and those who were now buried in the graveyard.

Greta, however, did not visit the old house. She stayed in her room despite the beauty of the warm and sunny Viena summer. When she occasionally appeared on the verandah, she stayed only a short while, and went back inside proclaiming that she hated the weather as well as the scenery.

Ilja spent a lot of time outdoors. Almost every day he took the boat and rowed far out on the open bay. Twice during the first week he had asked Teppana to heat the sauna, and had enjoyed it for hours, swimming every once in a while. Katri, too, had become used to the lonely figure, whom she often saw walking along the shore or in the forest.

Aniviisu refused to see anything redeeming about the man. An inexplicable hatred pulsated in the girl's soul. Each time she saw Ilja Huotari, or even heard his name mentioned, her face turned sullen and her gaze revealed poorly veiled contempt. The girl's aversion toward her *buobo* increased each day – she had even begun to blame him for the death of her parents. If *buobo* had really cared for his son, the accident would never have happened ... How it could have been prevented – even Aniviisu could not explain.

During the summer Aniviisu befriended Kaarlo with all her soul. The boy proved to be worthy of her friendship. Almost every day they met in the forest by the pond. The two of them walked to the rapids and they sat watching the foaming water, or they walked on the shore talking. Sometimes Kaarlo took his violin along to the shore and played it there. Its sound would stop the Huotari people at their work, it was part of life on the point, just like the boy himself.

Katri felt a pang of joy when she looked out the window one Saturday evening in July and saw two familiar figures in the yard, Henrik Meinander and Kaarlo. She hurried out to greet the visitors. All day they had expected a thunderstorm, but the ominous clouds that had gathered in the sky had passed by, sprinkling only a few drops on the shore. The Meinanders did not want to venture out on the lake in their boat because the wind still showed signs of an impending storm.

They were standing in the yard when a rowboat appeared around the point. Ilja Huotari was sitting in the boat; he had grabbed a fishing rod after taking a sauna and rowed out on the lake. Henrik looked with curiosity at the man he had heard so much about.

"What's he really like?" he asked Katri.

"A very reserved person, but otherwise completely different from what I imagined. Much friendlier and warmer."

"Do you think I could go and introduce myself?"

"Sure," Katri said. "He seems lonely. One would think he would like to exchange views with someone; he has a large library and I believe he is well-read."

Henrik nodded pensively. They watched as Ilja's boat veered in the direction of Uhtua. The man rowed with steady strokes and the fishing rod swayed at the stern. Katri found the situation somehow odd: going fishing on a Saturday evening after his sauna? Henrik's conversation distracted her and she did not ponder the question any further.

Ilja saw that Outi's sauna was being heated. Outi had spoken the truth: smoke escaped from every crack of the sauna – as if the whole structure were steaming. This was his invitation to steer his boat to shore.

Ilja rowed to a little cove near the house and guided his boat under the weeping birches. He had to smile at his fishing rod in the stern; a shallow cove was filled with vegetation: reeds and yellow and white water lilies. It would certainly have been a pretty sight had he begun to fish there. From here he could see Outi's sauna ... What was it that drew him here? He smiled again – what a question for an adult man to ask himself.

When the sauna seemed to be ready and no more smoke poured out, Outi came to the shore and sat down on the bench next to the blackened log wall. Ilja could clearly see the woman was waiting. He pushed the boat out from among the reeds and rowed towards the sauna. When the boat touched the dock, Outi looked at her visitor in the eye.

"You could have come earlier – the child and *buobo* are asleep."

There was joy and laughter in the woman's voice.

Only a few drops of rain had fallen, but it seemed to have rinsed the dust off the leaves of the trees and the grass. The air smelled fresh and clean.

"Let's go rowing," Kaarlo suggested.

"Let's," said Aniviisu eagerly. "Let's take along fishing rods, the fish might bite well tonight."

They ran from the path to the yard. Kaarlo placed his violin case on the table in front of his father.

"We're going fishing."

"Don't stay too long," Katri said. "Nasti is making dinner."

Aniviisu remembered something, and her face clouded over.

"He's not in the sauna, is he?"

Katri shook her head.

"Your *buobo* already had his sauna. He appears to have gone out on the lake, too."

"What direction?"

"Toward Uhtua."

"Good," said Aniviisu. "We'll go in the other direction."

The youngsters ran to the shore, Katri and Henrik gazing after them.

"When do you have your sauna?" Henrik asked.

"I have the entire summer night," Katri said. "It is a simply fabulous sauna; when you heat it all day, it's still hot enough to have a sauna the next morning. The three of us: Nasti, Aniviisu and I always have saunas together."

Henrik looked at her with a smile.

"It is good to think that you and Aniviisu will come to Sortavala. Kaarlo has found a friend in her. What does Ilja Huotari have to say about the matter?"

Katri thought about it for a moment.

"He was hurt that Aniviisu wasn't willing to move in to his fancy house. But he doesn't intend to prevent her from going to Sortavala, and that's really good. He's a modern man and doesn't object to education for women. I wish Aniviisu, too, could see that side of him."

Aniviisu grabbed Kaarlo's arm.

"Hey, that's *buobo*'s boat! Over there at Outi's dock … Quickly, row out on the bay, I don't want them to see us."

Kaarlo turned the boat, and soon they were fast on their way toward Huotari Point. They both had a hunch why Ilja's boat was tied to Outi's tilting dock. Kaarlo noticed tears of anger in Aniviisu's eyes.

"Do you know Outi?" the boy asked.

"Is there anyone who doesn't," Aniviisu snorted. "There are always men going there, I've seen it myself. They never go all the way to the house, they stay at the sauna. Your aunt Elma once told Mother that Outi is the most notorious woman in Uhtua."

Kaarlo nodded with a grave face. By now their boat was far away from Outi's shore and they started fishing. Kaarlo spit on the worm and cast his line far out. Aniviisu leaned against the sideboard and said nothing, but every once in a while her gaze would turn to Outi's sauna.

"I wouldn't want to the kids to see me leave," Ilja said to Outi at the sauna entrance. "Surely they must have recognized my boat."

His head was still hot, his ears buzzing. He felt he couldn't speak or even think properly. He had never experienced anything like the love-making with Outi a while ago. She sat in front of him by the window with a short shirt on; she was laughing away quietly.

"Now, Ilja Huotari, you will come here every week," Outi said. "I'll make your life worth living."

The man didn't answer. Outi continued.

"What do you care about the youngsters, just take your boat and row home."

"But what if they talk …"

"What the hell do you care, they'll talk anyway! They'll say Ilja Huotari's wife is too pale and bloodless, that's why he took Outi who is a real woman. What do you care what people say; you've got money. People's mouths have been silenced with money before – even here in Uhtua. Build them the road, that'll shut them up. They'll even forgive me if you give them the road."

Ilja gave Outi a long look; she sat there before him virtually naked, without shame, and spoke wise words. She was some woman.

"What you say is true," Ilja said aloud. "Last week I spoke about roads to the police chief. Did you hear about it from him?"

"I won't put out for the police chief," she snorted. "I hate Russians. But you will get it, you'll get it every time you come to see me. But bring money …"

Ilja went to the dock and looked out over the lake. The children's boat was still there. He untied his boat, waved his hand at Outi, and rowed decisively to his own shore. The youngsters came to shore much later, only when Ilja had gone to his house, and sat down in his library, with his mind still in turmoil.

"Katri, Ilja Huotari's boat was at Outi's shore," Aniviisu said indignantly as she came into the living room.

"Oh my goodness," Katri said, disturbed.

"I wish he would die," Aniviisu said. "I wouldn't cry over him."

The next day Kaarlo arrived in his boat to Huotari Point cove quite early in the afternoon. Nasti had brought out a white tablecloth for the table they had carried out into the yard. Katri and Aniviisu were sitting there having tea and planning the fall and their impending trip to Sortavala.

Ilja Huotari had not been seen since Saturday night. Katri smiled inwardly; she could appreciate that he did not like the idea that the children had seen his boat on Outi's shore. Yet it was only to be expected, Katri thought; there wasn't a man in Uhtua that Outi had not snatched up. And this latest capture appeared to have been one of the better ones …

The new house cropped up in conversation all the time. Mrs. Huotari generated the most curiosity; she wouldn't venture out even accidentally, not for a walk nor for a trip in the rowboat. She just kept sitting indoors.

"She is not a well person," said Nasti with empathy.

"How does she pass her time?" Aniviisu wondered.

"Maybe she reads or does handicraft," Katri suggested, which made Nasti snort loudly.

"Believe it or not, but she'll soon be on her way back to Canada," she said. "And that's probably why Ilja Huotari makes sure he has a woman somewhere nearby."

Nasti's view of the world was uncompromising. When she heard about Ilja Huotari's visit to Outi's sauna, her opinion of him plummeted. Such a whoremonger … She often came back to this topic and saw her opportunity at the very moment Aniviisu noticed Kaarlo's boat and ran to meet him. It wasn't proper to speak of these things in front of the child.

Kaarlo fastened the boat to the dock and the youngsters went along the path to the shady forest, Kaarlo first, Aniviisu following. Suddenly the boy stopped abruptly and Aniviisu bumped into him.

"What is it?"

The boy put his finger across his lips, and Aniviisu was silent. She looked in the direction Kaarlo pointed and her face darkened. On the shore of the pond, on their very own tree trunk sat – Ilja Huotari.

Aniviisu was about to shout at the man to go away, but something held her back. There was something very sad about his appearance, sitting there with his face resting on his palm, oblivious to the newcomers. What sorrows could he have? Aniviisu tried to harden herself, even though she knew he was lonely. But she did not like Ilja Huotari, rather she was afraid of him. That is why she grabbed Kaarlo by the sleeve and whispered, "Let's turn back, let's go away."

Just then the man noticed them with a start.

"Excuse us, we don't want to disturb you," Kaarlo said.

"Oh, there is room enough here," Ilja said standing up. He nodded to Aniviisu and looked questioningly at the boy.

"Good day, my name is Kaarlo Meinander," Kaarlo hurried to introduce himself. "From Uhtua … or actually from Sortavala."

"So, from Sortavala?" Ilja said. "Come and sit down, the forest around here is beautiful."

- You go, Aniviisu said and dashed off running before the boy could do anything.

Kaarlo looked helplessly after the girl, but then turned around to greet the man.

The man and the boy felt a peculiar sense of kinship as they sat there on the tree trunk talking about all kinds of things. Kaarlo thought to himself that he had never talked in this adult fashion with his own father. Ilja again thought he would really have wanted to have a son like this. But he no longer had a son …

"Can you tell me what is bothering the girl?" Ilja asked abruptly. "Why is she avoiding me and why does she run away all the time?

Why doesn't she want to move in with me, even though I've done everything I can for her enjoyment?"

Kaarlo looked at the man's serious and troubled face. How could he tell him? Then he decided he had to speak his mind. Who else would do it?

He told him what an enormous sorrow the drowning of Aniviisu's parents had caused her. It was nearly impossible for her to get over it.

"And her opinion of you comes from her father," Kaarlo explained. "He in turn had never understood why you didn't come to Finland to see him. That's why Aniviisu doesn't accept you."

"My son had good reason for his criticism. I'm not defending myself, I can only say that we each have our reasons, which outsiders cannot know."

"Aniviisu doesn't want to get to know you because she hates you," Kaarlo said straight out. "You have not said one word of consolation to her, and so she feels that the death of her parents hasn't meant anything at all to you. She thinks you are a cold and heartless person."

These were harsh words. Ilja had not expected such frank words from the boy.

"I will try to make it up to her. I would like to talk to her, but she doesn't give me a chance."

There was almost despair in Ilja's voice. Kaarlo looked at him with sadness.

"I cannot help you," he said quietly.

They walked slowly toward the old house, came to the cart road, and saw Katri, Aniviisu, Nasti, and Teppana sitting by the table having tea. Kaarlo stole a glance at the man walking beside him and saw him looking toward the yard with a sorrowful, almost teary-eyed gaze. Perhaps he would have liked to be part of this group, sit in the yard of his old childhood home looking over the sun-kissed water of Lake Kuittijärvi.

Kaarlo felt very sad as he looked at the man walking away. The man knew that everyone sitting in the yard was staring at his back – and now he could even guess what they were thinking.

Ilja sat on a rock on the shore. He could not go in quite yet; Greta would soon guess his state of mind and say something seemingly innocent yet insidiously cruel. Today he would not be able to endure it.

He tried to steady his feelings. Everything was actually fine, he assured himself. During a few short weeks he had got to see everything he had dreamed about for years. But his heart was squeezed by anguish and there was no one he could talk to. He would have liked to open his heart and talk about all those years when he had run away from everything – most of all himself. Now he had the courage to admit it – and also that he was fleeing again. Here he was in Uhtua, he greeted the people he met, but he did not get even close to striking up a conversation with anyone. Outi was the only one he had managed to talk to as they lay relaxed recovering from their sensual pleasures. But Outi did not listen, she was not interested in his anguish. And now he had been able to talk with this schoolboy. Where will all this end?

When Ilja opened the front door to his house and stepped in, he stopped in the hallway and looked around him bitterly. All this wealth and abundance – for whom? Would he one day die alone in this house with no one to mourn him …

A boat was moving on Middle-Kuittijärvi. A young girl sat on the stern seat drawing lines in the water with her hand. A boy, a few years older than the girl, was at the oars. He put all his energy into the rowing and paid no attention to the girl. They said nothing to each other; they were strangers to each other – and shy. Kaarlo Meinander had seen the girl in Lamminpää in Uhtua. He knew the girl's name was Anja, and that she was the daughter of school teacher Darja Mihailovna and a classmate of Aniviisu. The day before, as Kaarlo and his father were walking northward along the shore of the Uhtua River, had they run into the teacher and her daughter near the school. The teacher had been curt and churlish. The daughter always behaved like a deaf-mute in her mother's presence; she never said a word, just walked behind her. The girl had pretty, red cheeks but was wearing a black scarf.

Henrik Meinander had spoken to the teacher, making conversation and had asked if she had been to St Petersburg lately.

"No I haven't, my sister lives in Sortavala nowadays."

"Natalia? I remember her – she was a nurse. I heard from Katri Jääskeläinen that your daughter will be going to school in Sortavala. Will she be living with your sister?"

"Of course," the teacher had blurted out. "I can't afford to get separate accommodation for her. And Natalia is morally obligated to take the girl in!"

Kaarlo had noticed the girl's expression change. She obviously had wanted to protest, but Aniviisu had told him that Anja never dared oppose her mother, never even opened her mouth when her mother was speaking.

"We are poor people!"

Henrik Meinander had stared at the woman in front of him. She had shot her words like an accusation with fire in her eyes. Henrik had felt himself becoming irritated; most everyone here in Uhtua was poor. Yet they were not harbingers of bad news like this one – she even dressed in black all the time, and persisted in dressing her daughter the same way. The girl was never dressed in bright colors like other girls in Uhtua.

"What's that Ilja Huotari like?" the teacher had asked in an indifferent tone of voice. "Rolling in money, I hear. That money, of course, has been carved off the backs of the workers – and then he comes to flaunt it in starvation-plagued Viena. Builds a house fashioned only to mock the poor …

"That's not quite the case, Henrik had tried to interject, but the teacher was not to be interrupted.

"I have no appreciation for that kind of a man! The pleasures of the rich are bought and paid for with the suffering of the poor.

The teacher's words were followed by an awkward silence, which was broken by Anja. This was rare.

"Mother, could I go with this boy tomorrow to see Aniviisu?"

Darja Mihailovna threw a glance at Kaarlo.

"Why is this boy going there all the time?"

"Why wouldn't I? I am off school, Kaarlo answered cheerfully." The woman eyed her daughter once more, then she said to everyone's surprise, "All right, you can go."

At the same moment, the woman turned on her heels and started walking away with long strides. The daughter scampered after her. Kaarlo had to shout after them, "Come to the Likopää shore late tomorrow afternoon, around six."

Father and son looked at each other. Henrik Meinander shook his head. He had a pensive look on his face.

"That is one devil of a woman," he said. "A veritable agitator." A dangerous woman …

His father's words remained with Kaarlo and they bothered him the next evening as he was waiting for Anja on the Likopää dock. Dangerous – in what way dangerous?

Anja did not appear dangerous in the least as Kaarlo looked at her secretly. The girl was like a frightened bird, on her guard every moment.

People had generally become more cautious in Viena. Kaarlo had himself made note of the fact that he and his father were increasingly looked upon as strangers – even in places where they had visited in previous summers and spent time. His father said it was because the Russian civil authorities, officials and police, had given the Czar's directives to teachers and priests and they had subsequently taken it upon themselves to Russify all of Viena. And because the people of Viena lacked the strength to oppose them, they were silent …

Aniviisu waited for them by the sauna. Kaarlo got a warm feeling deep inside him as he looked at her. Aniviisu had changed during the course of the summer; she had shot up in height, and the childish roundness had begun to give way to the figure of a young woman. The girl laughed out loud as the boat came into view.

"I'm bringing a visitor!" Kaarlo shouted from afar.

Aniviisu waved her hand.

"Anja! Is it you!"

Kaarlo steered the boat to the shore and Anja hopped ashore with her shoes in her hand. Before greeting Aniviisu she put her shoes on. Then she reached out her hand, a little shy, but smiling.

"I came to see you, since my mother let me be accompanied by that boy."

Kaarlo pulled the boat up on land. He looked at the girls, who were difficult to perceive as friends, so different were they. Aniviisu positively radiated joy of living and energy; Anja on the other hand was introverted and somehow altogether colorless. Kaarlo concluded that socialism must be an austere outlook, since it branded an entire personality like that. No wonder his father opposed it with all his heart.

The youngsters spent the evening sitting in the yard of the old house. Even Katri and Nasti took time from their chores to join them. Once in a while Aniviisu sneaked a glance at Anja, who appeared more listless than usual and who seemed to withdraw deeper into her shell as soon as the conversation became a little more lively. She had begun to look very much like her mother, which Aniviisu thought was sad.

"Why is Anja so quiet?" Katri asked before long. "What is your aunt like? Do you like her?"

Anja blushed, as everyone's eyes focused on her. She shrugged her shoulders helplessly.

"I don't know … she's just like my mother. I'm a little afraid of the fall term."

Aniviisu went up to her friend and put her arm around her shoulder.

Don't be afraid, Katri will be there, too. If you don't get along with Natalia, you can always come and stay with us. We already know where we are going to live; it's the Alhainen house at the end of Seminary Street. Where does your aunt live?

"On Karelia Street …"

"Now listen, girls," Katri said. "You will be entering a tough school with long and glorious traditions. An exciting and interesting time in your lives is about to begin."

"Even Kaarlo goes to school there," Aniviisu said to Anja.

"My school is next door to yours," Kaarlo said. "But you have no business there any more than I in your school. Fortunately they don't supervise us during our leisure time!"

In this manner this warm and happy summer evening passed. Soon these evenings would come to an end, and the trip to town and school would become imminent. However, during these summer days, Aniviisu's pain stemming from the death of her mother and father began slowly to diminish in her heart. She had noticed that Kaarlo had become more and more important to her. She had noticed something else as well: Anja was jealous of the boy. That dimmed her joy.

The script of Greta Huotari's life's was altogether confused. She felt she had no grip on life at all – as if she had in vain tried to hold on to something that was slipping away. True to her habit, she had woken up around noon – to the same sense of unreality as on other days. Listless, she looked around her pink room.

She hated this place: the whole house and especially its surroundings, the lake and the forests – even the sunny sky, which arched appallingly clear and blue. Why did Ilja have to bring her to this wilderness? To torture her, to torment her. Ilja himself fled to the outdoors, leaving her with two decrepit old fools.

There were people in the old house, but Greta did not want to go there. She could sense their coldness. And why should she care for those people anyway? They were peasants, uncivilized clodhoppers, they were probably even illiterate. They had no manners, marveled at the simplest things and asked stupid questions. Was she supposed to befriend such boors? Never!

Greta was unhappy and lonely. At the same time she felt hatred toward Ilja. The man had lied to her; he had said there was a ten-year-old boy here who would move in to live with them and whom she could care for. During the long journey she had seen the boy in her mind's eyes. But what awaited them here – a girl! A silly peasant girl, who brought her impudent aunt along to insult them. How did they dare! And Ilja had just stood there mute, he who otherwise was definitely mighty and cocky enough! They all just wanted to humiliate her …

The girl had been ordered to move in, but she hadn't; she hadn't even been to visit in the new house. A few times Greta had seen her rowing on the lake and heard her cheerful laughter at the sauna shore. That only added to Greta's sadness.

She felt tired though she had only just woken up. Ilja was already gone, gone fishing, Samuel said. Fishing!

Greta could not understand how he could all of a sudden get interested in something like that. Was Ilja turning into a child again? Out fishing almost every day ... No, she had to get away from here before she went totally crazy.

Greta sighed. She would not have anything else to do today than walk from one room to another in this large house, to look out of the window and to have coffee on the verandah. In Canada she had enjoyed reading; here she had opened a book, read a page or two and put the book back, utterly bored. Nothing felt worth the effort.

For days now Greta had not bothered to get dressed. Even now she was walking around in her housecoat. She went into the room that was intended for the boy. She had planned the interior herself, chosen the furniture and the objects down to the globe and the miniature rifle. She had recalled all the things her own son had wished for when he was ten – all the things she could not afford to buy at that time. And the girl had not even bothered to look at the room. Now it was a room without spirit, full of things that no one touched or used – like a tomb.

"The graveyard of my dreams ..." Greta said almost out loud.

"Oh dear, Madam should't worry about such things!"

Greta turned around. Mrs. Jenny had appeared at the door without Greta noticing her.

"Does Madam want breakfast?"

Greta shook her head.

"You didn't eat anything yesterday either, you'll get sick if you don't eat!"

"I miss my home and my son," Greta said. "It's so boring here. I'm dying of boredom!"

Mrs. Jenny understood, she nodded, took her by the arm and sat her down on the sofa.

"You should go rowing, the weather is gorgeous," she chatted. "Or should I ask Samuel to heat up the sauna? It's a wonderful sauna although it is first full of smoke. The steam is very gentle … Afterwards you could have a swim. Sitting inside makes you listless."

Greta smiled dejectedly and left the room. She went to the dining room to have a cup of coffee and then returned to her room upstairs. Jenny had made her bed and opened the windows in the meantime. The brilliant sunshine penetrated into the room through the thin curtains. The light hurt Greta's eyes. Quickly she closed the door, closed the heavy drapes and bent down to rummage about in a drawer of the dresser in her dressing room. She finally found what she was searching for. She pressed the bottle against her cheek as if to comfort it, pulled the cork and took the first long drink. A warm feeling spread all over her chest and she closed her eyes, sighing with pleasure.

At some point Greta realized she would have to get dressed and take her suitcase and the money she had put away for a rainy day. She was swaying while putting on her clothes, but her brain was clear. A few dresses into the suitcase … the photograph of her son … a couple of books … underwear … She saw Mrs. Jenny walk over to the old house, and she had asked Samuel to heat the sauna. It's now or never.

Greta took her suitcase and staggered down the stairs. There was no one in the hallway. She hurried to the front door. On the steps she looked around, but neither of the servants was anywhere to be seen. Almost running, she rushed around the corner with the suitcase. She stood for a moment in the shade of the wall waiting for her breathing to calm down. She took a swig from the bottle, put the cork back and hid the bottle carefully in her summer coat. Then she took her suitcase and started to walk with wobbly, but hurried steps. Before long she came to the cart path and began to walk along it away from the house. Now she would only need to find someone to take her to Vuokkiniemi – from there she was sure she would somehow make it to Helsinki. Luckily she had money!

"Thank God – I am free!" She kept on repeating to herself as she hurried forward.

Greta had decided that she would not be brought back, not even in shackles. Even if the journey took half a year, one way or another, she would return to Canada. Ilja Huotari would get his freedom, too – but not a divorce. Greta had decided that. He could just boil in his own stew, lonely and forgotten. Why had he dragged her here on false pretenses! And drunk wine at every meal …

Greta would never forgive him for that humiliation.

"Madam has disappeared!"

The shout greeted Ilja, as he was pulling the boat onto the shore upon his return from Uhtua. Samuel ran down the path to meet him.

"We have looked all over, sir, but she is nowhere to be found."

Ilja's face hardened with anger. He had been through this experience before. Greta must have had a bottle, maybe two, hidden away somewhere. The woman must have gone somewhere in a drunken stupor, sneaked away somewhere just like she had done on many occasions in Toronto – only to be found a couple of days later who knows where; once in a closed concert hall, dead drunk between the rows of chairs; once in the Salvation Army night shelter, where she had registered under her maiden name; and once in jail.

Ilja's anger was mixed with concern. There were no concert halls or night shelters here in the wilderness. There were only impenetrable forests, wolves, bears, and goblins. Did Greta have an accomplice or would she be found dead this time?

"Let's take it easy," he told Samuel. "This isn't the first time …"

The old man was clearly beside himself.

"There is nothing but gloomy wilderness around here!"

"Go and tell Teppana what has happened."

"He has already gone to look for her," Samuel said. "The entire household has been calling out and combing the forest nearby. The girl thought she saw footsteps on the cart path to Pistojärvi."

"She is aiming for Vuokkiniemi," Ilja said. "And to think that the woman never stuck her nose outside. Well, I have always said that Greta is a thinking person."

He looked at his old servant.

“I believe Mrs. Huotari has decided to leave us once and for all.”

“I’m afraid so, too.”

Ilja patted the old man comfortingly on the shoulder, and they walked together to the old house, where everyone else had already gathered. They were waiting for Teppana and his news. The women somehow managed to make coffee before Teppana finally arrived in a state of excitement.

“An Uhtua man told me he had rowed Madam across to Vuokkiniemi. Madam had asked him to tell us she was safe and on her way to Helsinki …”

Teppana became silent and unhappy, and looked around furtively. Nasti ordered him to go on.

“Well then,” Teppana continued meekly. “He also told me she had said to say she would not be coming back. She is going to Canada …”

Ilja’s face remained expressionless, but in his heart he sighed heavily. So this is what eventually happened … He noticed Aniviisu who was standing a short distance away looking at Teppana. He tried to guess what she was thinking: now you have no relatives other than me. She did not say anything, however, she just stood there looking. And Ilja did not guess her thoughts correctly; only one thought kept pounding in the girl’s mind: punishment … now you got your punishment, it serves you right, my *buobo*. Now you can live there in your big house all alone. Katri and I are leaving for Sortavala and you will stay here alone!

July turned into August and it was harvest time. The people from the old house toiled in the fields from morning till night with Kaarlo as their helper. One day, Ilja joined them. Strong as an ox, he cut the grain with his scythe. He bound sheaves so quickly that the others could not keep up. At night he had a sauna later than the others and grunted something about going fishing.

"Thank God there are enough fish in the lake," Katri said with a laugh to Nasti at the sauna shore. Nasti smiled in answer.

But Aniviisu heard it – and understood.

"Starting tomorrow morning I want to be called Anna Liisa," the girl said quietly.

Childhood was now behind her.

PART THREE

Youth

Anna Liisa looked at the photograph in which all the students of the Sortavala Girls' School had gathered for a group photo in front of the school. She and Anja were in the front row, sitting side by side almost in the center of the picture. Anja's mouth was tight-lipped and her thin braids were hanging down on her shoulders. She was wearing the same gray coat she had worn last summer in Uhtua; her hands rested in her lap and she looked serious. Anna Liisa had a broad smile on her round face. Her blond hair was parted in the middle and had been pulled into one braid in the back. She had placed her hands in her lap the same way as Anja because being photographed had felt like a very exciting event. She remembered well the clothes she had been wearing: a dark coat with a white lace collar that she had folded over the coat collar. There they sat, one stern, the other one smiling, and wearing funny-looking boots, which fortunately did not show under the hem of their coats. They were in sixth grade, for they had been allowed to start at the Sortavala Girls' School by skipping a grade.

There were no other pupils from as far away as Uhtua. During that first year everyone asked: "Why did you come here all the way from Uhtua ..." What were they supposed to answer to that? The reason was probably that Anna Liisa's Aunt Katri Jääskeläinen was a teacher in the teacher's seminary, and Anja's Aunt Natalia was a nurse in the general hospital. They came to live with them because with them, each girl had a home away from home and also someone close for security.

Anna Liisa could not bring herself to put the photograph away quite yet. It had almost two hundred people in it. The teachers were there as well, of course, even the male ones. The girls from the higher grades were standing in front of the steps; they were dressed much better than the girls in the lower grades. Many of them wore hats with a brim and stylish coats. Quite a few of them had braids. The male teachers wore black coats and felt hats. Anna Liisa remembered how her heart would skip a beat when occasionally one of the male teachers would tip his hat to her out on the town.

How childish it all had been! And how unbelievably wonderful. They had really learned to rely on each other. Anna Liisa and Katri had never forgotten their first day in the city, when Anja had run from Karelia Street a couple of blocks away to their apartment, choking with tears.

"Aunt Natalia has the night shift four times a week! I'm afraid to be home alone. Now, too, she has the night shift ..."

Katri solved the problem easily. Natalia was just as stern as Anja's mother, but Katri was gentle: she gave Anna Liisa permission to do her homework at Anja's place in the evenings. When it was time to go to bed, Katri would pick her up from the house on Karelia Street and also make sure Anja went to sleep and that the door was properly latched. Anna Liisa remembered how she had thought it odd that Natalia had never said a word of thanks to Katri, but instead had acted as if Katri did not even exist. She had her reasons, of course: Katri sang soprano in Mr. Mikael Nyberg's church choir; Natalia in turn sang alto in the Workers' Association mixed choir. Anna Liisa had a photograph of each choir and in them it was easy to recognize both Katri and Natalia.

In the picture of the church choir, the handsome Mr. Nyberg and his wife sat in the center. Their little daughter wearing long braids sat in front on the ground. The women standing around all looked stern, especially one who was wearing a blouse that was buttoned up to her chin and who was sporting a lorgnette. Katri, too, had a collar on her dress so wide and high that her head was unnaturally erect. In the back row stood handsome-looking men, a particularly good-looking one just behind Katri's shoulder. Even Anna Liisa could have been attracted to someone like that. Katri, however, did not take a fancy to anyone. She taught school during the day, came home for the evening, cooked, took care of Anna Liisa and Anja until they were in bed, and made sure they got to school in the morning. There was no room for a man in that kind of a life. "They are married, almost all of them," Katri had answered when Anna Liisa asked about it.

The third fascinating photograph also depicted Sortavala. It was from the last years of the 19th century. It was a picture of the Workers' Association chamber choir. Anna Liisa had received the photo from Anja. There were eighteen people in it, ten of them women. And one of the women was Natalia Stepanova, the sister of Darja Mihailovna, born in Salmi. She was standing farthest to the left, almost turned away from the others. Her small face was expressionless, but the dress was pretty, and Natalia looked slender and girlish. Anna Liisa looked at this particular photo often. It felt strange to think that Natalia was a socialist, a revolutionary. That was a subject Anna Liisa had not talked about with Anja.

The three of them had been awaiting the end of the school year for a long time. Anna Liisa was not, however, quite certain whether she would continue school the following fall. The headmistress of the school, Anni Saukko, had called her into her office in the afternoon of the day before. Anna Liisa had gone there with her heart racing, fearing that she might inadvertently have committed some offense.

"Sit down, Anna Liisa," the headmistress had said to her in a kind voice. "What is it I have been hearing, that you might not continue school next fall? What kind of talk is that? Of course you'll have to graduate from high school; you have such a good head on your shoulders. And what will your grandfather say! He's coming to town tomorrow, isn't he?"

"Yes, he'll be staying at the Seurahuone Hotel."

"Ask him to come and see me when school is out," the headmistress had said with a smile. "Maybe it would be good for you to be present as well. Or do you have other plans?"

Yes, she did, she had other plans indeed. Now that Kaarlo was moving to Helsinki to study the violin, she wanted to go with him. It was so natural for them to be together always. She could not even imagine staying in Sortavala alone. But how could she have told the headmistress that? A young pupil of the Girls' School was not allowed to have private affairs – the headmistress had reiterated that numerous times.

"You can always become a teacher," the headmistress spoke as if to herself. She had taken Anna Liisa's silence as a sign of agreement. "Your grandfather told me the last time we met that he will have a Finnish school built in Uhtua. Of course, he will want you there as a teacher, although you don't meet the formal requirements. But my dear girl," the headmistress shook her finger, "doesn't the matriculation cap mean anything? And university?"

Yes, it does, of course it means something, Anna Liisa had thought as she stepped through the door out into the yard. But she felt as if she was about to be torn in half: Kaarlo and Helsinki pulled in one direction, *buobo* and Uhtua in the other.

A swarm of girls surrounded her on the steps. With a bleak little smile she let the girls by. It felt like such a long time since she, as a lower grade girl, had scampered in front of the big girls. These youngest ones always moved as one flock, swarming forward without seeing anyone, and laughing at any little thing. Anna Liisa turned to look at the school building, which had become so dear to her. The years she had spent there were happy years, and she felt gratitude toward the school. And she knew that even if she weren't to continue studying there, her years at school would crop up in her memory in vivid images, which would trigger a yearning and a mixture of joy and sadness: the gatherings for morning prayer in the assembly hall, the sound of the old harmonium … the smell of chalk and the blackboard sponge … the walks on Pitkäsilta bridge with the girls… and Kaarlo at the boys' high school located between the Girls' School and the church. How often she thought she could spot Kaarlo's figure in the crowd of boys in the yard – and how her heart then had jumped for joy … and this School Street, which was so familiar that she knew every house by heart …

Anna Liisa slowed down her pace instinctively and took a deep breath of the fresh spring air. The other girls had gone home already, including Anja.

Anna Liisa thought she would surely catch up with Anja if she walked more briskly, yet she dallied on the way. She was already near the church, but Anja was nowhere to be seen. And in fact she wanted to think about her situation alone; she could not talk about it with anyone. During the spring she had noticed that she sometimes became annoyed when Anja clung to her. Otherwise, too, so many things had happened: Anja's move to the Alhainen house to live with Katri and her, the quarrel with Natalia. And then there were Anja's political activities, which even the people at school knew about. Twice Anja had been about to be expelled from school. Anna Liisa still shuddered when she remembered how she had had to defend her friend.

"What kind of home circumstances does she have?" the headmistress had demanded to know with a steely look in her eyes. "Anna Liisa will now tell us everything without hiding or embellishing anything!"

"Her mother is a teacher in the Ryhjä school in Uhtua," Anna Liisa had explained. "They lived by themselves, the two of them."

The headmistress had been shuffling the papers on her desk.

"Darja Mihailovna … a Russian?"

"Yes, from St Petersburg."

"Does her mother take part in political activities?"

Anna Liisa had been squirming inside. What could she answer to a question like that? But the headmistress had been relentless.

"Anna Liisa will go ahead and tell us!"

"I guess so, I don't really know," Anna Liisa had tried to evade the question. "At least when I was a child people whispered …"

"That she is a socialist, correct?"

"Yes."

"And what about Remisova's aunt? Is she a socialist too?"

"Well, I don't know!"

"You must know that, Anna Liisa! Just go ahead and tell us!"

"I only know she sings in the Workers' Association choir."

"Does Miss Remisova sing in the choir too?"

"Yes, she does."

A big fuss was raised over that. It was not appropriate for Girls' School pupil to belong to any political association or participate in any political activities – not even in a choir.

Anna Liisa and Katri had spoken to Anja, tried to persuade her, and finally pleaded with her, to give up the choir and concentrate only on her studies. Anja had withdrawn into her shell like a clam, pressed her lips together into a bloodless line – but nevertheless she obeyed them. She had gone to discuss the matter with the headmistress, but never told anyone what had been said in the office.

"Your grandfather has arrived!"

Anna Liisa had slipped inside into the apartment, which by now had become so very familiar to her, on Seminary Street in the Alhainen house. She heard Katri's voice; she was in the kitchen cooking. Katri's voice was so happy and content, it was positively bubbling. And no wonder – tomorrow was the last day of May, the last day of school.

Anna Liisa went to wash her hands and upon her return, she stopped to look down at the street where young women were hurrying toward the seminary. She leaned on the windowsill peering out between the white curtains. Such happy-looking women …

Katri came to the door.

"Where have you been? Anja came home a good while ago."

Anja had lived with them since last fall, when her relationship with Aunt Natalia had broken down once and for all.

"I just walked slowly," Anna Liisa said evasively.

"I met your grandfather today," Katri continued. "He's coming to visit tonight. He has been on the road for three days."

"Is everything all right at home?"

Everything was fine. Except Mrs. Jenny had fallen and hurt her hand and had it bandaged for a couple of months in the spring. In the meantime, the men had had to cook their own meals.

"Samuel is good at that," Anna Liisa said with a laugh. "But who did the housecleaning?"

"Oh, your grandfather didn't say anything about that," Katri said. "Maybe Outi ..."

Anna Liisa gave a quick smile.

"Don't say that, Katri, that's history now."

"Oh, history has a way of repeating itself," Katri muttered, a little embarrassed. "But why am I talking such nonsense, matters of no consequence. Have a sandwich. I have a roast in the oven for the evening; we'll have a full meal then."

"*Buobo* is probably bringing wine," Anna Liisa said all the while looking at Katri, who combed her hair quickly in front of the mirror, threw her apron on a chair, grabbed her purse and hurried out the door.

"Are you talking to yourself?" Anja said, sticking her head out from her room in the hallway.

Anna Liisa raised her eyes. She had so many things to talk about with Anja. But would there be enough time? The day after tomorrow they would all go to Uhtua for the summer. Anja had to go with them because a trip like that was very hard to manage alone. Anja had been difficult all winter. She had not tolerated any criticism, not even half a word. She had fretted and fumed like a little child. And so Anna Liisa was on her guard now when Anja came to talk to her.

"Just think of all the years we have spent at the Girls' School," Anja said in an unexpectedly nostalgic voice. "When we came here that first fall we were just children – and now ..."

Anna Liisa bided her time before she asked a question that had been bothering her:

"Anja – what do you know about Artturi Kangas, the boy from the seminary who is now being held prisoner in St Petersburg?"

Anja's body tensed. She looked at Anna Liisa searchingly.

"Why do you ask? He was no longer at the seminary when it happened, he wasn't there at all last year ..."

"But he gave rousing political speeches around here! And you were with him. That's why you don't want to finish school because you are going to St Petersburg from here. You pretend to be engaged in more important matters than finishing school."

Anna Liisa noticed that she had raised her voice. Red patches appeared on Anja's usually pale face.

"I don't pretend to, I do," she retorted.

They stood face to face as if sizing each other up. Anja had adopted her usual uncommunicative expression, which meant there was no point continuing the discussion. Anna Liisa was annoyed both with her own level of agitation and with Anja's obstinacy. Could this unfortunate creature not leave politics alone?

"If Finland ends up under Germany, times will be many times worse than they are now," Anja said finally, as if in answer to the question her friend never gave voice to.

"But what if Finland becomes independent!"

"Maybe it will, but not while the Czar is in power," Anja said. "Finland will not receive its independence until Russia is freed from the yoke of the Czar. Don't you see, Anna Liisa, what's happening in the world? The time is soon ripe for a world revolution!"

Anna Liisa rolled her eyes.

"Oh, my dear Anja, I'm not interested in a world revolution; I'm interested in this day here in Sortavala! What possesses you to have to talk about such horrible things in school and at the seminary? You were close to being expelled last fall. Have you already forgotten that? What are you planning to do with your life? You quit school, you go to St Petersburg for the summer, and when you come back from there you'll start the world revolution in Uhtua – is that it?"

Anja was going to answer at first, but then she turned on her heels and went back to her room at the end of the hall. Anna Liisa rushed after her, yanked her door open and continued her ranting.

"Now listen to me for once, Anja, to what I'm telling you! If Katri hadn't taken you in, you would have had to fight with your aunt all winter and spring. And how have you shown your gratitude? By taking advantage of her kindness! Katri and I vouched for you so you could stay in school. And you said you would stop. But now I can see it was only the beginning. And now you stand there looking like you want to shoot me!"

Only actually uttering the last sentence made her realize how deep her rage was, yet she went on.

"You went over there to the seminary that one night – just admit it! That was when Katri was so worried. One of the teachers had seen the light in the office go out suddenly. It was you in there. What were you looking for?"

Anja couldn't get a word out of her mouth – she just stared at Anna Liisa. How did she know all these things? And why did she now, on the last day of school, make such a fuss about it? Why didn't she let old matters rest?

"You don't have to answer, I can see the guilt in your face," Anna Liisa said. "I am just so disappointed in you. You stole Katri's keys to get into the office. I remember how Katri was looking for those keys. How could you?"

Anja stared at her friend, first with a desperate look in her eyes, then her expression hardened and she recovered her ability to speak.

"I am not going with you to Uhtua, I'm going straight to St Petersburg.

"Makes no difference to us," Anna Liisa said cruelly. "What will we tell your mother? She'll come to Huotari Point in any case. Are we to tell her that her daughter has gone to St. Petersburg to start the revolution?"

Anja didn't answer. After a moment of silence she said, "You hate me, Anna Liisa, but why? What is so bad about trying to help the poor and the exploited? I am speaking on their behalf, not on behalf of you rich people."

"And you say that after taking advantage of my *buobo*'s support for five years! Has his money now suddenly laid a curse over us?"

Shaking with anger, Anna Liisa marched out the door and slammed it shut. She went into the kitchen and sat down on a chair by the table. She felt like crying.

Anja threw herself on the bed and closed her eyes. She felt such infinite fatigue that her head swam. Anna Liisa's lecture had a lot of truth to it, although she did not want to think about it. She felt as if she were caught in a strange web. For the first time she had fears about the game she had got involved in.

Artturi Kangas, who was now sitting in jail in Špalernaja, had managed to send her a letter:

> *Anja!*
>
> After school is out, come directly to St. Petersburg. Go to NA's apartment, you know where it is. Try to get to visit me. They will have to release me, they have no evidence. We will make Russia free, we will liberate her from the Czar's oppression. We will also liberate Viena, but differently from the Finns, who are also planning to free Viena.

Anja felt her thoughts calming down when she thought of Artturi – his brown eyes, his broad shoulders and his deep voice, which was commanding even when he spoke quietly. Anja had got to know the boy a couple of years ago when she went with her Aunt Natalia to the Workers' Association. The people there were workers, not socialists.

Anja had immediately seen that Artturi was of a different breed, a revolutionary. The youngster lived dangerously, quit the seminary for a year, then he was captured and taken first to the Vyborg provincial prison. From there he was taken to St Petersburg and that is where he still remained. Anja did not understand how she could help him. She would have to go first to Uhtua to discuss the matter with her mother. Then they would go to St Petersburg, the two of them, but first they would have to arrange for someone to milk their cow. They would have to travel together because Anja was afraid to travel alone.

Now even Anna Liisa had tried to put her down. Anna Liisa had never even seen the people's poverty and distress. She had always been a privileged child, who before the arrival of her *buobo* had been spoiled by her parents, Nasti, and Teppana. Then came Katri in the place of the parents and finally Ilja Huotari, filthy rich, straight from Canada.

What did they know about the daily life of the disadvantaged? Anja was completely horrified the first time she visited the new house on Huotari Point. So much space for so few people. Books, paintings, valuable rugs and furniture; for the price of one single item one could feed a poor family for many weeks. Anja had immediately felt such a strong aversion toward Ilja Huotari, that even now she did not feel like meeting him that evening. What if she was to go for a lengthy walk on her own? Tomorrow would be her last day in Sortavala; she could say goodbye to the lovely trees in Vakkosalmi and climb to the top of Kuhavuori to think about Artturi with whom she had been there the previous fall. How terrible it must be for him to languish in prison.

The Girls' School had been everything to Anna Liisa. It had guided her from childhood to an awareness of life. She did not know how she could live without the school, the teachers, her classmates and friends. The school was demanding and its rules and regulations were strict and uncompromising, but at the same time it was a comfortingly safe place. She had never found the school's discipline to be oppressive, but had realized immediately that it was a necessary condition for successful work and intellectual development. This is why deep inside she could not understand Anja, who had broken the rules and engaged in activities that the school community did not condone.

Anna Liisa still remembered the night when Anja did not come home to Seminary Street. She had told Anna Liisa during recess that she would spend the night at a classmate's house. Anna Liisa recalled how she had wondered who that classmate might be, because she did not know a single girl in their class who would conceivably invite Anja to her home. But Anja had explained late that afternoon that it was a girl from a completely different class. It had been a plain lie, Anna Liisa understood that now, but since they had never lied to each other before, she simply could not suspect even such a blatant deception. And so Anja had left.

Before going to bed Katri had begun to look for her keys. As usual, she had sat at her desk until late at night marking the essays of future female teachers at the seminary, when she suddenly noticed that the keys to the office were missing from her purse. She had looked all over, even come to wake up Anna Liisa who was already asleep.

"I must have forgotten them at school," Katri had finally concluded, shaking her head, and she had gone to bed.

Anna Liisa couldn't go back to sleep immediately. She had been lying awake wondering at whose house Anja was spending the night and why. Anja had broken all ties to Aunt Natalia, so she certainly could not be there.

In the morning they had both overslept and woke up only when Anja came to get her books. Just as they were leaving for school, Katri had noticed the keys on the floor next to the little table in the hallway.

"So that's where I dropped them!" she had said with a sigh of relief. "I was so sure I had forgotten them at the seminary."

When Katri returned home that afternoon, she had immediately told the girls that someone had broken into the office and rummaged about in the papers. One of the teachers had seen a faint light in the office and hurried over to look. She had knocked on the window and then the light had instantly been turned off. Who had been in the office at that time of the night remained a mystery. In the morning a thorough investigation was conducted but nothing was found to be missing.

Now Anna Liisa knew that Anja had stolen the keys that evening from Katri's purse, gone to the seminary office together with someone else, rummaged about among the papers and spent the rest of the night somewhere – perhaps with that boy, Artturi Kangas. In the morning she had come home while they were still sleeping and had dropped the keys on the floor in the hallway. Anna Liisa was quite sure of it, and she shuddered to think of the dangerous business Anja was involved in.

How could she do it? Didn't she give any thought to how compromising even Katri's situation would be, should it all come out in the open? Even though no one would really suspect Katri of anything improper, it would still be a scandal. And how ungrateful Anja was! Here she was allowed to live with them, yet she acted against them!

The thoughts upset Anna Liisa to the extent that her face became flushed. She took the plates from the cupboard and began to set the table for the evening. Then she went to her room, changed into her light-blue dress, combed her hair and took her purse. In the hallway she shouted to Anja:

"I'm going to the Seurahuone Hotel to get *buobo*. The table is set, watch that the roast doesn't burn! And could you please peel the potatoes ..."

Anja did not answer.

The lilacs in the back yards of the houses along the street were in full bloom; there was such an abundance of them that the fragrance of the blossoms appeared to fill the entire town. The people on the street were dressed in summer clothes and looked happy. What a lovely town Sortavala was with its small wooden houses and its gardens! Having walked a few blocks, Anna Liisa noticed her mood improving. She felt bad about the quarrel with Anja. But she couldn't help her temper, that was simply the way she was: quick to anger and quarrel, but just as quick to reconciliation and forgiveness. She had been the same way with her *buobo,* Ilja Huotari.

The Pitkäsilta bridge was swarming with school children sauntering back and forth. She saw Kaarlo gesticulating at the end of Rantakatu Street and she stopped at the shore to wait for him. How tall and muscular Kaarlo looked, more like an athlete than a violinist. Kaarlo and three other boys had started a string quartet while in fifth grade and since then they had performed, accompanied by Mrs. Naëmi Starck, the doctor's wife, at many festive occasions. Now, in their graduating year, they had had to decline performance requests. There was nothing else in Kaarlo's life but the violin – and the love of his childhood and youth: Anna Liisa. Kaarlo came up to Anna Liisa and stopped to catch his breath. He looked at the girl's hair which was loose.

"Where are your braids? What if one of the ladies comes upon you and says that it is not appropriate for a young girl to walk around with her hair flowing freely?"

Anna Liisa laughed.

"That will end tomorrow! But I will still have to go with *buobo* to talk to the headmistress after the commencement. She actually talked to me already."

Kaarlo nodded knowingly.

"Continuing school ... What if you were to continue in Helsinki?"

They were standing in the middle of the street and passersby had to go around them. Kaarlo's words added to Anna Liisa's confusion. She looked at his tanned face whose blue eyes radiated with joy and confidence. How could anything go wrong between them? Anna Liisa did not answer, just squeezed Kaarlo's arm.

They walked hand in hand across the Pitkäsilta bridge, sidestepping the laughing noisy school children who, aware of their impending departure for the holidays, were becoming increasingly reckless and boisterous in their play. They hurried toward the Seurahuone Hotel, but stopped for a moment to watch the ships in the harbor.

"One of those goes to the Valamo Monastery," Anna Liisa said, deep in thought. "It is now three summers since I've been there."

"Would you like to go there now?"

Anna Liisa shook her head.

"I want to get back to Uhtua as soon as possible. I miss it so very much."

In the park Kaarlo pulled Anna Liisa to sit on a bench. He held her hand firmly in his.

"I would like to tell you," he started, but paused for a long while.

"What?" Anna Liisa asked softly.

"That I love you. I have loved you from the first moment I saw you sitting in the forest behind your old house. I guess I decided then and there that I would marry you one day. And last fall I decided that I would buy you a ring the day I graduated from high school." Kaarlo took out a small box and opened it. Inside on top of a black velvet was a turquoise ring, with two small diamonds. Tears welled up in Anna Liisa's eyes.

"Are you proposing to me although I am only sixteen ..."

"I am over twenty," Kaarlo said quickly. "To me it is of no consequence what age you are. I have decided to marry you and I intend to propose marriage as soon as it is materially possible and as soon as you feel ready."

"Will you support us by playing the violin?" Anna Liisa asked.

"I'll take a job playing in some orchestra," Kaarlo said. "Or else I'll give private lessons. I may even become a concertmaster."

Anna Liisa looked at the ring and slipped it on her finger. Kaarlo was right, why should they start worrying about the differences in their ages now; it had never bothered them before.

"Thank you, Kaarlo. I have never owned a ring. You don't need to think that you should mark me in some fashion to make me remember you; I will remember you always; for years you have been the only one for me in this world. You are dearer to me than Katri and *buobo* ..."

As they continued walking arm in arm, Kaarlo suddenly asked, "By the way, anything new with Anja? You haven't talked about her in a long time."

"And I'm not going to talk bout her now either," Anna Liisa said. "Not on an exquisite day like today."

Kaarlo looked at her in surprise, but said nothing. He drew Anna Liisa closer.

Ilja Huotari was waiting for them in the little park in front of the Seurahuone Hotel. Pensive, he sat on a bench, a white straw hat in his lap. He was wearing a light summer suit, and under his chin a blue bow tie. He had closed his eyes, letting the sun warm his face. As he heard steps crunching on the gravel he opened his eyes.

"*Buobo*!" Anna Liisa exclaimed and ran to hug him.

"Careful now," he said with a laugh. "Don't crush my straw hat."

"We'll buy a new one!"

He laughed again and rose from the bench to shake Kaarlo's hand.

"Nice to see you, too. And congratulations!"

"Oh, it's not until tomorrow," Kaarlo said almost embarrassed.

Smiling, Anna Liisa watched the men. She still couldn't understand that for more than a year she had hated her grandfather so much she wouldn't even talk to him.

"Now let's go to our house," she said, grabbing her grandfather by the arm. "Katri has a roast in the oven."

"Before we go I'll get the wine from my room. Wait here."

"How many bottles did you bring?" Anna Liisa asked.

"Five."

They walked slowly, stopping to lean against the railing on the Pitkäsilta bridge, and to look at the lapping of the waves and the glittering reflections of the sun. Anna Liisa had slipped her hand under Ilja Huotari's arm, while Kaarlo walked behind them carrying the winebag. Anna Liisa talked incessantly; she was too happy to be silent.

"Have you heard anything from Greta?"

Anna Liisa's question made Ilja serious.

"Nothing except that she is still at the sanatorium – and that she will probably never get out of there."

"No divorce proceedings under way?"

"That will never happen ..."

Anna Liisa nodded seriously. Her grandfather would not divorce Greta, but would take care of her financially for as long as she lived. To *buobo* it was a matter of honor. To Anna Liisa it was a horrible thing, for she knew well Katri's and her *buobo*'s feelings. Their love had been kindled the second summer they had returned from Sortavala to Uhtua. Anna Liisa had been contemplating all winter the real reasons why she did not want to move into the new house, and she had felt vaguely guilty about the whole thing. When they had arrived at Huotari Point by way of Vuokkiniemi in early June, *buobo* had come to see them in the old house and asked them both to move into the new house.

"I have been so very lonely all winter," he had told them honestly. "You, Anna Liisa, would have your own room and you, Katri, could take my wife's room. She will never return here again ..."

Ilja had then told them that Greta was a patient for the chronically ill ("drunken insanity" he had grunted to Samuel upon first hearing the news) in a sanatorium north of Toronto.

"She has decided to drink herself to death," Ilja had said.

The women had sat in the yard of the old house that evening, pondering what to do. The following morning they had gone to see Ilja and had told him of their decision: they would indeed move into the new house. That summer Anna Liisa had made peace with her *buobo*. And that summer Katri and Ilja had fallen in love with each other.

"You know what," said Ilja as they reached the corner of Rantakatu Street. "I know of no more beautiful town in all of Finland. This is a real summer town."

"What's new in Uhtua?" Kaarlo asked.

A look of fleeting irritation crossed Ilja's face. The topic was not a pleasant one.

"The Russian authorities order the people around as if they had whips. The people don't have a will of their own anymore. I have tried to instill some moral strength, but it's like talking to the walls. That's why I have increasingly begun to live like a hermit. I feel like a stranger in Viena."

"That is unfortunate," Kaarlo said seriously.

"It's even worse to see the debasement of the people of Viena," Ilja added.

They walked some distance in silence, then Anna Liisa asked:

"*Buobo,* did you know that two men from the seminary have left to join the Jäger battalion? They are now in training in Germany. Fortunately Kaarlo is not interested."

"In a soldier's profession?" Kaarlo said. "Certainly not. I don't understand anything about military drills or fighting."

"One can serve one's fatherland in many ways," Ilja said. "The power of a small people lies above all in education and culture. A nation also needs artists."

"But does it understand that? Anna Liisa asked quickly, which elicited a smile from the men.

"Why don't you come and see our house," Kaarlo suggested. "There is a local lady there preparing for tomorrow's celebration. We could have some juice in the garden swing. What time does Katri get home from the seminary?"

"At six," Anna Liisa replied. "And it's not even five yet, we've got plenty of time."

And so they turned onto Rantakatu Street and started walking toward the Meinander house.

Kaarlo had lived alone in the house all winter. An old woman from town had come every day to clean and make food for him. This was the reason that Anna Liisa and Kaarlo had been able to see each other unhindered. In the course of the winter their relationship had become a love relationship. Anna Liisa had hurried after school to Kaarlo's house, and he had escorted her home just after six o'clock in the evening. The high school boys were not allowed to keep company in the evenings – and also, one of the school's teachers lived in the same block as the Meinanders. Anna Liisa and Kaarlo spent their afternoons together: Kaarlo practised his violin, while Anna Liisa sat by the window, listening and doing her homework. Kaarlo's closeness had infused Anna Liisa with a sense of well-being and security. Even an outsider might have noticed how the girl had changed during the winter; her childlike appearance and her childishness were gone forever; the girl had turned into a charming woman. Henrik Meinander, who had spent many a weekend in Sortavala, had also noticed the change. Meinander himself had been quite fond of Katri, but she had made her choice already four years ago. Now, during the last winter, he had paid fewer and fewer visits; it had begun to hurt him just to see Katri.

"By the way, what's new with Anja?" Ilja asked suddenly. He had no idea what train of thought his light-hearted and innocent question set in motion in both of his companions.

Anna Liisa had sometimes marveled at how strangely the fates of the people in her inner circle were intertwined.

The same could be said of Anja's life, for Artturi Kangas had been Kaarlo's classmate in high school. The boy had dropped out of school and gone to the teachers' seminary. Then he had quit that, too, and soon thereafter he had ended up in prison. Anna Liisa was not aware that Kaarlo knew of Anja's infatuation with this black sheep of the high school, who obviously had socialist leanings. Kaarlo had never spoken about it but he had become cautious in his dealings with Anja. He found it strange that she was so austere and that she spared no effort to be ugly; she even dressed like a man, as if she were ashamed of being a woman. Anna Liisa had detected a peculiar friction in the relationship between Kaarlo and Anja.

Anna Liisa had never realized that she herself had always come across like a princess, as the center of all attention – and Anja as her "lady in waiting," always on the side or in the background. Anna Liisa was sociable and smiled a lot; Anja was withdrawn and serious. A bystander might have thought that Anja was embittered by having to eat the Huotari's bread of charity. In reality, however, what embittered her the most was that Anna Liisa and Kaarlo never took her along in the afternoons to the Meinander house.

"There is nothing much new with Anja," Anna Liisa answered without looking at her grandfather.

Nothing more was said about the matter for they had already entered Meinander's garden. Next to the swing stood a pair of wicker chairs and a table. They sat down to talk and Ilja thoroughly enjoyed himself. The trees offered shade, and the breeze coming from the direction of Vakkolahti carried the fragrance of the sea, cooling and caressing. Time, however, was merciless, and soon Anna Liisa hurried them again to move on. The dinner table was all set and awaiting their arrival at the Alhainen house.

They all noticed how distressed Anja was. The girl was busying herself at the stove in the small kitchen. She cleaned up after herself, she emptied the potato peels from the wash-basin into the garbage can, then she tested with the point of a knife whether the boiling potatoes were cooked through. When she saw Ilja Huotari, she wiped her hands on her apron and came forward to greet him.

"Oh, it's Anja," Ilja said with a broad smile. "Don't you look healthy and vigorous. And why not, now all your worries are behind you."

Anja cast her eyes down with a faint smile.

"I don't think I'll be able to avoid one failing grade – the Russian language gave me trouble."

Ilja looked at the others, who also seemed surprised.

"The Russian language? But isn't that your mother tongue?"

Anja shook her head.

"My mother felt it was important that I learn Finnish. I do know how to speak Russian, but the writing and the grammar are another matter altogether."

"Just admit that you hate Russian like the rest of us!" Anna Liisa shouted from the next room. "Are the potatoes ready? I for one am starving."

Anja did not answer. She emptied the water from the potato kettle and put the potatoes in a white porcelain dish. Katri had already placed the roast and sauceboat on the table. Kaarlo had opened a bottle of wine and served everybody.

"To summer!" Ilja said, lifting his glass.

"To a wonderful summer!" Anna Liisa exclaimed. 'Soon all of us will be in Uhtua and we won't return until autumn!"

They enjoyed the dinner in a cheerful atmosphere. They savored the roast and drank glowing red wine brought in from the wine cellar of Ilja's new house. Their conversation was lively; they discussed the past winter and made plans for the coming one.

Ilja tried to talk Anna Liisa into staying in Sortavala for the university-bound classes, but did not have any success, at least not yet. Then Anja dropped a bombshell, which silenced them all.

"Mother wrote from Uhtua that I can serve as her substitute in the Ryhjä school despite lacking formal qualifications. Mother is going to St Petersburg next year to get medical help – you see, she is concerned about her lungs."

Anna Liisa's face exuded relief.

"That's great!" she exclaimed. "You don't want to continue toward university anyway. You've always wanted to go to the teachers' seminary. What could be better training than being a teacher's substitute at the age of seventeen."

Anja looked inquisitively at her friend, but the enthusiasm was genuine. Anja found it difficult to understand, particularly after Anna Liisa's sermon earlier in the afternoon.

"Would you be living in your former home?" Katri asked.

"Yes. I'll travel with Mother to St Petersburg next week, but only for a short time. Mother will stay there, but she would really like to go to Crimea. My uncle is a police officer there."

Anja fell silent and her cheeks were blushing; she had, in her own opinion, already spoken too much.

"Oh, Anja, we are truly happy for you," Katri said, reaching to pat Anja's hand.

"A toast to Anja's fortune!" Ilja said.

Anna Liisa looked at her friend as she brought the glass to her lips. A strange anguish dwelled on Anja's face; you could see it in her whole appearance and you could hear it in her voice. What on earth was wrong with Anja?

Anja looked intently at the others around the table, feeling strangely alienated. From the very beginning she had not felt she belonged with these people; she felt she was included only out of pity. Anna Liisa had made it plain this afternoon what she really thought of her. She feared those words of Anna Liisa's which had wounded her so. She had accused her of politicking, of taking advantage ... A crack had opened in their friendship. She felt like a complete outsider – like the poor relative you read about in books. But it was these people's lives that were poor – even now they prattled about boating in the archipelago and having champagne ... did they have any idea how precarious and dangerous these times were? That tomorrow everything would be different?

Intuitively, Anja felt that no one would notice if she were to disappear suddenly. She felt bitter and no longer tried to deny it. One ultimately had to choose whose camp one belonged in: the rich or the poor. The oppressors or the oppressed.

When Ilja again began to talk about Uhtua matters, Anja went into the kitchen supposedly to fetch more potatoes. She slipped into the vestibule, took her coat from the rack and sneaked out through the front door. Pulling on her coat she began to walk toward her former home. Before she noticed, she was standing in front of Aunt Natalia's door.

Natalia Stepanova's appearance caught no one's attention, but her personality was difficult to forget, once one had got to know it. She was stern and uncompromising in her demands, followed rules and regulations to the very last letter and had no sense of humor. In Nurse Stepanova's ward no one smoked tobacco, told jokes or complained. The ward was ruled by "Stepanova's law," with discipline and order as in a garrison, and many patients literally feared their nurse. Natalia Stepanova had a clear opinion why people became sick and did not mind expounding on it in front of her patients:

"All sick people are hypochondriacs or slackers," Nurse Stepanova proclaimed. "Man was not created to lie in bed all day long. Man was created to work! Get up! Get up! On your feet, walk around, that's the fastest way to get home."

Natalia Stepanova lived as she preached: she was a veritable workhorse. She demanded the same of others, and the nursing students avoided her like the plague. They were ready to swear that Stepanova did not have one human emotion. Anja basically agreed; when the aunt had become angry at her niece, she sent her away from her home without even asking whether she had any place to go. That had been a shock to Anja.

She had received her mother's letter a day or two ago. Her mother's suggestion that she become her substitute, while she was ill, seemed an excellent one. She had written that her strength had waned altogether during the winter and that she longed for her only daughter to come to her aid. Her mother apparently knew nothing about the break between Anja and Aunt Natalia. The envelope bore the aunt's address, but it had been pushed into the mailbox of the Alhainen house.

The yard on the block at the end of Karelia Street near the railway station was open and large, with lilacs and bird cherry trees. Natalia's little back yard cottage stood next to the sauna and was surrounded by flowerbeds. At the corner of the sauna was a garden swing and that was where Anja sat down. She was simply afraid to knock on her aunt's door; first she had to muster up her courage. The door to the cottage was open, and a pile of bedding lay on the chair by the door. As always on Fridays, her aunt was cleaning house. Anja took off her summer coat. The breeze felt chilly at first, but the sun shone warmly. She was sitting there, deep in thought, when her aunt came out and bent down to pick up the comforter. That was when she noticed the girl sitting on the swing. A contemplative expression appeared on her face.

"Come in Anja!" she demanded.

Anja was startled, hesitated a moment, but then obeyed her aunt.

The apartment was in the middle of housecleaning. Her aunt always cleaned house even when everything was impeccable. Not even dishes would pile up because if her aunt took a glass from the cupboard simply to drink a glass of water, she always washed and dried the glass immediately and put it back in the cupboard.

Anja stepped over the rugs that were rolled into bundles in the hallway and went to sit down on a chair in the little living room. She fumbled with the belt of her coat in her lap and looked at her aunt seriously.

"What did your mother write?" Natalia asked as she sat down in the armchair.

"She is ill."

"What's wrong with her?"

Anja shrugged her shoulders.

"She says Saša has invited her to Crimea for the summer."

"Is she suspecting tuberculosis?"

"I guess so. She has always feared for her lungs. Now she is asking me to be her substitute for the winter because she will have to stay in St Petersburg for treatment."

Natalia got up from the chair and walked to the window. The window was open and the wind was billowing the white curtains. She pulled the window shut, nipped a dried-out flower from the geranium, and tested the soil for moistness. Then she wiped her finger clean on her apron and turned to look at Anja.

"Is the boy in prison?"

Anja cast her glance down.

"Yes."

"Did you help him search the teachers' seminary office?"

"Yes, I did."

"How?"

"I took the office key from Katri's bag."

"Does Katri know?"

"Anna Liisa does."

Natalia sighed audibly.

"Didn't I tell you not to engage in politics at school?"

"Yes, you did."

"Why did you do it?"

Anja looked at her aunt with tears in her eyes.

"Because Artturi ..."

"You are in love with that boy!" The aunt blurted out the words like an accusation. "That is what controls your thoughts and your feelings. And you spent the night with him, I know it. At your age ...

I find it detestable! And then you had the audacity to claim that nothing happened! Do you still claim that?"

Anja shook her head without meeting her aunt's eyes. An almost triumphant smile swept across the aunt's stern face.

"Will you now admit that the boy led you astray."

Anja lifted her head, her eyes defiant.

"I will not admit that!"

Natalia's face darkened. She went up to Anja, grabbed her by the elbow and yanked her up. She shoved the girl in the back toward the hallway and out the door.

"Come and tell me when you are ready to admit it. Greetings to your mother."

The front door slammed shut. Anja stared at it, her whole body trembling. Again her aunt had rejected her although she had told the truth! Swallowing her tears she began to walk along the street toward the shore. There was nobody in this whole town who cared for her, nobody.

It was said about Anna Liisa that her *buobo* cared for her more than for anyone else. He had come from Uhtua to Sortavala specifically on this last day of spring. Ilja remembered how cold and distant his relationship with her had been five years ago when he had come back to his homeland from Canada. Almost immediately upon his arrival, Anna Liisa had left for the Girls' School in Sortavala and had not come back until the following spring. Katri and Anna Liisa had not come to Uhtua even for Christmas, although Ilja, with high hopes, had invited them to spend Christmas there. During the first year Katri had paid for the girl's tuition. Money had come from Ilja to an account he had opened for Anna Liisa at a bank in Sortavala, but they had not touched his money. Katri had kept the girl as her own, and Anna Liisa had projected onto Katri all the longing she felt for her mother at the time. Katri had understood how to bring her niece up wisely. She emphasized the right kinds of values, and thus Anja also got lessons in how to conduct herself. The aunt's firm discipline had always been a natural thing for Anna Liisa, but Anja had rebelled against it from the start, quietly, but all the more relentlessly.

Katri had often talked with Ilja about the differences between the two girls. In Katri's opinion, Darja Mihailovna had sowed the poison of bitterness in her daughter's sensitive mind. Ilja, for example, was to be loathed and hated because he was richer than others, "a potentate," Katri had once heard Anja call him. It did not help that Ilja paid for Anja's schooling as well. The second winter Anja's clothes had worn so thin that she simply had to get new ones. But did that make Anja happy? Not even close. Instead, Katri and Anna Liisa had needed to coax her for a long time before she agreed to accept the new clothes.

Katri had realized that Anja actually wanted to look poor and miserable compared to the other girls – since, in her mother's view, that was honorable. Katri had without hesitation thrown away all her rags, the tattered and matted wool sweaters, the socks whose heels were mostly clumps because of all the darning, the underpants that were held up by only one button, the winter coat whose fur collar looked like a rat that had drowned in a ditch. When Anja had seen herself in the mirror in her new clothes, she had almost shouted with joy, for she, too, was a normal girl who admired beautiful things. But when she had gone home, Aunt Natalia had criticized her severely.

When Katri and Anna Liisa had returned to Uhtua the first summer, things fell into place without extra effort. They had made peace with Ilja Huotari. In the beginning, Katri had been afraid of what Ilja would say about her staying in the old house because she no longer had any right to live there. Anna Liisa, however, had not wanted to go to Uhtua alone.

The women had taken a sauna and were sitting on the shore, wrapped in linen blankets, when Ilja's boat suddenly approached from the direction of Uhtua.

"Is he still catching well with his hook?" Katri had murmured to Nasti.

"He hasn't visited Outi since May," Nasti had answered.

Katri had been ashamed of her nasty remark as Ilja had rowed close to the shore and greeted the women very cordially. Then he had asked:

"Would it be convenient for you to come to my house for dinner? All of you from the old house."

Katri and Anna Liisa had secretly exchanged glances, but they could think of no excuse to decline. And so they had accepted the invitation. During the meal, Ilja had apologized for handling his relationship to Uhtua so poorly during his whole stay in Canada.

Katri had responded that he had by no means "handled his relationship poorly"; he had actually completely neglected everything. Only now had the man come to realize that he had a granddaughter. At first Ilja had nearly flown into a rage at Katri's words, but then he had started to laugh, and they had enjoyed the rest of the meal in a jovial atmosphere.

Anna Liisa had nevertheless tried to sulk with her grandfather for another week, but she finally gave in as she realized that her *buobo* was earnest and sincere. And so they had moved into the new house. Nasti and Teppana had remained in the old house and Ilja had promised that they could stay there as long as they lived.

It was around the same time that Katri had started to become absent-minded and more and more often was found sitting in the parlor under the chandelier, listening to Ilja telling stories of his colorful life. Anna Liisa had sometimes come to the door, but had not had the heart to disturb them, and had quietly tiptoed away.

Katri had noticed that she had become absorbed in her thoughts, and a smile spread over her face as she looked around her: these people had become a real family to her.

After the dinner the women began to wash the dishes and Kaarlo sat behind the kitchen table keeping them company. Ilja glanced at them from the door and then he asked Katri if she would join him for a walk. Katri accepted the invitation with pleasure.

In the small town of Sortavala everyone knew each other. When Katri and Ilja Huotari stepped into the street, Katri could immediately sense the inquisitive glances. She could even guess what the women they met were thinking – who was this handsome man she had in tow? She greeted the women serenely and thought how fortunate it was that they were going to Uhtua the next day; there would be no teachers' lounge nor any need to explain anything.

They walked to the shore, crossed the Pitkäsilta bridge and walked in the direction of the Seurahuone Hotel. A white hat was balanced on Katri's curls; Ilja looked at her with affection. As they sat down for a cup of coffee in the Seurahuone Hotel restaurant, Katri began to speak.

"I have received a letter from the police department in Helsinki," she said quietly. "My husband's murderers have been found. They are responsible for two other cases as well."

"Who are they?"

"Socialist revolutionaries ... They had some kind of a cell in Helsinki, although the leaders are in St Petersburg. Can you imagine that already seven years ago they had a long list of people marked to be liquidated. It included politicians, university people and who knows who else. Juhani's name was on that list."

Ilja's face turned serious.

"Now that the Jäger training has started in Germany, it means that the first steps have been taken toward complete separation of Finland from Russia ..." Ilja took Katri's hand in his and spoke even more quietly than before. "If the Jäger movement fails, you will not be safe."

"But the Russians themselves don't approve of the socialists!"

"Of course not, but this movement is strong and has support in all European countries. The Czar's visit to Helsinki in March was a sign that Russia won't allow any activities designed to advance independence. Governor General Seyn is just as exacting as was the late Bobrikov. Nothing has changed. And that means that the socialists have no chance yet in Russia."

They were quiet for a while as the waitress brought the coffee tray. Then Katri said, "I simply don't understand what my husband had in mind back then."

"The same as all activists, to get military training," Ilja said "They just didn't dare say it out loud in those days. I have since come to understand that Juhani Jääskeläinen was one of those who had already received Jäger training by then. That made him dangerous."

"Dangerous enough to have to have him murdered?

"Those who are for violent revolution are fanatics," Ilja responded.

Katri fingered her napkin; it was obvious that she was nervous.

"Do you think … Do you think I have reason to be afraid? It's after all seven years since my husband's death."

Once again Ilja took Katri's hand.

"You don't need to be afraid of anything," he said. "I'll take care of you. As far as I understand, Sortavala is a perfectly safe town, and if anything were to happen here, you'll leave your job at the seminary and move in with me in Uhtua for good."

Katri gave a relieved smile, and for a moment they concentrated on drinking their coffee, but then Katri said:

"I was supposed to tell you that the boy Anja is infatuated with, that Artturi Kangas, has been arrested and imprisoned in St Petersburg. I am worried about Anja, she is always so strangely isolated – and quite odd at times. It's still difficult for me to believe that she really sang in the Workers' Association choir. That is completely unheard of; no school girls around here have ever participated in political activities."

"She is her mother's daughter," Ilja said.

They looked at each other seriously. Then Ilja smiled.

"Let's leave sad things be. I am happy that I am getting both of you to Huotari Point. You cannot imagine how long this winter has been."

The man's eyes filled with such tenderness and passion, that Katri blushed.

"If only I could get divorced," Ilja continued quietly. "I'd give my right hand to have you for my wife."

"Don't torment yourself," Katri said. "What of it if people talk in Uhtua; deep inside I know our relationship is right."

"They talk about Outi too …"

"You know what," Katri said leaning forward, closer to Ilja. "It doesn't bother me. Since we found each other, you havn't seen Outi once."

"No, I haven't – and I won't. I have come to value fidelity."

On the first day of June the school town of Sortavala awoke to a bustling morning. Wherever one looked one saw only students dressed in their best finery, hurrying forward alone or in groups. There were light summer dresses, brimmed hats, and white shoes. Some of the boys even had dark suits and bow ties under their chins. The cheerful youngsters filled the Pitkäsilta bridge, making it difficult to pass by. After the commencement ceremonies, some of the students would go by boat on a summer outing to the islands. Others would climb up to the lookout tower, but most would go to the train station and travel home for the summer.

The youngsters' faces radiated relief and joy, although among them were, of course, those who would have to go to summer school or be held back a year. All in all there were only a few, and the majority rejoiced as they walked along.

They had woken up early in the Alhainen house, too. Their hair had been done already the night before, after their sauna, and now all three women were dressed in festive outfits. A smile played even on Anja's face, which usually was so morose.

"Well now," said Katri. "You are very pretty when you smile!"

"This is such a beautiful dress," Anja said, twirling around so that the hem of her skirt swished to and fro.

Katri smiled with contentment. She had sewn the two-part dress from a flowered fabric. The skirt was wide and long, the sleeves of the blouse came down to the elbows, and around the neckline was a red-striped ribbon.

Anna Liisa, too, was pretty. She had on a blue and white sailor's dress. She put on Katri's white straw hat when they left.

"Smile, smile," she told Anja as they entered the street from their yard. "You won't be getting any failing grade! Just think this time tomorrow morning you'll be on your way to Uhtua! And then you'll get to go to St Petersburg, too. Isn't that reason enough to smile?"

"The trip to St Petersburg is no fun-trip for us," Anja said warily. "We'll be living in a boarding house in some small dirty room."

"But St Petersburg is still St Petersburg," Anna Liisa said. "With any luck you'll see the Czar or the Czarina or perhaps the Grand Duchesses. You can stand at the corner of the Winter Palace and look at the Neva River. I actually envy you. And you just make a wry face. Wake up, Anja!"

Anna Liisa stood with her certificate in hand by the wall of the auditorium. Anja stood beside her, her whole being reflecting relief and with a happy expression on her face. She had not failed Russian and otherwise too her report card had exceeded all her expectations. The school choir sang Merikanto's "Easterly Wind" and Järneflet's "It Was Summer for Me." Anna Liisa saw how her *buobo* closed his eyes – he was visibly enjoying the clear female voices, which sang of summer's glory.

Anna Liisa came to, as if from a spell, when the headmistress began to speak:

"Summer has come to Karelia! The swallows have returned, the lilacs have opened their blossoms, and soon the midsummer roses in our gardens will fill the air with their fragrance. The graduating class will leave the Girls' School, which has become so familiar to you, and go out in the world; you are leaving us, and we will miss you. Some of you will leave us after the middle grades; to you I say: preserve in your hearts what this school has taught you. This beautiful building has been your home; here you have followed house rules whose aim has always been to benefit you. Often, as we get older, we wonder why something at some stage of our lives did not turn out the way we would have wanted. Only as the years pass do we come to understand that everything happens for our own good. Girls, let us be silent in a prayer on this last day of spring."

All heads bowed, and hands holding report cards rose to their hearts.

"We thank you, Lord, for your word, for the lantern at our feet, and for the light on our road. We thank you for our fatherland, our home, our school, and all the worldly goods that you have bestowed upon us. We thank you for this school building, which has guided our steps into the world of knowledge and civilization. Bless the students of this institution, both those who are leaving and those who are entering; bless these seedlings of your garden and the teachers who nurture them. Bless, oh Lord, our ruler, our country, and our people, its homes and schools. Bless our beautiful Karelia, bless and enlighten those in whose hands the school is so that your will may prevail and your glory shine. Amen."

The headmistress raised her head and looked over the auditorium.

"Dear students, we will end this last day of school with hymn number 336, thus saying goodbye to the graduating class and those who have ended their school work.

Solemnly and with moist eyes, they sang:

Oh, Lord, look after me
and prevent me from falling.
Comfort me in my sorrow
With your boundless mercy.
My hope and my protection
My shelter against danger,
Leave all sorrow in your realm.

Kaarlo Meinander had returned from the podium to his seat with his violin. Every now and then his hand rose inadvertently to touch the graduation cap he had placed on his head just moments before. He sat by the window, letting his glance stray onto the back yard and beyond, to the Girls' School building whose windows glittered in the sunshine. There was Anna Liisa, his girl, who would be thinking of him ... Never before had he played as well as a moment ago, thinking only of Anna Liisa. They had before them the whole of a wonderful summer in Uhtua; Lake Kuittijärvi with its clear water, fishing trips, walks in the forest by the rapids ... His music studies in Helsinki would begin in the fall.

Kaarlo turned to look at his father. If only his mother had still been alive to experience this day.

Katri Jääskeläinen listened to the choir and thought about all those years she had spent in the seminary. Upon finishing her teacher's training she had worked for a couple of years as a teacher here at her old alma mater. She had taught many young men and women, and each spring had sent many to start their careers as teachers in Finland's towns and villages. The majority always went to Karelia, often to the Lutheran areas, but sometimes also to the Eastern Orthodox regions. Once in a while she received letters from former students: one had got married, another had had children, someone had become ill, someone had become widowed. They always wrote to Katri, and they always received a reply when they needed advice. Katri felt responsible for these people, who were trusted with the mission of enlightening the people of the Grand Duchy of Finland, of instilling in them a patriotic mindset.

The expression on the faces of the teachers sitting in the auditorium this spring was grave. The officials who had succeeded Bobrikov had chosen the teachers' seminary in Sortavala for special surveillance. During the past year, Governor General Seyn himself had issued an ultimatum to the seminary through the civil officials. Over the winter, many inspectors had come to investigate the quality of the Russian language instruction. Attention was also paid to the teaching of religion. In the religious studies classroom was a large and, at least in Katri's opinion, beautiful picture of Christ. The inspectors had recommended taking it down, because it did not comply with the doctrines of the Russian church. The picture still hung on the wall, however; it had not been exchanged for an image of the Mother of God. Geography and history were also under suspicion. The inspectors were afraid that the wrong impression was being given of the relations between the Grand Duchy of Finland and Russia. An order had been issued to furnish each teachers' seminary with a picture of the Czar, and to make the Russian language a mandatory subject. The libraries were also issued stern directives.

Katri knew that fear reigned among the teachers. No one knew in advance whether the inspectors would suddenly show up, for example, at this commencement to listen to what was being said in the speeches at the Sortavala seminary. Any one member of the audience could be a spy, who would report the content of each prayer for the fatherland.

Katri could not help but conjure up an image of Anja in her mind. She knew now that Anja had taken the office keys from her purse, given them to Artturi Kangas and brought them back in the morning while Katri was still asleep. Deep inside she had probably known the truth of the matter all the time, but after Artturi had been arrested and transported to St Petersburg, Anja's behavior toward other people had turned openly hostile. She had been especially rude toward her and Anna Liisa as if they had somehow had something to do with the arrest. Anja's behavior had opened Katri's eyes and at the same time hurt her feelings, because for five years she had been a mother's substitute for the girl. She had listened to the girl's sorrows and worries. Offered her a home when her aunt put her out in the street. Not one word of thanks had ever come from Anja; it seemed as if the word "thank you" did not belong to the girl's vocabulary. This made Katri particularly sad, not because she craved to be thanked, but because Katri had failed in teaching her the most basic rules of behavior and because the girl's ingratitude revealed a hardened heart. And furthermore, it also offended her because she had never despised Anja or considered her inferior to Anna Liisa. She had demanded of both girls adherence to the same rules: civilized behavior, participation in housework, diligence and conscientiousness in schoolwork. And she had not, in her own opinion, been particularly strict; the girls had to come home at the agreed-upon time, of course, but she had always emphasized the importance of different hobbies and urged them to go to concerts and to the theatre club.

Katri made an effort to concentrate on the poem that a girl in a salmon-pink dress was reciting with great stress on the trochaic meter.

Soon, however, her thoughts were on Anja again. She recalled the quarrel over the fact that Anja sang in the Workers' Association choir. "Is it somehow not as good as the seminary's choir?" Anja had yelled at her. Katri had felt she had to search her mind, but in her opinion the matter was a simple one: in the workers' choir Anja had to sing workers' songs and their contents were political. Yet Katri had been ashamed to look Anja in the eye. She had felt she was a real fossil from another time and a very narrow-minded person – not at all the modern woman she had imagined herself to be.

In one matter Katri had to admit having been partial, and that was in her relationship to Kaarlo. She had permitted the courtship, allowed Anna Liisa to go to Kaarlo's home on Rantakatu Street after school, although she knew he lived alone. She simply did not want to keep watch on the youngsters or serve as their chaperone. She knew instinctively that they did not have sexual experiences, that they were only young people who were deeply and romantically in love and who had decided to spend the rest of their lives together. And so she had not put any limits on Kaarlo's and Anna Liisa's courtship, but to Anja's and Artturi's relationship she had had to set limits. Anja had become very angry at that.

"Why is everything allowed for Anna Liisa, but not for me! Why do you let Anna Liisa go to Kuhavuori for a walk after six o'clock, but I am not permitted to go with Artturi to listen to the Workers' Association concert? Why are you so unfair?"

What could Katri say to that? Anna Liisa and Kaarlo walked on Kuhavuori hand in hand dreaming and talking about their future. On the other hand, who knew what kind of people Anja would meet at the Workers' Association concert. But how could she tell the girl that socialism was a bad idea. And was it? Yrjö Koskinen himself had written that it was somehow unclear how socialism would want society to be organized. How then could an ordinary teacher have known? Katri had tried to circumvent the entire issue and had forced Anja to study Russian, her stumbling block in school. Anja became embittered and began to lean even more on Artturi, a robust boy with brown inquisitive eyes and broad shoulders whose blond hair was a tousled mess like the hair on the head of the character Juhani in the novel *Seven Brothers*. Why did Katri find even his outward appearance irritating? Did she have such strong prejudices against the world of ideas the boy represented?

The choir began to sing, and again Katri tried to pull herself together. The last days of May had been busy both for the teachers and for the graduating seminarians. First they had held two days of exams with thorough oral examinations, then on the third day musical performances and singing examinations. People came to listen to these from all over Sortavala and its environs.

When the principal began to hand out certificates, Katri looked at the graduating students with affection. Next fall they would begin the routines of a real teacher, which included much that could not be taught at the seminary – all that they would have to learn in practice.

In the evening there was still a reception that the principal put on in his apartment, and then she would get to go home. Then to the first summer day's concert at Vakkosalmi and in the morning – to Uhtua.

The Girls' School's auditorium was decorated with flower garlands and green branches. The headmistress was in the middle of giving her salutatory speech, but Anja, who sat next to Anna Liisa, could not bring herself to concentrate on it. In her opinion the headmistress was mouthing only meaningless phrases and pure nonsense. Instead, she thought about herself, the following day, and the impending trip to St Petersburg. She thought about her quarrel with aunt Natalia and wondered why her aunt felt such a strong aversion toward Artturi. Anja could not understand it. Why was her aunt so implacably angry with her? Four years she had lived with her aunt in the small back yard cottage, been compliant and obeyed every order. Then Artturi Kangas had arrived and everything had changed.

What might it feel like to be in prison for one's political views? Most likely bitter. Artturi was a young man whose mind was filled with huge visions for the future. And now he was behind bars. She felt bad thinking about it. Why was the world so complicated? There was a lot of talk about Finland's independence – that is what the Jägers, the activists and the civil guard wanted. But so did the social democrats and the revolutionaries. Why was their patriotism not as good as the others?

What had Artturi actually done? Organized illicit meetings, spoken against the Czar, defended the poor and the dispossessed. What was wrong with that? Wasn't it every Finn's duty to fight against the arbitrariness and oppression of the Czar's officials?

Anja had to admit that they had entered the seminary's office on their own initiative. But Artturi had not taken anything from there; he had only wanted to check some individuals' personal records. "One must know the background of both one's friends and one's enemies," Artturi had said.

Who might be the ones who had betrayed him?

Artturi had been labeled an enemy of both Finland and Russia. A bolshevist … Anja remembered someone using that word. And she remembered Artturi's own speeches whose fervor had sometimes frightened her. Dark predictions of what was to come, maybe bloody altercations …

Suddenly Anja shuddered severely; it felt as if an icy cold breath had run through her. She felt like everything was unreal, and the feeling was so strong she became scared. It was as if she were watching herself from the outside and saw herself as a stranger sitting at the convocation of a Girls' School. And at the same time she saw her future, but she did not dare look … She was overcome with anxiety. She clutched her chest because she felt as if she could not get enough air.

"What's wrong?" Anna Liisa whispered alarmed. "You're totally pale, are you about to faint?"

Anja shook her head; she did not know where she was.

"No … I just became nauseated."

Anna Liisa grabbed her friend by the shoulders.

"Just lean against my shoulder. Let me know if you pass out."

Anja had already recovered enough to smile at Anna Liisa's joke.

"How can I tell you if I have passed out?"

"Take a deep breath."

The girls around them began to whisper and the headmistress' speech was disrupted.

Anja stood up and left the auditorium hastily, almost at a run. Everyone noticed that her face was pale. It happened often during morning prayer that some girl would faint, but at commencement – that was quite exceptional.

Having got out into the fresh air, Anja sat down on the steps of the school. She pressed her head against her knees and took deep breaths of the cool morning air. What had happened exactly? It was as if she had had a strange and threatening vision … What might it signify? Had something happened to Artturi? Maybe he had been sent to Siberia or something even worse – shot. Anja squeezed her eyes shut as if she could thus expel the haunting images. No, she would have to heed her aunt's and Katri's warnings. She was crazily in love with a man who had only taken advantage of her.

Then the doors to the school opened wide and the girls pushed into the yard. Anja was surrounded by cheerful laughter and chatting. The girls were kissing and hugging each other.

"Remember at midsummer – at our summer place!"

"Hey, when is your ball again – 5th of August?"

"I'll be going to Helsinki tomorrow!"

Anja listened to the girls' exclamations in a state of numbness. What about me? she thought. What expressions would the girls' faces wear if I were to throw in that I'll travel to Uhtua tomorrow and from there to St Petersburg to spend a month in some derelict boarding house, where a retired civil servant with bread crumbs in his beard sits across from you at the breakfast table. Then I'll return home to care for a thin and ugly old cow only to start working as a teacher without the formal qualifications but with a ready-forged reputation of being peculiar.

"Anja, what's wrong with you?"

Anja raised her head. Anna Liisa stood before her in her crisp sailor's outfit, with her straw hat in her hand. Her round face looked worried.

"Are you ill? Can you walk? We have to go to the boys' school to wait for Kaarlo. He has already got his graduation cap!"

"I can walk," Anja said, rising to her feet. She grabbed Anna Liisa by the hand. "You won't believe it – All of a sudden I started feeling so bad, everything went cold inside."

Anja's eyes still looked frightened. Anna Liisa wrapped her arms around Anja's waist in a motherly fashion and pressed her toward her side.

"Let go of your worries!" she commanded. "You didn't get a failing grade and the sun is shining!"

Kaarlo saw Anna Liisa and Anja coming to the boys' school yard and hurried toward them. The whole yard was swarming with people, new graduates and their well-wishers.

Kaarlo immediately noticed that something was wrong when the girls stopped in front of him. Anja looked even more withdrawn than usual and completely pale. Anna Liisa in turn glanced every so often at her friend with a worried look in her eyes.

"What is it?" Kaarlo asked.

"What is it ..." Anna Liisa said and her face broke into a broad smile. She wrapped her arms around Kaarlo and pressed a kiss on his lips. "Only this – congratulations to the new graduand!"

Kaarlo's cheeks blushed and he looked around quickly. But all around the atmosphere was wild and cheerful; nobody paid any attention to them.

Anja's congratulations were of a much more sedate kind, but she, too, placed a light kiss on each of Kaarlo's cheeks and looked with a serious expression at the roses and the white cap.

"But you're totally pale," Kaarlo said.

"I began to feel dizzy in the auditorium," Anja explained embarrassed. "I had to leave in the middle."

"Well, you'll soon get a glass of champagne," Kaarlo said laughingly. "That will bring back the glow of health to your cheeks."

Only then did Anna Liisa notice the trio standing by the fence: Katri, Ilja Huotari, and Henrik Meinander.

"Hoy, we're over here!" she shouted waving her hand.

A coffee reception had been organized at the Meinander house for a small crowd of people. A couple of Kaarlo's fellow graduands were also present; they had already had champagne at a few receptions earlier and wanted to sing many songs with their arms around each other's shoulders:

They sang "The sun descends among the red flowers of the west," and a song in German:

Grau, theurer Freund, ist alle Theorie,
nur grühn des Lebens goldner Baum.

Kaarlo looked at Anna Liisa who was sitting on the sofa between Katri and his father with a cup of coffee in her hand. She was so beautiful, so lovely ... a charming smile on her lips, and a happy sparkle in her deep blue eyes. In the afternoon she was to go with her grand father to see the headmistress of the Girls' School. That made Kaarlo nervous because he wanted her to continue her studies in Helsinki. Anna Liisa would live in their large apartment and Kaarlo would be able to see her all the time. They would be together always, for it was obvious they would get married as soon as Anna Liisa came of age. They were, in fact, secretly engaged already ... Kaarlo would become the world's most famous violinist, he would go abroad to study and perform, and he would bring Anna Liisa with him. He did not understand why Anna Liisa continually talked about teaching the poor children of Uhtua, when she could live in the capital in a fine house, attend concerts and the theatre, and travel abroad whenever she wanted to. Henrik Meinander was a professor at the University of Helsinki; he had a large apartment and a good salary.

Nobody knew the full extent of Ilja Huotari's wealth, but it seemed he could give his only grandchild the moon! They really were fortunate, he thought to himself as he saw his father standing up with a glass of champagne in his hand.

"Kaarlo – now university student – may I have your attention please! As your father and only relative, I want to propose a toast in honor of this magnificent day. Today, if ever, life is before you in all its glory, like an overflowing glass of champagne. And let it overflow today, it will settle in time. From now on, each day will be filled with work and worry about the future, but today - today no newly graduated high school student needs to think about tomorrow; today is today, filled with roses, champagne, sweet kisses, and the singing of the nightingale! Cheers – a toast to my son – I am so proud of you! And so would your mother have been ..."

"Cheers!"

By evening everything had been settled. The headmistress of the Girls' School had met with Ilja Huotari and Anna Liisa at the school. The discussion concluded with an agreement that Anna Liisa would continue her university-bound studies there in the old school. The headmistress was a wise woman; she realized that if Anna Liisa were to go to Helsinki with Kaarlo, neither of them would get any studying done. It would be a senseless waste, for they had their whole lives ahead of them. Anna Liisa pondered the headmistres' word for a long time because her grand father had left the matter for her to decide. Finally she came to the conclusion that the adults were wiser than she, at least in this matter. And she would still be able to be with Kaarlo every summer. Otherwise everything would continue as before: she would live with Katri in the Alhainen house and attend the Sortavala Girls' School. It actually didn't feel like such a bad idea, Anna Liisa reflected as she walked homeward arm in arm with her grandfather. One thing, however, did bother her.

"*Buobo*," she said slowing down her pace. "I am worried about Anja ..."

"Why?" Ilja asked surprised. "She didn't get any failing grades, and she'll travel with us tomorrow to Uhtua and then on to St Petersburg. In the fall she starts teaching in her mother's school, where she knows the children and the work very well. Why are you worried?"

"Anja has been involved with dangerous people," Anna Liisa said. "With Bolsheviks!"

Ilja stopped and looked at his granddaughter.

"Could you somehow next fall ..." Anna Liisa began to say a little irresolutely ... she did not quite know how to express herself.

"Since I'll be here and all ..."

"Look after her? Of course I will."

"She fell in love with a boy named Artturi Kangas," Anna Liisa explained. "Or actually he is already a man. He went to the seminary but dropped out in the middle. I happen to know that he was spying on the seminary people. Then the police arrested him, and now he is in prison in St Petersburg."

"So Anja has got herself entangled in that kind of thing," Ilja said pensively. "She has indeed changed somehow lately – she's quieter and even more serious. She doesn't speak much."

"I'm scared," Anna Liisa confessed. "She criticizes anybody who has any wealth; she speaks of revolution and workers' ideology. She doesn't even go to church any more."

"Did you have problems during the winter?"

"Only once, but that has now been cleared up. But I feel so bad. Anja no longer likes me as before, to her I am a rich, spoiled bourgeois girl. *Buobo*, say it isn't so!"

Ilja stopped and looked out over the bay. The sun was still high in the sky and there were lots of people in the park by the shore. They could hear music from the direction of the Seurahuone Hotel.

"Don't you worry, you're the same old Anna Liisa you have always been," Ilja said comfortingly. "Anja has got many of her values confused. I'll speak to her in the fall when she starts teaching. There is to be no politicking there, that's clear. I will do it considerately, you can count on that."

The evening was warm and light; the sun made the surface of Lake Airanne glitter. It appeared as if all of Sortavala had gathered in Vakkosalmi park to listen to the concert of the joint choirs and orchestras. A leafy birch alley led from the gate to the performance field on the edge of which the music pavilion was located. The stand across from the singing platform was erected against the rocky wall of Kuhavuori hill, and so the place had naturally good acoustics. The outdoor restaurants and cafeterias were open and packed with people. Most were out with their whole families.

The performers were beginning to file up to the platform, and the musicians were tuning their instruments when Ilja looked for seats for his companions. Anja looked at the singers standing next to the platform and suddenly she startled.

"Aunt Natalia!"

Katri too turned her head.

"Is the Workers' Association mixed choir performing here, too?" she wondered. "Sure enough, there's Natalia Stepanova."

Katri did not dare look in Anja's direction. She could guess the girl's feelings – a Girls' School student was not allowed to sing in a choir that was accepted to perform here and celebrate the first day of summer together with other choirs.

Fortunately, at that moment the first notes rang out, the murmur of people's voices quieted down and the people began to listen to the music. The orchestra played the waltz "Sounds of Spring" by Strauss. Some of the younger people marked the rhythm by swaying, and suddenly a popping of a champagne bottle sounded from somewhere. No one minded even that on this beautiful day.

"Quite a characteristic sound of spring," Henrik Meinander whispered to Anja who sat next to him, and she showed a faint smile.

After the intermission, the string quartet formed by Kaarlo and the other high school students performed. For their repertoire the boys had chosen old waltzes that suited the atmosphere of the summer evening perfectly. The familiar tunes inspired the audience to hum along and the atmosphere in the large auditorium-like stands became almost intimate. Anna Liisa looked around discreetly and saw only smiling, happy faces. She herself was happy too – and so proud of Kaarlo.

When everyone had joined in to sing the Karelians' Song at the end of the concert and the audience expressed their appreciation and admiration for the choirs and the orchestra, Ilja motioned for his companions to get moving.

"Let's go! I have reserved a table at the restaurant at the Seurahuone Hotel."

This last evening they spent together, all of them. It was an evening of youth, joy, and happiness. A nightingale sang in Vakkosalmi park, oblivious to the cheerful noises of the young people. Hotel Seurahuone filled with festive parties and the champagne corks popped more and more frequently. Anna Liisa looked at her loved ones, she was filled with love toward all of them. She felt she had her whole life ahead of her.

PART FOUR
Toward Maturity

The moon was in the shape of a sickle and its color was mysteriously red. Katri looked at it pensively, and although she assured herself that she wasn't the least bit superstitious, she had to admit that the moon's color was somehow eerie. Maybe a contributing reason was that the moon had been red already for many weeks and the old people had repeatedly predicted that bad times were in store for Viena.

"All times are bad for Viena," Ilja Huotari had growled to one such prognosticator, "as long as its people remain passive."

Katri agreed, but when she walked across the yard of Huotari Point, she could not refrain from looking at the sky again. She would not go so far as to cross her heart, as Nasti who walked beside her did. One thing was certain, however: times were bad and no one dared expect anything good from the future. War raged in Europe and peoples and nations murdered each other. And brother had risen against brother with rifles in hand in Finland.

Later in the evening, as was her habit, Katri read the newspaper to Ilja in the parlor. Wearing her glasses, she sat down on the bench by the window and looked inquiringly at Ilja, who was sitting on the dark-red sofa, smoking his pipe.

"Go ahead and read!" he urged her. "You have such a beautiful voice."

Katri thumbed through the paper. After the events of the last year, one had the feeling one might find anything in the news. She wondered whether any future generation would ever experience a year like 1917 had been. A revolution had taken place in Russia, and Finland had gained its independence. Those kinds of events had been talked about, even planned, but it still felt unbelievable that they had actually come about. But soon the joy of Finland's greatest hour had died when the Civil War had broken out at the end of January.

Katri had not yet got used to the thought and that was why reading the newspaper had recently become unpleasant. She did not want to think about the fact that Finns, having finally become independent, were now killing each other.

Ilja noticed where Katri's thoughts had strayed once again. At times he felt as if the red moon actually had an effect on people. He put down his pipe in the ashtray and said gently:

"Why don't we forget the newspaper, read me something else. Something pleasant."

Katri gave him a grateful glance. She put the newspaper away and went into the library. At the door she turned to ask, "What should I read? Would Samuli S. be all right with you?"

"But of course."

Katri returned with a thin volume in her hand. She sat down on the sofa beside Ilja, looked over some pages and began to read:

"The sun was very hot; it shone relentlessly. No wonder then that all of nature seemed to have fallen asleep. No clouds, not even a white wisp of cloud, had risen into the sky. The birds did not sing, they did not even make a sound; not a leaf stirred in the trees, not even the leaves of the aspen. The yellow road alone was allowed no respite. A cart came rolling down the hill, rattling along the sharp gravel ..."

Late in the afternoon, teacher Anna Liisa Huotari skied from the school toward her home on her clumsy skis. The woods were packed with snow. It had snowed so much that Anna Liisa had to switch from riding a horse to skiing already at Christmas time. Skiing was slow and took her so long that during January and February she had spent the weekday at her school and only come home to Huotari Point to spend the weekends with Katri and her *buobo*.

Her small school was on the shore of Kuittijärvi near Jyvälahti; it was a Finnish-language school. Anja's school in turn was closer to Pistojärvi, and there the language of instruction was Russian. Anja had sometimes said laughingly that they should have switched schools, for Anna Liisa had graduated from high school a couple of years earlier and her Russian skills were quite good. Anja had quit school and had always feared she would fail Russian. She had taught as her mother's substitute the first year in Uhtua. After that she got her current position as the teacher of an old Russian school in a small village with only a few derelict cottages, a dilapidated church, and a graveyard.

"I wish Mother had stayed in Crimea," Anja had sometimes sighed.

Darja Mihailovna was still carefully attending to her former duties – just as morose and efficient as ever.

Anna Liisa's thoughts moved with the rhythm of the pushes with her ski poles, bouncing from one thing to another. So much had happened in the last two or three years. Fear and agony were part of Viena's fate, armed men had come from different directions, calling themselves liberators. Anna Liisa wondered whether she had become cynical; she had become more and more certain that most of those who had come there had only their own interests at heart.

Last weekend she had learned from Nasti and Teppana that a government official had come from Kemi to Uhtua Inn. He had gone to the town hall office and shouted at the clerk, who had not reported the names of some young men in the area to the military authorities. Anna Liisa knew the boys who were hiding somewhere. People just kept quiet about everything. The Russian police chief was feared and despised; the same was true of other officials. An additional problem now was the fact that nobody could tell, whether they were still the Czar's servants or had become Bolshevik agents.

The previous spring, after the Russian revolution, demands had been expressed at a large gathering for Karelia's independence in Suomussalmi. Another suggestion had been that Karelia be annexed to Finland. Anna Liisa had been at the meeting, together with Katri and her *buobo*. She too had become excited by the idea that Finland buy Karelia from the Russians for a price equivalent to the value of its forests. But the Finnish politicians were against it; the whole Karelia issue didn't seem to interest them much.

"They are so used to bowing and scraping before Russians," Ilja had growled.

Upon returning home, Anna Liisa had read Ilmari Kianto's war poem to the children in school:

May Viena Karelia rise up high,
Rise from its oppression!
May freedom come, and light,
And to the people might!

The children had looked at her, asked who Kianto was, and run out into the yard to play. Anna Liisa could only shake her head. Maybe the children actually knew how to put things in the right order of importance.

And now what they had feared most had happened.

Civil War had broken out in Finland. Rumors of different acts of violence and riots had reached Uhtua soon enough. Anna Liisa was afraid to think about the whole matter.

Kaarlo, too, had joined the Civil Guard. He was now fighting against the Reds – he, an artist! Anna Liisa simply could not fathom it. How could a sensitive person whose entire life had been devoted to music suddenly exchange his violin for a rifle – and then kill! Anna Liisa was not at all surprised that Kaarlo's letters were bitter in tone; between the lines she could plainly read that the man was scared to death.

Anna Liisa had already regretted that she had strongly insisted on a teaching position for this school year. If she had moved to Helsinki, as Kaarlo had wanted, he would most likely not have joined the Civil Guard but continued his studies at the conservatory. She had reproached herself many times over.

The previous week Katri had read in the newspaper that the main body of the Jäger battalion had arrived in Vaasa from Libau on the steamship *Arcturus*. A welcoming parade had been held in Vaasa market square. The parade had been received by the commander of the White army of Finland, General Mannerheim. Anna Liisa had received a letter from Kaarlo where he described the parade. Kaarlo had written that the Jägers were to disperse to different parts of White Finland. "And I will myself come to Viena on special assignment during the spring," the letter said at the end.

Special assignment? What could that be? Anna Liisa was on the one hand eager to see Kaarlo, but on the other hand she was outright angry that the Jägers and the Civil Guard were coming to Viena to mess up their lives. We don't need any soldiers here. We had peace here, and people lived together in harmony.

Gliding down the slope onto the ice of Kuittijärvi, Anna Liisa again felt a longing tug at her heart. She had not seen Kaarlo since last fall, since he did not even get a Christmas break, having joined the Civil Guard.

After skiing a mile and a half along the shore, Anna Liisa instinctively stopped at the spot were she could first see her home, Huotari Point. She remembered how she had hated the house when it was first built on the point. Now she thought it was the most wonderful house in all of Viena Karelia. Now she longed for it, her own light-blue room with its furniture brought from Canada and the book cabinet full of books.

She kicked her skis forward again. She tried to look for the trail she had left last week, but it had snowed so much it was completely covered.

Was she up to being a teacher? She wondered about that as she skied along. She was now nineteen. After graduation from high school she had taught small children all winter although she did not have the formal competence Katri had. In her own opinion she had done well. Katri no longer taught school; she had moved to live with Ilja Huotari – surely for the rest of her life. Anna Liisa knew that Katri's feelings toward her *buobo* were not the great love of her life – her great love had been her ruthlessly murdered husband. But Katri loved Ilja warmly and tenderly.

"What would you say if I were to resign from the seminary and move in with your *buobo*?" Katri had asked her the previous fall in Sortavala.

What could she say to that?

"I mean what do you think if ..." Katri had cast her eyes down, "if you see me and your *buobo* in the bedroom together?"

Anna Liisa had laughed at her modesty and told Katri she was happy that they would be able to wake up together every morning.

"That is the most wonderful thing I know!" she had said.

And Katri had moved to Huotari Point last fall at the same time as Anna Liisa.

Suddenly, Anna Liisa stopped again. Something was moving far out on the open lake. She focused her eyes in the Uhtua direction and discerned a cluster of horses and sleighs. They curved around Huotari Point and continued at a high speed. Who might they be? There were four sleighs and they were all coming straight toward her.

Anna Liisa became rigid from fright. What should she do? There wasn't enough time for her to reach the shore and the shelter of the forest. Who could they be? Whites – or Bolsheviks?

Where were they going? To Jyvälahti … Terror squeezed her chest and she could not move; she only stood there, awaiting her fate. Did she have her identification papers with her? Yes, they were in her knapsack.

But why would anyone want to stop her here on the ice and inquire who she was? Nothing of the sort had happened before.

With keen eyes, and almost without breathing, Anna Liisa followed the approaching horses. They came galloping, whirling up snow around them. She tried clumsily to step to the side and give them room to pass even though all around was shoreless open expanse of lake. Then they noticed her, or maybe they had seen her earlier, for an order to halt rang out from the lead sleigh. Before she knew it, the sleighs had surrounded her on all sides. The horses' nostrils flared and blew steam into the cold air. Anna Liisa had to close her eyes. She pulled her scarf from her hair down on her shoulders and stood there motionless while the afternoon sun played on her blond hair.

She lifted her head although her fear had not subsided at all. The sun was shining from behind her, blinding the men in the sleighs. She saw the man in the first sleigh shading his eyes with his hand.

"Your name! Who are you?" the man roared, trying to see with whom he was talking.

The man spoke plain Finnish! Anna Liisa realized the men were Whites from Finland. Her fear subsided.

"What gives you the right to shout at me?" she said, her voice quivering a little. "Here in Viena anyone can travel both summer and winter without anybody demanding to know their name."

"Please state your name!" The man repeated his request, now in a more moderate voice. "And where are you heading?"

Anna Liisa swallowed her annoyance.

"Anna Liisa Huotari," she said. "I'm on my way to the house on that point. That is my home."

"What are you doing on the ice?"

"I move on the ice or in the forest when I feel like it!" she said angrily, holding her head up high. "I'm returning home from the Syrjäkylä school where I teach."

"Just a minute, men," a shout was heard from another. "No need to interrogate this woman – this is the wrong woman."

The man rose up from his sleigh and came to stand in front of Anna Liisa. He was a tall man whose height was further accentuated by his fur coat, which reached all the way to the ground. On his head he wore a high white fur hat. There was a foreign accent in the man's Finnish, but the voice had a dark, pleasant tone.

"We have received a report about some teacher who agitates around here, but it is not about Miss Huotari. You are Ilja Huotari's granddaughter, aren't you?"

Anna Liisa nodded silently. Many thoughts crisscrossed in her mind. Did the man mean Anja? He must have meant either Anja or Darja Mihailovna. Anna Liisa shuddered. What if Anja had been here now instead of her – she did not dare finish her thought. This was like a bad dream. *Buobo* had said something about some detachment coming from the other side of the Finnish border, but it had sounded quite distant. These men must be from Malm's detachment. But why did this one man stand there in front of her looking amazed?

"I would like to go home," Anna Liisa said with her most teacher-like tone of voice. "Could you kindly ask these gentlemen to pull their horses back so I can pass through."

She looked at the man sternly. His face was thin, his features regular, and his blue eyes had a strangely penetrating gaze. The white fur hat was set at a rakish angle. For some reason this irritated Anna Liisa. Was this now one of the Jägers who had come from Libau?

"Is your grandfather home?" The man's question caught Anna Liisa by such a surprise that she became momentarily confused.

"Oh, yes … he is expecting me home right now."

"I have something I need to talk to him about," the man said. "We are now going to Jyvälahti, but we'll be back in the evening. Tell your grandfather that I will stop by your house."

"Excuse me, but who are you?" Anna Liisa said. "I don't know if my grandfather will welcome strangers."

Anna Liisa stared angrily at him. This man was a boor, even if he was a Jäger.

"Please forgive me, I am Lieutenant Gilbert Weissenberg," the man said and saluted her. "Finnish citizen of German origin."

Anna Liisa nodded. Gilbert Weissenberg … Had Kaarlo ever spoken about a man by that name? Anyway, his conduct was outrageous, inviting himself to our house …

"Very well," Anna Liisa said, bending down to reach for her ski pole on the ice. "I will tell grandfather you have promised to visit him in the evening. May I go now?"

The man nodded, gave a quick salute, jumped back into his sleigh, and then the horses curved impatiently back onto the open lake. Anna Liisa stood there for a moment as if paralyzed and then began slowly to ski toward the tip of the point. Tears ran down her cheeks. The fear returned, making her almost hysterical. Her thoughts were confused, but again and again she heard the man's voice:

"This is the wrong woman."

What if she had been the right one? What if it had been Reds stopping the granddaughter of the rich Ilja Huotari. What would have happened then? She did not want to think about that.

Wet snow began to fall from the sky making the skiing difficult. Anna Liisa was soaking wet when she finally reached the sauna shore. She untied her skis and leaned them against the sauna wall. Then she hurried home with quick steps. Only once did she turn around to look and in the direction of Jyvälahti she saw the horses only as small dots, just about to disappear into the horizon. At that moment she had a horrifying realization: Good Lord – Anja! Anja was alone at her school in Pistojärvi …

She found it difficult to believe that this was all true. Did one have to start to be afraid here the same way as in Finland, where innocent people were being killed!

"This is the wrong woman!"

The sentence pounded in Anna Liisa's head. The men must have been looking for Anja. There were no other teachers in the villages south of Uhtua. Except of course Darja Mihailovna. Anna Liisa found herself wishing the men were looking for Darja and not Anja. After the revolution, Darja had openly proclaimed Bolshevik doctrines and made her schoolchildren sing the Marseillaise and the International. But why would the Finnish Whites be looking for her? To interrogate her? But why? Why would they interfere with people's political views?

When Anna Liisa reached the yard, Nasti and Teppana had just returned from their ice-fishing hole. They were lifting the fish basket onto the steps and looked frightened at the girl who rushed toward them with her scarf falling to her shoulders, her hair wet and disheveled, and her chest heaving with heavy breathing.

"Did you see them? Did you?"

Anna Liisa's rapid breathing made it nearly impossible to get the words out intelligibly. Nasti and Teppana looked at her, bewildered.

"See what?" Nasti asked.

"The horses! Four sleighs with Whites! They came from Uhtua and stopped me there on the ice. They started interrogating me!"

Nasti and Teppana had come straight from the south to Huotari Point and had not met anybody.

"They stop everyone who is out on the ice," Anna Liisa explained. –"Soon nobody will dare move about there."

"What are you talking about – interrogating?" Teppana said nervously. "That's the damnedest thing! We have to go fishing, that's for sure. If you have to dig the papers out every time – Hell, that won't do."

Nasti began to guide Anna Liisa inside.

"Do go in poor child, your *buobo* has probably started a fire in the fireplace. Then you can go to the sauna, it's heated up."

"Will you come with me?"

"I'll be having a sauna later with Teppana, but I'll go and get the water ready," Nasti chatted. "You must be exhausted after such a long ski trip; the sauna never feels as blissful as after a ski trip."

"There is no way you are going to Syrjäkylä alone on Monday," Teppana said, standing by the fish basket. "I will go with you."

Anna Liisa turned and looked at Teppana with affection.

"So you will … I know you!"

Samuel met her in the hallway and helped take off her coat. He was old and clumsy, but seemed to continue working from morning till night.

"There was a letter from Canada," he said. "Your *buobo* has been sitting in the tower all day."

"Where is Katri?"

"In the kitchen."

A letter from Canada, Anna Liisa thought as she went into the kitchen. I wonder what that means. She stopped by the kitchen door: she was enveloped by the wonderful smell of freshly baked bread.

"Oh, you're here already!" Katri exclaimed, red-cheeked from behind the oven. "Would you like to eat or are you going to the sauna first?

"I'll go to the sauna first. I'm so glad it was heated this early."

"Miss will have a sandwich now anyway!"

Mrs. Jenny stood in front of Anna Liisa with her tray. She was not taking no for an answer. Anna Liisa squeezed her shoulders and took a sandwich. Then she walked up to Katri and gave her, too, a hug.

"I just had a shocking experience out there on the ice," she said as she took a bite of the sandwich. "A group of soldiers with horses stopped me. They wanted to interrogate me. There was a Jäger lieutenant among them who said he wanted to see *buobo*. He said he would come by this evening."

With floury hands, Katri tucked back some hairs that had come loose from her bun and looked at Anna Liisa with a serious expression on her face.

"Ilja is upstairs in the tower," she said. "He got a letter from Canada, and evidently it is something quite serious. I haven't wanted to disturb him."

"Then I won't go there yet either," Anna Liisa said. "First I have to wash my hair and get changed into clean clothes. There was no water at the school, can you imagine! The well was frozen. I haven't been able to have a sauna all week."

"What did you say about some soldiers with horses?" Katri asked.

"I'll tell you later."

Anna Liisa hurried back to the hallway and ran up the stairs to the second floor. By the door to her own room, she stopped and looked toward the steps leading to the tower. There was *buobo's* own kingdom, where no one else went – unless invited, or if *buobo* needed something urgently. If there was something extremely urgent, one could ring a bell that was located halfway up the stairs. Anna Liisa pondered for a moment whether she should ring the bell, but then she decided that this matter was not important enough. She would have time to tell her news at the dinner table after having a sauna.

Upon entering her room, she immediately noticed two letters that had been placed on her bed. She opened one of them immediately. It was from Kaarlo, written at the end of January.

Anna Liisa, My Love…

This is a rushed letter I can send with a friend of mine who is coming to Kajaani. Terrible things have happened here, there will be war for sure, no doubt any longer! I was in Vaasa when we stripped the Russians of their arms. A fight erupted and I ended up in it as well. The Bolsheviks are planning to help Finland's workers obtain their revolutionary goals. Fortunately, we have as our commander-in-chief a certain Mannerheim. He has been highly praised. I am still for the time being here in Vaasa, but I will end up fighting, no doubt about that. Don't worry. But know the fatherland is in danger.

Soon spring will come and we can be together again, of that I am certain.

Your Kaarlo

Kaarlo had to get involved in the fighting! For a moment it was difficult for Anna Liisa to breathe. She would not be able to take it, if something were to happen to Kaarlo. What would this all lead to? Will Viena, too, end up in war?

Between the new house and the sauna was a wide path. It continued a little narrower from the sauna to the old house. Teppana had cleared it with his own homemade plow. The path was wide enough for the water sled to advance on it. While Anna Liisa glided down to the sauna, Teppana lit his pipe.

"Now go in there, and you'll get wonderful sauna vapors." The old man went sauntering toward the old house and Anna Liisa slipped into the sauna. In the front room she took off her sauna robe and entered the hot sauna. Nasti was preparing the water and looked up with squinting eyes.

"Did you know Teppana's old ailment has cleared up?"

"Good Lord – what is it?"

"I'm not telling. I'll be going now."

Anna Liisa had dried herself, done her hair and put on a new dress. When she come out from her room, the door to the tower opened and Ilja Huotari appeared on the stairs.

"Would you come here, Anna Liisa, please," he said.

Anna Liisa began to climb the stairs. She looked at her *buobo's* features. They were usually stern and reserved, although during the last year a happy smile had played on his face more often than before. Otherwise, he had not changed during the eight years he had been in Uhtua; he was the same strong man, former seaman and gold prospector, an authority figure, nowadays respected by the Uhtuans, a man of his word.

Time had been wasted at the beginning when they had not understood each other. Then had come the wonderful school years in Sortavala during which they had found each other. Anna Liisa would never forget her high school graduation, when *buobo* had taken them all to Helsinki and from there by ship to Stockholm. But her appreciation did not stop there. She was grateful to her grandfather for having given her so many great opportunities to study and improve herself.

When Anna Liisa entered the tower room, Katri was already sitting there. Anna Liisa never stopped marveling at the room; to her mind it was the strangest room in the world. The ceiling was steep (like a four corner Lappish hat), each wall had a window, one facing each direction. In the middle of the room was a large table. The walls had shelves for books and papers. Next to the table were a sofa and chairs and a small narrow table with a sculpture of a ship standing on it. The objects in the room reflected the fact that the occupant had sailed the seven seas. The paintings on the walls depicted sailing ships; even the glass on the liquor cabinet doors was decorated with anchor engravings.

"Sit down, Anna Liisa, I have something to tell the both of you."

Ilja Huotari sat down across from the women. Anna Liisa thought he was still a handsome man – only his hair had become gray. He still dressed with style, "like a foreigner" as the Uhtuans would say, but nowadays they said it approvingly, even with pride, for Ilja Huotari had turned out to be the kind of man the Uhtuans needed. He had the Syrjäkylä school built, which had been on their wish list for decades: a Finnish-language school. The people in the Kuittijärvi region did not mind in the least that their first teacher was Ilja Huotari's very own granddaughter – quite the contrary, what could be better than getting a teacher who was born and raised in Uhtua.

Ilja Huotari had done other things as well for Uhtua; in particular, he had financed the building, repair, and improvement of the roads. He had hired workers for road construction and managed to develop the beginnings of a network of roads around Uhtua. The Russian officials had followed these road projects with disfavor because the road led, not from Uhtua east toward Viena's Kemi, but toward the Finnish border. The police chief had publicly accused Ilja of agitation in favor of the Finnish cause, but his efforts had gone awry. Ilja had grabbed him by the hand and thanked him loudly, pretending to take the accusation as praise – he really wanted to be an advocate for the Finnish cause.

Anna Liisa looked at her *buobo* affectionately, but at the same time she was filled with worry. She thought she saw an anguished glance in his eyes. Every so often he glanced at the letter in his hand.

"It was brought here this morning," he said at last. "You, too, had some letters, Anna Liisa."

"So I did, from Kaarlo."

"What about your letter, Ilja?" Katri asked quietly.

Ilja turned toward her.

"It affects you as well."

"Me?"

Ilja took a look at the letter as if to check what he was about to say.

"Greta has died in the mental hospital," he said. "It happened on the 27th of November. Her son wrote to me; he says he was with her the whole time."

Ilja was silent for a while, then he looked at Katri.

"I am now a free man."

Silence fell over the room; all three of them seemed to be deep in their own thoughts. Then Katri broke the silence.

"I have never cared whether you are free or not. We have in any event lived together like husband and wife."

Anna Liisa wondered why this news seemed to affect all of them, despite the fact that Greta had not been part of their reality for years. Anna Liisa had only a few vague images of Greta in her mind, and she knew that Katri had not met the woman more than once or twice. *Buobo*, however, had lived with her for years, and, furthermore, he had clearly had pangs of bad conscience after Greta's departure – maybe he still did; then sorrow is always multiplied.

Anna Liisa grabbed her *buobo*'s hand and put it against her cheek.

"So, now it has finally happened. It surely must be a great relief for you. We will not grieve for her now, only pray to the Mother of God that Greta's soul may find peace.

Anna Liisa walked to the window toward the west and looked at the evening twilight.

"*Buobo*, I have to tell you what happened to me this afternoon as I was skiing on the ice on my way home," she said. "Four sleighs with men in them came toward me … they stopped me."

"They stopped you?" Ilja rumbled. "What are you talking about? What men?"

"Finnish soldiers, Jägers, I guess," Anna Liisa said. "One of them began to interrogate me, who I was and where I was going. I told him no one has ever interrogated people around here for going about their own business. Then a man jumped up from another sleigh saying I was the wrong woman. They were looking for some teacher with a different name. You can imagine how terrified I was. He said his name was Gilbert Weissenberg, and he said he would be coming to see you tonight."

"Weissenberg…" Ilja tested the name. "No, I don't remember hearing about anyone by that name. This is unheard of! Harassing innocent people. Who do they think they are? They come here from Finland and believe they can do whatever they like!

"Should we be going downstairs?" Katri asked. "If the man comes …"

"Samuel will let us know," Ilja said. "Where were they heading?"

"To Jyvälahti," Anna Liisa said. "Which one do you think they had in mind – Anja or her mother?"

"This is a peculiar thing," Ilja said and put the letter in the safe, which was in the bookshelf behind the books. "I think Darja Mihailovna is a difficult person to deal with, but nobody has the right to start interrogating her just like that. Even the Bolsheviks have human rights."

Katri shook her head with a worried look.

"Let's go down," she said. "Dinner is ready."

Fear filled Anna Liisa's mind again when she heard the front door open and Samuel wishing the visitor welcome and asking him for his coat.

"The Huotaris are waiting in the parlor."

Then they could hear Samuel's feet dragging on the floor, and the sharp sound of boot heels. The visitor's steps were long and determined and they stopped on the threshold. Anna Liisa refused to look that way.

Ilja was sitting on the sofa next to Katri; he stood up and motioned for the visitor to come in.

The man walked with the same determined brisk steps across the parlor and stopped in front of Ilja. He was wearing a gray uniform jacket, German style trousers and shiny black boots. His face was narrow, the eyes strangely blue, almost icy. With one motion of his head, he swung his hair away from his brow.

"Sir, ladies," Gilbert Weissenberg began, presenting himself. "I do apologize for arriving at your home uninvited, but I wanted to introduce myself."

Ilja Huotari stretched out his hand and greeted him. Then he introduced the women.

"Katri Jääskeläinen from Sortavala."

Katri gave him her hand and smiled. Weissenberg pressed a gallant kiss on her hand.

"Madam, would you happen to be Juhani Jääskelainen's widow?

"Yes, I am," said Katri surprised. "How do you know him?"

"All Jägers know him. He was one of the activists who did great service for the cause of the fatherland. I lived in Berlin for many years after graduation from high school. They knew your husband there as well. It is an honor for me to meet you."

Anna Liisa could not take her eyes off the man. Was this the same boorish soldier who had interrogated her on the ice?

"My granddaughter, Anna Liisa," Ilja introduced her. "I understand you have already met."

"Yes, indeed, today in the afternoon," said Weissenberg turning toward Anna Liisa. "I beg your forgiveness, Miss, I could see that we frightened you."

Anna Liisa held out her hand and she, too, received a polite kiss on it. She did not know what to think as she sat down in an armchair.

Ilja bid the visitor to be seated. The expression on his face was inscrutable. Gilbert Weissenberg waited until his hosts had been seated; then he, too, sat down, on a chair at the side of the sofa.

The conversation was slow to start. Ilja was wondering why the man had come to see him; this surely was not a simple courtesy visit. Katri was wondering how it could be that the man had known Juhani – he was so much younger than they. And she could not recall Juhani ever having spoken about anyone by the name of Weissenberg.

Anna Liisa was in agony. She did not look at the man, yet felt his gaze all the time. It had a peculiar effect; it caused all her strength to dissipate.

Then Weissenberg began to speak.

"I belong to the Jäger platoon that came from Libau to Vaasa a week ago. Four of us officers were sent here to Viena to train others. We arrived only yesterday and I do not know anyone here yet."

"So you are Jägers, are you?" Ilja said, looking inquisitively at the visitor. "I do understand that Jägers are needed now in the White army in Finland since the Civil War has broken out, but I don't understand why you were ordered here to peaceful Viena.

Weissenberg listened attentively to Ilja Huotari's words.

"You know that it is time now to obliterate the border between Finland and Viena," he said. "It's our intention to rid Viena of Bolsheviks, Red guards and Russkis. We ask everybody with influence here in Viena to join us in a common front. That is why I came here, to ask your opinion and to listen."

"So you are interested to know if the Vienans want to be liberated. Interesting that no one came to ask us about that in advance."

Ilja Huotari got up from the sofa. He walked to the small table and poured cognac into two glasses. He handed one of the glasses to Gilbert Weissenberg. He had become a little agitated during the last exchange and clearly wanted to calm down.

"By the way, why are you talking to me about these matters?" he asked suddenly.

The very direct question did not throw Weissenberg off balance at all. He answered with perfect calm:

"Because we are asking you to finance our arms. There are Bolsheviks who have infiltrated the Uhtua region. They have a weapons cache here somewhere. We intend to eradicate them from Viena. I tell you frankly, Mr. Huotari, that we will join Viena with Finland. It is our duty!"

Ilja Huotari tilted his glass and took a long swallow. When he began to speak again, Anna Liisa and Katri both noticed that he was nervous. The more nervous he was, the more quietly he spoke. His voice now was calm and quiet.

"I will never and under no circumstances agree to finance anybody's weapons. I hate weapons. I have during the course of my life seen so much violence and bloodshed that it sickens me just to think about it. I believe you are honest, Lieutenant Weissenberg. But I do not want Viena to become a theatre of war."

"You were all at the Uhtua Karelia celebration last summer," Weissenberg said, and, seeing the dumbfounded expression on the others' faces, he continued: "I saw you there. You participated in the large citizens' gathering drafting for the interim government a proposal for an autonomous administrative region for both Viena and Aunus. You therefore hope to liberate Viena from under the yoke of Russia. Now we have an opportune moment – the Reds are being defeated in Finland, and it is time to act here as well.

Ilja Huotari shook his head.

"The road of violence is not the right road."

Gilbert Weissenberg's eyes flashed; he lifted his shiny boot over his knee and tossed his head to the side.

"The best Russki is a dead Russki," he said dryly.

Ilja squeezed his cognac glass so hard Katri was afraid it would break.

"Nothing is that simple. I am afraid there are many Vienans whom you and your kind consider Russkis. What would their fate be? The same as that of America's Indians? 'Good things' were done to them as well until they were near extinction. You have already today given us a foretaste of your methods. You scare women who have always traveled on Viena's waters and paths without ever having to fear anybody. You stop free people and you interrogate them! I know your methods – if someone disagrees with you, they pay with their lives."

Ilja's voice had turned dangerously quiet; he was on the point of exploding. Lieutenant Weissenberg realized this and turned to Katri.

"What about you, Mrs. Jääskeläinen? Your husband spoke of liberating Viena already nearly ten years ago. He was murdered exactly for the reason Mr. Huotari just mentioned – he dared to disagree.

Katri did not dare look at Ilja. The lieutenant had put her in an awkward situation. There was something charming about the man, yet at the same time he exuded dangerous coldness.

"Yes, my husband was an activist as you know and he did indeed speak on behalf of Viena's freedom. But his life's philosophy always favored peaceful solutions. I am certain that if he were alive today he would oppose armed intervention in Viena's affairs."

"How on earth can you expect support for peaceful resolution from Lieutenant Weissenberg – that's completely illogical," Anna Liisa said, suddenly joining the conversation. "He is a soldier trained in Libau, not a pacifist."

Gilbert Weissenberg turned to look at his newly found defender. His face broke into a most delighted smile.

"Thank you for those words, Miss Huotari. You are closer in age to me, and therefore you understand ..."

"The lieutenant is saying that Ilja Huotari and I are fossils," Katri said.

The atmosphere, which had become quite tense, relaxed and the conversation took on a lighter tone, although the topic remained serious.

Anna Liisa realized to her horror that she could not resist the charm of Lieutenant Weissenberg. The man spoke with passion and got his listeners to believe his words.

Anna Liisa noticed that she was comparing the lieutenant to Kaarlo. It felt both unfair and embarrassing, but she could not help herself. The lieutenant was a soldier and an officer, used to giving orders and making demands, and something of that aggressiveness entered ordinary conversations as well. He looked deep into the eyes of his conversation partner and did not relent until he had his way. Kaarlo was an artist, sensitive and a romantic – he was soft, and would rather give in than demand.

"I refer again to the citizens' meeting at which the decision was made to demand of the government that the Karelians, Sami, and Veps of Viena, Archangel and Aunus be formed into the republic of Karelia!"

Gilbert Weissenberg challenged Ilja Huotari with his gaze.

"Lieutenant Weissenberg perhaps didn't notice that the Vienans did not make any public statement in favor of joining together; the speeches were made primarily by the Kuusamo people who were born in Viena," Ilja answered, still disagreeing with the young man.

Time passed; the evening grew dark. The lieutenant took out his pocket watch and looked at it. His horse was waiting at the sauna shore – he still intended to travel to Uhtua for the night. He kissed Katri on the hand, bid farewell to Ilja Huotari with a deep bow, and then took Anna Liisa's hand between his hands.

"You are a teacher – at which school?"

Anna Liisa tried to answer the man's gaze calmly, but there was something insolently intimate in his eyes, which confused her thoughts.

"At the small Syrjäkylä school," she said. "I don't have a teacher's certificate. I am only a high school graduate."

"You have an important mission as a Finnish-language teacher of Viena's children," the lieutenant said looking deep into Anna Liisa's eyes. "You can teach them the right kind of patriotism, unlike some Uhtuan teachers, who teach the children Bolshevism. We have to work to weed that out."

Anna Liisa escorted the man to the hallway, while Katri and Ilja remained seated in the parlor. In the hallway Samuel handed the lieutenant his fur coat and helped him put it on. Then he bowed and withdrew. For a moment, Anna Liisa was alone with the lieutenant.

"I am glad to have met such civilized people as you all are," Lieutenant Weissenberg said. "I am especially glad to have met you. I didn't recognize you at first in the afternoon on the ice, only after you said your name. I saw you last summer in Uhtua, and I haven't been able to get you out of my mind. If we were in Helsinki I would ask you out to dinner, but since we are in Viena I invite you for a sleigh ride. Will that be acceptable to you?"

Anna Liisa did not know what to say. She could feel her cheeks blushing. Should she accept? That would probably not be dangerous. She just nodded.

When Anna Liisa returned to the parlor Katri, too, was holding a glass of cognac. Anna Liisa flung herself into her chair with a brooding look on her face.

"He invited me for a sleigh ride; he said if we were in Helsinki he would invite me out to dinner."

"Do you trust him?" Ilja asked with a gentle glance at his granddaughter. "I am jealous of you. Isn't one man enough? Does another one have to show up and court you?"

"No one will fool Anna Liisa," Katri said calmly. "Furthermore, Lieutenant Weissenberg was a most pleasant young man, so polite and civilized."

"Too civilized," Ilja growled, staring at the women from under his thick eyebrows.

"I believe you really are jealous," Katri said with a smile.

"And surely not only of me," Anna Liisa added.

The women looked at each other and burst into cheerful laughter. Ilja stared at them, a little embarrassed.

But then Anna Liisa's face became serious. "I don't quite understand what they are saying about Uhtuan teachers. *Buobo*, what does it mean?"

"Persecution, interrogations ... interfering in the lives of the Uhtuan people," Ilja said quietly.

Katri nodded. She understood Ilja. He was an honest man and he held absolutely firm opinions about most things. He was also very particular about the difference between good and evil. He detested violence and weapons. Katri already knew that the Jägers would not get any monetary support from Huotari. If it was up to Ilja, Viena would not be liberated with arms.

"Fanaticism is never a good thing," Ilja said. "And it has also been said that patriotism is the last hiding place for many a scoundrel. I can understand somebody like Malm, bringing his troops here. His grand father fought in the Finnish War, and he has military traditions to keep up. But I am afraid of these young officers who have been trained in Germany – they have the skill, but do they have the wisdom to use it?"

Anna Liisa looked at her grandfather with surprise, maybe even a little agitated.

"*Buobo*, now I don't understand you. You, too, want Viena separated from Russia!"

"Yes, I do. But I also want what's best for Viena! There has been a storm in Russia and the heaving waves have not yet died down. We don't know what will ultimately happen. How does Bolshevism differ from Czarist rule? Finland got its independence, but already they are fighting a civil war! Do we wish the same fate for Viena? Do we want Viena to be liberated in a way that leads to its ultimate destruction? Even the very thought is horrifying to me."

Anna Liisa nodded earnestly. *Buobo* was quite right; she had simply given in to Lieutenant Weissenberg's enthusiasm. Reality was something entirely different: the horrors of war. And Kaarlo was in the midst of them. Anna Liisa's heart ran cold when she recalled Kaarlo's second letter, which had been written much later than the first one:

My little darling!

You can't imagine all that I have encountered. This is a soldier-to-soldier combat war and not a guerrilla war. I was in Vaasa just a few days ago when the 27th Jäger battalion arrived from Libau by ship. That was only the main group. The reception was magnificent. I saw General Mannerheim, the supreme commander of the White army at close range. They are saying that the Jägers are being dispersed as training officers to various parts of Finland. Perhaps some will be coming to Viena, too, for there is a lot of talk of Greater Finland.

I think of you, there's no summer like last summer! It's like a dream and I live in that dream. I live as long as I see you. It's hard for me to be a soldier because I am a violinist. But even a violinist has to take up arms for his country. Without you I would die. Only the fact that you exist gives me strength to fight for my existence.

My treasure, Anna Liisa – yours only!
Kaarlo

After her *buobo's* words, Kaarlo's letter tore Anna Liisa's heart even more. It was agonizing to think that a sensitive artist must kill and fight. A Gilbert Weissenberg could do it, he was trained as a professional fighter. But Kaarlo was trained to magically conjure up lovely melodies on the violin …

The day's events felt very confusing and even oppressive to Anna Liisa. Her world had been safe ever since the moment her *buobo* had moved to Uhtua. This house had been her haven, both concretely and symbolically. Now everything had changed in the course of one year. Nothing old and nothing of what had been held to be true could be trusted to be right any longer. It still felt completely unbelievable that the Czar had been toppled from his throne and that the old Russia no longer existed. And how she had rejoiced last December when Finland declared its independence.

Now the joy had turned into tears and sorrow, and nobody knew how long the killing would continue in Finland. *Buobo* was right – it would be terrible if war came to Viena.

Anna Liisa tried to dispel the oppressive thoughts from her mind. She tried to think of Gilbert Weissenberg. *Buobo* might well be right about the cause, but he had judged the lieutenant wrong … So the man had visited Viena last summer - and remembered her … The thought set her in turmoil.

She bid her *buobo* and Katri good night. She looked at them from the door: they sat near each other holding hands …

Snow had begun to fall outside in large floating flakes. First they almost melted as they touched the ground, then they began to harden already in the air, and suddenly the whole region was in the middle of a heavy snowstorm. Samuel sauntered to the door and remained there.

"What is it?" Ilja asked.

"Oh, just this snowstorm," the old man said. "Like on the Atlantic in the old days. Do you remember, sir?"

"How could I forget?"

Samuel's wrinkled face was wreathed in smiles.

"We couldn't see more than a hundred yards ahead."

"Fifty yards!" Ilja said. "And another ship almost touching the side!"

"That was some snowstorm," Samuel chuckled. "And it was in the month of May! The African guys came out on deck to marvel; they had never seen snow before at that latitude …"

Samuel enjoyed a few more moments of his reminiscences, then he said: "I'm going to bed, I've already locked the doors."

"Locked?"

"I thought that would be best. There seem to be all kinds of people roaming around at this time."

"All right, in that case. Good night."

Samuel pattered across the hall to the room behind the kitchen. He pulled his jacket off while walking and coughed a couple of times as if to clear his throat.

Mrs. Jenny came to say good night as well. She set the dining room chairs in their places, and wiped the table with the hem of her apron.

"We'll let the girl sleep in tomorrow morning," she said. "She's exhausted, the poor thing."

"Yes, let her sleep," Katri said smiling. "Good night."

Ilja had poured himself some more cognac. He warmed the glass between his hands while looking out at the snowfall through the curtains. The blizzard was impenetrable. Snow seemed to be whirling everywhere – the whole world was white. Fortunately, one can get to Uhtua along the shores; otherwise the Libau man might have got lost in the snow.

"There's quite a drift already in front of the door, and the veranda seems to be full of snow as well," Katri said as she returned to the parlor.

"If we can't get out in the morning, Teppana will dig us out for sure."

"I hope he doesn't hurry very much," Katri said quietly.

The embers in the fireplace were dying out. The snowstorm had let up for a while, and when Ilja opened the heavy drapes, the whole room lit up from the glitter of the snow.

Katri sat on the sofa with her feet pulled up under her. Her hair was tousled and her cheeks still glowed red.

She looked at the man's leisurely pace and suddenly felt enormously happy.

She remembered how difficult the relationship between her and Ilja had been at the beginning. How gloomy the fall had been when she had left with the child for Sortavala; Ilja had been disappointed by their departure. The hatred had run so deep in all of them at that time that they had not even tried to resolve anything. She also remembered what people were saying after Greta's departure. They said Ilja Huotari had had Outi as his mistress for quite a while. And he probably had; from Huotari Point to Outi's place was only a little over half a mile. Ilja had never spoken with Katri about Outi, nor did he have to. In Katri's view no one was obligated to give an account of their previous life, whatever it may have contained. Deep inside, everyone is accountable to themselves – that is enough. Katri had been exceptional also in that she had invited Outi to Huotari Point when Ilja was gone. People had been ready to award her a halo for it, but Katri had refused to accept it. She felt great sympathy for Outi, specifically as a woman. Outi's lot in life was not an easy one. She had only wanted love, and men had exploited that need. Outi had aged too; her child was a teenager and her old father had died. She tried to survive the best she could in her little cottage. Katri had got involved to the extent that Ilja now inconspicuously funneled money to Outi so she did not have to starve. And why shouldn't he do that; he helped many other Uhtuans as well.

"What are you thinking?" Ilja asked as he came back to the sofa …

"Oh, my …" Katri was startled. "I was thinking about Outi … How she might be doing in her ramshackle house, if anybody is shoveling snow and if she is warm enough? Her daughter, by the way, is Darja Mihailovna's pupil in Ryhjä."

"Is she? I wouldn't know the girl, I've probably never even seen her," Ilja said. Then he looked Katri in the eyes and continued: "Before Outi I had never met a woman who didn't demand something from me. And after Greta left, my hunger for a woman was huge. I have never wanted to deny that."

"You liked Outi a lot."

"Yes I did – but now I have learned to love."

It was quiet for a while in the room – only the howling of the wind was heard from behind the window panes. Suddenly Katri felt the man's arms around her. She looked up and saw Ilja's eyes, which were filled with affection.

"Katri, I am now a free man. Will you marry me?"

Anna Liisa, too, heard the wind howl. She had been lying awake, staring in the dark at the bluish ceiling and trying to restore order to her thoughts and feelings. But she felt as if she were a winter night's wind gone astray, a wind that roamed aimlessly in the roof structures and the desolate crowns of the trees and could not seem to find its way to the open expanse of the lake where the shores could not be seen.

Finally she lit a candle and sat up. From the stairs she heard steps and muffled speech. She tiptoed to the door and opened it slightly: *Buobo* was walking with Katri at his side toward their bedroom door and then they stopped. Anna Liisa saw them kissing. She sighed silently: *Buobo* had finally proposed marriage, she thought. She returned to her bed and blew out the candle. Darkness enveloped her smiling face.

Sunday morning dawned snowy and clear. The front door could in fact not be opened before Teppana came and cleared the snow from the veranda and the area in front of the door. So much snow had come down during the night that the drifts reached to the eaves of the sauna. Huffing and puffing, Teppana began to clear the path to the sauna.

Anna Liisa came downstairs first. *Buobo* and Katri were still sleeping. Anna Liisa waved her hand to Mrs. Jenny.

"Come and have a cup of coffee with me."

Mrs. Jenny was neat and starched, as if she had not taken off her lacecap or her apron all night. The breakfast was set on the side table in the dining room: fresh wheat bread, bacon, eggs, and coffee.

"Already?" Mrs. Jenny whispered, guessing from her expression what Anna Liisa had on her mind.

"I believe so," Anna Liisa whispered back. "I saw them last night as they came upstairs. They kissed at the top of the stairs like a young couple. You mark my words, we'll have a wedding soon."

"Oh my goodness, I say – at their age!"

Anna Liisa laughed out loud.

"You should have married that Samuel yourself," she said. "How nice it would be now to wake up all warm and snug together."

"You be quiet, girl. Listen, I had myself such a husband that compared to him Samuel is just a beggarly old thing. But Kustaa died there in the Copper Cliff mine."

While they were talking, Katri and Ilja appeared at the door. Anna Liisa instinctively rose to her feet.

"Well … tell us, tell us!"

"What on earth should we tell you now?" Ilja asked.

"Don't be a tease, *buobo* … Did you propose to Katri?"

Ilja looked sternly at Anna Liisa.

"Now listen to that child! No respect at all …" Then a broad boyish grin spread all over his face. "Well, I did propose to her! And you'll get your wedding! So what do you think now that your aunt will be your step-mother?"

They all laughed together. Anna Liisa rushed to embrace the engaged couple.

"*Hospody*! What an unforgettable Sunday!"

In the afternoon Anna Liisa pushed through to the old house through a new snowstorm. She shook the snow off her clothes in the vestibule and ran into the old living room in her socks. Nasti and Teppana were already waiting impatiently for they were in the habit of reading the *Tales of a Field Surgeon* every Sunday, when possible. They had coffee first, and then Anna Liisa went to her old bookshelf and took out a thick book. Nasti got comfortable in her chair and Teppana moved a little closer on the bench. Anna Liisa opened the book close to the end. She showed them the last pages.

"Today we will come to the end," she said.

" Don't you babble now, just read," Nasti said.

And so Anna Liisa read:

"As the revolution spread over the entire city and Stockholm heaved like a sea in a storm, Paul Bertelsköld hurried with thumping heart to the Marquise d'Egmont's hotel. At the gate he met the guard, standing calmly with a rifle at his shoulder. No assault had been made; there was no danger in sight. In a considerably calmer state Paul ran up the secret stairs. The door was closed. He knocked. No one answered …"

"Don't stop!" Nasti sighed as Anna Liisa paused for a moment.

"The beautiful Frenchwoman lay there dressed in her pale-colored morning dress, yet herself almost paler on the small chaise longue, which was upholstered with light-blue silk. She seemed to be sleeping, but her chest did not rise. Her thick brown hair spread, half unbraided, over her naked shoulder. The diamond hairpin, which held her ribbon head-dress in place, glittered in the sun; a white rose was pinned to her bosom ..."

Anna Liisa read on, looking once in a while at Nasti, who listened with her mouth open but without uttering a sound.

"Is there a letter?" Nasti asked

"Yes, there is a letter."

She continued: "Your Highness, My Love! If we cannot be together, why should I live? Do not get angry with me that I part with my life at the same time as I part with you. My life has not been of any use; I wish that my death at least will be of some use. You should know, therefore, that I have procured for the King of Sweden both the time and the money without which he could not have saved his kingdom. I have procured them by an oath that I cannot break. I have sworn that from this day on, I will give myself to a man whom I detest. But Herminie d'Egmont does not sell herself. My creditor will receive only my lifeless body."

Large tears rolled down Nasti's cheeks. Teppana, too, had to cough in his palm. Anna Liisa wanted to smile, but kept her expression serious.

"The book ends with a poem," she said. "Shall I read it to you?"

"Read it," Nasti managed to say despite her emotions.

And Anna Liisa read:

In Ester's house,
A home of gold.
No happier abode
Could one behold.
The sweetest court
Was Ester's home,
An orphans' port
That was her dome.
Joy's greatest place
Was her embrace.

Anna Liisa closed the book. She had now read to the very end. Nasti sat with her hands in her lap, looking very unhappy.

"What about next Sunday?"

"I'll bring another book," Anna Liisa promised. "I'll look for something exciting, something just as good as the *Tales of a Field Surgeon*."

Nasti sighed. Teppana nodded. The Sundays were nothing without these reading sessions. Anna Liisa got up, hugged Nasti and stroked Teppana's thin hair.

"I am off again in the morning."

"I'll go with you on my skis," Teppana said. "You won't be going alone, that's for sure. Let's ski in a row, I'll open the track."

The Sunday came to an end, but not the snowstorm. As far as the eye could see, the open expanse of Lake Kuittijärvi was covered with, heavy new snow. And it kept coming down incessantly.

The weight of the snow had broken off branches, and the path Teppana had cleared had disappeared by evening.

Anna Liisa woke up early on Monday morning. She got dressed in warm clothes, ate breakfast, and threw on Katri's old wolf's fur. Teppana was already waiting in the kitchen. He had a heavy rucksack on his back, which contained food for the Syrjäkylä school for the week. Anna Liisa's knapsack had food for the children. Teppana had brought the skis to the veranda; he tied them to Anna Liisa's felt boots and then they started their struggle toward the lake through the snow.

Katri and Ilja stood by the parlor window watching as the travelers pushed along onto the ice of Lake Kuittijärvi.

The skis sank into the snow – the wet snow stuck to the bottoms of the skis in big clumps. Anna Liisa became exhausted almost immediately. Luckily, Teppana was skiing in front of her; it was a little easier to ski in his tracks. Slowly they made their way forward along the shore of the lake, until they finally got to turn into the shelter of the forest.

It was oddly quiet in the forest, for the snow had muffled all sound. They skied forward as if in a strange wonderland.

“If you still can make it another couple of miles, it’ll ease off,” Teppana said once in a while comforting her. “Just tell me if you run out of breath …”

Anna Liisa clenched her teeth. She could take it, she wasn’t that weak! She lifted her skis, one after the other: left foot up, thump it into the snow, right foot up, thump it into the snow. A deep furrow was left behind them. After two hours of trudging through the snow they caught sight of the Syrjäkylä school between the snowy trees. The log house had one classroom and a storage room and at the other end of the building two rooms for the teacher to live in. There was a small sauna by the shore. There were no neighbors; the nearest houses were a mile and a half away.

As Anna Liisa skied into the yard after Teppana, she saw three children already waiting there. They rushed to help their teacher, to get her knapsack off, and her skis upright against the wall.

“How did you get here from your faraway village?” Anna Liisa asked. “You too, you little rascal,” she said to a boy who never seemed to cease grinning.

“Palaga isn’t coming, he broke his ski,” the boy announced.

“Well, that’s too bad,” Anna Liisa said. She took the rucksack from Teppana and asked him to come in.

“I’m not coming in quite yet,” the man said. “I’ll get a shovel and start shoveling. I’ll check the well, too, while I’m at it.”

By mid-day Teppana had finished the shoveling. Twelve kids had waded to school from the remote villages this morning. Most had come on skis, two on sleds, and someone had trudged through the snow on foot.

Anna Liisa made tea as her first chore. The children had traveled to school in deep snow, and needed to get something hot to drink. The classes started a little late, but otherwise it was a terrific day. By mid-day the well was usable again, the yard cleared of snow, and the fire-wood carried in and piled beside the stove. Teppana shouted from the doorway that he would be back on Wednesday to check on things. Anna Liisa hurried to the window to wave to him. For a short moment she felt wistful as she saw that familiar figure disappear toward the school's sauna shore, but then she looked at the children's bright eyes and said:

"Take out your pencils and erasers! Hey, you rascal – don't chew that pencil!"

At the end of the school day, Anna Liisa always felt dead-tired. She sat at the teacher's desk for a long time in the twilight. She marked tests immediately, for she didn't really have anything else to do here. Now when it was impossible to move about outdoors, she took the interior route to her living quarters. Before that, however, she locked the door conscientiously.

Her small apartment was cozy and neat. The larger corner room, whose window looked toward the lake, had a white writing desk, a narrow bed, two soft armchairs and a table, a bookshelf that covered a whole wall and beside the bed a white washstand. The kitchen had more space; there were cheerfully motley ragrugs on the floor, white chairs around the kitchen table, cupboards, and a stove for cooking. In the hall was a pantry, whose shelves got filled regularly on Mondays when Anna Liisa returned from Huotari Point.

She had been alone at her school since the previous fall. Teppana had transported everything Anna Liisa needed here by horse; there were books, one shelf after another, clothes so she did not have to bring them back and forth, a sewing basket for needlework and an ornamented rose-patterned dinner set for four. The stove was her *buobo's* invention and simply excellent; Anna Liisa made herself dinner every evening. She baked for the children, made soup that they ate at least for two days, and the children in turn helped her with the dishes and cleaning the rooms. Anna Liisa knew that for some of the children from the wilderness villages the meal they had in school was the only warm meal of the day. They were all like a large family. Occasionally some mother would make pies; sometimes someone brought milk or bacon. Most often the children would bring salted fish that was available during winter.

It was lonely at the school, but Anna Liisa had never been afraid there. Not even late in the fall when the dark forest sighed like a horde of ghosts. Anja's school was six miles away, and Anja was not afraid either. All the houses were familiar; there were no strangers roaming in the forests.

At least there had not been, Anna Liisa thought. Had the situation changed now?

The dusk of this winter day had enveloped the solitary school building. Only a faint light in the window reflected onto the snow. It comforted the skier who sighed with relief pushing forward the last few feet with her ski poles. She undid her bindings, and stood the skis up against the wall. Then she looked around. On the empty yard she saw crisscrossing paths. Anja glanced at them with envy. Someone had been here to help Anna Liisa – she herself had to do even the heavy work at her school. The Marjavaara school was old and dilapidated despite the fact that Ilja Huotari had ordered repairs to be made there as well. But Anna Liisa's school was new ... logs that still looked quite fresh, large windows, a veranda. Anja once again felt that familiar bitterness; it was so ingrained in her that it sometimes frightened her. There were only about six miles between their two schools, but they had not seen each other very often during the winter.

Anja shook her clothes clear of snow by the corner of the building. Her old fur coat was worn bare in some spots, but it still kept her warm.

She knocked on Anna Liisa's kitchen door and just in case, she announced who was behind the door. She could hear steps immediately.

"Open up! It's me – Anja!"

"Oh, my goodness!" she heard from inside the door, and then it was pulled open and Anna Liisa's surprised face appeared. "Anjuška! This time of the week! Come in, my dear friend."

Anja left her fur coat and her felt boots in the vestibule and walked into the warmth of the kitchen. There she stopped and sniffed the air.

"You have been baking – what a wonderful smell!"

"You're staying for the night, aren't you?" Anna Liisa asked and bid her friend to sit down. "You won't have enough strength to ski back to Marjavaara any more tonight."

"No, I really don't. You can't imagine how much snow there is in the forest."

"I know it; I skied here only this morning from Huotari Point. A horse won't get anywhere in those drifts."

"How are they at Huotari Point?" Anja asked a little timidly. "Are they all well?"

"Yes, they are fine."

Anna Liisa put the water kettle on the stove.

"What about you?" She said. "Has anything happened? I have been a little worried about you."

"Nothing much. I just felt like I had to come here. I need someone to talk to."

They had tea and ate pasties that Anna Liisa had baked. Anja recounted news from her own school. To Anna Liisa she looked healthy and happy, for her body had filled out since the days at the Sortavala Girls' School and she looked altogether prettier. She had let her brown hair grow and nowadays tied it in one long braid at the back. But she had not learned to dress. Anna Liisa sighed inwardly as she looked at her friend. She looked like a Russian matuška.

Then her glance met Anja's gray-blue eyes, and she thought she saw something that Anja tried to conceal.

"Are you afraid of something?" asked Anna Liisa, putting her knitting down in her lap and looking intently at Anja. "You talk and talk, but never get to the real stuff."

Anja lowered her gaze; her face had grown serious. Silently she nodded.

"Tell me, tell me everything!"

Anja started in a quiet voice:

"They have been to warn my mother. They said that unless she quits speaking about socialism, she will be arrested. There are Whites in Uhtua ... Oh, Anna Liisa, I just learned that they have founded a Karelian Liberation Association. They are planning to get 25,000 members, can you imagine! And Mannerheim has reportedly promised to rid Karelia of Bolsheviks. Do you know what that means? There will be war here, too! And you and I are on opposite sides!

Anja burst into tears. Anna Liisa stared at her friend stupefied, and was unable to say anything at first. What did she mean – opposite sides? Aloud she asked, “What do you mean, opposite sides?”

Anja raised her teary face. Had Anna Liisa really not understood?

“Oh, you poor innocent thing,” she said. “You probably think you are neutral at Huotari Point, but in a class war there is no such thing. There are only two sides, the oppressors and the oppressed.”

Anna Liisa’s face darkened. Again Anja was talking politics. She tried to interrupt but Anja motioned for her to be quiet.

“You were born the granddaughter of Ilja Huotari,” Anja said. “That already makes you upper class. I again am the daughter of Darja Mihailovna, the strange Bolshevik teacher. That determines what side I am on. I couldn’t become anything different. Mother made me this way. But so that you would understand, I would like to explain her motives, why she became a Bolshevik. She isn’t crazy even though people say she is.

“Of course not,” Anna Liisa mumbled.

Anja told her mother’s story.

“In Russia in 1887 when Darja Mihailovna was a little girl of nine, her father belonged to a revolutionary terrorist party, which called itself The Will of the People. On the first of March, the party tried to assassinate Czar Alexander III. The attempt failed and fifteen students who belonged to the conspiracy were arrested. The court sentenced five of them to death. One of the five was little Darja’s father. He was hanged in May. Darja’s mother was left alone with six children. Darja never forgot what happened to her father. While she went to school in St Petersburg, she joined various organizations whose goal was to topple the Czar by terrorist means and establish a democracy in Russia.

My mother and father came to Uhtua to teach when I was two. Father soon died of consumption, but mother stayed on. She fed me revolutionary ideas – or poisoned me, as those who think differently would say. Aunt Natalia’s teachings were similar, although she was a social democrat.”

Anja looked seriously at Anna Liisa.

"To tell you the truth, I, too, can never forget the fact that my grandfather was executed."

Anna Liisa had not known this story. But even if she had known it, nothing would have changed in her attitude toward Anja.

"On the one hand I understand you, on the other I don't," Anna Liisa said. "It is after all more than thirty years since your *buobo's* death. It happened before you were born."

"Some wounds never heal," Anja said.

Anna Liisa shook her head.

"No," she said. "I cannot accept your way of thinking. If people don't learn from the past, they are doomed to repeat the same mistakes over and over. You, too, should know that the Finns and the Vienans will not accept the Bolsheviks in power – they are Russians, and what we want is freedom from Russia."

"Socialism does not know national borders."

"It seems to me that it does not know anything – at least not what people think," Anna Liisa said. "People want to live in peace. Nobody wants war."

"Unfortunately you are wrong," Anja said quietly. "There is a big industry that thrives on war."

Anna Liisa became silent. She felt uncomfortable; Anja took the discussion to topics that she had never even thought about.

"You haven't yet told me what you are afraid of," she said trying to bring the discussion back to its original topic.

Anja rubbed her forehead; her hands were shaking.

"The Jägers are saying publicly that the Bolsheviks will be wiped out in all of Viena. If they get the upper hand, they surely will go ahead and do it. Then they will also wipe out Mother and me."

Anna Liisa's heart ran cold. She had not dared to formulate the matter in her mind in such concrete terms. But Anja was speaking the truth. She had seen the men's expressions herself; they would have no mercy on anyone.

"You must be more careful with what you say," she said to Anja. "You don't have to fear the Uhtuans – we know you and your mother. But it is best not to provoke the Finns. I at least am afraid of them."

Anna Liisa told Anja about the incident that had taken place the previous Saturday on the ice of Lake Kuittijärvi. Anja knew immediately who the right woman was they were looking for.

"I will have to be careful," she said. "Fortunately, I have friends here."

The words sounded threatening to Anna Liisa's ears. Anja must mean Reds or Bolsheviks – so they were somewhere in the area! Suddenly she, too, was overcome with irrational fear. What if Anja told the Bolsheviks about her, that she opposed them?

"Anja ..." she managed to blurt out. "We cannot be enemies. We have been friends since childhood."

"In this war even friends may end up under different flags."

"Is that right in your opinion?"

"What is right is what a person's conscience feels is right."

A great silence descended between them. Then Anna Liisa made a bed for Anja on the kitchen floor and went into her bedroom. Anja sat at the kitchen table for a long time, resting her cheek on her hand and looking into the dark night.

By Friday the snowstorm had died down altogether. The sun began to shine from a clear blue sky. There was more snow everywhere than Anna Liisa ever remembered having seen. In the schoolyard the children had shoveled anew the paths that Teppana had made. The snow banks, which lined the paths, were so high that when one of the boys went to fetch water from the well, only his hat was visible.

Together with the children Anna Liisa had peeled potatoes, and while the potato soup was boiling on the stove, they had held a mathematics test in the classroom, talked about America, and practiced penmanship.

While the children concentrated on their writing, Anna Liisa had already been thinking of Saturday. She looked forward to going to Huotari Point more eagerly than usual, for she wanted to hear what was happening in the world. No news arrived at the Syrjäkylä school, but her *buobo's* house got all the news. Ilja Huotari's house had always been ahead of its time. Various newspapers from all over Finland came to the house by express mail, because Ilja had greased the paper carriers' palms with money.

Syrjäkylä, which is Finnish for "remote village," was aptly named. Anna Liisa had often lamented in her mind that she felt as if she lived in a sack. The days at school were always the same: the morning began with morning prayers according to the Eastern Orthodox practice, and then classes; then in between they ate and in the afternoon, around two o'clock, while it was still light in the winter, she sent the children home.

That is how this Friday had passed as well. When the children had left, Anna Liisa had locked the doors because a vague fear had been planted in her mind. She had washed, changed into lighter clothes, and now she sat writing a letter to Kaarlo:

My Darling Kaarlo,

How difficult it is for me to picture you with rifle in hand, fighting there in Ostrobothnia against your own countrymen. My darling, I don't understand the meaning of this civil war. I would perhaps understand it if the fighting men were trained soldiers, but not when men who are strangers to violence are forced to wage war. You are in my thoughts day and night. When I go to bed I press the icon of the Mother of God of the Konevitsa convent against my forehead and pray that you are alive and well.

We have had a terrible snowstorm. When I skied here to Syrjäkylä behind Teppana, I almost drowned in the snow with my skis. The snow has been coming down for five days in a row, but now the storm is over. Trees have snapped under the weight of the snow. The paths in the schoolyard are deep as trenches. The children are well. Fortunately they are diligent and don't give me much worry. I do worry about Anja. She came here to see me and talked about things that have made me scared. A platoon of Jägers have come here from Vaasa. One of them said he had come to Vaasa from Libau. His name is Gilbert Weissenberg, he is a lieutenant. He came to visit my *buobo* last Saturday. I am scared, although I am not quite sure why. The atmosphere here has become so tense. I miss you, I will never forget last summer and what happened to us. I was so happy then.

Your Anna Liisa

As evening came she again sat down by the window with her knitting. Sometimes during moments like this she yearned for someone to talk to about what had happened during the day. During her lonely evenings, she had often thought about her mother and father, about their death. Would her life have been different if they had lived? Now Katri and *buobo*, and Nasti and Teppana had taken the place of her parents. Actually she had had more security than any other young woman she knew. She thought of Anja who had never had anyone but her mother. She was still bothered by Anja's depression; she felt she was partly to blame, too. Why couldn't Anja be like others?

Suddenly, she heard the snorting of a horse outside. Anna Liisa was startled and rushed to the kitchen window. A horse-drawn sleigh had stopped at the other end of the building. It was already dark out, but the moon lit the yard enough so that she could see a man get out of the sleigh. She pulled away from the window and rushed into her bedroom to blow out the candles. Then she tiptoed to the vestibule. She could only hear muffled sounds from outside. The newcomer was tending to his horse, putting a blanket over its back and a sack of oats before it. Then she heard steps, they circled around the school and then stopped in front of the teacher's apartment.

Anna Liisa's heart was about to stop when she heard the first knock, quite near. She did not budge, the house was dark, maybe the visitor would go away … Then she heard a second knock, a little harder. Anna Liisa covered her mouth with her shawl and crept into the corner, into the darkness. After the third knock she heard a voice:

"Miss, open the door! This is Gilbert Weissenberg!"

Weissenberg!

Anna Liisa hurried to the door. The man was familiar – it was no bandit after all. She pushed the door latch to the side and opened the door. The man stood there in front of the steps, and in the moonlight Anna Liisa recognized his face. She motioned for him to come in.

"It's dark here. I put out the candles when I heard the sound of the horse."

The man took off his fur coat in the kitchen while Anna Liisa groped in the dark for matches and the candles. He did not say anything, just cleaned his boots on the kitchen doorstep and then hung his fur coat on the rack. Then he came to the bedroom door. Anna Liisa was just getting the first candle lit.

"I apologize for frightening you, Miss," he said. "I was over in Jyvälahti and someone gave me directions to the path leading here to the school. There's an enormous amount of snow and the horse is totally exhausted; it almost didn't make it all the way wading through the snow. I stripped the horse of its harness by the corner of the house."

"Please come in," Anna Liisa said. "May I offer you something?"

"Thank you, to tell you the truth I haven't had anything to eat all day," the lieutenant said. "I would be most grateful if you were to give me a piece of bread."

Anna Liisa had fresh bread that Teppana had brought, jam that Mrs. Jenny had made, and ham and salted fish. She looked furtively at the man as he ate at the kitchen table with concentration and in silence. When he was finished he thanked her, stood up, and put the dishes in the washtub.

"Thank you, you saved my life," he said smiling. "I would have had a trip of several hours to Uhtua; luckily I found you."

Anna Liisa did not know how she was supposed to treat her guest. Now that the candles lighted up the room, she felt shy. The man made himself at home, spoke and laughed, looked around at the cozy little home, and let his eyes wander over the rows of books in the large bookshelf. He was wearing the trousers of his military uniform, but instead of the uniform jacket, we wore a high-necked gray sweater.

"Anna Liisa," he said and smiled a little bashfully. "Can I call you that? 'Miss Huotari'sounds so formal to me. Just as I thought, you know how to make your environment cozy. What are you reading – Ah, Puškin! Lermontov. And of course *Tales of a Field Surgeon*."

"I know that book by heart," Anna Liisa laughed. "I have been reading it to our servants Nasti and Teppana on the weekends. We just finished it last Sunday. My aunt Katri bought me the book when I was eight years old."

"Besides being beautiful she is obviously also a wise woman."

Anna Liisa nodded and touched her hair discreetly. She had tied it together with a thin ribbon.

"You look very much like your aunt," the lieutenant said. "Your mother must have been very much like her."

"Yes, at least so far as I can remember," Anna Liisa said. "My mother and father drowned when I was nine."

"I didn't know. I'm so sorry."

They were quiet for a while, then Anna Liisa gathered enough courage to ask a question that had been bothering her.

"You said you were in Uhtua last summer. Were you not in Libau?"

"I went to the celebration and I saw you there," the man said. "Since then I have been thinking of you all the time."

It irritated Anna Liisa that he did not give a straight answer. But perhaps he had his reasons.

"Why did you come here?" she asked sharply.

The man raised his hand as if giving an order not to say anything, not to ask anything; everything would be all right.

"I was looking at the moon when I rode here earlier," the lieutenant said suddenly. "Red moon over White Sea ... The sky is so full of stars over here and the air so clear, so crisp ... When I rode my horse on the ice, I saw the most beautiful blue moment of my life. I thought then that I love this land, and its silence."

Anna Liisa listened in amazement. The man she had thought to be a gruff soldier spoke like a poet. Why had he come here, what was his business here?

"You didn't answer when I asked why you have come here?"

The man sat down across from Anna Liisa and looked in her eyes for a long while.

"You are not really that naïve," the man said. "Surely you know I came because you are a lovely woman."

Now Anna Liisa got a hold of herself.

"There certainly are countless lovely men in the world, but I definitely don't rush to seek them out."

"Of course not," the lieutenant said. "You are a woman who has had an old-fashioned upbringing and who would never do anything that would be considered improper. And what is more, you are engaged."

"How did you reach that conclusion?"

"I just happen to know, is that not enough?"

Anna Liisa looked at him at length. What was this man driving at?

"Even if I had not received an old-fashioned upbringing," she said, "I would consider it improper that you come to my home uninvited.

Especially when you know I am spoken for. You strip the horse of its harness and prepare it for the night. You take it for granted that your horse will be allowed to rest here overnight."

"And I as well," the man said "I am at least as tired as my horse."

All of a sudden, the talk had turned tense and cold. The man's indescribable impudence angered Anna Liisa. She glanced at the envelope on the table, which she had left there to be mailed. The man noticed her glance and took the envelope in his hand.

"Kaarlo Meinander," he said. "He is a brilliant violinist, one of Finland's most talented at the moment. I congratulate you, your fiancé is a fine man. He is fighting on our side, even though he is not a trained soldier."

"Thank God he isn't!" Anna Liisa said with flashing eyes and snatched the envelope from the lieutenant's hand. "I love him and he loves me. We will get married as soon as this damned war is over."

The lieutenant laughed quietly.

"You don't have to prove anything; I believe you," he said. He was silent a moment and then he said in a firmer voice. "But don't call our war damned, it is Finland's liberation war. Many a good man falls for freedom and fatherland. And soon you, too, here in Viena will have to make up your minds."

"Don't start lecturing me," Anna Liisa snapped. "Would you be good enough to stop immediately. I am not on the side of your patriotic enthusiasm! You come here to Viena and ask for weapons. You want to kill people of Viena and don't care what kind of horror you spread around you."

"Do you know who our common enemy is?" the lieutenant asked. "Its name is Bolshevism."

"I don't want to hear it!" Anna Liisa said sternly. "Go away, Lieutenant Weissenberg. I did not invite you here."

Anna Liisa went to the door and opened it. The candles in the room reflected a strange light – the shadows on the walls swayed as if they had been dancing. Gilbert Weissenberg rose and walked up to Anna Liisa. He kicked the door shut and took the girl's hands in his and bent down toward her.

"You cannot chase me out in the middle of the night," he said. "It is soon midnight and the horse is sleeping. You know it's at least a three-hour trip to Uhtua after this snowstorm."

That was true. Anna Liisa pushed the man away and went into the bedroom. She took a mattress and dragged it to the kitchen floor. Then she got a blanket, a pillow and sheets from the bedroom. While she made the bed for him, he stood by saying nothing. When she was finished with the bed, Anna Liisa cast a cold glance at the man and said curtly from her bedroom door: "There you are, sleep well."

She closed the door and latched it shut from inside. Then she got undressed and went to bed. For a while she heard the sound of steps from the kitchen; then it was silent.

When Anna Liisa woke up the next morning, she moved about very quietly in order not to awaken the man. Having dressed, she peeked into the kitchen; it was empty. He had left. The bedding had been folded neatly in front of the closet, and on the table was a slip of paper:

> *Beautiful Anna Liisa,*
> Thank you for the accommodation for the night, I slept really well. I will mail your letter, I promise. I will return next week to Jyvälahti. Even though you do not care for me one bit, I will still come and visit you.
>
> *Your Gilbert*

"Your Gilbert!" He is not mine, Anna Liisa raged inside. Why did he come here to mess up my life! May he stay away – far away!

The daily life at Huotari Point had now been shaken up once and for all. Ilja Huotari, who had had a proper road built behind the house to Uhtua, now watched day after day as different military detachments marched along the road. Now they came riding their horses, particularly the Whites from Finland; now by horse-drawn sleighs like a band of brigands with sleigh bells ringing.

Ilja Huotari had also heard that there were French-English troops in Murmansk. The Finns were reportedly not allowed to engage in battle against them, but had to try to maintain friendly relations and negotiations and make it clear that the White guard from Finland had come there on the invitation of kindred people in Viena to liberate it from Bolsheviks.

Ilja had growled contemptuously when he had heard those motivations, and his voice was just as challenging now as he talked to the group of men standing by the door.

"Who has invited whom! I am just asking."

The men belonged to the same detachment as Lieutenant Weissenberg. Some of them were Jägers; some from the civil guard. They had volunteered to go to Viena to kill Bolsheviks and to train others to do the same.

"No one here in Viena has asked for you or your weapons," Ilja said.

The men were devastated. Ilja Huotari was the richest man in Viena, a capitalist, and therefore more likely than anyone to support the White side. Why then this uproar? The section leader was Ahtiainen who hailed from the Kuusamo area. He finally had to ask directly:

"What are you grumbling about, Mr. Huotari? Are you on the side of the Bolsheviks?"

Ilja Huotari looked into the man's serious and honest face and said:

"I am on nobody's side. I already told you so. I just don't want people to start fighting here. Viena has to be developed, of course, but it will have to happen by peaceful means."

"One wouldn't think that a man who has seen the world would speak so naïvely," Ahtiainen said with a laugh. "You, sir, have so much earthly wealth that if we were to leave the area, and the Bolsheviks came here, they would order you out into the yard, stand you against the wall and shoot a bullet through you. That's the way it is, Mr. Huotari. That's their idea of peaceful means."

"Violence breeds violence," Ilja said.

"He who lives by the sword, will die by the sword," Ahtiainen replied. "The world is full of phrases. But when the Reds come and force you to look on as they rape your women, a phrase is a pretty poor weapon. They have tasted blood now and they are dangerous."

Ilja Huotari looked inquisitively at Ahtiainen; he was no fool. He knew he was in hot water because in times like these, people believed in words that appealed to emotions.

Ahtiainen noticed Huotari's perturbation and quickly added in a more moderate tone of voice:

"It would be good for you to remember, sir, that we are not a pack of bandits like the Bolsheviks. The Civil Guards are now part of Finland's defense forces and are precisely for law and order."

Ilja Huotari's eyes flashed, but he said nothing.

"Besides, the war is already here," Ahtiainen said. "Last Thursday enemy troops were seen at the eastern end of Lake Paanajärvi. They have a weapons cache somewhere around here."

"I can only repeat what I have already said," Ilja responded. "Independence is of course important also to Viena, but it seems to me that Finland is interested in Viena only so it can have a buffer between itself and Russia."

He was quiet for a while, then he added in a tired voice, "But of course, all of this talk is for naught, if the war truly is here already as you say."

"Unfortunately, that's the way it is," Ahtiainen said in a conciliatory voice. "Malm, the chief of the Civil Guard district, has been named supreme commander of the Viena Karelian troops."

Ilja Huotari nodded; he knew the man.

"I have heard he has arrived with his troops in Uhtua via Vuokkiniemi. And before them came a group of Finnish Reds, who have been scaring people by telling them that the Whites rob villages and burn them to the ground. We've had a big job calming people down."

Ilja nodded, looking at the same time out on the lake. The ice road was the only road to Uhtua from the west. He would still see many military detachments marching along it here in the heart of Viena. He turned once again to look at the group of six men by the door. What did these men want from him? Of course, he knew the answer. They wanted him to adopt a positive attitude toward them because Ilja Huotari's word had some currency around here. But why did they not understand what he was saying? That the people of Viena consisted of poor, dispossessed people who did not understand high-flying speeches. These people needed the means to live and to make a living, and those requirements could not be fulfilled by waging war. Was that so hard to understand?

"I do know what the government of Finland and the headquarters want," Ilja Huotari told the men. 'In Finland, they want the Vienans to take up arms and begin actively to work toward joining Finland. But I tell you straight: Viena's people don't want war; you will not get a single man from here."

Ilja saw the men's expressions harden, and so he continued more moderately.

"It's no use for you to imagine that I would be on the side of the Reds. Never! I love and respect this land enough never to change sides. But leave me alone. I will not participate in any armed struggle, nor will I support it in any fashion."

Ahtiainen realized the discussion was finished.

"Goodbye!" he said and saluted. Then he turned around and went ahead of his men to the hallway. Samuel had already stumbled to open the door.

Katri came into the parlor when the men had left. Ilja poured himself a cognac. He looked out the window to the lake as the group of men on horseback disappeared behind the point in the direction of Uhtua. Then he turned to face Katri.

"Did you overhear us in the library?"

"I did and I agree with you. They have not been invited here, the Vienans are not ready for war …"

"Who would be," Ilja said with a joyless smile. "The damage has already been done – they have managed to sow fear among the people. People are afraid of robberies by the Whites, and they are afraid of the Germans – All the people of Viena know that Finland is allied with Germany."

Katri pressed herself against Ilja's back and wrapped her arms around him.

"Let's try to forget all the bad things," she said.

"That's true," Ilja said. "Tomorrow is the most important day in our lives."

"That's right," Katri said with a laugh and gave the man a squeeze. "You know, I think it's wonderful to get married at the age of thirty-eight!"

"I wanted you for my wife already six years ago," Ilja said. "You are my only love and my heart's desire. Whatever happens in Viena, my love for you will remain. It would be sad if we had to leave this place, but at least we would be leaving together and starting a new life in Sortavala."

Sunday dawned beautiful. Two horses with sleighs left from Huotari Point. Ilja Huotari sat in the first sleigh, with his wife-to-be, Katri, and Anna Liisa. Teppana sat on the driver's seat, looking self-important. In the other sleigh Samuel was holding the reigns, and behind him sat Nasti and Mrs. Jenny wrapped in thick coats. The frost bit their cheeks as the horses turned onto Lake Kuittijärvi.

"Look, *buobo*," Anna Liisa exclaimed and removed her hand from the muff. "Somebody has lined up little spruces to indicate the road on the ice. This is the first real road to Uhtua."

"But it does not run on land," Teppana pointed out, making the others break into a cheerful laugh.

Road projects had always been close to Ilja Huotari's heart. Already as a young man he had been fed up always having to go by boat or to trudge along causeways. During the winter there were of course the ice roads, but in the summer the villages were isolated. And so he had had a road built on the north side of Lake Kuittijärvi all the way to Uhtua. Many people from the remote villages now used it.

The ice road was fast. Soon they could see the islands near Uhtua. They saw soldiers on the shore, on horseback as well as on foot. The further they went, the more soldiers and vehicles they saw. Ilja Huotari's facial expression turned stern. The information he had received was obviously correct: war had caught up with Viena. You could draw no other conclusion from these preparations.

The horses ran on, sleigh bells ringing, then rose onto the shore and continued toward Ryhjä village.

Not many people were in the church – only a small choir in addition to the people from Huotari Point. The wedding ceremony was performed by a Russian priest, Father Alexander, who was not very much liked in Uhtua, despite being quite civilized and pleasant in manner.

Here, too, public opinion was anti-Russian, and the Eastern Orthodox priest with his long hair and black cassock was a perfect symbol of everything Russian.

Father Alexander looked gently at the couple standing before him: Ilja Huotari, born in Uhtua a long time ago, then for decades living abroad, and then returning to his childhood region – next to him an attractive woman, with candle in hand. Katri's eyes were serious as she received the blessing for the marriage.

"God's servant, Ilja, is hereby crowned with God's servant, Katri, in the name of the Father, and of the Son, and of the Holy Spirit. Amen. Lord, our God, crown us with honor and respect. You will place golden crowns on their heads. They asked for their lives from you, and you gave it to them."

Katri Jääskeläinen had become Katri Huotari – in the name of the Father, and of the Son, and of the Holy Spirit.

Nasti and Mrs. Jenny stood side by side behind the bride and bridegroom, handkerchiefs in hand. Beside them stood Anna Liisa, who was also trying to hold back tears. Teppana and Samuel had remained farther behind. A small choir had been put together from the church singers and they sang with clear voices. Then Father Alexander said the blessing and the ceremony was over.

Ilja Huotari kissed his wife's hand and led her out of the church.

There were soldiers in the yard of the nearby school. The snow came up to their knees, and their horses stood by the post, blankets slung over their backs. Ilja Huotari recognized Ahtiainen among the men, the Jäger who had visited Huotari Point yesterday. The man waved his hand and, surprised, came to greet him.

"At church at this time of the day? Is there a service going on?

"No, only a wedding," Ilja said. "And I was needed there. I am, you see, the groom."

Ahtiainen lit up with a smile.

"Dear Madam," he said reaching his hand out to Katri. "May I congratulate you! I had no idea yesterday that it would be such an important day for you today."

Katri nodded smiling. Ilja was already waiting by the sleigh, ready to help the women.

It was then that Anna Liisa noticed Gilbert Weissenberg, who came out of the school door. He saw them, too, and began to walk toward them with long strides and with the hem of his fur coat trailing in the snow. When he had reached the sleigh, he greeted the women and asked how they were. Anna Liisa followed the man from the corner of her eye. She could not understand why this man unsettled her so. Everything within her told her she could not stand the sight of him, but still she felt flustered, almost feverish. Then, to her dismay, she heard her *buobo* say:

"You are of course welcome to join us for dinner, Lieutenant."

"Thank you, I would be pleased to accept," the Lieutenant replied. "Tomorrow we will continue to Lake Paanajärvi."

Then he turned to shout to one of the men on the steps to the school:

"Kaarnamo, go and get the lady's letter!"

A moment later the man came running toward them and handed Anna Liisa a letter. It had got mixed up with the mail coming to Uhtua. Anna Liisa recognized Kaarlo's handwriting on the envelope. Blushing, she stuck the letter into her muff. This was too much! It irritated her to no end that Lieutenant Weissenberg mailed and delivered her letters.

The horses began to run again and soon Ryhjä village was left behind as Teppana steered his horse to trot onto the ice road with the other sleigh following. Anna Liisa held back for a while, but then she could not refrain from asking:

"*Buobo*, why did you invite him to dinner? I don't like the idea one bit."

Ilja Huotari was in the middle of straightening his fur hat and looked at his granddaughter astounded.

"Why shouldn't I? It's our wedding dinner, and furthermore, Lieutenant Weissenberg is a very well-mannered man and a worthy companion."

"But I don't need a companion," Anna Liisa said curtly, sinking deeper under the furs.

"Is the letter from Kaarlo?" Katri asked.

"Yes – he is now in Vaasa. Or at least he was there when I last heard from him. Unless he has succumbed to the Reds' bullets."

"*Hospody*!" Katri said. "Don't say things like that out loud."

In the afternoon they ate lunch together in the large dining room. Nasti and Teppana were seated on one side of the bride and the bridegroom, and Mrs. Jenny and Samuel on the other, because they were wedding guests. Anna Liisa did the serving, despite Mrs. Jenny's protestations. They stayed at the table for a long time. There might be only bad news coming from the outside world, but happiness and sweet peace reigned today in the Huotari house.

In the early evening, Ilja stood by the window looking out on the lake. He saw a group of soldiers riding along the ice road toward

Jyskyjärvi. One rider separated from the group and steered his horse through the snow toward the tip of Huotari Point.

"Lieutenant Weissenberg is on his way!" Ilja told the women over his shoulder.

Kaarlo's letter gave an unembellished description:

My Little Girl,

It is late at night and a soldier friend of mine, Kaarnamo, is off to Viena. I don't want to scare you, but the latest battles have exhausted my strength. I am now at Savitaipale, near Lappeenranta. We will continue our trip from here to Vyborg. This is fratricide, that is my sole opinion about this war. We know that there are 15,000 Reds on their front. Last week terrible battles raged without interruption along the entire front. Fortunately, we have managed to win in defensive battles; the Reds have been considerably weaker. I know I shouldn't write to you about these things, but I do it because I know this letter will come to you directly.

Anna Liisa, my love, is it true that I will never again be able to pick up a violin and play? God knows, I would like to. I am no soldier; I am an artist, and an artist cannot kill another human being! The world situation now gives cause for great concern. According to the information we have received, Germany is now supporting the independence aspirations of the areas surrounding Soviet-Russia. But there is something odd in the peace agreement, despite the fact that the Germans occupied Livonia and Estonia last week. If only this war would soon end! I will send you word as soon as I have met some Jäger going to Viena. It is possible that I, too, will go there one day. You are so far away, my love – too far. I would like to marry you immediately as soon as this war is over – only that way will I be able to protect you.

Your Kaarlo

Anna Liisa had read the letter as soon as they got home from Uhtua. She had sat in her room for a long while with her face buried in her hands. She felt Kaarlo's pain and the longing in his heart as if they had been her own feelings. She would have given anything to be near her man.

But she had to go downstairs, take part in her *buobo's* and Katri's wedding luncheon as if nothing had happened.

Now, looking tired, she looked at Gilbert Weissenberg who had brought German wine as a gift of courtesy. The bottle was opened immediately and a toast was proposed to the wedded couple. Ilja took note of Anna Liisa's reluctant expression and remembered what she had said on the trip home: "Why did you invite him to dinner?" Yes, why?

Ilja could not answer that question. But why not – the lieutenant had interesting views on diverse issues and he knew how to conduct a civilized conversation. Ilja liked to see such people around him, but, with the exception of Ilmari Kianto and a few ethnographers, the educated classes had not discovered the remote Viena.

Ilja had to admit that he had invited the lieutenant to dinner for purely selfish reasons. What was wrong with that?

For dinner they had lamb, which Mrs. Jenny had prepared the Canadian way, and then they moved to sit in the parlor. Anna Liisa took the tray from Mrs. Jenny and poured coffee for all four of them. She felt she was like a sleepwalker; everything was unreal. The whole time she sensed and knew what the lieutenant was thinking. The man did not let her out of his sight for a minute; he even touched her hand when she poured the coffee. Anna Liisa knew that the touch on the hand meant so much more in imagination, a much more intimate embrace. She noticed that she thought much more about this man than about the one whose letter she had read this afternoon in such agony in her room. She was in agony now as well, but in a different way. The man confused her completely.

Anna Liisa could not avoid participating in the conversation. Then she had a chance to look at him openly, at his bright blue eyes and blond hair, which occasionally as he moved his head fell boyishly over his brow.

"It has been said that the Red terror is a weapon used against a doomed class, a class that does not understand that it should disappear from the stage of history," the lieutenant explained passionately. "That is the view of the Reds. They want to speed up the demise of the bourgeoisie. What then is the mission of the Whites – only to slow down the rise of the proletariat? According to the Reds, that, too, is an attempt to turn back the clock."

"Why should the bourgeoisie have to die?" Anna Liisa asked.

"There are many reasons why the Reds hate the bourgeoisie," the lieutenant said. "They are educated, they own and control the commerce and industry, and the leadership positions in politics, and they control the capital and the banks. In short, they represent civilization and money."

"Now you are oversimplifying things," Anna Liisa said. "I cannot for for the life of me believe that even the Reds would think that way. Finland's parliament has had a social democratic majority. The country has had a socialist Prime Minister, Tokoi, who is an educated man and who has been a worker, too. *Buobo* has actually dug for gold with his own hands in the same gold fields, together with Tokoi. From my Sortavala days, I know many poor people who are well-read and cultured. Why they are poor is another question altogether. What are the causes of social injustice? Why does some upstart and, to put it bluntly, stupid boss get to be rich while a brilliant poet must remain poor as a church mouse. Why does an honest working class woman never earn enough to buy nice clothes? Is she a lesser woman than some senator's wife who doesn't do anything? I believe the Reds use the word bourgeoisie only to personify these social injustices. Thinking anything different is conscious distortion of facts. Or stupidity."

Anna Liisa was short of breath when she finished speaking. Ilja laughed.

"There you go, Lieutenant! Anna Liisa has her very own thoughts on things; even I haven't had any say over them."

"Should you have had any?" Anna Liisa asked. "You have traveled the world, seen misery and poverty, and now you live here in poor Viena in superabundance. It is easy for you to say whatever you want. I, too, believe I know the nature of the Finnish working man: he doesn't make trouble without reason, except perhaps when drunk. But he will rise in rebellion only when forced into a corner. If his children are hungry. If he no longer has any other solution. That is why I am appalled by all this talk about ridding Viena of Bolsheviks. Why do you want to beat the downtrodden? Give them circumstances worth living, work and bread – and they won't rebel. Lieutenant Weissenberg, why do you want to eliminate those who dare think differently from you?"

When Anna Liisa was finished, an absolute silence had descended on the room. Lieutenant Weissenberg's cheeks were flushed, and for a moment Anna Liisa thought he might leave in anger. But then the lieutenant gave a forced laugh. "Miss Anna Liisa," he said, "if I were not right now sitting in this gorgeous parlor of this magnificent house, I would, on the basis of the words just spoken, have been prepared to swear that you are an agitator for the Red side. I don't understand why you defend them."

"I am not defending anybody," Anna Liisa said. "I do know that the Reds are capable of cruelty and wrongdoing. Human beings behave like wolves if the situation is allowed to reach the state of war. I was only trying to say that generalizing is always dangerous. And I hate war!"

"I don't," Lieutenant Weissenberg said coldly and raised his wine glass. "Composure," he added to Anna Liisa whose voice had kept rising more and more.

The atmosphere was spoiled. Katri tried with her gaze to calm down Anna Liisa whose eyes flashed with fire. Lieutenant Weissenberg tried diplomatically to change the direction of the conversation, exercising restraint and speaking gently.

"I believe your heart is on the side of the White army."

The lieutenant's sudden meekness was a sign to Anna Liisa that he was belittling her.

"I am on no one's side," she answered curtly. "I read Kaarlo's letter this afternoon; he wrote about the senselessness of this war. He is an artist and can't understand this kind of killing."

"Dear Miss Anna Liisa," Lieutenant Weissenberg said, "you forget one thing and your fiancé forgets it as well; his participation in the war on the White side is completely voluntary. Nobody has recruited him or forced him to fight. His own sense of honor keeps him there. I know from experience that many volunteers are ready to flee when the war becomes real. In the beginning they are fanatical; only later do they understand the reality of war."

For a moment it was quiet in the room, then Ilja Huotari said:

"You are of course right. Everything is based on voluntary choices. But you know well that the young men don't have even the faintest idea what the reality of war is when they first sign up. They get tired and scared, yet they cannot change the course of events, which they have in a sense dedicated themselves to. That would brand them as cowards. We can only hope that the war will end before they lose their lives. But in the face of Bolshevism we cannot yield – that is my opinion, too."

"I don't wish for Viena to end up in Bolshevik hands," Anna Liisa said heatedly. "But you don't even want to understand what I am saying."

"We do understand," Katri said, entering the conversation. She had sat quietly, listening, and now looked at Anna Liisa gently, understanding her views better than the men. She tried to mediate:

"You wish that people would analyze matters before taking any action. That is wise. But what can we do when actions have already been taken – perhaps very hastily and without justification? Then prevention doesn't work any more, and you have to address the problem directly. I assume that is what Lieutenant Weissenberg meant. The Reds have certainly suffered many real wrongs; but in the middle of a war you cannot undo wrongs, you first have to bring the war to an end."

"That is right," the lieutenant exclaimed.

"In Viena it is still possible to end the war before it escalates," Katri said. "You come from Finland, supposedly to help, but your assignment is difficult, because people are not willing to cooperate. It must be discouraging. I remember well the moral battles my late husband had to go through."

"Finland lived then under Bobrikov's oppression," the lieutenant said. "Now we are threatened by Bolshevism. It must be destroyed! We have the right to do that."

"Who gave you that right?" Anna Liisa asked quietly.

"We did. We gave ourselves that right. Someone has to have the courage to take responsibility."

The atmosphere was tense. Anna Liisa had clearly forgotten the code of proper conduct and had started to pick a fight. The lieutenant stood up, and took a step toward Katri, intending to say goodbye.

"No, no, don't leave," Katri said. "I invite you to stay the night; we have several guestrooms. Teppana took your horse to the stable, didn't he? It's already past ten o'clock. It doesn't make sense this time of night for you to ride out onto the ice when it's pitch dark."

Lieutenant Weissenberg bowed.

"I would be pleased to accept your invitation," he said. "I will continue in the morning to Jyskyjärvi, actually all the way to Vuokkiniemi."

Ilja Huotari and Katri bid goodnight and went upstairs. Anna Liisa darted after them and caught up with them in the hallway. She threw her arms around her grandfather's neck.

"*Buobo*, forgive me! I am just an awful person!"

"So you are," Ilja said with a laugh. "Just like me when I was young. Fortunately, you get over it as you get older; I am a good example of that."

"Katri ..." Anna Liisa looked pleadingly at Katri.

"You know what, my girl?" Katri whispered. "I totally agree with you! Good night. This happens to be our wedding night, and we now want to be alone just the two of us."

No one cared about Anna Liisa's pangs of remorse. She returned to the parlor. Lieutenant Weissenberg sat in an armchair next to the candelabra and the light reflected on his face. He rose to his feet as Anna Liisa entered the room and he sat down only after Anna Liisa had sat down. He looked at the girl seriously.

"Why do you feel such a great aversion toward me?" he asked. "You said things you don't mean in order to hurt me."

Anna Liisa looked at the man in surprise.

"What are you talking about?"

"You know what I mean," the lieutenant said. "Deep inside you hate Bolshevism just as much as I do. If my words were coming from Kaarlo Meinander's mouth, you would agree with every word. But me you object to."

The lieutenant looked at Anna Liisa in silence for a while, then he continued:

"And furthermore, you pretend. In reality you like me very much."

Anna Liisa looked at him sharply.

"I have never met such arrogance before. You are nothing short of shameless!"

"But I am right," the lieutenant said without flinching. "You know as well as I do that there is strong electricity between us ..." Seeing Anna Liisa's reaction he raised his hand. "No, no, I beg you, hear me out. You are worried about your fiancé, but if you were honest, at this moment you don't even remember he exists. You are a strange woman – the fire in you fascinates me. You're not even aware of it yourself, and you also don't know how beautiful and how exciting you are when you roar your opinions. An enchanting woman!"

Anna Liisa was unable to say anything; she was panic-stricken. She tried to get up from the chair, but the lieutenant stopped her.

"Don't go, I don't know the way to the guestroom – you have to take me there. And you also have to make the bed for me, like you did at the school."

Anna Liisa walked to the door.

"Wait here," she said coldly. "I'll go and make the bed. Can I bring you something from the kitchen?"

"No, thank you. It's your company I want. I'll wait here."

Anna Liisa ran quickly down the hallway and to the guest room behind the library. The bed was already made, for Mrs. Jenny always kept the guest rooms tidy and ready. Anna Liisa lit the candles and put towels on the bed. Then she opened the door to the bathroom in the corridor. She stood in the corridor for quite a while, trying to calm herself down. She couldn't understand what was wrong with her. Why on earth was she so excited? She finally had to return to the parlor; she walked in and sat down on the sofa.

Gilbert Weissenberg had taken out a cigar from the humidor on the table and used the candle to light it. He turned to look at Anna Liisa and then slowly blew out the smoke.

"How well do you know the teacher at the Marjavaara school?"

The question took Anna Liisa by surprise; she was startled.

"Quite well ... of course I know her well, she is a schoolmate of mine and a friend. She is a good teacher ..."

"She is a Bolshevik," the lieutenant said. "Don't try to say you didn't know that."

The man's aggressive tone made Anna Liisa completely flustered.

"I ... I don't know, I can't be sure, we haven't been talking about such matters!"

"Her mother Darja Mihailovna is also a Bolshevik."

"Yes, that's what people say."

The lieutenant chewed on his cigar and stared intently at the glowing end.

"I will give you a piece of advice. Avoid their company. Stay far away from them. That way the Reds will not get their eyes on you. This warning is for your own good. I don't want you to have to suffer."

"Why would I have to suffer?" Anna Liisa asked. "I have nothing to do with this war or with politics."

The lieutenant came to sit next to Anna Liisa on the sofa. They were now very close to each other. Anna Liisa tried to move farther away, but the man was like a magnet and pulled her toward him.

"Now listen to me carefully," he said, putting the cigar in the ashtray. "This is no ordinary war, and this war is not fought by knights. In this war nobody respects women; everybody shoots at everybody. In Finland they have had to execute some Bolshevik women who had been guilty of unspeakable cruelties. They had been completely fearless and unscrupulous. If you are known to keep company with Anja

Remisova, both the Whites and the Reds will draw their conclusions from that. Behave as if you didn't know her; that is my advice."

"I may be naïve, but I don't see any problem here," Anna Liisa said. "We are teachers, not agitators. Her school is a Russian-language one, mine a Finnish-language one – that is the only difference. We have been friends since childhood, and I know her inside out. I don't understand why this war makes her dangerous."

"All Reds are dangerous," the man said. He leaned closer to Anna Liisa and suddenly he took her face between his large hands. "You are a lovely woman – too lovely."

Anna Liisa tried to wriggle free, but couldn't. A warm mouth pressed against hers and she was in an embrace the like of which she had never experienced before. Then the man let go of her and looked into her eyes.

"You are as delicate as you are reluctant. But I don't apologize, I think it is wonderful to kiss you! I understand your apprehension, because in reality you are afraid of your own feelings. I am very much in love with you – I recognized that this evening. I will come and visit you at the school this week, when I return from Vuokkiniemi. And now – good night."

When the Huotari people awoke in the morning, Gilbert Weissenberg was already gone. He had left early in the morning without awakening anyone. The front door was carefully closed, and he had woken Teppana up at five o'clock.

Anna Liisa, too, left early for her school, this time with a sleigh and her own horse. As she drove through the snowy landscape, she tried gingerly to examine her heart. Something irrevocable had happened. Despite her diligent attempts, she could not get Lieutenant Weissenberg out of her mind, not his eyes, lips, embrace ... But now she had to concentrate on her work; she had to take care of the children. And behind it all was her worry about Anja.

Teacher Darja Mihailovna was teaching her first class of the morning in Ryhjä school. She had been a teacher for almost twenty years, and spent most of that time in Uhtua in Viena. The last couple of years she had nursed her consumption at her brother's in Crimea, but when she returned last fall to Uhtua, she had felt so much better, that she had resumed her old job. Her daughter, Anja, had taught as her substitute during her absence and had lived in her house on the shore of Uhutjoki River taking care of their only cow in addition to teaching. Last fall Anja had got a substitute teacher's job in the old school in Marjavaara, and so they both, mother and daughter, had a job this year.

Darja Mihailovna looked out the window in the middle of the class period and suddenly jumped back. The children noticed this and looked out to see why the teacher was so anxious. They saw a large group of riders coming into the yard from behind the church. Some of the children got scared, but Darja Mihailovna calmed them down. There was no danger: the riders were only gathering together. She tried to keep her voice steady and continued to teach:

"No one could have predicted that Russia would become Soviet-Russia," she said. "There is no Czar any more, his autocracy is gone and the voice of the people can now be heard all through Soviet-Russia. Ljuba – who are now governing in Soviet-Russia?"

"The Bolsheviks!"

The pupil was just about to sit down again when the class room door was wrenched open. A group of uniformed men entered.

"Who are you?" Darja Mihailovna asked in a stern voice. "Why are you barging into the class room in the middle of my lesson?"

"We came to listen to what shit you are teaching the children," one of the men snarled.

“You are not to use that kind of language in front of my pupils,” Darja Mihailovna said. “Please leave the room.”

“Shut your mouth, bitch!” one of the men commanded. “We are staying and we’ll be listening to every word you babble. If we hear as much as one word of Red propaganda, you’ll be looking down the barrel of a rifle.”

One of the children started crying from fear, and soon the anxiety spread to the whole class. A couple of little girls ran to the podium, seeking shelter behind the teacher. Pale faced Darja Mihailovna stared at the men. Then she walked to the middle of the room and gathered the children around her.

“Now, calm down,” she comforted them and then she turned to the men. She raised her voice:

“How dare you, brutes, come here to scare the children! Don’t you have any compassion? What have these children ever done to you?”

The men stared at the teacher, sneering openly. Darja Mihailovna saw through the window that there were at least twenty men with horses outside. Somewhere in her soul an image of Anja flashed through her mind. Had they been there already, had these liberators of Viena gone there, too? How will Anja survive?

For a short while nothing happened; then the man nearest to the door turned and went out, and the others followed. Darja Mihailovna took a deep breath. She knew that the fear, if it were to come at all, would come now as a delayed reaction. She knew that nothing would have happened in front of the children, but what about the times when the children were not there. She had to walk every day, morning and night, along the river to her little house in Lamminpohja village. Anja would be coming home on Saturday. They would have to talk, because the hunt for them had begun.

Darja Mihailovna let her children go home early in the afternoon. For the first time in her life, she was afraid to go home. For some reason the group of horsemen had not left the school yard. The horses stood by the post, and the men were standing around, smoking and talking.

Darja Mihailovna tied the black scarf around her head, took her black jacket from the peg and put it on, and finally she threw her empty knapsack onto her back. She stood in the dark classroom for a good while before she could bring herself to go out.

When she had arrived in the morning, she had put her skis up against the wall next to the front door. She had to get them now to go home. She stepped outside with her head erect, locked the school door and turned to get her skis. Suddenly, it was quiet in the yard. The men were standing in a circle looking at Darja Mihailovna. She was frightened; they stood there like executioners. They looked at her and waited for her to leave. What did they have in mind?

She threw the skis to the ground and pushed her black boots into the toe-straps. She bent down to pick up her ski poles and turned to push off in the direction of the village.

There were no Uhtuans out at this time of the afternoon. Or they had stayed inside for fear of the horsemen. When Darja Mihailovna began to ski toward the river, the men jumped onto the backs of their horses and came closer. Suddenly Darja realized that she would have to ski from the yard along an alley formed by the horses. She pushed calmly with her poles and the men's eyes followed her. Nobody spoke, but there was an unmistakable threat in the air. Darja Mihailovna skied toward a house straight ahaed of her, fixing her eyes on it.

Now she would have to keep a cool head. ... As she reached the house she could see the terrified faces of Mrs. Parviainen and her daughter-in-law in the window. She raised her hand, and signalled: do something, get help ... Mrs Parviainen had put her hand to her mouth, for she realized the teacher's panic.

For an instant, Darja Mihailovna thought of skiing into the Parviainen's yard, but then she thought she had to get home, milk her cow, feed her cat, and heat her little house. The riders had slowed down their pace as if they, too, had seen the Parviainen woman's frightened face. The horses were now at a walking pace, following the woman who struggled forward on her skis. Darja Mihailovna pushed and pushed with her ski poles. The fact that the horses were no longer breathing in her ears gave her renewed strength. The Ryhjä houses were left behind, the Uhutjoki River bed went straight north. That's where she now had to go.

The sun was already setting, its reddish disk still visible far beyond Lake Kuittijärvi. The wind had packed snow on the ice on the river and the riverbank. On the highest point of the riverbank, the children had made a ski trail. Along this trail Darja Mihailovna skied with arms that were getting tired. She could no longer see the horses and she sighed with relief. Scaring a lonely woman like that; they wanted to show their might. But soon she would be home, as soon as she crossed the snowy field.

Suddenly, she heard the sound of the horsemen again. And before she knew it they had surrounded her. She looked up in fear and recognized the same men who had charged into her classroom. The men didn't say anything; they just sat there up high riding at a walking pace beside Darja Mihailovna. Darja was afraid. Her arms and legs became paralyzed from fear and suddenly one of the ski poles slipped from her limp hand. She bent down to grope for it, but one of the horses pushed her with its head and she had to leave the pole and continue with only one. She stumbled on her skis, shaking from fear and exhaustion. When she tried to ski faster, the horses also picked up their pace, and when she slowed down, they, too, slowed down. They traveled that way more than half a mile in silence; only the snorting of a horse could be heard once in a while. Darja Mihailovna finally caught sight of her village on the other side of the river and the open field. She let out a sigh mixed with sobs.

But she had not even reached the corner of the nearest house when one of the men threw a rope around her. Darja Mihailovna let out a strangled sound, her other pole fell out of her hand, one of the skis fell off and suddenly she realized she was lying on the ground tied up with a rope like a lassoed animal. The man sitting on the horse shouted something and the horse suddenly shot forward at full speed. Darja Mihailovna screamed in terror, as she realized she was speeding behind the horse. Her face plowed the snow and her limp body tossed about from one side of the bank to the other. She screamed in agony, as the icy surface of the snow gashed her face and tore her clothes. She struck against a rock, but the horse did not slow down; it was now galloping around the field in a large circle. At some point Darja Mihailovna lost consciousness, and when the horse finally came to a stop, she thumped like a bundle into the snow and remained lying there. The man threw the rope from his hand and rode to join his friends. The unconscious and mangled Darja Mihailovna lay motionless in the snow. Two men from a house by the river ran out into the field to the woman. They gave a fearful look at the soldiers who sat on their horses looking threatening, like gods of doom. One of the village men loosened the rope from around Darja Mihailovna's body.

"*Hospody*!" he whispered crossing his heart. The woman was bloodied all over.

"Is she alive?" whispered the other man, equally horrified.

Darja Mihailovna was alive. She opened her eyes when she heard one of the horses snorting again near her.

"This is what you get for teaching the children of Viena Russki ideas!"

On Monday, Anna Liisa let the children go home early in the afternoon. She took her horse and lifted the children with skis and all onto the sleigh. She jumped onto the runners and urged the horse to a trot. The children were shouting with joy.

Anna Liisa drove each one all the way home, even to the remotest house. Left in the sleigh with her was a rascal who lived next door to Anja's school. The mother had wanted her son in a Finnish-speaking school although it made the trip to school quite long.

"Remember to wait for me by the field around eight in the morning; I'll pick you up then," Anna Liisa had reminded the children.

It seldom happened that they would get a ride from the teacher, but the teacher was now on her way to Marjavaara to visit the other young woman teacher.

"Only paying a visit," Anna Liisa had told the school children at the end of the day.

"The teacher is paying a visit!" They were tasting that unusual expression.

"Oh, my children," Anna Liisa had thought with affection as she let the horse trot along a little path, whose snowy surface was packed hard and firm. The houses she saw in the forest were miserable hovels with a cow or two, a horse, a cat and a dog. The fathers were away on peddling trips, while the mothers did all the work around the house and looked after the children. Each year a new child was added to the household although the men were nowhere to be seen. The houses in this remote village were poor and miserable, so poor, that in their eyes, Uhtua was like a miracle with its fine houses and churches. Despite the poverty the children had a great desire to go to school and learn things. Anna Liisa had three pupils whom she should one way or another get to go to middle school in Finland. They had the enthusiasm and the intelligence, although they were materially poor. Perhaps the sharpest mind was this boy who was the last one in the sleigh, that Anna Liisa called "rascal." His nose was running from morning till night, his hands hopelessly dirty, his clothes his brother's too large rags, and his felt boots inherited from his mother. But if you just asked him about math – let's say you ask him to multiply a six-digit number by another six-digit number – and he'd tell you the answer with shining eyes as if he had snatched it from the air. The boy was also quite apt at explaining things.

"When there is poverty," the boy had once said, "all things sink in like a knife into butter. Then things that aren't so good may also get lost. You don't realize then that one could go around things – so that when you don't have meat, you get fish, and if you don't get any fish, you shoot a rabbit."

Anna Liisa had sometimes, quite shocked, thought about this speech by this little "rascal." What incredible optimism was shown by this boy who was the poorest of the poor. And the boy was never in a bad mood or mean; he always had a grin on his face and his nose in a book.

And now they were supposed to be wary of what they taught the children. Anna Liisa had been thinking hard about that, because Lieutenant Weissenberg's warning had made her fearful. She could not remember ever having taught anything that could be construed as political. Had she ever spoken to the children about Russia or Soviet-Russia?

Certainly not. Why would she have spoken of such things?

Anna Liisa pulled the reins tighter in an attempt to get the horse to go faster. She had to warn Anja, tell her what Lieutenant Weissenberg had said.

The road had become better and the sleigh was now moving with good speed in the dusk of the forest. On both sides of the road stood tall spruces covered with snow.

A little before she got to the school, she stopped and let the "rascal" with his skis off. The boy grinned his thanks cheerfully and skied to the front yard of his home. The village of Marjavaara was small; within the radius of half a mile there were only four houses in addition to the school, the "rascal's" home next door, and an old farm. Behind the school in the forest was a clearing which had always been called the "square".

Surrounding the "square" were large boulders that were like seats. The clearing was surrounded by some old beard-lichen-covered spruces, which gave it a mystic feel. The road to the school passed by the "square." Anja had sometimes taken her children there, and even held classes there. There was an old platform high up in one of the large trees. It could not be seen easily, and not many knew about it, but Anja had once come upon it quite by accident and showed it to Anna Liisa, too. Together they had pondered why the platform had been pulled up so high in the tree. Anja thought it was intended for bear hunting, but they had never had it confirmed.

The school itself was a one-story building whose logs had blackened over the years. It was the second public building in the village; the first was a church, which was about to collapse. It had not been used in decades; its door hung loosely on its hinges and all kinds of rubbish had gathered inside. Anna Liisa thought it was the saddest church she had ever seen.

The graveyard next to the church was also neglected; rotted tree trunks lay across the graves, and in the summertime there was so much trash and brushwood that the graves were difficult to see.

The sleigh swept around the corner of the school. A little distance away was a dilapidated sauna intended for the teacher and next to it a row of newlybuilt outhouses. Anja had made improvements happen here; previously, the children had had to go to the bathroom in the woods; now the men in the village had managed to build outhouses. When Anna Liisa took the harness off the horse, Anja hurried out of the door to the yard.

"How come you're here on a Monday evening?"

"You came to see me a week ago Monday," Anna Liisa answered with a laugh.

She brought with her pasties and jam that Mrs. Jenny had made as a present. They went into the classroom, which had three rows of desks. The walls were covered with geographic prints in Russian and children's drawings. The Syrjäkylä school that Ilja Huotari had had built was new and modern, but Anja had many things that had been left behind by the previous teacher and which Anna Liisa had not managed to acquire: good slate-pencils and slates, good white chalk and sponges, with which it was easy to clean the board.

They walked around the school, looking at the books and the notebooks, speaking together like two teachers – about their children and about their school. Anja was, however, on her guard all the time; she knew there had to be some reason for Anna Liisa's surprise visit. They went to Anja's quarters. The apartment was quite neat even though the building was such a hovel. Anja asked her visitor to sit on the chair. She made tea, placed the tea things on the tray and came to sit as well.

"So, tell me, why have you come?"

"Can't you think that I came just because I missed you?" Anna Liisa smiled.

"Not on a Monday night! On a Wednesday maybe ..."

They laughed cheerfully. When they finally stopped, Anna Liisa looked affectionately at Anja. She had suddenly recalled their Sortavala years. How different she had been then, thin like a whisp. Now she was somehow womanly – her white skin and roundness became her.

“What is new with Artturi Kangas, I wonder,” Anna Liisa suddenly thought out loud. He came to mind now because of the Sortavala memories. “Do you know anything about him?”

Anna Liisa noticed to her great surprise that Anja blushed and looked guilty.

“So you have heard something about him. Tell me!”

Anja hesitated, but then she said:

“I have seen him. He was here for a week at Christmas time. He is now in Finland, fighting for the Red Guard.”

Anna Liisa couldn’t believe her ears.

“What are you saying! He was here?”

“Yes, just now at Christmas. I told you that I would be going to my mother’s house for Christmas, but I was here with Artturi. It was the happiest Christmas I’ve ever had. We had only salt fish and fresh bread, but we were happy.”

“Anja – so you do know …”

“I know … I could die tomorrow, but I have lived beautiful moments. They will never return.”

“Why wouldn’t they?”

A sorrowful expression marked Anja’s face.

“I am positive he will die in action. I got a letter from him yesterday. He writes that men are falling like flies, because the German Jägers have arrived. He is now in Tampere, which the Reds have decided to hold on to. The last battle between the working people and their oppressors will be fought there.”

Anna Liisa looked at her friend almost frightened; her face had an ardent, almost fanatical expression. Anja was whipping herself into a rage.

“What on earth are you talking about,” Anna Liisa said cautiously. “The Reds have practically lost the war. They are now setting up detention camps for the Reds …”

Anja took the letter that was leaning against the flower vase on the table and opened it. Her hand shook as she read it to Anna Liisa:

“Listen …”

"I write this to you, Anja, so that you will be careful and defend all that is most important in life for you, for your mother, and for me. The Whites and the Jägers are terrifying; they kill us around here with cruelty and determination. I have heard that there are prison camps being set up for us. I will likely end up in one of those myself, but may our cause help me survive it. Always remember, Anja, that more important than our friendship is to fight on the barricades against the oppressors. Only that way will we achieve equality and self-respect."

Anja put the letter down in her lap and stroked it gently. Anna Liisa said nothing. Anja's face was glowing and she was looking somewhere into the distance. Finally, she folded the letter carefully in four and put it back in the envelope.

Anna Liisa moved closer and took Anja's hands in hers. She spoke quietly as if the walls had ears.

"Listen closely … I have to tell you that a Jäger lieutenant has visited us at Huotari Point a couple of times. He warned me that I must not keep company with you or see your mother. Otherwise the Reds might get interested in me – and of course also the Whites, because it is known that we are friends. He also told me that the Reds kill even women in Finland. Oh, Anja, you have to flee from here! Couldn't you go to St Petersburg for example?"

"Why should I flee? I have my job here. I teach children. Don't be afraid on my behalf – I'm strong. But you are right; we can no longer meet. It would put you in danger. We have to wait until the situation calms down. I won't come to your place and don't you come here either."

Anna Liisa stared at Anja in shock.

"How will you survive here in the middle of the wilderness?"

Anja laughed.

"The same way as you in Syrjäkylä. Your school is even more isolated than mine. I at least have a couple of houses within view; you have no one even nearby."

"But I can ski down to Lake Kuittijärvi immediately if danger lurks!"

"What can you do on the ice?"

Anna Liisa became disturbed – nothing, of course.

Anja had begun to pace back and forth across the floor, quite nervously.

"Anna Liisa … I must tell somebody, if something were to happen to me after all …"

"What would happen?" Anna Liisa whispered.

"If I am taken away somewhere."

"Where? And who would take you?"

Anna Liisa was overcome with anxiety, but Anja motioned for her to be quiet.

"There are weapons here at the school," Anja said quietly. "They have been hidden in the sauna, under the sauna benches. The sauna is old and the sauna benches warped. I put the guns under them and a few boards on top."

"Why on earth do you have guns?" Anna Liisa asked perplexed.

"They are not mine; they belong to the Bolsheviks. I would like to get rid of them, but on the other hand – there they are; and if the Whites come – I have ammunition, too." Anna Liisa stared at her friend wide-eyed. "Good Lord – do you know how to fire a gun?"

She did not know what to think. Anja was a real Bolshevik after all.

"I had to tell someone," Anja said. "In the event something were to happen."

She looked at Anna Liisa almost with pity. If only her friend knew what she had been taught in St Petersburg during the summers – not only shooting, but everything worth knowing about terrorism. Anja was almost shocked how naïve Anna Liisa was. "Couldn't you go to St Petersburg …" As if she would go to St Petersburg now that the revolution was coming to Viena. Never!

At that very moment there was a knock on the door. Both girls jumped.

"Who could that be?" Anja wondered, frightened.

"Let's go together and see," Anna Liisa whispered.

Anja ran to the hallway first, Anna Liisa following. Anja stood in the dark hallway for a moment, then she shouted:

"Who is there? What do you want?"

"It's Teppana Jyrkinen from Huotari Point. Is our Aniviisu there?"

Anna Liisa's face quivered. Aniviisu – that name had not been used in years. She went to the door past Anja and opened it.

Teppana stood at the door with his worn fur hat pulled down to his eyes. At the corner of the school stood a horse and sleigh next to Anna Liisa's horse. Teppana came in and closed the door behind him. He did not even remember to take off his hat. Anna Liisa got frightened. She knew Teppana inside out. Now something bad had happened!

"*Buobo* sent me to get you," Teppana said. "Teacher Darja Mihailovna has been attacked in Uhtua; you must go there immediately, Miss Anja."

Anja was struck by panic.

"Mother ... My mother? Who did it?"

"They didn't say. They just said that Miss Anja must go there immediately."

The girls got into their clothes quickly and ran out into the yard.

"What do I do with my horse – do I take my own horse?" Anna Liisa agonized.

"You take your horse, and Miss Anja can go in your sleigh," Teppana said. "We'll first go to Huotari."

In less than two hours the horses were at Huotari Point. Teppana rounded the tip of the point with his horse and Anna Liisa followed suit. Teppana then went to take the horses to the old house and the girls hurried inside.

"*Buobo*!" Anna Liisa yelled in the hallway so that it echoed in all parts of the house.

Everyone rushed to the hallway: Katri and Ilja Huotari from the parlor, Mrs. Jenny and Samuel from the kitchen.

"*Buobo*, come with us!"

Ilja asked the girls to sit down for a minute. Katri went to get his fur coat.

A neighbor of Darja Mihailovna's in Lamminpää came to tell us," Ilja explained. "He said the teacher had been assaulted and was unconscious, that she had been dragged behind a horse. She is in bad shape, they are afraid that …"

"Oh, Good Lord," Anja said quietly and looked at Ilja Huotari in a state of shock. "Behind a horse … tied up …"

"I think I can guess who are to blame for this," Ilja Huotari said seriously. Katri brought his fur coat and helped him put it on. Soon they were outside by the horses and then the sleigh turned around the tip of the point straight out on the lake. The horse trotted in the twilight along the ice road, which was marked with spruce branches. Ilja sat in the sleigh with both girls beside him. Anna Liisa was greatly relieved that her grandfather had come along, for she felt much safer now.

"Now the expedition has shown its true colors," Ilja said mostly to himself. "They attack innocent civilians. That is not the work of liberators; that is what occupation forces do."

"Why isn't everyone allowed to live and think their own way?" Anja said in a soft voice.

"Anja." Anna Liisa looked at her seriously. "Similarly people in Soviet-Russia would have mercy on those who are not Bolsheviks."

Uhtua came into view; the houses rose dark in the shelter of the embankment, and the church was dimly visible, lighter and farther away. The sleigh glided past Likopää toward Ryhjä village and then along the river to Lamminpää.

Where were the soldiers from Ryhjä village? Where were the troops who had swarmed all over Uhtua on Sunday? Did they move on when they found out that they weren't getting any men to occupy Viena? The heroes accomplished only as much as teaching a lonely, unarmed woman a lesson …

Ilja Huotari felt a strange ambivalence inside him. He was openly on the side of the Whites, yet here he sat in a sleigh on his way to help a Red agitator, for that is what Darja Mihailovna was. But people were allowed to agitate, proclaim their own doctrines, and believe in what, in their own opinion, was the right belief.

The order of events had been established and the newcomers brought up to date. They could not understand that something like this was even possible: that soldiers would force their way into the school while the lessons were in progress, how Darja had skied and been tormented by the horsemen … "Is this how Bolshevism is eradicated?" Ilja asked angrily. Is this what Mannerheim meant when he proclaimed: "I will not let my sword rest in its sheath before the last of Lenin's warriors falls and every hooligan is deported from Finland as well as from Viena Karelia. This was the deed of hooligans and bandits."

They could see immediately that Darja Mihailovna had received serious injuries. The woman was conscious, but was not strong enough to speak. She opened her eyes slightly, then fell back into semiconsciousness. Her face was badly mangled, she had broken ribs, and her legs had several deep open wounds. In addition, she must have had a concussion because she had complained of a severe headache. "Do you know how to dress wounds?" Ilja Huotari asked the old woman who had been fetched to care for the woman.

"*A vot*, I have herbs," the old woman said with a toothless smile.

Darja Mihailovna moaned, and Anja stroked her hair.

"Mother will have to be moved to my apartment in Marjavaara," she told Ilja Huotari. "She can't stay here."

"She isn't strong enough to be transported there," Anna Liisa said immediately, looking at her *buobo*. "Maybe you could get Darja Mihailovna to Anja's place when she has gained some strength and recovered a little bit. They wouldn't dare stop your horse."

Ilja nodded in agreement.

"We'll see to it with Teppana that she gets to Marjavaara. It's too risky to leave her here. We won't leave the woman to die."

"Not even if she is a Bolshevik," Anja said quietly.

What could she now do for her mother? Tears welled up in her eyes again, when she looked at her mother's mangled face. It had been their intent to kill her; there was no doubt about that. She now had to return to Marjavaara and get everything ready so that her mother could be brought there as soon as her condition allowed for her to moved.

Anna Liisa wrapped her arms around Anja's shoulders. There was nothing more they could do for Darja. The horse had to go back to

Huotari because it would soon be night time. The old woman stayed to look after Darja, to milk her cow and to heat her house. Ilja Huotari promised to come and see how the patient was doing the day after tomorrow.

"Look after her well," he said to the old woman and paid her a good amount of money. "Keep the door locked and don't let anyone in. Teppana will visit tomorrow. If something happens before then, just send word to Huotari."

A clear sky full of stars lit their dispirited way home. There was no longer any sign of a red halo around the moon. Anna Liisa noticed this and suggested to the others it was a good sign.

"I at least believe Darja Mihailovna will recover!"

"I don't." Anja said gloomily. "Tomorrow the whole moon will be again red! Everything will get colored by blood!"

Anna Liisa and Ilja exchanged a glance, but neither one said anything. Anja's words silenced them all, and when Anna Liisa looked at the edge of the moonlit forest, it seemed to be filled with ghosts grinning diabolically.

All week Anna Liisa was strangely listless, and the classes were very taxing. She also felt terrible that some of the children had waited for their teacher's horse Tuesday morning not knowing that she had forgotten her promise to pick them up. When four girls had still failed to show up at the school at nine o'clock, Anna Liisa had taken her skis and gone to get them. The girls had been waiting for her at the side of the road in the freezing cold weather.

"Where is your horse, Miss," they had asked. "Did you go home last night already?"

"I had to take the horse back last night; now hurry to school. I am sorry I couldn't get word to you."

They had returned to school skiing in a row, and Anna Liisa let them go home earlier than usual.

At night her mind became even more restless – and she knew why. She was waiting for him to come. She waited with such passion that her eagerness frightened her. But Lieutenant Weissenberg did not arrive, although he had said he would come when he returned from Vuokkiniemi. Had the rumor of their trip to help Darja Mihailovna already reached his ears? But that was simply Christian charity for one's neighbor. One cannot abandon a human being. Everyone should understand that … Or did anyone understand anything anymore?

The man did not come during the week. On Saturday afternoon a sleigh turned into the schoolyard, and Anna Liisa's heart started thumping. But it was *buobo* and Teppana. Anna Liisa had been waiting for them as well. She ran out into the yard to welcome them.

The March day had been sunny and warm. Water was dripping from the eaves and the wet snow seemed to evaporate visibly.

Ilja Huotari gave Anna Liisa a hug, feeling relieved when he saw that she was all right.

"We took Darja Mihailovna to Anja's apartment," he told her.

"How is she doing?"

Ilja shook his head.

"Quite poorly. She complains about her heart and is unable to walk. She does nothing but sleep."

"How will it end?" Anna Liisa asked with a worried look as they went inside. "Fortunately Anja knows how to care for her, so she'll at least have emotional support. *Buobo*, I'm scared that Anja is there all alone."

"We were just talking about that very same thing with Katri," Ilja said as he sat down on the armchair. "We came to the conclusion that you'd better heed Lieutenant Weissenberg's advice and refrain from going to visit Anja. The Reds do value the fact that we went to help Darja Mihailovna, but with that act we upset the Whites. I'm not worried at Huotari Point, but you, too, are alone here in Syrjäkylä – who knows what might happen. Starting next Monday, Teppana will come here and keep you company, whether you want it or not."

"Teppana! What would he do here?"

"He'll be sitting on the firewood box with a shotgun in his lap guarding you," Ilja said. He attempted to make his voice sound playful, but his expression was grave. "This situation can drag on for a couple of months. Then there will have to be a resolution, one way or the other."

Anna Liisa felt cold inside. So this is where we are now in Viena Karelia, too – daily fear?

"Very well, Teppana can come on Monday, we'll get along."

The plans for Teppana to come to Syrjäkylä were, however, cancelled already Saturday evening. When the men returned to Huotari Point late in the afternoon, Teppana still went out to fish on Lake Kuittijärvi and he skied into open water.

He did manage to climb up from the hole, but the trip home was so long that he almost did not make it back alive. Nasti came running to get help from the people in the new house when her husband had collapsed on the floor half frozen. During the course of the evening Teppana got a fever, actually such a high one that he had delirious all night.

"Pneumonia," Katri said as she changed cold packs on the man's forehead. During all of Sunday everyone in turn ran from the new house to the old one, and Nasti feared the worst. Teppana was, it's true, a sorry sight; it was difficult to understand how a robust man could be so helpless. Severe cold shivers shook his whole body, he coughed incessantly, and the fever rose so high his skin felt like a glowing wood stove. Then Ilja remembered that he had a stock of drugs in the tower room that he had used during his years at the seas. He rummaged through the case, and he finally pulled out the little bottle he had been looking for which said: "PNEUMONIA." The bottle contained a special cure for pneumonia, to be taken seven drops a day.

"This was given to the seamen when they fell ill with pneumonia," Ilja said. "Let's try it; it won't do any harm."

On Monday, Teppana's fever began to subside, but he still had to remain in bed. He was not up to being anyone's guard, for he would hardly have had the strength to hold the shotgun.

The occupiers of Viena from the Finnish side were not discouraged despite the fact the Viena people were suspicious and reticent toward them. They held different information meetings and program evenings, which automatically turned into political events.

Ilja Huotari had out of curiosity attended a few of these meetings and noticed that a couple of lists were passed from hand to hand for signatures. One of the lists was a petition for help against Bolshevism and an indication that the people accepted that Viena be joined with Finland. The other petition requested a complete list of the names of all Bolsheviks in Uhtua.

The petition to the Finnish government was signed by about three hundred Vienans. At the same gathering a Civil Guard branch was established in Uhtua. The other list remained blank, at least at this gathering.

Now Ilja knew where they were heading. They wanted to make Viena a part of Finland by force of arms. And then they had the audacity to talk of independence for Viena! Ilja had let them know what he thought of such a petition – and so no Huotari Point people's names appeared on the list.

That fact was of course duly noted by the Whites, and when the horsemen rode by Huotari Point along the ice road, some White officer would look angrily in the direction of the house. Ilja Huotari's reputation was no longer good.

This did not bother Ilja. He looked out from his tower window far out across the icy expanse. He knew that the invader did not have much time.

While Teppana was lying in his bed and Anna Liisa was busy teaching in Syrjäkylä, Ilja Huotari made the trip between Huotari Point and Syrjäkylä quite frequently to make sure that everything was fine with the girl. He also went to the Whites' meetings in Vuokkiniemi and Uhtua, despite the fact that he never signed any petitions or participated in the debate.

A few times he met Commander Malm of the Viena Karelia forces, face to face and then he criticized the selfishness of Finland's ambitions.

"I know what you want," he told Malm. "You want a union between Finland and Germany, but you forget that we, the people here in Viena, hate the Germans, and even if you were to order us with gun in hand to love them, it wouldn't happen. Furthermore, the young men in Viena are tired of war; they want to go peddling as they have always done. Do you yourself really believe in this talk of liberating Viena? I don't think you do. You are after all a thinking person. Is Finland full of war-crazy people? You have a civil war going on in your own country, yet you want to go to Viena to rattle your swords!"

"You want the Reds to govern Viena, do you?" Malm asked in an ominously quiet voice. "I would not have believed that of you."

"Of course I don't want the Reds to control Viena, don't speak such nonsense," Ilja Huotari said. "I want to develop and build Viena, create a more wholesome future for it – you know that. But you cannot build the future with arms or by waging war!"

Malm said nothing to that. Ilja Huotari knew that his words rang on deaf ears. And he was not surprised. In all wars, truth is among the first casualties.

The following week Anna Liisa got scared when one evening she heard a loud pounding on the door. She peered cautiously through the kitchen window to see who was there. A horse was standing by the corner of the house, stripped of its harness and covered with blanket. A hot tinge ran through Anna Liisa. She knew who was behind the door.

"Lieutenant Weissenberg," Anna Liisa said as she opened the door. She felt relief and fear simultaneously.

The man's face was serious as he entered the house. He took off his overcoat and threw it on a chair.

"I have been unable to come earlier," he said with an apologetic smile. "I was fighting in Paanajärvi all week."

"How many did you kill?" Anna Liisa asked quietly.

The lieutenant's eyes flashed as he answered:

"Two."

Anna Liisa adopted a sweet facial expression.

"Lieutenant Weissenberg," Anna Liisa said. "How does it feel to be a killer. Not a very good catch for a week's work. Did you drag anyone behind your horse?"

Weissenberg did not answer; he just sat down in the armchair in the bedroom and took off his boots without asking permission.

"Do you intend to stay overnight again."

"That's what I thought," the man answered. "You can't bring yourself to throw me out anyway. Besides, we have a lot to talk about. I haven't seen you since you and your grandfather played Good Samaritan."

"You know about that?

"I do. I know that, and I know many other things. We have time to talk. But have mercy on me and give me some food!"

Anna Liisa had prepared food, she boiled potatoes, carved a roast, and brought pastries and raisins to the table. The man had eaten voraciously, and she had looked at him with sidelong glances. She had wondered in her mind what kind of a man he really was? Where was he from? What were his parents like? Did he have sisters, brothers? The man had appeared somehow vulnerable while he was eating and had eaten with gusto, with full concentration. When he was finished eating he thanked her, then grabbed Anna Liisa's hand and said:

"Let me sleep an hour, then I can hold your hand for the rest of the evening."

But Gilbert Weissenberg did not hold Anna Liisa's hand an hour later. He slept for many hours and such a deep sleep that every once in a while Anna Liisa had bent down to check that he was still breathing. The man would probably not have woken up all evening if the snow hadn't started to slide off the roof of the school. It came down with such a rumble that even Anna Liisa got startled. The man sprang to his feet and stared around him with a frenzied look in his eyes.

"It's just the snow sliding off the roof," Anna Liisa said calmly.

"How long did I sleep?"

"Three hours."

"Why didn't you wake me up?"

"Why should I have woken you up?"

"Because I want to be awake when I am with you."

"I, however, like you better when you are asleep."

"Anna Liisa … Why are you so rude to me?"

Anna Liisa was embarrassed. Was she rude? Yes, she was. Maybe they should talk about it …

"I believe that you want to stir up my mind and my soul in one way or another," Anna Liisa said. "You are trying in every way possible to turn our relationship – no, what am I saying, this is no relationship!"

"Come and sit here beside me," the lieutenant said. "Yes, yes, don't be afraid, I promise to behave."

Anna Liisa sat down beside the man. Now they were close; their faces were close and their knees were close. Why had she sat down here … She could have gone to sit on the chair opposite him. What was it about this man that he could control her with his words? Anna Liisa tried to get her thoughts to settle down. She loved Kaarlo. He was her whole life. She would marry him, will bear his children and would live her life happily with Kaarlo!

The lieutenant appeared to read Anna Liisa's mind.

"I know you are engaged to Kaarlo Meinander," he said. "I don't know whether you love him. I only know that you did not want to free yourself from my embrace that evening. You would have liked to stay there. Please, let me be close to you."

"Let's talk about something else," Anna Liisa said. "For example, why you came here tonight."

"I came because I wanted to see you," he said. "But you are right, we also have to talk about the things that have happened since we met last."

"Do you mean our trip to Darja Mihailovna's house?"

"That among other things," the lieutenant said, "and also about the fact that you went to visit that woman although I advised you not to. Why did you go?"

Anna Liisa felt ill at ease. Did the man not understand?

"You cannot forbid me to meet with my childhood friends! She is there in the middle of the woods all alone. I would be a frightfully bad person if I were not worried how my friend was doing in a place like that. You and the rest of the soldiers are the reason that people have to be afraid here these days!"

"Weapons have been hidden in Uhtua and surrounding villages," the lieutenant said. "As soon as the Bolsheviks get their hands on them, they will use them to shoot us. We have not yet found any weapons cache, but we know that the people who are hiding those weapons include a woman.

Anna Liisa gave a nervous laugh.

"A woman ... You are saying that a woman is hiding weapons!"

"If you know something about the weapons cache, you are well advised to tell me immediately. If you are harboring a secret like that, it is a dangerous secret."

The lieutenant's voice, too, was dangerous. Anna Liisa had to turn her eyes away secretly; how could she betray Anja! She heard in her ears Anja's frightened voice when she told her about the guns. She would not betray Anja – no! If she were to inform on Anja, this man would leave from her side immediately and go to the Marjavaara school and then ... But she had to do something. The man was clearly watching her expressions and reactions.

Anna Liisa turned to look the man in the eyes, with sparks of anger in her gaze.

"Don't you speak to me about weapons," she said. "I teach small children humanity and peace. Leave us alone!"

"I certainly will," the man said hastily. "I believe that you don't know anything. And how could you know anything; you are like a child, just as trusting. When someone speaks to you in a friendly manner, you believe what they say. But you have to realize that those who take their orders from Moscow are completely amoral and unscrupulous. Their only aim is to get the world on its knees. They want to govern everything – also Finland and your beloved Viena."

Anna Liisa's lips quivered – she was afraid. She was afraid the man would uncover her secret. Why did Anja have to confide in her? Why didn't Anja keep the weapons cache as her own secret – what could Anna Liisa do with that knowledge? Quietly, almost invisibly, she began to weep. Tears welled up in her eyes, then they began to stream down her cheeks. The man was baffled. He took Anna Liisa in his arms and pressed her to his chest. Anna Liisa buried herself there. Should she now tell him the tears came from fear. What did he think it was? She wept because at this moment she hated Anja for having put the burden of this knowledge on her conscience. In the midst of her weeping she realized that he had lifted her lightly to the bed amidst soft pillows. And before she had a chance to wipe her tears, the man had enveloped her in gentle tenderness the like of which she had never imagined. Suddenly, everything else in her life became unimportant – only this moment had meaning.

Why did Weissenberg always leave secretly? That had happened twice before, Anna Liisa thought. She woke up in the morning and noticed immediately that he had gone, leaving a note on the table and just taken off. How had she been able to sleep like this – without waking up! Then she remembered the night before and right away she was wide awake. She closed her eyes again. Today she was different from yesterday. Today, nothing was what it had been before.

Darja Mihailovna rested in the inner room of her daughter Anja's apartment at the school. Anja had helped to put a white night gown on her. Darja Mihailovna saw her own hands on top of the blanket – they were pale and thin. She had unbearable pain in one of her knees. She touched her face with one hand – it was not her face … It was not at all her face, only coagulated blood, contusions. She felt how her mouth was twisted, her lips so swollen she could not use them to speak. Her eyesight was also poor because her daughter had tied a bandage over an open wound on her forehead. Her shoulders ached, her entire body felt as if it had been whipped, one arm had several deep cuts. How sharp ice could be – it cut like a knife! She listened to her pains, the continual pounding ache in her knee, the unbearable pain at the back of her head, which did not let up even for a second. The headache was the worst; it was about to drive her insane. And now she began to feel pain in her heart. It had started at night. First she had felt nauseated, then severe pain in her chest. Her body could not be her body; how could it have had room for so much pain. A cup of water stood next to Darja Mihailovna's bed. She tried to reach for it with a shaking hand but was too weak even to touch it with her fingertips. Anja would soon come from her lesson. Anja would help.

After a long and nightmare-filled sleep, Darja Mihailovna finally woke up with a fever. Her whole body was burning. Why was she here, in Anja's bedroom? Who was taking care of the cow in Lamminpää? And the cat? Innocent animals had to be taken care of, they had to be fed. Who was taking care of the children in her school? She had to get out of bed and go to the school; she had worked there for decades. Then she remembered the horsemen – they had come after her as soon as she had got her skis moving on the river bank. She closed her eyes, squeezing them shut, but could not make the image disappear. The horses came closer, her ski poles fell down … She thought they were only teasing her, but then she felt the rope around her … Darja Mihailovna curled herself up into a small bundle in the bed and let out a quiet whimper, like a child crying in her sleep.

The children were outside at recess, and Anja hurried to look after her mother. Darja's eyes looked feverish and her bruised face was burning hot.

"Mother, how are you doing? Drink some water – are you hungry?"

"No …"

Darja Mihailovna drank the water eagerly. She had not been able to eat anything for several days.

"The animals," she whispered.

"They are being cared for."

"The children …"

"The children are off school. They are waiting for you to come back."

Darja Mihailovna tried to sit up in bed.

"Anja … if I die … remember your grandfather ... he was murdered …" She paused a little, then she continued with an even more choking voice: "The weapons … tonight from the sauna … to the woods …"

The colors of the snowy forest ranged from blue to bluish red. As the evening turned into night the temperature plummeted far below the freezing mark. The crusty snow glittered. During the day the eaves had been dripping with water; now they were festooned with large icicles.

It was already past midnight when the door to the school opened and Anja stepped out. She locked the door carefully and put the key in her pocket. She halted by the corner of the building, withdrew into the shadow of the wall and stood there listening for a good while. Not a sound was heard – the forest was silent as the grave.

Anja got going. She made her way to the sauna, pulling the water sled behind her. Every now and then she stopped to listen, and then she continued on. Finally, she stopped by the sauna door, looked again over her shoulder and then began to pry the door open. It creaked quietly. After many attempts she managed to get the door open enough for her to go inside. She slipped into the sauna room and returned soon, carrying two elongated bundles. She placed the bundles on the sled and went back into the sauna. She did this three times, and finally there was a whole heap of bundles on the sled. With her cheeks red from the exertion and with her heart pounding, she started pulling the sled onto the path and then toward the church in the forest.

No one was awake in the village at this hour. People were sound asleep, having gone to bed already around eight o'clock. But Anja was nevertheless on her guard. She looked behind her to check if she could see the tracks. Of course she could: every single one. But the villagers used the path too, fetched water, looked for firewood in the forest – why shouldn't the sled tracks show. And who would be looking for them? She hauled water herself along this road every single day. But her fear made her suspect even the most natural things. She left the water sled on the path as if she had been there to fetch water; she did not want to make tracks to the church with it. The church looked desolate at this time of night. Half of the roof had fallen in, and the stars shone through it. Anja lifted the bundles one by one in her arms and carried them to the church hallway. She found a closet at the bottom of the steps and moved the bundles there. The planks were loose on the floor and she had to make a strenuous effort to get them to budge. They had frozen to the ground and she had to get a sturdy stick with which she managed to pry them loose. Between her exertions, she stopped to listen for sounds from the graveyard or near the church. Everything was quiet; she only heard her own frightened breathing.

She hid the bundles under the icy, loose planks. She put the planks back in their place carefully and made sure she left no trace of her visit. Then she pulled some rubbish in front of the closet door, and with her mittens swept away any traces of snow left by her felt boots. After inspecting the floor closely in the moonlight, she slipped out through the rickety door and checked her tracks in the snow in front of the church. Everything was neat; nothing let on that the guns had been relocated. Calmly, she returned to the sled.

When she returned to the school it began to snow, a thin veil of dry, cold snow. Intermittently the snowfall got heavier and her tracks were covered. She knew, however, that she could not assume that the falling snow had saved her. Everything still depended on luck. She was so frightened that when she reached the shed at the school, she sat on the sled for a long while calming her breathing.

Finally, she closed the door to the shed and tiptoed into her home. Inside, in the hallway, she pressed herself against the door and closed her eyes.

"Anja ..." Darja Mihailovna's pained voice spoke from the bedroom. "You were not seen, were you ..."

Gilbert Weissenberg was riding alone in the forest, when he saw the enemy. They approached in a group along the ice, talking quietly among themselves. The sight alerted all his senses. He steered his horse deeper into the forest, tied a bag of hay in front of it, and continued on foot. He had to get away from the horse because if it were to neigh, the men on the ice would hear it immediately. He found a spot in the shelter of trees where he had a good view of the lake. Eight … nine … ten … eleven Reds! The whole group rode closely together near the shoreline where the wind had blown the snow up on the embankment. Each man had a rifle flung over his shoulder; some even had holsters at their sides. Others had packs on their backs, while some had bags of hay hanging on the horse's flanks. The lead rider had binoculars hanging around his neck. The group moved forward very cautiously as if they knew they were being watched. The lieutenant had experienced the same feeling: an intuition that told you that the enemy was near. The group must be on a reconnaissance mission. The Reds apparently knew that some of Malm's troops were still in Vuokkiniemi, on their way to Sorkka by way of Paanajärvi. How could they know that? Some Vienan person must be a spy, someone close to their group …

The riders came closer and Weissenberg hid behind a large boulder. If the Reds were to go into the forest, they would come upon his horse … His forehead broke into a cold sweat. What if the horse were to neigh or snort, what if its hay were to run out and it wanted more. Holding his breath, Weissenberg watched the men coming closer. Just before they reached his hiding place, they stopped. Weissenberg could not take his eyes off the group. Rough-looking men, bearded and weather-beaten. Their equipment was bad, but their horses were good. Why were they dawdling there? Had they stopped for a smoke? Yes indeed, the men dug out their hand-rolled cigarets, having first ascertained that everything was quiet. Even now they put two men on guard. Weissenberg could smell the strong tobacco and could make out a sentence here and there as the men were talking rather quietly.

"Someone should contact the school ... one can't go there in the daytime ...

"Whites. We have to be wary in the village ..."

The wind muffled most of the words however hard Weissenberg pricked up his ears. Suddenly he realized: they were of course speaking about the weapons cache. They were out to gather the guns! Oh, if only he could hear more.

But the horsemen were soon on the move again, and before long the group was far away. They went straight in the direction of Jyskyjärvi and Paanajärvi.

Weissenberg rose to his feet and gathered his thoughts. The school ... That was now the first real clue. But of course there were several schools in the area.

Anna Liisa received a letter in the morning delivered by the "rascal":

> Destroy this note immediately upon reading it.
> Mother is here, in bad shape. She has a terrible headache and throws up every now and then, although she has not eaten in days. She also complains about her heart. I am afraid she won't make it. Remember that we are being watched, both of us. For your information, I am free of them.

Anna Liisa wrinkled her eyebrows, and then she realized. Anja was rid of the guns! Thank God – someone had come to take them away. She turned to the boy:

"Did you meet the Marjavaara teacher?"

"Yes, she's the one who gave me the letter."

"Don't bother telling the others that the teacher sent me a letter."

"I won't ever tell. Mother forbade me."

"Your mother forbade you?"

"She said that now I am not allowed to say anything about anything."

"Your mother is right."

As soon as she got inside, she burned the letter in the classroom stove.

Terror is a peculiar thing; once it has got a hold on a person, it does not let go lightly. Anja worked as usual, held classes with the children, went out with them during recess, sometimes escorted some of the youngest children to their homes after school – all the time with her heart in her mouth, if she heard even the faintest unusual rustle somewhere. One day she went with the children to the graveyard and at the same time, she checked that no tracks could be seen near the church. She walked among the children, talked to them about seemingly important matters in nature, but always she was on her guard – she felt as if some invisible threat was following wherever she went.

Quite late one evening as she was returning across the yard to her apartment from a visit to the outhouse, a man who had slipped into the shed summoned her there in a low voice.

"Where are the guns?" he asked.

With quivering lips Anja told him.

"Take them away as soon as possible," she pleaded. "I don't want to have anything more to do with them."

The man promised; he said the Reds would come one night to take them away. They needed weapons right now.

After this, Anja's fears abated somewhat, but did not leave her completely. Especially in the evenings, dread stole into her heart. One day a neighbor woman brought a letter to Anja upon her return from Uhtua. It had gone to Darja Mihailovna's home. Anja looked at the envelope, but the handwriting was unfamiliar. She opened the letter and read it. It was from one of Artturi Kangas' comrades, who wrote that Artturi had died in a street battle in Tampere. Anja stared unseeingly at the piece of paper. A chilling frost entered her soul. She felt totally empty, as if life had fled from her body as well. She could not even cry, but stood there with dry eyes on the teacher's platform, not seeing or hearing the children who were busy with their math assignments. Everything was now over, she knew it. Her life no longer had a purpose – from now on everything would be as in a fog. I loved that man, Anja thought, and she knew that Artturi had loved her. Their love was not of the passionate physical kind, but rather respect for each other, working together, believing in the same dreams and fighting for them. How great their plans had been – and now they had all come to naught; crushed by a few awkward words: Artturi was dead.

Anja's eyelids ached, and she hoped the tears would come. But they did not come, and she sank deeper into depression. Like a machine she worked till the end of the school day.

In the evening she poured out her heart to her mother, who still had a high fever. No medication had helped and Darja Mihailovna was tired of her aches and pains.

"Don't you give up," she whispered to her daughter in an almost inaudible voice. "If those butchers come to power, they will kill all of us. They murdered your grandfather and look what they did to your mother. They are dogs ..."

"Mother ... Don't leave me alone!"

Darja Mihailovna reached out her hand to touch her daughter's cheek.

"We have been alone all of our lives ... We have always been shunned ... Don't worry about that. Many people wander about their whole life with no purpose. We have always had a purpose ..."

"A Bolshevik is a Bolshevik, be it a man or a woman!"

That is what Lieutenant Weissenberg told Anna Liisa one night when they were together again.

Anna Liisa would have liked to object, but she could not. Her heart was almost bursting when she felt his body against hers. Gilbert could have said anything and she would just have agreed. She loved this man so much that her world was all mixed up. She lived her days as in a dream, waited passionately for the evening, performed her job poorly, and was lost so deep in her own thoughts that even the children noticed it. She even forgot her fears because when evening came, she put a candle on the windowsill as an invitation to Gilbert. She had never experienced this kind of passion; just thinking about the man made her want him. She worshipped him with such fierceness that it scared her. How could a feeling like this last; this was no longer normal!

She had had to write a letter to Kaarlo. It was as if some evil spirit had entered her and forced her to write. While she was writing the letter, she was painfully aware that it would hurt the man deeply. Kaarlo would never be able to recover from the letter. Nevertheless she had to write:

Dear Kaarlo

I know I can never be forgiven for the enormous wound I am inflicting on you with this letter. I will not even try to explain. It just happened: Gilbert Weissenberg has stolen my heart. I love him with a great passion, and my love for you, compared to my love for him, is but a sisterly affection. His and my relationship is serious, it is a relationship of lovers, and therefore, that which was missing from yours and mine has

> found its fulfillment between Gilbert and me. I am returning your ring. I hope you will one day be able to play the violin again. Please forgive me Kaarlo – But I love him beyond reason!
>
> *Anna Liisa*

She had sent the letter a couple of weeks ago. She did not want to think about it, particularly not now.

"Do you know what you have done to me?" Anna Liisa asked at night, when Gilbert had returned from Vuokkiniemi and was planning to move on early in the morning.

"I do," the man said. "I have taught you to love."

"That, too. But you have laid on my shoulders such a burden of guilt that I will never be rid of it."

"Why do you feel guilty?" he asked quietly. "You can control countless things in life but your feelings are not among them. You and Kaarlo drifted into your relationship simply because you had got to know each other already in childhood. You thought it was love, and maybe it was, but only now do you glow. Did you know, woman, that only in my arms are you really radiant! When you ask me what I have done to you, I answer that I have made you a woman."

Gilbert had captured Anna Liisa's full attention. She had not been to Huotari Point in a week and she had not wanted Teppana to come to guard her, although he had recovered from his pneumonia and it had been agreed a long time ago. She did not have time to talk to her *buobo*, even though he had sent her a message that she should come and visit. During the days she was busy with the children, but in the evenings she sat by the window looking out on the lake. Would he come tonight, would he come tomorrow? Had he had to fight? Would he be transferred to Viena Kemi? No – he was still here in Uhtua and rode almost every night along the edge of the forest to the Syrjäkylä school. Early in the morning he was off again. He was just as crazy – perhaps even crazier in his love. And dangerous.

"Gilbert ... I know nothing about your family. You haven't said anything about them."

Anna Liisa asked this question again even though she knew it irritated him.

"My family ..." the man growled indifferently. "Father in Germany, mother in Helsinki. We can talk about that some other time. I will introduce you when the time comes."

"When will it come?"

"When this war has been won and we have created Greater Finland," Gilbert said.

"I have had an old-fashioned upbringing," Anna Liisa said. "I can't have a relationship with someone who doesn't have clear plans for the future. Do you, Gilbert?"

The man pulled her underneath him.

"Now shut your beautiful mouth, I want to love you ... make love to you until the morning without thinking about the future! God only knows how long we'll be alive ..."

They did not sleep, nor did they talk; they lay so close to each other that their breathing blended with each other's. Every time Anna Liisa opened her eyes, the man was looking at her in the moonlight.

In the morning he was gone, and Anna Liisa was quieter than usual.

The next day after morning prayers, as Anna Liisa was giving out assignments to the children, Teppana came riding into the yard. Anna Liisa looked out the classroom window and felt annoyance. Why was he coming here uninvited? Had she not said she did not need anybody to watch over her.

His steps echoed in the hallway and Anna Liisa opened the door.

"Teppana, what is it?"

The man motioned for her to come to the hallway.

"Close the door to the classroom. You have to come home – there is a visitor for you."

"A visitor ... What are you talking about? Who?"

"There just is a visitor," Teppana said with an expressionless face. "Your *buobo* said you have to come."

Anna Liisa looked straight into Teppana's eyes, and his gaze penetrated deep inside her. It tried to communicate something, and suddenly Anna Liisa understood. She went back into the classroom.

"Children, you can go home now and there won't be any school tomorrow either. I have to go home. Come back to school on Monday!"

The children got all excited and began to look for their things. They banged the lids of their desks, and even a little scuffle was about to erupt. Anna Liisa could not, however, be bothered. She and Teppana she put the room in order together and then she hurried to her apartment to change clothes. In the meantime, Teppana smoked a cigaret outside. The horses were waiting in the shed. Teppana had prepared Anna Liisa's horse for the trip.

"When did he come?" Anna Liisa asked as she mounted her horse.

"Early in the morning."

They began to ride along the muddy forest road.

"Why did he come?" Anna Liisa asked. "Isn't he in Vaasa fighting?"

"He's done fighting wars," Teppana muttered, looking accusingly at Anna Liisa. Teppana was angry. Anna Liisa saw Teppana angry now for the first time in her life. So everybody at Huotari Point had banded together against her ... Gilbert's and her love affair had been found out.

"Is he wounded?" Anna Liisa asked, shocked to discover how cold and unemotional she was.

"Yes, he is wounded."

Mrs. Jenny was standing in the hallway with Samuel when Anna Liisa arrived. She threw her coat to Samuel, but he did not manage to catch it and it fell on the floor. Anna Liisa gave her knapsack to Mrs. Jenny – it contained only an empty milk jug and some dirty laundry.

She stopped at the base of the stairs and asked: "Where is everybody?"

"In the library," Samuel grunted.

Anna Liisa's eyes narrowed. Even that old gnarled man! The whole household was against her, as she had guessed. Now she would have to confess her love for Gilbert. She would do it coldly and deliberately, for there was no alternative. She knew she would be pressured. What would be Kaarlo's strategy? Would he elicit pity ...

Anna Liisa went to her room. She got undressed and went into the bathroom. There was no hot water and so she washed in cold water. Then she got dressed, brushed her hair and put indoor shoes on.

"Anna Liisa, are you there?" Katri asked, knocking on her door.

"Come in."

Anna Liisa was sitting at her vanity and looked at Katri in the mirror. Katri walked to the middle of the room and sat down on the chair. She did not come near Anna Liisa, did not hug her, did not kiss her as always before. Anna Liisa turned to look at Katri.

"All right, you can start your reproaches," she said calmly.

"That tone of voice isn't necessary," Katri said. "Nobody is going to chastize you, you are a grown woman."

"What has happened to him?"

"Come and see for yourself," Katri said and went to the door. She stopped there. "But Anna Liisa, please don't be scornful. He didn't leave you, you left him."

Is that really Kaarlo, was Anna Liisa's first thought. A thin, bearded man with hollow eyes was sitting in an armchair. His whole appearance was ragged and he had a dirty bandage around his arm. Anna Liisa stopped as if she were stuck to the floor. Kaarlo looked at her with a despondent look on his pallid face.

"What has happened?"

Ilja Huotari was standing by the window and turned to look at Anna Liisa.

"Kaarlo was ambushed by the Reds, but managed to escape."

Anna Liisa approached Kaarlo cautiously. She tried to search deep within herself for some old feeling, but found only pity and a kind of disgust that focused on the man's dirty and unkempt appearance. She thought she would not have recognized Kaarlo had she met him on the street, looking like this.

"How come you are in Viena?" Anna Liisa asked

"I was sent here to deliver a message to Malm," Kaarlo said in a listless voice. "I left from Vaasa a week ago. There were six of us who were ambushed by the Reds in Vuokkiniemi.

"But you managed to escape."

Kaarlo smiled joylessly.

"My horse startled and ran into the forest with me on its back. The Reds fired a few shots after me and I got this flesh wound in the shoulder. I hid in the forest for two days, for I couldn't orient myself toward Uhtua. A White reconnaissance patrol found me and brought me to Uhtua."

Kaarlo cast a peculiar glance at Anna Liisa.

"I got your letter there."

"In Uhtua!"

"It had not yet left. Mail delivery has been difficult. I read the letter only yesterday.

Anna Liisa could not look Kaarlo in the eyes. She could not have prepared herself for something like this. Why did Kaarlo not say anything more about it? Why did she have to send that kind of a letter!"

"Your bath would be ready now," Mrs. Jenny said from the door.

"I'll come and help you," Anna Liisa said, when Kaarlo maneuvered himself up from the chair.

"No need. I can manage."

When Kaarlo had washed himself and changed his clothes, Katri and Mrs. Jenny dressed the wound and bandaged the shoulder again. Once again Ilja's medicines in the medicine cabinet in the tower came in handy. The pain eased, for luckily the wound was only a superficial one.

Kaarlo lay down on the bed in the guestroom, curled up, and retreated into his own world, beyond reach. Anna Liisa entered the room and tried to get him to talk, but his anguished eyes stared out the window. Anna Liisa was unable to get through to him; she tried and tried but Kaarlo withdrew into himself.

She had moved her chair next to the bed and tried to take Kaarlo's hand. Kaarlo pulled it back.

"I have nothing more to say to you," he said. "I don't want to listen to your love trouble, that topic is the ultimate triviality compared to all else that's happening in this world."

"Do you think I am a fool?" Anna Liisa said. "I have no love trouble."

Kaarlo stared out the window.

"You are not my Aniviisu," he said. "You are a different woman. Your gaze, even your eyes are different. You have the outward appearance of the old Anna Liisa, but on the inside you are a stranger."

"What are you trying to say – do you want to decide my feelings?" Anna Liisa asked.

Kaarlo sat up on the bed and looked Anna Liisa sternly in the eye. Anna Liisa looked at the thinned out face whose eyes were filled with anguish, and had the look of a hunted animal. The look on his face was tormented and accusatory, as if Kaarlo alone had been affected by the war.

"I will have to stay in Uhtua, for I have been stationed here. But don't worry, I won't bother you."

"Kaarlo – please forgive me for the letter. it must have hurt you very much."

"Why do you apologize?" Kaarlo said in a bitter voice. "What happened that changed you in one week? I know – you have experienced something new with him. I have loved you with the kind of love that is made of truth, respect, and affection. But you could afford to throw away a love like that. At the same time you threw away seven years of our lives. The war is finished in Finland – I don't have to go there any more. I will carry on here now."

He was silent for a moment, then he continued:

"In time I will return to Helsinki. I don't want to hear anything from you ever again. I will travel abroad on a concert tour as soon as my shoulder heals. And I'll try to forget you."

"You'll try ..."

"Yes, I have to confess, it will be difficult! I had thought that I would ask you to marry me and take you along on my tours when this wretched rebellion was quelled. Now you will obviously stay here as the Libau Jäger's mistress! That's what you wanted!"

"Mistress!" Anna Liisa shouted. "What do you mean!"

A scornful look appeared on the man's face.

"Did you think you were the only woman in his life?"

"You are disgusting! Disgustingly jealous!" Anna Liisa said in a rage. "You want to hurt me on purpose! You can't accept the thought that the man loves me and I love him. I don't believe you – I don't! I'm leaving now – try to stay alive. We will not meet again."

Anna Liisa turned to look at the man. His face was like ice, the eyes accusing and angry. What right did Kaarlo have to hurt her! Without looking back she closed the door.

"Do you have to leave this late in the evening? Ilja asked, trying to coax her into staying. "Aren't you worried that the platoon of Red horsemen might still be out there in the Kuittijärvi region. A known White woman, or should I say a known White officer's woman, is an excellent target for pursuers.

"Don't be mean?" Anna Liisa said in a tired voice. "I am not afraid. I just want to get to the school."

"I am not being mean," Ilja replied. "It is you who have a guilty conscience. I hear you gave the children tomorrow off?"

Anna Liisa could not contain her agitation.

"You are all silently accusing me. Very well – I'll say it aloud so that you both know it: I love Gilbert Weissenberg more than anyone else in this world. He needs me!"

"You reject Kaarlo's faithful love for a man you don't know and whom you know nothing about?" Katri sad.

"I do – and Kaarlo rejects me. He is going abroad as soon as the war is over."

"Do you have a future with this lieutenant?" Katri asked, still calm. "Has he spoken to you about the future?"

“We only met a month ago. Why would he talk about the future so soon?

“Very well,” Ilja said. “You know what you’re doing … I have to remind you that we will soon have a civil war here in Viena just like in Finland. The schools might have to be closed, all White officers are being sent to Viena Kemi, and this house may be a stop over point for them. The officers won’t have time to woo girls, your beloved Lieutenant Weissenberg may have to get involved in real war. I predict that he’ll be here in Viena still a couple of months, so you will be alone soon enough anyway. So go – maybe you’ll meet him today. Teppana will get you your horse – we cannot prevent you from going.”

“You certainly cannot stop me from going.”

“I know you are expecting that man tonight. Ride through the forest, in any case, because they are for sure keeping an eye on the shore line. If anything happens, remember I warned you. Good night, Anna Liisa.”

Anna Liisa felt that her *buobo* and Katri were abandoning her. She left the room without saying goodbye.

Kaarlo, Anja, Gilbert ... Anna Liisa thought about these three people while she was riding along the dark forest road. Small Bird Grove and the rapids were already far behind, and she was now riding along the river toward the north. She had never before had to use this route to the Syrjäkylä school, it added almost six miles to the distance. She had been crazy to make this trip.

Was she otherwise in her right mind? she asked herself. No, she had not been in her right mind ever since Lieutenant Gilbert Weissenberg stepped into her life. How easy and simple it had all been! Fall in love, give in, forget everything in the past, Kaarlo, and the future and replace them with this unbelievable frenzy. So keen was her desire, so filled with longing for this man was she that she could not go away from the school for fear that he might come there while she was gone.

She suddenly recognized the wilderness meadow in front of her. From here it was three miles to Marjavaara. And immediately she thought she could now go in the cover of the evening's darkness to visit Anja and see how her mother was doing. Would she dare? What if there were a bunch of Red horsemen there? She made her decision quickly: she would take the horse to the shed at the neighboring house. It was the "rascal's" home, and she could well have some reason to talk to his mother.

Somewhere a branch rustled and a big bird took flight, frightened, with wings flapping. Anna Liisa's horse, an old mare, was used to moving in the forest; it knew the way to Marjavaara village. At a tranquil pace it carried its light load. After half an hour Anna Liisa discerned the church and the few houses in the darkness. She rode into the yard of the old farmhouse by the edge of the forest, near the school. She took her horse straight to its shed. The farm was poor and typically Vienan – people lived at one end of the building, the animals at the other. The farm wife came from the hay barn out into the farm yard and stopped there when she recognized the person who arrived.

"The teacher ..."

"Good evening, Moarie, can I bring my horse here? I was going to visit the teacher."

Moarie nodded, but looked at Anna Liisa somehow helplessly.

"Is there some news from there?"

"She died last night. The Russian teacher's mother. I don't know if you can go there now. There were horses there this afternoon."

"Oh my god," Anna Liisa said and went into the house at the woman's beckoning. The "rascal" came to meet her at the door and grabbed the hem of her skirt.

"Oh it's the 'rascal.' Why don't you go out for a while, I have things to discuss with you mother."

The little boy looked in Anna Liisa's eyes as if he had understood. Then he went out.

"Listen, teacher ..." Moarie spoke quietly as if she were afraid to talk to Anna Liisa. "Horsemen have passed by here a couple of times. My husband says they are Reds. Why are they going to the Russian teacher's house? She is probably a Red herself."

Anna Liisa knew she was, but could not say so. She also knew about the guns and guessed that the Reds moved about around here because of them. But didn't Anja write that she was rid of the guns?

"I would like to visit the school," Anna Liisa told Moarie. "It may be dangerous. Where will she bury her mother? Can she bury her in the Marjavaara graveyard?"

She'll have to be buried there, Moarie thought. But who is going to dig her grave and who will bless her?

Do the Reds bless their own? Anna Liisa wondered in her mind. Aloud she said:

"Maybe in this case it will be enough to just lower her in the grave. Anyway, someone should help the teacher."

"Nobody in Marjavaara dares help her any more," Moarie explained. "She is a Russki and we know about Russkis around here.

We used to help them before. Mind you, she hasn't done anything to me. You just go there, leave the horse in our shed. I'll tell the boy to give it hay and water. But when you go to the school, you better stay clear of the village road; walk along the edge of the cemetery in the shadow of the big spruces. Don't go inside the school; there might still be some of the horsemen there."

The dusk outside had thickened into darkness. Anna Liisa stopped at the corner of Moarie's house and looked around. The school building stood about three hundred feet away, and farther away loomed the cupolas of the ancient church. Not a sound anywhere. Still, Anna Liisa sensed the presence of some unidentifiable threat in the village. The feeling was so persistent she was filled with apprehension. She inched cautiously along the fence and finally slipped into the forest.

She was almost at the church when she suddenly saw the horses. They were tied to a tree, altogether six horses. Their owners were inside the church; Anna Liisa could hear muffled voices. Her heart pounded in her chest. She could no longer go back because if anyone happened to come out of the church they would spot her immediately. She withdrew even deeper into the shade of the large spruces. Her heart pounded so hard she was afraid someone would hear it.

Then the men came out. They spoke among themselves in low tones. Anna Liisa heard enough of their conversation to realize they had added to their weapons cache.

"Finally we have everything hidden away," one of the men said. "No one is going to suspect a half-collapsed church."

"Except of course some of the locals," another grunted.

The men went to their horses and untied the reigns from the tree. Then Anna Liisa saw Anja running up to the men. Anna Liisa heard her ask:

"Did someone dig the grave?"

"It's dug, all right."

"Who should I say dug it, if someone were to ask?"

"Say you dug it yourself."

"With my strength ..."

"Women have had to dig graves before. Be careful, we are now off to Vuokkiniemi – through the woods. We'll return here in a few days," one of the men said. "One of those White bandits managed to escape, although I hit him with one bullet. Look out for him, he might be hiding in the woods. You just stay behind locked doors. We'll get your mother's murderers yet."

Anja said nothing. She just stared at them. In the moonlight her face looked unnaturally pale. She was standing about sixty feet from Anna Liisa's hideout and gazed on as the horsemen rode off. Then she turned and began to walk to the school.

Anna Liisa stopped by the door to the shed, which was slightly open. She stuck her head inside.

"Anja ..." she said softly.

Anja turned around quickly, for she had recognized Anna Liisa's voice.

"What are you doing here! Quickly, go away ..."

"What are you doing yourself?" Anna Liisa asked and stepped inside.

Darja Mihailovna's coffin was in the shed surrounded by small spruces. Next to the coffin, which was made from rough-hewn boards, stood the water sled; Anja had just been trying to lift the coffin onto the sled.

"I'll help you," Anna Liisa said.

Together they lifted the coffin onto the sled. Anna Liisa found it sad to think that inside was the tormented and mauled body of a mother. Anja's mother. She wanted to cry or scream in rage. She was obviously experiencing the same emotion as the man who a few minutes ago had said that they would avenge Darja Mihailovna's murder. But was vengeance the solution ...

"A grave has been dug in the graveyard," Anja said. "Would you help me take Mother there?"

"Yes, of course."

Anja pulled the water sled, while Anna Liisa pushed. There was only a little snow left on the ground, but enough so that the sled moved forward. The snow had melted completely in the graveyard, and they had to pull the sled on bare ground. The grave was in the right-hand corner. The girls carried the coffin for the last few steps. It was now much heavier. Anja's face was cold and calm, but hot tears were streaming down Anna Liisa's cheeks. She was crying because a fellow human being was being taken to her grave like this, in the middle of the night and secretly ... The grave was not deep. Using all their strength they managed to get the coffin into the pit, but one end fell in first despite their caution. As Anja reached for the spade that was beside the grave, Anna Liisa said quietly:

"Wouldn't you want a blessing for her final journey?"

"We don't use blessings."

"Let me ..." Anna Liisa did not recall anything suitable by heart, but she began to grope for words: "Let us ask for a Christian ... pain-free, honorable, and peaceful end to our lives ... When we have remembered The Holiest of Holies, The Purest, The most Blessed, the Comforter, the One who gave birth to God, the Blessed Virgin Mary of All Saints, let us place ourselves, each other and our whole lives in Christ God's hands. Amen."

Toward the end her voice grew stronger, and the last sentence she pronounced with a clear voice. Anja stood with the spade in her hand and looked down at the coffin at the bottom of the hole. She could see its contours clearly in the moonlight; it looked awkward and defenceless.

"Thank you," Anja said softly.

The soil that had been thrown up on the edge of the grave was frozen and lumpy; it made a hollow sound as it fell down on the coffin. The sound so shocked Anna Liisa that she had to make a major effort to stay there until Anja was done shoveling the earth. Finally, the grave was filled. They stood silent for a while. The moon shone from between the clouds, and once again Anna Liisa thought she saw some red around its rim. Or was she only imagining it? This much she knew, however, that she would not dare ride to Syrjäkylä tonight; she would have to spend the night at Anja's apartment.

Anja stood with her head lowered for a long while. Then she turned away in anguish and wiped her eyes quickly.

"Let's go," she said quietly.

They stayed awake until the morning hours and talked and talked. Anja told Anna Liisa about her mother's last moments.

"It seems to me that she gave up – she died out of fear. As if she had known that something even worse might still happen."

"What could be worse?"

"Mother said all of this was only the beginning," Anja said. "She said a civil war tears a people apart and when the war is over it will be time for revenge. It is a chain reaction without end. The Reds are now behind barbed wires in prison camps in Finland.

Anja stopped and then she looked at Anna Liisa

"Artturi avoided that fate, he died in Tampere."

"He died …?" Anna Liisa had difficulty speaking because of her shock. "When?"

Anja did not answer – she only gazed far into the distance.

"You loved him?"

A smile lit up Anja's face.

"If I were to die tomorrow, I would think of him. I feel that for one week I experienced something that I can never experience again."

Anja had to clear her throat before she could continue.

"No one else other than my mother has ever loved me," she said. "I am ordinary and homely. But I know that Artturi loved me and that's why I still derive strength from him."

Anna Liisa's eyes had filled with tears. She could never have guessed that Anja felt and thought this way.

"You don't believe it perhaps, but we have always loved you. Although sometimes we had the feeling that you did not want our love."

Anja nodded quietly, and they were silent for a good while. Finally Anna Liisa asked:

"Didn't you get rid of those guns?"

Anja started and looked sharply at her.

"You didn't tell anyone, did you?"

"Of course not," Anna Liisa said, almost hurt. "I am just afraid for you."

"No need for that," Anja said. "I know exactly what I'm doing. The Whites have killed all my loved ones. I have to avenge their deaths."

Anna Liisa did not know what to say. The word "avenge" scared her. This side of Anja would likely always remain incomprehensible to Anna Liisa. Why should she bother to warn her when she wouldn't accept any warnings?

Anna Liisa went to sleep on a mattress that had been brought to the kitchen floor. She could not go to the bed in the alcove, because the night before Darja Mihailovna had died in it.

"Anja … I have broken our engagement," Anna Liisa said when they had lain in the dark for a while. "Kaarlo knows it already."

"What are you saying?" Anja shouted from the bedroom.

"You heard me – it's over now."

Anja appeared in the doorway.

"What do you mean? Have you left him?"

"Yes. And I don't want to talk about it any more."

"I would never have thought it possible," Anja said. "You were so solidly tied together ever since childhood. Kaarlo is a fine man. He was always very friendly toward me, too. What happened? What drove you apart?

"Another man," Anna Liisa answered.

"Who?" Anja wondered; then she realized: "The man from Libau, the Jäger?

They looked in each other's eyes, and Anna Liisa nodded. Anja's eyes turned ice-cold. She spoke quietly:

"That same group killed my mother. For murder is what it was! What kind of barbarians can drag an old woman tied with a rope behind a horse? I hate the Jägers!"

"The Reds are guilty of exactly the same kind of barbaric acts in Finland," Anna Liisa said.

"Are you defending those men?"

Anna Liisa could say nothing. Of course she wasn't defending the men who had tortured Darja Mihailovna. She did not mean that. But what did she mean?

Anja paced fast around the room. Right now she was not a mourning woman who had just buried her mother. She hated everything Anna Liisa represented.

"This demonstrates clearly that there really is a gulf between us; we just haven't always remembered it."

"Do you mean that you and I could be each other's enemies?" Anna Liisa asked.

"Yes, I do," Anja said.

They lay down again to sleep, but neither of them could sleep. Anna Liisa racked her brain as to how she could assure Anja that she had never done or intended to do anything bad to her. Anja again wondered why she could never accept the love the people of Huotari Point had always shown her – or had they? And how could Anna Liisa love both her and a man who had been party to her mother's murder?

They both woke up early, having slept only a couple of hours. Anna Liisa lifted the mattress and the blanket onto the bed and got dressed quickly. Anja had already come in to make tea. She had lit a fire in the stove; the birch wood crackled. Anna Liisa put on her overcoat.

"I am leaving now."

Anja did not answer, just looked at her with weary eyes. Anna Liisa went out the door, and in the hall she heard Anja's voice behind her. She thought Anja said:

"Take care of yourself."

Anna Liisa did not turn around, only said as if to herself:

"You, too, take care of yourself."

The Viena people had been following the events in Finland with a fear that was not far from panic. All kinds of wild rumors spread fast, and they were virtually impossible to repudiate. Most of all the people were afraid the war which raged in Finland would spread to Viena as well. One day there was a rumor that Finland will be annexed to Germany and that a German king would be governing the Karelians, too. Another rumor claimed that all foodstuff in Viena would be sent to war-ravaged Finland.

Gilbert Weissenberg laughed when he heard these stories, but then he became serious when he realized that the Viena people took them to be the truth and not a joke.

"Can't the agitators of the Karelian Cultural Association speak so that these people understand?" he asked at his Uhtua headquarters. "You should explain the Finnish position on the Eastern Karelian issue and not scare people unnecessarily."

The agitators defended themselves:

"When even a man of Ilja Huotari's caliber opposes everything we say, then what do you think the ordinary Vienans will do? They have had to grapple with propaganda from the Reds, the Bolsheviks and the allied forces."

The officers were sitting in the back room at the Uhtua Inn debating these kinds of issues when a horseman galloped full speed into the yard. Gilbert Weissenberg looked out the narrow window and recognized the man. He sat down behind his desk with somber expression on his face. He asked the others to leave. He tried to assure himself that this would only be a routine meeting, but did not believe that even himself.

When Kaarlo Meinander stepped inside the Inn's back room, which had been converted into an office, Lieutenant Weissenberg pretended to thumb through some papers on his desk.

"Good day – greetings from Vaasa!"

Meinander's voice was more comanding than his appearance, which was somehow cold and indifferent, partly tense, too, and did not at all seem to befit the tall, thin body and the dreamy-looking eyes. He was wearing a shabby uniform. Weissenberg lost his equanimity for a moment.

"Please have a seat."

Then they looked each other in the eye, long and hard. Weissenberg detected only hatred in the other man's eyes. It was a pure even a frightening hatred, because it emanated from a pair of eyes whose basic characteristic was gentleness. Meinander's face was pale and one arm was in a sling.

"Why were you sent here?" Weissenberg asked.

"I have spent all the summers of my childhood and youth in Uhtua, and I know these people. They are not ready for our cause."

"So they sent you to be an agitator," Weissenberg smiled. "But it sounds like you do not intend to agitate for our cause, but for your own. We only want one thing: that these people stop resisting us and come over on our side."

"The headquarters have the wrong picture of the Karelian people," Kaarlo said calmly. "I participated in a meeting of the Karelia District staff, where the situation was discussed with the East-Karelian committee."

"How many men do they have?" Weissenberg queried gruffly.

"Almost a thousand men for the Aunus project, organized into ski companies in Sortavala, Salmi and Joensuu," Kaarlo said. "And in addition, about three hundred volunteers, mostly from Salmi and Suojärvi for the purposes of a voluntary occupation.

"Ski companies!" Weissenberg yelled. "It's almost April and the snow is melting."

"I am only the messenger."

The official part of the visit was now taken care of. Would they still have something to discuss? During the course of their conversation, Weissenberg had changed his mind about Meinander. He wasn't just some insignificant fiddler as he had thought. He was a man's man, and no mere artist. They were equal contenders for Anna Liisa's love.

"Where did you get that scratch?" Weissenberg asked, pointing at the bandaged arm.

"I was ambushed by the Reds, but managed to escape. It's only a flesh wound – the internal wound does not show."

Internal, Weissenberg repeated in his mind. "Do you call it a wound! You behave like a man whom one does not expect to have any internal wounds."

Kaarlo Meinander's cheek muscles became strained.

"Lieutenant Weissenberg – if we were officers of the former Czar's Imperial Bodyguard, I would ask you right now: swords or pistols? I find it degrading to speak with you about my feelings; you treat people as toys. Therefore, I do not want to talk about the matter even though it concerns my fiancée. This I will tell you: If you hurt her, I will kill you with my own hands even if it were to lead to a lifetime in prison. Do you understand?"

"I understand your emotional outburst," Lieutenant Weissenberg answered. "I can assure you that I will safeguard Anna Liisa as my most precious treasure. The last thing I advised her was not to have anything to do with that Russian teacher ..."

Kaarlo's face looked anguished.

"The death of Darja Mihailovna does not do the Finnish soldier proud," he said. "I can imagine that somewhere in the heart of Asia people might commit such acts of barbarism. But not here. Torturing an old woman will only make the people morally angry and thirsty for revenge. It casts a shadow over the entire Finnish army."

"You do have fancy words," Weissenberg said. "But Bolshevism will not be quelled with high-sounding phrases. And it casts the shadow of death over the whole free world – if you will permit the adaptation of your metaphor. Bolshevism must be crushed by force before it spreads like a world fire."

"It has already spread," Kaarlo Meinander said. "It is a pest that pollutes everything. A Red death."

"That we agree on, fully and totally."

After a moment's contemplation, Weissenberg began to speak again:

"We know that the Reds have hidden guns somewhere here in the Uhtua region. It's said to be a large weapons cache. The matter is of great concern to me for we know, both of us, whom these guns would be used against. Has Ilja Huotari said anything to you? I don't know what he thinks of all these things. He went to visit that teacher at the Marjavaara school and had his hired hand drive Darja Mihailovna there. I have myself heard the Reds speaking of some 'school.' Could the mother and daughter be hiding the weapons?"

"That I don't know, but one thing I do know: Ilja Huotari is a Viena patriot through and through. He is neither White nor Red, but a Vienan. If he hasn't spoken with you, it is because he doesn't trust you. That is what I meant when I said that headquarters have the wrong picture of the Karelians.

Weissenberg looked at his visitor at length.

"On whose side are you yourself?"

"On the side of Viena."

Anna Liisa had heated up the sauna. When she went to have a sauna bath, she instinctively latched the door on the inside and only later realized what she had done. She had never before been afraid at the Syrjäkylä school. Darja Mihailovna's fate had changed everything. It had demonstrated that when the laws of war rule, no one is safe. She would have liked to discuss matters with Anja, unburden her mind and ponder on things aloud. But Anja had declared a kind of war on her. At first it had offended her, but then one evening as she gave the horse some hay, she realized she had declared the same kind of war on *buobo* and Katri. Otherwise she would have taken the horse and ridden to Huotari Point to spend the evening there; the snow had now melted in the forest.

But she could not bring herself to go.

In the evening she had time to think seriously about her own affairs. She had decided to forget Kaarlo, yet she could not get his exhausted appearance out of her mind. Why had he been talking about a mistress. Did he perhaps know something? Did Gilbert have someone else – had she been only diversion to him. Was she not his great love after all? Anna Liisa smiled faintly, sitting on the sauna bench. Great love … What was that?

She was still thinking about it while she was getting dressed in the sauna front room. For years she had thought Kaarlo was her great love. She would never have believed that there ever could be anyone else, that incomprehensible passion like this existed.

She left the sauna and walked slowly to the school. The forest smelled of approaching spring. She realized that even now she was on her guard and that she kept looking around her in the waning light. It was quiet everywhere and a slight breeze came from the lake. She slipped inside her apartment, locked the front door, and pulled the curtains.

She had not spent a Saturday night at school in a long time. To defy Katri and *buobo,* she had decided to stay away from Huotari Point, even though she vaguely expected Teppana to arrive. She felt she had let Teppana and Nasti down, too; she had not visited the old house in weeks even though she knew they were expecting her to come and start reading a new exciting book as she had promised. She had a guilty conscience, but she simply could not help but think of herself and Gilbert all the time.

Her musings were interrupted by the arrival of a horseman in the yard. She quickly blew out the candles and hurried to the window. It was Gilbert. Anna Liisa rushed to open the door, and Gilbert came in, rifle in hand. He placed it in the corner of the entrance hall and took Anna Liisa in his arms.

"Don't be afraid," he said. "I'm keeping it here just as a precaution … Soon I must be off to Vuokkiniemi."

They stayed awake all night. Talked, made love. Anna Liisa still couldn't bring herself to ask what was weighing on Gilbert's mind. The man was serious and somehow distant, even apprehensive. Anna Liisa had never seen him like that before. At long last he managed to blurt out:

"Kaarlo Meinander came to see me on business. We first discussed the business, then we shifted to private matters. He threatened to kill me if I ever hurt you."

"How could you hurt me?" Anna Liisa asked.

Gilbert's face began to show distress.

"I thought I loved her … Eva," he explained quietly, his gaze fixed on the floor. "But it wasn't true. It was an arranged engagement – my parents wanted us to marry. Oh, Anna Liisa – I cannot stand being away from you, not any more."

Suddenly Anna Liisa felt totally cold inside. She looked at the man as if he were a complete stranger. She had all along believed Gilbert to be unattached! Anna Liisa was quiet for a long time. That is what Kaarlo was referring to; Gilbert's engagement was public knowledge. But so was Kaarlo's and her engagement. Anna Liisa could see the paradox: they were both engaged but not to each other.

"Kaarlo wanted to marry me immediately once the war was over," she spoke to herself rather than to Gilbert. "We quarreled, I screamed at him, and he told me coldly that I would remain a mistress to you."

"Did he say that?"

Gilbert turned toward Anna Liisa and took her face between his hands.

"I am so worried about you. When I return from Vuokkiniemi on Monday, we will go to all the houses to announce that the schools will be closed for a while here in the Uhtua region. As long as the Reds go from house to house in search of Whites, you must not teach at this school, not one day more. We know that they have hidden guns here in the vicinity of Uhtua and we will start a major search tomorrow. We managed to capture one Red, and the boys are right now extracting information from him. We have already heard that they have vowed to revenge Darja Mihailovna's death – and you would be a good target for those bandits."

"Bandits …" Anna Liisa said with a faint and joyless smile. "Those who killed Darja Mihailovna were the same kind of bandits."

She could feel Gilbert looking at her inquisitively and turned to look at him.

"What is it?"

"Your eyes narrowed when I mentioned the guns," Gilbert said calmly. "Do you know something about them?"

"No, nothing," she answered. All too quickly, she thought. She could still feel Gilbert's gaze.

"Just admit that Marjavaara teacher has something to do with them."

Anna Liisa had decided she would never betray Anja. She owed her friend that much, even if their relationship had ended for good.

"Don't harass me, Gilbert," she said quietly. "I know nothing about any weapons cache. I have already told you so. Now let's sleep. It'll be morning soon."

Anna Liisa waited for Gilbert all Sunday afternoon. With a cold heart she sat reading a newspaper while waiting for the day to turn into evening. She had cleaned the classroom, now that the school would be closed for the time being. When dusk began to deepen, she thought for a moment she would go to Huotari Point, because the thought of spending the night alone scared her. If Gilbert didn't come ... If the Reds caught up with her somewhere in the forest off Lake Kuittijärvi and shot her. One horrible image followed another in her mind's eye and Anna Liisa could not stand them.

Early in the evening a boy from Marjavaara, not the "rascal" but someone a little older, came to Anna Liisa's school. Anna Liisa saw him standing at the door as she came back from the well. The boy stuck a letter in her hand and took off.

Anna Liisa did not have a chance to ask him anything.

In the kitchen, behind locked doors, Anna Liisa opened the letter:

Anna Liisa,

Forgive me for making you leave like that last time you were here. I value it very much that you helped me carry my mother to her grave. Come to visit tomorrow afternoon, we'll have coffee and talk.

Anja

Anna Liisa put the letter down in her lap bewildered. What did this mean? She pondered over it many times throughout the whole evening while waiting in vain for Gilbert to arrive. Once she was about to put on her overcoat and go and get her horse, but then reason prevailed and she remained sitting in her bedroom. She stared in the direction of the forest where the last few snowdrifts gleamed in the darkness of the night. She felt like going to Marjavaara. Anja had apologized, she wanted to talk. Then she tried to think through what it was Anja wanted to apologize for. That she held Bolshevik beliefs while Anna Liisa's beliefs were bourgeois? That did not make any sense. Anja was perfectly free to hold those views as long as she didn't demand that Anna Liisa adopt them. Anna Liisa knew she could never think the same way as Anja. Yet she, too, had the ability to empathize; she could imagine how the oppressed and the poor felt. And of course she was opposed to a world in which a daughter had to bury her mother like a run-over dog, in a frozen hole in the ground.

The evening felt endlessly long. Every rustle from the outside made her start. Was it because she was thinking about death? She did not want to go to bed, but curled up on the wooden box in the kitchen.

And there she fell asleep fully dressed. At first she slept restlessly; she was startled out of her sleep several times, but finally she fell into a deep sleep from which she awoke only in the morning, when the cheerful shouts of the children awakened her.

Ilja Huotari sat in his tower. It was his private world, where no one else was allowed except when something of prime importance came up. This was such an exceptional moment. Ilja opened the door to the tower, went down the stairs to the hall on the second floor and called for Katri.

"Are you there ..."

Katri came out from the bedroom where she had been cleaning.

"Would you come upstairs for a minute, please," Ilja said.

It was not that unusual that Ilja had asked her up to the tower. Lately, he had often needed to talk with Katri because the matters he had to deal with were challenging.

Ilja was wearing smoking jacket with dark green, quilted silk lapels. Around his neck he wore a foulard, which in Katri's mind was the mark of a snob.

"Well, here I am," Katri said.

She sat on the chair ready to listen; for living with Ilja she had learned to listen.

"I'll show you how to open the safe," Ilja said.

Katri became alarmed. She had not been expecting anything like this.

"Why are you doing this?" she asked.

Ilja explained: "If something were to happen, if they come to get me for some reason, you will have to see to it that you take the papers in the safe with you."

"Why would they come to get you?

"In Finland estate owners have been killed," Ilja said. "The Reds walked straight into their parlors, dragged the men outside and shot them. I don't see anything that would indicate that the same thing couldn't happen here. And it's always good to prepare for the worst."

It was not difficult to open the safe. You turned the knob on the number reel first four times clockwise, then four times counter-clockwise and *voilà* – the door opened. The safe contained documents pertaining to the house, bank papers, money and checks, and some of Katri's jewelry. Ilja placed them all in a cloth bag, which would be easy to take along if they had to leave the house in a hurry. He asked Katri to try to open the safe again and was pleased when she succeeded on the first try.

"If I'm not here, you can hide the bag under your clothes," he said. "The safe is never to be opened with any stranger present."

Katri agreed. She sat across from her husband.

"What kind of serious matters are going on?"

Ilja told her briefly, and Katri understood that these were really serious matters. Viena still had reason to fear that war would break out. The frost-damaged roads so far had held off any occupation expedition, but the plans had not been cancelled, rather they were being developed further all the time; for example, a network of East Karelian agents was set up to spy on the activities of the Reds.

"There is fighting in Paanajärvi against Mannerheim's orders," Ilja said. "But otherwise the Finnish forces are reluctant to cross their national border. They are even reported to defy their company commanders saying that they had been called to arms to defend Finland, but not to conquer the Russians.

"They are right about that," Katri said. "I think there is no justification for war ever. Is it true that there is fighting in Viena Kemi?"

Ilja nodded.

"There are reportedly three hundred Reds there. They are also saying that an icebreaker is on its way from Archangel but nothing is known about its crew. You mark my words, the Finns will withdraw again and will come to Uhtua."

Katri was going to say something, but at that moment the ship's bell above the door rang. Katri and Ilja looked at each other. They hurried to the door and saw Kaarlo at the bottom of the stairs. He was quite agitated.

“Both the Reds and the Whites are on the move here now,” Kaarlo said with panic in his voice. “The Reds are planning to revenge Darja Mihailovna’s death. The Whites have caught one of those who have hidden weapons. Our men have been ordered to clear the entire region. We have to bring Anna Liisa and Anja here to Huotari Point from the wilderness. God only knows what’s happening there.”

“Go and tell Teppana to get them,” Ilja said and ran down the stairs.

“And tell him to saddle up a horse for me, too,” he shouted.

Anna Liisa could not believe that she had fallen asleep on the box. But there she was and outside it was just another morning. There was nothing anywhere now to be afraid of. She heard the happy sounds of the children outside.

While brushing her hair, she wondered if it was the loneliness at night that brought about all those scary thoughts. Was there any real reason to be afraid?

In the morning it was easy to answer no, but she knew it would be totally different again at night. Why had Gilbert not come? Why hadn't he even sent a message …

No, this has to stop! she thought. All this pondering and wondering was nothing more than an escape from reality. Of course, Gilbert had had a perfectly legitimate reason. She would have to stop creating problems out of nothing at all. That was what she was thinking as she hurried outside where the children awaited her, making a racket.

"Miss teacher – we thought you'd gone to Huotari," someone shouted. "The girls already went inside to warm up."

Then the rest of them went inside and Anna Liisa played the morning hymn on the harmonium. Then they said a prayer, before they got to the geography lesson. The subject of the day was Germany.

"Teacher, Germany is our enemy, isn't it?"

Anna Liisa sighed. Well, how did one explain it?

There was no hot lunch for the children today, because Anna Liisa had not had the time to get any food from Mrs. Jenny last time she was at Huotari Point. Today she fed them sandwiches and boiled some tea in the samovar. They put salted meat on the bread because they had quite a lot of it at the school. The children at the Marjavaara school ate the same meat as well.

During lunch, Anna Liisa explained to the children:

"We have been told that the schools will be closed for the time being because of the war. It means that when the order goes into effect tomorrow, you will not be coming to school until you are told differently. Stay home and don't go into the forest."

"Where is the war?" the 'rascal' asked. "I haven't seen a single soldier."

"You can't see it here; the fighting is at Paanajärvi and Kemi."

"They are fighting against those Bolsheviks."

"Listen, 'rascal,' Anna Liisa said nervously. "I'll go with you to visit your village. Let's all go together."

Anna Liisa continued her geography lesson. She thought it might be a good idea to go with the children to Marjavaara. Even the Reds would not start shooting at a bunch of children.

Around mid-day she was overcome by strange fatigue. Every once in a while, she thought of Anja and her letter. Why did she now suddenly apologize, even though she had been so cold and curt? Anja had told her in no uncertain terms that they were enemies. She could not help it; the letter made her uneasy.

Anna Liisa ended the school day just after noon. She went to get her riding clothes and locked the doors to the school.

One of the boys had harnessed the horse in the shed, and Anna Liisa mounted onto the saddle. She lifted two little girls to sit behind her and a third, even smaller one, in front of her. And so they went, the whole gang into the forest, the horse at walking pace, the children walking, hopping, or skipping from one tussock to the next. The schoolhouse was left behind, and so, too, Lake Kuittijärvi, which had not yet shed its ice. Anna Liisa looked around. Spring was truly making progress, the sun was shining high in the sky, and the snow had melted into puddles on the path. In front was a causeway; the "rascal" went bravely first, then the horse with its load, and last the horde of children.

Most of the children lived in the nearest village and waved goodbye to the teacher, who had now taken "the rascal" to sit up on the horse and continued. Three other boys walked along for another half mile.

"You can do the lessons on your own," Anna Liisa advised the boys, "and do help your mothers with their work. This won't last long; then we'll continue school again."

She dropped three boys in the next village and her only remaining companion left was the rascal who smiled, happy to get to ride with his teacher.

At last they could see the houses of Marjavaara. Usually the horse walked along the familiar path around the little wilderness meadow behind the Moarie farm, but now when they reached the end of the path, Anna Liisa noticed it was under water.

"Look how much water," she said to the rascal.

"I guess we'd better go around the meadow on the north side," the rascal said like an adult. "I know."

"So you know, do you …" Anna Liisa said, suppressing a smile. "Well, since you are so sure, I guess we'll do that then."

They circled the meadow and arrived at the barn behind the Moarie farmhouse. Then the boy whispered: "Teacher …"

A group of eight horsemen came riding on the other side of the meadow at the edge of the forest. Quickly Anna Liisa backed up her horse into the shade of a spruce, trying to see who the men were. She could not even make out their uniforms, much less their faces. She could not tell whether they were Whites or Reds. They rode toward the village with the hems of their coats swaying.

"What do we do now?" Anna Liisa said in a trembling voice, transmitting her fear to the boy as well.

"To our shed, quick – along the field," the boy said. He obviously controlled his nerves better than the teacher.

Anna Liisa tugged at the reins and the horse went into a slow trot toward the Moarie house. The horsemen rode toward the church ahead of them, but so far away that they neither heard anything nor looked back … The horse walked more calmly now. Anna Liisa gave a sigh of relief when they entered the shed.

"Go and tell your mother that I am here," she told the youngster quietly.

Anja sat behind the teacher's desk wearing a gray wool sweater because she had been cold all day. When she had woken up in the morning, she was already shaking as if an invisible wall of ice had frozen inside her. She read again the note that Ilja Huotari had sent her this morning: "Anja, come to our house to safety immediately!" She had sent her answer instantly with the man who had brought the letter: "I thank you for your concern, but I do not need it." What kind of safety could Huotari Point have offered?

The silence in the room as the children were writing in their notebooks made her drowsy. Anja thought of Artturi again, she kept his last letter in the pocket of her wool sweater. It gave her strength amidst her fear. Suddenly, she heard noises from the yard. She rushed to the window and saw eight horses. The men had dismounted and were tying the horses to the post in the yard. Then they sauntered toward the front door. She could see that they were Whites.

Anja gathered the children around her. She had always thought she would be brave in a situation like this, but now when she heard the heavy steps in the hallway, she was scared.

The door was wrenched open and four men appeared in the doorway with rifles in hand.

"Teacher Anja Remisova, follow us!"

"Why?" Anja asked with the children around her.

One of the men took a step forward to chase away the children.

"Kids!" he said. "You'll stay in the classroom until someone comes and lets you out. Is that clear!"

The children drew closer to their teacher. One of the girls wrapped her arms around her. Two boys stood leaning slightly forward as if ready to charge.

"Step aside from there!" The soldier said with a commanding tone of voice.

"Let the children go," Anja said gently, loosening the children's hands from around her. She looked at the soldiers. "Where are you taking me?"

"Shut up!"

Two men stepped forward from the door and, frightened, the children withdrew further. One of the men grabbed Anja so heavy-handedly that he tore the sleeve of her sweater. The second man was on Anja's other side, and they led her out.

"The teacher's coat!" One of the girls shouted. "How can you take the teacher out without her coat?"

"She won't be needing a coat," one of the soldiers said with biting irony.

Anja was not aware of how she was pulled out of there. She felt as if she didn't have any legs at all. She was carried to the middle of the yard and the men encircled her immediately. At that moment, she realized she would meet the same fate as her mother. She closed her eyes because her heart was pounding so fast that she was dizzy. If only she could withstand the torture and survive. She would gladly suffer pain for months if only she could stay alive …

The men got on their horses and began to escort Anja to the forest. The whole time, she expected the noose to tighten around her. She looked around, but the entire Marjavaara village appeared dead; not a single villager to be seen anywhere. The horses jostled her and she was forced to run. Once she stumbled and fell but somebody yanked her to her feet by her hair. It hurt terribly and tears streamed down her cheeks. They took her toward the graveyard. The horses pushed even closer; a hoof hit her leg and she almost fell again. She no longer looked around her. She tried to look at the sky and the sun, but they no longer existed. Then they were at the graveyard and the horses stepped aside. She saw the guns, which had been placed in a row on the ground in front of the church.

The men dismounted and dragged Anja to where the guns were. Now they started an interrogation in which she could say nothing, because they allowed her no time to respond.

"Did you hide these weapons?"

"Did you do it alone?"

"Who brought you the guns and where did they come from?"

"Are they intended to be used against the Whites?"

"Answer!"

How could she have answered. The men stood in a circle around her and were shoving her. She fell and someone kicked her but she was pulled back onto her feet and the pushing continued. She was thrown around like a ragdoll and could neither see nor hear anything anymore – the men's mocking shouts and the horses' neighing all blurred together. Her nose was bleeding and her clothes were muddy. Again someone hit her in the face and her eyebrow was cut and blood streamed over her eye. She saw the men's faces, their staring eyes and gaping mouths through a red haze. When she fell down, she was pulled up and they pushed her down again. Then they grabbed her by the arms and started to drag her on the ground. She realized she was being dragged to the "Square"; she saw the large rocks and the tall trees. She was pushed to the ground and the men surrounded her again. She tried to scream, but was hit in the mouth and she had to swallow blood in order not to choke. Then two men grabbed her skirt and ripped it off her. She tried to twist away realizing that her lower body was bare, but she was held down by strong hands and other hands pried her legs apart. One by one, the men dropped their pants and raped her. She did not know how many men came on top of her. She saw everything as if through a fog and was conscious only of her excruciating pain, as if she had been split in two. Then she saw a rifle with a bayonet. She tried to scream but the pain that pierced through her stomach was so strong it blanketed out everything else. She lay still and motionless in a widening pool of blood and was unaware that the men, drunk on blood and rut, stomped on her with the heels of their boots and the butts of their rifles, until they had put out the last spark of life. Death finally came – mercifully.

Anna Liisa looked at Moarie in shock."What are you saying – guns?"

"They came by here this morning and said they had found the guns last night in the old church. They said the Russian teacher was guilty and would be killed. They came to warn us that everybody in this village who does not tell everything they know about the guns will be killed. Be they Whites or Reds …"

Anna Liisa had to grab the door for support.

"I must go and warn Anja," she said. "I'll leave the horse here in your shed. I'll walk …"

"Be careful, teacher, they say the Reds are coming to retaliate."

"Revenge, revenge, revenge!" Anna Liisa screamed almost hysterically. Frightened, Moarie took a couple of steps back.

Anna Liisa slipped out from the shed. It took a while for her eyes to get used to the light because the sun was shining from a clear blue sky. She sneaked behind the Moarie house and walked in the lee of the houses toward the school. Then she ran to the forest and started to go around the church protected by the trees. Her heart was pounding from fear as she advanced from one tree to the next. Finally, she was in the shelter of the forest – but at that moment she saw a rider approaching. She tried to dash into hiding, but it was too late – the rider was already close. Anna Liisa looked up in horror and whispered:

"Teppana! Thank God!"

Teppana had seen Anna Liisa. He stopped and jumped down from his horse.

"Oh Lord, how I have been looking for you! What the hell are you doing here?"

Teppana was angry; his voice was actually trembling.

"Anja sent me a letter asking me to come …"

"It was a trap! I ran into some Reds in the forest but they didn't see me. They are on their way to the Syrjäkylä school to take you prisoner. Who knows, maybe even to kill you – for revenge. Now go and hide, anywhere, Moarie's shed, for example."

"My horse is there ..."

Anna Liisa couldn't breathe because for fear. She let Teppana lift her to sit on the horse. When she was seated properly he gave her a rifle.

"Let's go around the graveyard; it's the only way out of here. Then they saw the horses. There were eight of them and they were galloping fast toward Uhtua and soon disappeared out of sight. Teppana and Anna Liisa moved cautiously toward the school and were soon behind the church. Then Anna Liisa saw the guns. They had been placed in a straight line in front of the church. There were dozens of them. Here and there were some gaps as if somebody had grabbed a few guns from there.

"Were there that many of them," Anna Liisa said surprised, which made Teppana look angrily at her.

"What did you know about the guns?"

"Anja knew. The children! What are they running here for!"

Anna Liisa jumped off the horse and ran toward the children. They were scared, one of the younger ones was crying.

"What's happened?" Anna Liisa asked.

"They took our teacher. The soldiers came and took her."

"Where did they take her?"

"Over there!" One of the boys pointed toward the "Square." "I watched through the window, they took her between their horses."

A horror-filled suspicion hit Anna Liisa. A little girl tugged at the hem of her skirt.

"The teacher left without her overcoat."

"Children – you must go home right away," Anna Liisa told the children who had gathered around her. "Start running and don't stop until you're home."

The children nodded and started to run in the direction of the Moarie house.

"Come and sit behind me on the horse," Teppana said and helped Anna Liisa up. "We have to find that girl."

The horse began to run toward the "Square." Teppana guided the horse deep in among the large spruces and put a sack over its head.

"It's used to it, it won't neigh."

They returned to the church and approached the "Square," looking searchingly around. When Teppana came to the large boulders and peered on the square, he covered his mouth with his hand, choking back a groan. He tried to prevent Anna Liisa from looking but she had already seen it. Anja's naked white body, what was left of it, lay on the ground in an unnatural position. Blood had splattered everywhere, even on the branches of a nearby spruce.

Anna Liisa had vomited everything she had inside but could not get her nausea to subside. Teppana had held on to her and whispered:

"Calm down, calm down, we have to get away from here."

Anna Liisa knew she would never forget the sight she had seen at the "Square" however long she lived. And she would never forgive the men who had perpetrated this atrocity. She would not rest until they had been punished for their crime.

Suddenly, Teppana put his finger to his lips. They heard the sound of horses. Were the murderers returning to the scene of their crime? Teppana was afraid Anna Liisa would scream. He lifted her in his arms and carried her to safety behind the large boulders.

Teppana took a cautious peek. He saw six riders stop in front of the church by the guns. One of the men cursed loudly. Teppana looked more closely at them and realized they were Reds. He could feel a cold sweat beading on his forehead. He pressed Anna Liisa flat to the ground. "They're coming here," he whispered. "If you want to stay alive, don't move."

The men rode toward the "Square," on their guard and looking around cautiously. Then they noticed the body. They jumped down quickly from their horses. One of the horses became nervous and started to circle around the "Square," snorting madly. It could smell blood.

Anna Liisa had buried her face in Teppana's side. Teppana took a deep breath. If they were discovered they would reach the end of their lives in an even more gruesome manner.

"Oh Hell, guys! The girl's been raped and speared ... It's the White hounds' doing," one of the men said nearly in tears.

The men stood by the body for a long while. They appeared to hold a moment of prayer. From their hiding place, Teppana could see the girl's bloodied face, the stockings that had slipped down to her ankles, a round arm, and her hair spread out on the muddy ground. What little snow remained had been colored red. The men were standing ominously still. Then one man took off his long coat and two men lifted the girl's body carefully onto the coat.

With extreme gentleness, the man wrapped the coat around the girl and lifted her into his arms.

"Now off to the Syrjäkylä school," one man said in a harsh voice. "That Jäger's slut will see the end of her days before sunset! And her death won't be any easier than this one!"

Teppana pressed Anna Liisa's head against his chest so she would not hear what the man was saying. The horses started to move, the lead man holding the wrapped body in his arms. Anja's arms and legs hung down below the coat. Teppana thought they looked awkward ...

When the men had left, Teppana did not waste any time. He left Anna Liisa for a moment behind the boulders and slipped into the forest. He untied the horse and brought it behind the church. Then he ran to the "Square" and pulled Anna Liisa from behind the boulders. He carried the girl to the horse and lifted her to sit in front of him.

"Now let's go to Uhtua," Teppana said. "We'll go via Ohdanjärvi through the wilderness. There are some big marshes – are you up to it?"

"I am ..."

Ilja Huotari's horse got almost entangled in its own legs as it was racing to take its master along the path on the shore of Lake Kuittijärvi to the Syrjäkylä school. They did not dare go out on the ice any more, for it was all covered with water. The horse trudged in the forest trying to find solid ground under its feet, but there was none. Ilja tried not to yell at the horse but every now and then he just had to swear at it, because his mind was tormented by the terrible fear that he would not get there in time.

Finally, they reached a kind of path that led straight to the Syrjäkylä school. Ilja could not understand how Anna Liisa had managed to make this trip all through the fall and winter. Of course she had sometimes skied and sometimes ridden along the ice on Lake Kuittijärvi – but still! That girl was certainlt not short of guts.

The horse stopped again, breathing heavily from exhaustion. Ilja patted its neck and spoke into its ear:

"Try to make it a little bit farther. Anna Liisa is in danger."

The school's sauna came into view first, then the schoolhouse. It was built in a beautiful spot, and Ilja himself had had it built. It was the Viena people's own school and there the instruction was given in Finnish – or more accurately in the Karelian dialect the children understood in Uhtua.

Ilja steered his horse straight to the schoolyard. He was afraid no one would be there. He knocked and pounded on the door to Anna Liisa's apartment but it did not open. Looking in through the window, he could see that the apartment was empty. The classroom door was also locked. Anna Liisa must have let the children go home and she had gone somewhere herself … Ilja stood in the yard, irresolute, wondering what to do next. Where was Anna Liisa? Then a terrible fear seized him: maybe the Reds had got here before him?

While he stood there indecisively next to his horse, five horsemen emerged galloping behind the outbuilding and into the yard. The men quickly surrounded Ilja and he recognized them as Reds. Nobody spoke; they just stared at him with cold eyes until a sixth horseman joined them. He held in his arms an oblong bundle.

"Ilja Huotari himself!" he said and lifted his bundle in the air.

Then Ilja saw the arm of a girl, which dangled out from the coat. He got such a shock he could not breathe for a moment. He leaned heavily against his horse. Anna Liisa … dead …

"Good God!" he said and stared at the man.

"Come and have a look," the man said and got down from his horse with the bundle in his arms.

Ilja could hardly move his legs – he stumbled and looked at the man pleadingly.

"Are you proud of what your kind has done?" the man asked quietly.

He lifted the edge of the coat just a little, but Ilja recognized Anja's body immediately. He could not help but let out a sigh of relief, despite the tremendous shock it was to see the body.

"Be that the work of the Whites or the Reds, it surely isn't the work of human beings," he said.

The men had dismounted and hurried to the school. They smashed in the door and searched the entire building but it was empty.

"Where is that Jäger's woman? Where did you hide her, Ilja Huotari?"

"I have not hidden anyone – she isn't here," Ilja said. Then he pointed to the body on the ground. "Shouldn't she have a coffin soon? You're dragging along a dead woman! Is that a way to honor the deceased?"

The men became confused. They looked at each other but no one said anything. The horses snorted impatiently, for they wanted to be on their way. The wise animals they were, they probably instinctively felt the tension in the whole situation. Everything was confusing right now; the seed of hatred had been sown, and no one knew any more which came first, the crime or the revenge.

Ilja watched the men calmly. He knew he would now be taken away. Since they hadn't captured Anna Liisa at school, her grandfather would do as the target of their revenge. But where were Anna Liisa and Teppana?

If these men were to come upon them in the forest, what would be Anna Liisa's fate?

Seeing Anja's body had horrified Ilja. Were her killers beasts? Is this what Viena had come to – that people tear each other to death like the beasts of the forest? If the Finns were to remain here much longer, customs and habits would become barbarized to the extent that centuries of progress would be wiped out. And they claimed to be harbingers of enlightenment!

"Let's go," said the leader of the Reds.

"Where to?" Ilja asked calmly.

"We will take you to Paanajärvi – to be interrogated by our superiors."

"You can interrogate and shoot me right here," Ilja said. "I have nothing to hide. My granddaughter is not at the school as you could see for yourselves. I don't know where she is. Maybe your people have already taken her, an innocent person. Where does this crazy urge to sink to the level of animals come from?"

"You tell me," said the Red leader. "Or do you consider those who killed this girl to be human beings? Do you want to see the details?"

Ilja turned his head away.

"I already said it's not the work of human beings. It cannot be defended by anybody."

The men mounted their horses. Again one of them took it upon himself to carry Anja's body. They waited until Huotari had mounted his horse; then the whole group rode toward the forest.

"If they went to find you at the Syrjäkylä school, it'll take them a whole hour. For that hour we are safe," Teppana explained to Anna Liisa, who was sitting behind him on the horse.

They had gone straight north from Marjavaara toward the large marshes. Teppana searched out the most difficult route in the hope that possible pursuers would get tired and give up, at least when it got dark.

Teppana knew these regions well. He knew every fishing hut, every wilderness cabin, the fields and the meadows, the rapids and the ponds. He knew that the Reds did not have detachments north of Uhtua and that the Whites had set up headquarters of sorts in Uhtua. Therefore he had to get Anna Liisa there to safety. He had to find a hiding place for the girl and then get help from Uhtua. That would be the easiest way to save her life. If the Reds captured him alone, they'd let him go; what would they want with an old saphead like him. But if he and Anna Liisa were caught together, they would nail him to a tree to watch what they did to her before they killed her …

They were in such a dense forest that the rays of the setting sun could hardly find their way there. Teppana knew there was a river behind the forest. They would have to get across the river and then they would reach a solitary meadow. There was an ancient fishing hut that Teppana had discovered once as a young man – it had been abandoned already then. He would leave Anna Liisa there and continue alone to Uhtua.

Anna Liisa was so exhausted that Teppana was afraid she would fall off the horse. Since the nervous strain had continued for over twenty-four hours, her mind was quite confused. Suddenly she started talking to Teppana in an agitated voice:

"Kaarlo always plays his violin here in the forest. He brings his violin along and just plays and plays. Kaarlo can't live without me. Teppana, where is Kaarlo?"

Anna Liisa's speech became intermingled with weeping, and Teppana tried to sooth her:

"Calm down now, Aniviisu. I'll take you to Kaarlo. You must not speak now; you must be completely quiet. Otherwise you'll disturb the forest spirits."

Anna Liisa became silent and closed her eyes.

Teppana found the river and the horse waded across to the other side. Then they started to trek along the river down toward Lamminpää.

Katri was sitting in the kitchen with Mrs. Jenny who had baked bread and prepared more food than usual, just in case. Katri could not sit in one place for long – she had to get up and pace around. She had not felt safe since her husband had left that morning.

"Does Master Huotari have any dangerous papers?" Mrs. Jenny asked suddenly.

"What do you mean?"

"Well, papers, that should be hidden if the Reds were to come here."

Katri stopped and looked at her.

"Do you think they should be put somewhere safe?"

"I think that you, Mrs. Katri, should go to the Whites' headquarters to be safe, with papers and all. And I will go there, too.

Suddenly Katri came to life.

"I'll go up to the tower," she said and was already on her way through the dining room in the hallway. Mrs. Jenny watched her go.

For the first time Katri went to the tower alone. She knew where the key was, for it was hidden under the handrail. She opened the door and left it ajar. Her eyes glanced over the bookshelves, cabinets and glass vitrines which contained miniature models of different types of ships. She pulled open drawers and shuffled through the papers. They were not important; the important ones were in the safe.

She went to the large metal cabinet and turned its ring-like lock first four times clockwise, then the same number counterclockwise. The door opened. She took the cloth bag, which held all of the most important things. There was also money in the safe; with the bundle of money in her hand, she thought it for a minute, then she took the money, too. She closed the safe quickly, locked the room and hid the key where she had found it. Then she went downstairs and saw Lieutenant Weissenberg. He had just come through the front door.

"Mrs. Katri – where is Anna Liisa?"

Katri heard the worry in his voice.

"At the school."

The lieutenant's face darkened. He grabbed Katri by the arm.

"Gather all the important papers, all the things you would like to be safe."

"I just did," Katri said astounded. "What is it?"

"I will take you and the women of the house to safety in Uhtua," Lieutenant Weissenberg said. "We have an escort of five horsemen. I'm afraid it looks like the Reds have taken your husband captive. And nobody knows where Anna Liisa is."

"What's happened?" Katri asked in shock. "How can my husband be held captive?"

"Some of our people killed the teacher Anja Remisova in a brutal way."

"Hospody! Oh, Good God, have mercy!"

Katri instinctively made he sign of the cross in front of her face. She stared at the lieutenant with a horrified look.

"A large number of guns were found in the church next to her school," Weissenberg explained, ill at ease. "The Reds are now looking for Anna Liisa to take revenge. She is not at the school, but neither was your husband who reportedly went there. You must surely have realized that this house is no longer safe."

Katri nodded. She put on her large cape under which she hid the cloth bag and the money. Mrs. Jenny had quickly packed foodstuff in a basket and was already standing outside. Samuel refused to go anywhere.

"If they kill me, it's about time anyway," he said.

Nasti was also absolutely firm: she would not leave the cows and the other animals.

And so Katri and Mrs. Jenny were helped onto the back of a horse which had been brought from the old house. Accompanied by Jägers, they began to journey along the forest path to Uhtua.

Twenty-three men rode alongside Ilja Huotari. The Uhtua forests were full of galloping horses at this time. Ilja did not know whether they were taking him to the Reds' headquarters. He looked closely at the path along which the horses were advancing. They were headed east. That made sense since Uhtua was full of Malm's troops. They were planning to circumvent them.

Ilja could not get Anna Liisa out of his mind. He refused to believe that anything bad had happened to her. She must still be with Teppana. During the course of the day, it had become clear to Ilja what had happened because the men talked freely about things in front of him. He learned that the Whites found a weapons cache in the old church in Marjavaara. They took out their anger on the teacher of the school next door, by torturing and raping her – and finally they had killed her in a cruel manner.

The Reds did not know where those Whites were right now. But they had made plans for what they would do to them when they caught them. Ilja wanted to forget what he had heard.

Anja Remisova's body was buried during their journey. They stopped by a village on the shore of Pistojärvi. The men found a spade in an old shed. One of the men dug a grave in the back yard of an old gray cottage, and another man kicked a few boards loose from the walls of the shed and built a coffin. The lowering of the body into the grave was performed in silence, no one said a prayer, no one sang, no one said blessings to send Anja off on her final journey. The men's faces were drawn tight and they did not make the sign of the cross but instead fingered their pistol holsters. But Ilja Huotari made the sign of the cross in blessing over the grave.

"You'd better rest a while," Teppana said quietly and helped Anna Liisa down from the horse.

Teppana looked at her. Her face was pale and there was panic in her eyes. She obeyed everything Teppana asked, behaved as if she had absolutely no will of her own.

Teppana realized that he should get her to a place of refuge as soon as possible.

"Listen to me," Teppana spoke gently and propped her up to sit against a tree stump. "Let me explain. I have to get you to a hiding place and I have a plan. Believe and trust me; has Teppana ever let you down? No he hasn't. Teppana has never let Anna Liisa down. Teppana is the most faithful of the faithful."

They found the old fishing hut by a bend in the river. Half of it was covered under the branches of a huge weeping birch; the other half had almost collapsed into the water. Teppana left his horse some distance away in the forest; he did not want to leave tracks to the hut on the damp ground. He took Anna Liisa by the hand and led her along the river embankment to the hut.

The threshold was high. Anna Liisa climbed in with Teppana's help. Then she took off her shoes and stepped over some rubbish to the back of the ancient firebox. That is where Teppana wanted her to stay. Anna Liisa made herself invisible and Teppana placed a few pieces of wood next to the firebox. Contented, he looked around, nobody would suspect that someone was hiding in the hut.

Teppana quickly made a birch bark basket and filled it with water from the river. He took it to Anna Liisa and looked toward the rear of the firebox – nobody would find her there.

"Aniviisu," Teppana said softly. "I am leaving now to get help from Uhtua. If you hear the sound of horses, don't be alarmed; just stay absolutely quiet. Remember, I'm getting help. If you don't hear from me by tomorrow, only then can you get out. In that case, walk along the river."

Anna Liisa nodded.

Teppana left Anna Liisa in her hideout and walked to his horse without leaving any tracks. He guided it down along the river and came to the wilderness meadow. There he stopped to listen. From somewhere he heard a group of horses approaching.

Teppana pondered for a minute and then he detected an old hay shed at one end of the meadow. He hurried there, gathered hay for the horse and grabbed an old wooden shovel that was lying on the threshold. Instinct told him he should do that. He listened again – the voices were closer. He jumped into the ditch that was leading away from the shed, dug mud from the bottom and smeared it over his face and clothes. Then he began to shovel mud with the appearance of a ditch-digger.

The sounds of the horses came closer; there must be a large number of them. Teppana let out a deep sigh – now he would have to pretend to be a dumb farm-hand. He started digging the ditch, glancing to the side occasionally. The riders came closer and he could tell they were Reds. The group came straight toward the shed. They had apparently detected Teppana. He shoveled mud without looking up, and when he finally did look up, he stared straight into Ilja Huotari's eyes. Ilja's eyes signaled a warning.

"What are you doing in the ditch?" the Red leader shouted.

"Well, I'm ..." Teppana grunted. "You can see for yourself, damn it ..."

"Have you seen any horses around here?"

"Horses? Well, I have mine in the shed over there."

The commander snorted.

"Where are you from?"

From Tsiksa," Teppana replied without hesitation.

"Where is the best place to cross Uhutjoki River?"

Teppana pushed his hat back with his thumb, wiped his upper lip and thought feverishly. No use to lead them astray, they'd only come back and kill him. And so he said honestly:

"About a mile and a half east of here, turn down where there's a collapsed hay shed; there's a shallow spot there in Uhutjoki River. Where might you be heading?"

"We're taking this prisoner to Paanajärvi."

"Oh, a prisoner," Teppana said and lifted a good chunk of mud. "I'm kind of a prisoner here, too, shoveling this ditch here."

"You should join us," the commander said. "The Whites are already killing women."

"Oh, they are, are they?" Teppana wondered. "Our women are all safe so far."

Ilja Huotari closed his eyes when he heard this. He had got the message. Anna Liisa was safe. God bless Teppana!

Anna Liisa lay curled up under her coat. She was shaking all the time, but didn't know if it was from cold or from fear. Exactly on the level of her eyes was a crack between the logs. She could see down to the river. Years of dead grass and clay. She felt lonely and anxious. Teppana had promised to come and get her, but what if the Reds found her first? She could not rid her mind of the image of Anja's naked body, the blood-covered thighs and the head's unnatural position on the ground. How much had Anja suffered? Had she been conscious to the end? She knew she must cry, cry away all the tears of agony. She didn't cry so much because Anja was dead, but because of the horrible death she met. How does it feel when the bayonet ... No!

She wanted to scream, but she only bit her sleeve. Anna Liisa closed her eyes. She did not want to think about it. But she could do nothing about her imagination. What if the Reds found her? She was trapped here behind a blackened and dirty firebox!

"Oh please, merciful God – help me," she moaned aloud.

Lieutenant Weissenberg stopped his horse at the corner of Outi's house. A half-grown girl came out with a slop-pail in her hand.

"Is your mother home?"

"Yes, she's home."

Katri hurried in with the lieutenant following. Katri had never been in the house before. She knocked on the door and a cheerful voice said:

"Come on in!"

When Outi recognized Katri, she got up quickly from her spinning wheel, blushing scarlet up to her hairline. Lieutenant Weissenberg took off his hat and bowed.

"Madam, please forgive us for pushing our way in like this," he said. "But we should get this lady here," the lieutenant pointed to Katri, "to Uhtua, because the Reds have taken Ilja Huotari prisoner. I have five horsemen with me here, but we were just informed that the Reds are taking Mr. Huotari to Paanajärvi. The women do not dare ride alone to Uhtua – would you lend us a horse?"

"Sure, I'll lend you one," Outi said and threw on her wool sweater. With red cheeks she ran out into the yard with Katri and the lieutenant in tow.

"That one ..." Outi said and harnessed the horse quickly.

"Could you yourself perhaps ride toward Uhtua with the lady," Weissenberg asked. "The other woman has never ridden before either."

Outi nodded, she could do that, no problem. It was better for three women to ride together than for one to ride alone.

Katri went up to Outi, took her hand and thanked her.

"I won't forget this," she said.

The lieutenant returned to the horses. He helped Katri to mount the horse Outi had given her.

"I will ride with you until we can see Uhtua," he said and took the lead.

They made an odd group. The lieutenant and Katri rode in front, and behind them Outi and Mrs. Jenny on the same horse. Riding side by side, the lieutenant and Katri had to make conversation.

"I have to confess that I have thought evil thoughts about you," Katri said. "My husband and I have not been able to understand why Anna Liisa broke her engagement. We know you had other plans for your life before you met Anna Liisa."

"I am in love with her."

"Have you given any thought to how these exceptional times affect people?" Katri asked. "In war, death is always near, and the nearness of death makes feelings of love stronger, and so people may think of what is normally considered infatuation as love."

The lieutenant did not answer, but he gave Katri's words serious thought. Suddenly he became alert: He heard the sounds of a horse's hooves ahead. Quickly, they steered their horses into the shelter of the trees.

The approaching rider had also noticed them, and he, too, steered his horse into the forest.

Lieutenant Weissenberg dismounted, took his pistol and gave it to Katri.

"Shoot him if he is a Red."

Terrified Katri looked at the gun.

"How do I know if he's a Red?"

"If he shoots at me."

The lieutenant knew the rider was hiding in the spruce grove by the road. He lifted his rifle to his chin and shouted:

"Come out with your hands in the air!"

He repeated his command and then, from behind the trees, came a man who was covered in dirt and who was holding a wooden shovel.

"Teppana!"

When Teppana recognized the lieutenant and Katri he dropped his shovel and was so overcome by emotion that he was almost unable to speak.

"I thought, I thought ..." he kept stammering.

"Where is Anna Liisa?" the lieutenant asked anxiously.

"On the north side of Uhutjoki river, in an old fishing hut," Teppana said. "She is well hidden there, but otherwise quite shaken and distressed, poor girl. We saw what they had done to Anja."

"Did Anna Liisa see Anja's body?" Katri asked horrified.

"We saw what was left of her."

Katri began to cry in the middle of the path, pressing the pistol against her side.

"Don't cry, Katri," Teppana said gently. "I saw Ilja Huotari alive.

Anna Liisa was lying behind the firebox in the fishing hut which smelled of smoke. She was still shaking from cold – or maybe she had a fever; she could no longer tell. She did not know what time of day it was either. Everything was confused except the images of the Marjavaara village in her memory. They flooded her mind constantly so vividly that she wanted to scream in horror. She could see Anja's body with her mind's eyes and could hear the shout in her ears: "Now off to the Syrjäkylä school!" What would they have done to her? Tortured, humiliated, raped, stuck a bayonet through her?

All that could have happened had she not left the school with the children in the middle of the day and if Teppana hadn't found her in the forest.

She had also been thinking about the letter from Anja. Had it been a trap? She could not believe that. But even if it had been a trap, it would have strangely made sense. Then Anja would have been speaking the truth when she said that they, too, could become enemies. Was there anything but enmity in the world.

Anna Liisa thought about the day when Gilbert Weissenberg had spotted her on the ice of Lake Kuittijärvi. Before that her world had been perfect. She had been happy; she had had someone she loved, Kaarlo; and her whole future had been clear. Then she had fallen in love with Gilbert, and with such passion that she still found it incomprehensible. It had been real love, she was sure of that. But what had it given her? Nothing but grief and pain …

Again the image of Anja's body returned to her mind. So naked, so defenseless in the middle of a muddy field … How could they do it?

Anna Liisa sobbed aloud. She did not want to let into her consciousness the question that had bothered her all the time: Had

Gilbert been among the murderers? She knew she would not be able to stand to hear the truth.

The sun was setting and the air became cooler. Anna Liisa shivered with cold and curled up even more. She closed her eyes and tried to sleep. But the nightmares started immediately. Had Teppana been caught? Was he being tortured? Would he reveal her hiding place to the Reds?

By this time she was already shaking hard, and she heard voices from all directions. She saw Reds who thrust their hands under her skirt and touched her all over. But then she opened her eyes and looked around in the darkness – she saw only Gilbert's face, felt only Gilbert's hands.

Suddenly Anna Liisa came to and sat up in her little nook. Now she was not dreaming! She heard the sounds of horses clearly and they were coming straight toward the old fishing hut.

They had found out that she was here. What was it like to die? Did it take long? More than death she feared the pain. Her entire body trembled when she thought that they would grab her by the feet or the arms, drag her out into the yard, and do the same to her as they did to Anja. She could no longer control herself, she shook like a patient sick with fever. Then she heard as if through a mist a cautious shout:

"Anna Liisa! Teppana here ..."

While swaying on the back of the horse, Ilja Huotari was still thinking about the funeral. It had been the humblest funeral he had ever seen. The young woman had been lowered into the grave, wrapped in her own torn clothes. And the coffin had almost been just dumped into the hole and some soil quickly shoveled on top. Was this the spirit of the new era?

When they returned from the Syrjäkylä school, the group stopped at the tip of Huotari Point. Three men went in with Ilja. The house was otherwise empty except for Samuel whom they found sleeping on the couch in the hallway. He was happy to see his master, but noticed soon that the accompanying men were hostile. To Ilja's silent question he answered:

"Mrs. Katri and Mrs. Jenny are in Uhtua."

Ilja Huotari could not help but sigh with relief. It did not matter what happened to him but he was worried about Katri and Anna Liisa. He did not dare ask about Anna Liisa and Samuel did not dare talk about her.

"A mighty wealthy house," reflected Orpana, the leader of the Reds. He came from Kemi. "We need money, Mr Huotari, you will be good enough to show us to the safe. I've heard that this house has such a thing as a safe. If you don't open it voluntarily, we'll break everything here."

Ilja had no choice but to show them to the tower.

When they entered the room, he saw to his great relief that the door to the safe was open; all the money and jewelry were gone. He pointed with his hand:

"As you can see, my wife got here before you."

"Damn it," Orpana said. "Do you have any other hiding place?"

"Do you think I would keep my valuables anywhere else but in the safe, which I brought here all the way from Canada! I sure don't, I wouldn't be that crazy," Ilja Huotari thundered.

Downstairs, Samuel had been ordered to bring out all the food he could find in the pantry. Slowly and clumsily, he collected the bread that was baked yesterday, a leg of lamb, and salt fish. He put it in a bag that one of the men threw over his shoulder. Samuel was left by the front door; no one was interested in him. Now as they pressed on toward the north, Ilja Huotari wondered whether he would ever again see this faithful man who had served him for decades.

During the entire trip to Lamminpää, Anna Liisa did not say a word. She sat in front of Lieutenant Weissenberg on the horse, her whole body still shivering.

"Don't be afraid, my darling, you'll be safe soon," Gilbert spoke softly. "We'll take you and Katri to the Finnish side of the border tomorrow. Huotari Point is no longer a safe place."

Anna Liisa did not answer. *Buobo* had been taken prisoner, the horrors still continued.

The horses galloped into the village of Lamminpää and passed by Darja Mihailovna's empty house. They rode in a long column all the way to Ryhjä village in Uhtua and stopped in front of the school. Anna Liisa slid down from her horse and ran into the arms of Katri who was standing on the steps. There she remained, crying hysterically, and Katri looked at Lieutenant Weissenberg, alarmed.

"We have to get her to bed, she has a fever."

"Where is *buobo*?" Anna Liisa asked as Katri took her into the room.

Nobody answered. At that moment Kaarlo Meinander entered. Anna Liisa took a step toward him and the shawl she had kept wrapped around her fell to the floor.

"Kaarlo, where is *buobo*?"

Kaarlo walked up to Anna Liisa and took her in his arms. "Our troops are following the Reds to Paanajärvi. I am certain that your *buobo* will be rescued. But you must calm down now, Anna Liisa, you must eat and sleep."

Anna Liisa did not see Gilbert Weissenberg, nor his jealous hatred of Kaarlo. She only felt an embrace where she felt safe.

As Kaarlo led her toward the bed, she freed herself from his arms and went to stand next to the table. Her cheeks glowed feverishly, but her voice was clear and audible, as she directed her words at Gilbert:

"Who killed Anja?"

Weissenberg did not answer.

"Gilbert – I am completely in my right mind," Anna Liisa said. "I want to know who killed Anja!"

Gilbert Weissenberg stood silent for a long time. His gaze glance wandered about and his voice betrayed his apprehension when he began to speak nervously:

"Well, our troops of course. That cannot be denied. Cavalry captain Malm issued an order to cleanse Uhtua, Pistojärvi and its environs. A weapons cache of considerable size was found in the church next to the school – and it turned out that the woman in question was the main culprit in the hiding of those guns. The men were enraged, the situation got out of hand … I am not trying to defend it."

"Were you there?" Anna Liisa asked quietly.

"No, I didn't make it in time."

She was quiet for a moment, trying to sort out her thoughts. Then she said:

"If you had made it there in time, would you, too, have participated in the raping and tormenting of Anja? Would you, too, have pierced her with a bayonet and ripped off one of her arms, which I saw about fifteen feet away from the body! Answer me!"

"Anna Liisa …"

"Don't touch me!" she screamed and suddenly she began to scream hysterically. She screamed and screamed until she burst into convulsive weeping. She wept her face distorted, and her whole body in spasms. Katri went up to her and slapped her on the cheek.

The crying stopped instantly, and Anna Liisa sat down on a chair.

"Lieutenant Weissenberg," she said quietly. "You are responsible for what happened to Anja, however much you try to deny it. You didn't make it there in time … Can you cross your heart and swear that you would have prevented that horrible act if you had been there? Where did you not arrive in time? You did not get there in time to kill and rape Anja."

Weissenberg did not respond. His face had tightened and become mask-like. Anna Liisa tried to control herself. She groped for Katri's hand as if searching for safety and said to the man in a monotonous voice:

"I do not want to see you ever again, Gilbert Weissenberg. Never, remember that. If I had a gun right now, I would kill you."

The long and tiring journey seemed never ending. Ilja rode in the middle of the group, quite exhausted. The sun had set and dusk was settling over the landscape. At one point the men had stopped and eaten the food they had taken from Huotari Point. Ilja was not given any food, he had to settle for plain water. Then the journey continued.

The horses trudged along in the forest, for the roads to Paanajärvi were just footpaths. Ilja could not quite understand why they wanted to take him somewhere to be interrogated. Why didn't they shoot him immediately? He didn't know anything about any weapons cache. And he could not understand how Anna Liisa had been linked with all of this – except by having fallen in love with a Jäger lieutenant. Anna Liisa and Anja had been friends since childhood, and Anja would never have wanted anything bad to happen to Anna Liisa. Why did these people not understand that? And where on earth was Anna Liisa! The uncertainty tired him out altogether. With a dull mind he examined his whole life, for he was certain it would end soon. He thought about his departure from home, the defiance and pathos of youth. He reflected on his marriage, the hysterical and alcoholic Greta. He had not given the woman anything except a little financial security, a home and beautiful clothes. He remembered the seas of the world he had sailed for years. What had he learned from that? Nothing. He recalled his time on the gold fields of Yukon in Canada where he had amassed his wealth. What did it profit him now? Nothing at all. He thought about his house on Huotari Point and Katri, his wife. He would have wanted to grow old with Katri; take her along to Canada to look at the places where he had dreamed of the future. And now he sat here on a horse on his way to his own execution.

The ambush happened so fast that the men in the rear did not even realize what was happening. The Whites who had stationed themselves on either side of the wide clearing opened murderous fire. Ilja realized that men were falling in front of him and behind him. He jumped off his horse and lay flat against the wet ground. The shots crackled like a wild forest fire.

Then it was silent. Ilja heard someone call his name. He rose to his feet with great difficulty, for the journey had stiffened his limbs. A man in a gray uniform jumped forward with his rifle pointed at him.

"Are you Ilja Huotari?"

"I am."

A happy smile spread over the young soldier's face. He turned to look at his friends.

"Mission accomplished," he shouted.

The Reds had been driven out of Uhtua, but Huotari Point was still being guarded by three riflemen. They kept a close eye on everyone who moved about on the lake. Ilja found his wife and Anna Liisa unharmed, but they had decided to stay at Huotari Point only a short while. They would soon move to Sortavala.

Anna Liisa asked Teppana to take her to Pistojärvi. Ilja forbade her the trip altogether, but Anna Liisa won out.

"*Buobo,*" she said quietly. "I have to go there. I simply must."

Anna Liisa insisted and Ilja had to go along.

Teppana brought the horses to the front door in the morning. As they rode, the three of them, toward Pistojärvi, *buobo* tried to tell Anna Liisa not to expose herself to futher torment.

"I have to," Anna Liisa said.

There was no more talk of Gilbert Weissenberg. He had returned to Vaasa without seeing Anna Liisa. He had written a farewell letter, which Anna Liisa had thrown in the fireplace in the dining room, unopened. Something was shattered forever. Kaarlo had left the same evening and Anna Liisa did not want to see him either. She wanted to be alone. She felt utterly exhausted, yet she could not sleep. Every night she woke up from nightmares. The schools were still closed. Teppana had collected Anna Liisa's belongings from the Syrjäkylä school. If it were to open next fall, it would have to be with a new teacher.

Anna Liisa thought about all of this as she rode toward Pistojärvi. Teppana rode in front, Ilja Huotari behind. Both men held a rifle across their saddles.

They came to a halt in the little wilderness village of Pistojärvi. Ilja nodded, there it was ... in the back yard. Anna Liisa went there alone; she didn't want anyone to go with her. With heavy steps she came to the back yard of the graying cottage.

The earth had begun to green, and buds were swelling on the birch branches. There was a mound – the black dirt stood out from the grass which had recently been revealed by the melting of the snow. A wooden plaque had been placed on the grave:

Teacher Anja Remisova
Born 3 May 1899
in Uhtua.
Died for her convictions
28 February 1918.

"Anja ..." Anna Liisa whispered. "I know your letter wasn't a trap. The only trap is life itself. Forgive the cruelty of human beings."

To my readers,

In the summer of 1991, I was able to visit the very Uhtua region where this novel takes place. In Pistojärvi I saw a mound in the back yard of a gray cottage that was surrounded by light-blue fence palings. An old woman who spends her summers in that cottage told me in a few words about a young woman, a teacher, who had been brutally murdered in 1918.

This novel was conceived when I stood by her grave.

The author